Catherine Lavallée

Be Careful What You Wish For

About the author

Alexandra Potter was born in Bradford. She has lived in the USA and Australia and worked as a features writer and sub-editor for women's glossies in the UK. She now writes full-time and lives in Los Angeles. Her previous novels are *Do You Come Here Often?*, *What's New, Pussycat?*, *Going La-la*, and the widely acclaimed *Calling Romeo*.

ALEXANDRA POTTER

Be Careful What You Wish For

HODDER

First published in Great Britain in 2006 by Hodder and Stoughton
A division of Hodder Headline

A Hodder paperback

11

A CIP catalogue record for this title
is available from the British Library

978 0 340 89961 8

Typeset in Plantin by Hewer Text UK Ltd
Printed and bound in the UK by CPI Mackays, Chatham ME5 8TD

Hodder and Stoughton Ltd
A division of Hodder Headline
338 Euston Road
London NW1 3BH

For Saar
Who proved to me that wishes really can come true

ACKNOWLEDGEMENTS

First of all I'd like to say a big thank you to my editor Sara Kinsella for believing in both me and this book and for all her enthusiasm and hard work, and my agent Stephanie Cabot and everyone at William Morris for their continued support.

This book came about at a huge turning point in my life and I'm lucky to have fantastic friends around the world who helped me along the way – thanks guys I couldn't have done it without you! I'd especially like to thank Lynnette for all our transatlantic phone calls and happy times at her flat in Fulham; Dana, whose kindness, encouragement and love of trash mags has gone a long way to making Venice feel like home from home; and then of course there's Barney, my feline friend, who kept me company on those long nights at my laptop (the Fancy Feast are on me).

As always, I'm forever grateful to my parents for all their love and support – they are quite simply the best mum and dad a girl can ask for – and to Kelly, for being a wonderful big sister and looking after me when I first came to LA.

And, finally, to Saar. What can I say without taking up the rest of this page? So I'll keep it simple and just say thanks luv – for everything and a whole lot more.

There are only two tragedies in life: one is not getting what one wants, and the other is getting it.

Oscar Wilde

Chapter One

What do you wish for?

World peace?

A cure for Aids?

Gisele's bottom?

Wincing with pain from my new diamanté thong sandals that have rubbed two blisters the size of jellyfish on my big toes, I press the button for the pedestrain crossing and wait on the kerbside. I mean, whatever it is, we all wish for something, don't we? Every single one of us. Unwrapping the yoghurt-coated flapjack that's my breakfast I stare down at my throbbing feet. And I'm no different from anyone else. Except whereas everyone else is busy benefiting mankind, changing the world and looking fabulous in a G-string bikini, I'm standing here looking at my blisters – and do you know what I'm wishing for?

'Ouch.'

As if on cue, a blister pops and fluid trickles between my toes. *Flip-flops.*

It's near the middle of July and the UK's in the grip of a heatwave. For most of the sunshine-starved population this means a blissful merry-go-round of sunshine and ice-cream, picnics in the park and deck-chairs in the back garden. For us Londoners it's hell. The city is sweating like an athlete. Stuffy offices, stinking traffic fumes and tube trains without air-conditioning make life miserable. Tempers are fraying. Noses are peeling.

And my feet are killing me. Cursing silently, I unearth a grotty piece of tissue and squat down on the pavement.

Chic, very chic, I muse, wiping a moustache of melted foundation from my top lip with my finger and stuffing the raggedy tissue between my toes. Sometimes I wonder why I even bother buying *Instyle* every month when I can put together such a stylish look myself.

Feeling a shove in my back I notice the lights have changed and standing up I begin hobbling across the road. Immediately I'm engulfed by a crowd of commuters, yakking on mobiles, smoking cigarettes, slurping lattes. Everyone pushing, rushing, jostling, bumping. A briefcase bashes me in the calf and I yelp. Not for the first time do I find myself wishing I lived by the sea. Instead of in the polluted inner-city hell-hole I've called home for the last six years.

Managing to make it to the pavement before the little green man disappears, I limp along Marylebone Road. To tell the truth, sometimes I feel as if I spend my whole life wishing for things. Not great big life-changing wishes – like discovering Brad Pitt's shooting his latest blockbuster in my neighbourhood and, guess what?, wants me, Heather Hamilton, to be his leading lady.

Yeh, right, I'm not talking about *those* kind of wishes. The close-your-eyes-and-make-a-wish-type wishes that involve throwing coins into fountains, watching for shooting stars or rubbing Aladdin's lamp. I'm talking about all the ordinary, inadvertent and, quite frankly, *boring* wishes I make a dozen times a day without thinking about them. For me, wishes have nothing to do with magic: they're just a part of everyday life.

Like I wish I hadn't just eaten that great big flapjack.

Suddenly aware that I'm holding an empty wrapper, I feel a stab of guilt. OK, so I bought it from a health-food store, and it was on the shelf next to the dried apricots and brown rice, but who am I trying to kid? I mean, I know it's not really healthy. I squint at the nutritional information. Oh, my God, *healthy*? This stuff should carry a health *warning*. Have you any idea how many grams of fat there are in flapjack?

Scrunching up the wrapper I stuff it hastily into my bag, which as usual is full of all the crap I carry around with me: leaky biros, stray Tampax, a lip gloss that's lost its top and is covered with bits of fluff. Oh, and a couple of those little tickets from the electronic weighing machines at Boots.

Which reminds me of another one of my wishes. I was only supposed to be buying some Tampax, but when I popped into Boots at lunchtime I couldn't resist stepping on to the scales and wishing the little digital display was going to say I was a couple of pounds under nine stone – and not, as it turned out, a couple of pounds over.

Well, all right – make that five pounds. But I'm sure my clothes weigh that much anyway.

Sucking in my stomach, I continue hurrying along the main road. In fact, now I'm thinking about it, I make so many wishes I'm not even sure I can remember them all. Take the last twenty-four hours for example. If I had to write them all down I'd end up with a whole wish list . . .

<u>I Wish</u>

- I'd stayed in last night instead of going to a karaoke evening with my best friend Jess.
- I hadn't started doing tequila slammers.
- the ground had opened up and swallowed me when I'd started yodelling Barbra Streisand's 'Woman In Love'. In B flat. With my eyes closed.
- that when I got home at two a.m. I hadn't texted the-bastard-ex-boyfriend.

I'm mortified at the memory. Sending a text message is one thing. But remembering what I put is quite another.

- I hadn't squeezed that spot on my chin in the loos at work.

But I did and now it's brought along a couple of friends for moral support.

- that when I overheard a woman on the tube reading out that article about multiple orgasms in *Cosmo*, I hadn't snorted, 'Huh, what are they?' just as the whole carriage fell silent.
- someone had warned me that on my thirtieth birthday I wouldn't automatically be given this amazing career along

with all the other presents to unwrap. [You mean that's not how it works?]

- men suffered from PMT.
- there was always an empty seat on the tube. No queue at Starbucks. And a parking space for my car outside my flat.

You know that joke about how women can't park because men tell them seven inches is this big? (It's that joke where you have to pinch your fingers together.) Well, last week I told it to the man who lives at number forty-two. Just after I'd tried squeezing my car into that space behind his new BMW. And reversed right into it. Unsurprisingly he didn't laugh.

- I'd win the lottery.

Admittedly a tricky one, having never actually *bought* a ticket. But that's one of the things I love about wishes. *They don't have to be realistic.*

- there was no such thing as 'a bad-hair day'.
- that yesterday when the yoga instructor was helping me do a handstand I hadn't chosen that exact moment to do a fanny fart.
- I could actually manage to drink eight glasses of water a day.

Eight whole glasses! I mean, it's just so boring, it doesn't taste of anything.

- I could meet a man whose hobbies include washing-up, monogamy and foreplay.

Instead of making a mess, cheating, and tweaking my left nipple backwards and forwards as if it's the dial on their car stereo and they're trying to tune into Capital Radio. Not that I'm referring to Daniel, my ex, or anything.

- I never have to fake another orgasm.

(See what I mean about them not having to be realistic?)

- anti-wrinkle creams actually did what they say on the jar.
- there are no calories in Häagen Dazs double chocolate chip.
- I hadn't believed the sales assistant when she said it was easy to do a St Tropez tan at home and that the secret was bodypolishing.

I glance down at my legs. Think orange stripes. Like a deck-chair.

- Dad wasn't married to the bitch from hell.

Whose real name is Rosemary, and who I refer to as proof that wicked stepmothers aren't just the stuff of fairytales.

- I hadn't borrowed my brother Ed's iPod to go rollerblading.

Or tried to look cool by skating backwards and falling flat on my backside. Correction: flat on the iPod. Which is now broken.

- My Visa card hadn't been refused at the checkout at Sainsbury's.

Embarrassing enough without being ushered into a little room by a sour-faced supervisor who'd called my bank, picked up a pair of scissors and cut my shiny, flexible friend in half 'on orders from your bank manager'.

- I'd realised the assistant at the local video store was being ironic by recommending *Swept Away* with Madonna as a 'classic'.

Phew-wheeh. I hear a wolf whistle and zone back in. Only to see a gang of workmen staring at my chest. Which brings me swiftly to the next wish on my list:

- that I was wearing a bra.

Putting my head down I attempt to stride past nonchalantly. OK, just ignore them, Heather. Don't make eye-contact. Just keep walking and pretend you can't see them. Just a few more steps and you'll have got past them . . . Easy-peasy. See, workmen aren't so bad.

'Oy, show us your tits.'

- I wish all workmen had small penises.

Blushing hotly, I hurry past, pretending to look at my watch to avoid their gaze. Which is when I see what time it is. Oh, fuck.

- and I wish I wasn't late to meet Brian at the register office at ten.

Because it's already twenty past. *And he's going to kill me.*

On the front steps of Marylebone register office, a slim, attractive, grey-haired man in a charcoal flannel suit, who could pass for his mid-fifties but is a decade older, is rocking backwards and forwards on the heels of his highly polished shoes. He checks his watch, looks up and down the road, then sighs and turns his attention to his button-hole. The pink carnation is wilting in the heat and he fiddles with it agitatedly.

That's Brian, and although he can't see me hurrying towards him because of all the pavement traffic, I can see him. He cuts an awkward figure, standing alone and conspicuous in his smartly tailored suit, with someone else's confetti scattered at his feet. A few passers-by glance at him pityingly. Not that he notices. He's too busy checking his watch again and digging out his mobile from his breast pocket. He flips open the mouthpiece, taps in a number, forefinger stabbing the buttons awkwardly like someone who can't type, then presses it to his ear.

A hundred yards away, I hear a familiar tune. Sticking my hand into my bag I wiggle my fingers around until finally I locate my Nokia. Just as it stops ringing. Damn.

I yank it out, along with the hands-free earpiece which is all tangled up as usual, and stare at the screen. One missed call. Hurriedly I dial voicemail. 'You have one new message.'

As I wait to hear it I wave frantically at Brian but he's got his back to me and all I can see is the hunch of his shoulders as he lights a cigarette.

'It's me, Brian. I'm outside the register office and I'm getting a little nervous. And, well, not to put too fine a point on it, Heather, where the bleedin' 'ell are you?'

Oh dear.

As his voice hisses at me I realise I'm in big trouble. I hit reply and he picks up immediately. 'Heather?'

'Right here,' I gasp, sneaking up behind him and tapping his shoulder.

It's an attempt to defuse the situation with humour. Instead it nearly causes a heart-attack. Brian swings round clutching his chest, the lit Benson & Hedges wedged between his fingers. He glares at me accusingly. 'You're late,' he snaps into his mobile. Then, realising what he's doing, he curses, flips the mouthpiece shut and shoves the phone into his pocket.

'I know and I'm so sorry,' I apologise, then try to explain. 'My alarm didn't go off and the tube took for ever and I'd bought these stupid new sandals—'

'Well, at least you're here now,' he interrupts, grinding out his cigarette under his shoe and buttoning his jacket. Everything Brian does is rushed and twitchy. He reminds me of a bird, all ruffled feathers and darting eyes. 'But we'd better hurry up,' he's saying, smoothing down his lapels and picking off an invisible thread with the meticulous attention of someone who irons his underpants.

'Where is everyone?' I hurry after him up the front steps.

'Inside. Waiting for us.' He pulls open the front door and holds it for me. 'I've been here ages. When you didn't show up I came outside to look for you.'

'I'm really sorry,' I apologise again and duck my head under his arm. I'm a lot taller than Brian, especially in my new sandals, and I have to stoop as I step into the cool darkness of the lobby, where I pause to check my reflection in the gilt-edged mirror.

I'm your typical redhead, pale skin and freckles, lots of wavy scarlet hair, and painful childhood memories of being called

Gingernut, Duracell, and something unrepeatable that involves pubic hair and rhyming slang. Honestly, I'm surprised I'm not in therapy for the rest of my life. Not just at the hairdresser's having blonde highlights put in every six weeks to turn me into a strawberry blonde. Usually I blow-dry it straight, but today it's gone all puffy in the heat. I try to smooth it down. Which is when I notice Brian. In the mirror I can see him standing behind me, staring at the floor. 'What happened to your feet?' he demands.

Remembering, I look down. 'Fashion,' I quip, bending down and trying to hide the toilet paper that's sticking out from between my toes.

Usually he'd laugh, make some wisecrack, or quiz me about my latest shopping spree. Unlike most men of his age Brian makes sure he keeps abreast of new trends – he's always nicking my copy of *Vogue* even though he insists it's only to look at the photography – and is fastidious about fashion. But this time he huffs dismissively.

'Shall we?' he monotones, clenching his teeth. The muscles in his jaw twitch and he glares at me with flashing grey eyes. Despite his mood he's incredibly handsome for an older man.

'Yeah . . . I mean, yes . . . of course . . .' I gabble, feeling like a child who's misbehaved.

Together we cross the marble lobby, our footsteps unnervingly loud. Ahead of us is an impressive set of mahogany doors. Muttering something about how the next wedding party is due to arrive at any minute and if we don't hurry up the whole thing will turn into a shambles, Brian reaches for the brass door handle.

I place a hand on his arm. 'Hang on a sec.' Tugging a packet of tissues out of my bag, I tear open the Cellophane and hold out a tissue. 'I know how you cry at weddings.'

He frowns, not giving an inch.

I wave the little white triangle like a flag.

It's too much. He surrenders, his forehead unknots and the tension drains from his face. 'I'm sorry. I was beginning to think you weren't going to turn up.' Accepting my peace offering he tucks it deftly up his sleeve.

'What? Jilt you at the register office?' I whisper.

The corners of his mouth twitch. 'Mmm, something like that.'

We share a smile. He straightens his tie, smooths down his hair to disguise where it's receding and throws back his shoulders. 'Ready?'

I pull at the hem of my skirt and tuck a stray curl behind my ear. 'Ready.' I nod, feeling a jangle of nerves.

We both stare straight ahead, faces serious. I brace myself.

'OK. So, this is it.' Reaching for the door handle, Brian takes a deep breath. '*Showtime.*'

Chapter Two

A vista of multi-coloured hats, their ostrich feathers and silk netting fluttering in the wind from the ceiling fans, greets us as we enter. The room is absolutely jammed. The guests are sitting shoulder to padded shoulder, fidgeting uncomfortably in the stifling heat and trading family gossip. A couple of children have grown bored and are playing what looks like tag round the two huge floral decorations that are standing guard, like a couple of Calla lily bouncers, at either side of the doorway. Somewhere a baby is crying.

No one notices as Brian and I enter from the back, except, of course, the registrar who's waiting for us at the top of the aisle. In a garish shirt and open-toed sandals he flings us a look of relief and hurries towards us. Or should I say 'trots'. This is definitely a man who prays to the God of Graham Norton.

'Oh, my word, thank goodness,' he whispers loudly. 'I was beginning to think we were going to have a riot on our hands.' Scratching his goatee, he rolls his eyes round the room theatrically.

'Don't worry, the cavalry's here now.' Brian tugs a little black object out of his pocket, holds it out in front of him and points it in different directions.

The registrar stares at him quizzically. 'What's that?'

'A light meter,' I reply, and spot the pile of cases in the corner. Unzipping a black holdall, I pull out a tripod and begin to assemble it. 'We need to check the readings for the exposure.'

The registrar nods. 'Oh, I see.'

'As the official wedding photographer it's my job to make sure the happy couple get the photos they've always dreamed of,' interjects Brian, reaching for his camera and selecting a lens. 'Because memories fade . . .'

On hearing my cue I join in: '. . . but a photograph lasts a lifetime,' we chime together.

'That's the motto of Together Forever,' Brian continues, unable to keep the pride out of his voice. He passes me the lens cap and points the camera at the registrar. 'I thought of it myself.'

'You did?' The registrar looks dubious. 'I thought it was already a well-known saying . . .'

The shutter releases with a loud click, catching him by surprise. 'Oh, goodness!' Captured with his mouth wide open like a fish, the registrar stands blinking after the brightness of the flash. Which brings us to the attention of the wedding party, who turn round in their chairs in excited anticipation.

A hush falls as all eyes turn towards us. But I know they're not looking *at* us – we're just the wedding photographers – they're too busy looking *beyond* us, at the doors that are swinging open as someone presses 'play' on the tape-recorder. The sound of a sax fills the air and Whitney Houston blasts into 'I Will Always Love You'. As the registrar scuttles back up the aisle, Brian and I take our positions. Here we go.

I wait expectantly. This is the moment when the bride makes her grand entrance and you get to see the dress. It's my favourite bit. After all, most of us, at some point in our lives, have dreamed about what we'll wear to our own wedding. When I was about six years old my favourite game was dressing up in my white nightie and Mum's old wedding veil and pretending to marry Barney, my teddy. One day I fell over in the mud in the garden and my mum dried my tears and told me I looked beautiful anyway – because every bride is beautiful on her wedding day. It's only since I took this job that I've realised my mum told fibs.

Because, yes, I've seen lots of brides look beautiful in their dresses, but I've also seen big white meringues that make you want to cover your eyes with your fingers, family heirlooms that should have stayed in the attic, and corsets so tightly laced that the bride is literally spilling over the top like ice-cream in a cornet. Not to mention the dodgy veils, tacky tiaras and twenty-foot-long sequined trains. Believe me, Trinny and Susannah would have a field day. But, then, who I am to talk? I have loo roll stuffed between my toes.

There's a loud sob from the mother of the bride. Oohing and aahing from the elderly relatives. A stifled giggle from one of the boys who was playing tag, followed by a clip round his ear from his dad.

And a gasp from me.

Only this time it's not because of my blisters.

Before me, in a bright pink dress that looks like something worn by a Spanish flamenco dancer, is a bride who's old enough to be my mother. Actually, no, I'm mistaken. *My grandmother.*

'You look gorgeous, sweetheart,' gushes Brian, rattling off frame after a frame.

What can I say? This man is a pro.

'The dress is stunning . . . just a little bit to the left . . . truly stunning . . . Now, big smile for the camera . . .'

Passing him a new roll of film I watch him in admiration. Brian's been doing this for so long he's caught full-blown wedding fever. It doesn't matter whether they're big or small, traditional or themed, he adores every last one of them. He was married once, way back in his early twenties, to some model called Phoebe, but they divorced amicably after a couple of years (I'm not sure if that was before or after he admitted he was gay) and since then he's had a string of failed affairs.

Not that this has stopped him being a true romantic. If anything, it's made him even *more* romantic. He gets all misty-eyed at the first sight of a ribbon rippling on the front of a white Rolls. Can't listen to the Bridal March without dabbing his eyes with his sleeve, and borrowing tissues from the mother of the bride to blow his nose all the way through the vows. Honestly, he's a complete mess. By 'till death do us part' he has to go outside for some fresh air.

Which leaves me in charge. Officially I'm supposed to be his assistant, but I usually end up taking most of the pictures. Despite the unwritten rule in society that decrees women have to goo-goo over new-born babies, puppies, cuddly toys and – the *pièce-de-résistance* – weddings, they just don't have that effect on me. It doesn't mean I'm against marriage. On the contrary, I love the idea of falling madly in love and living happily ever after. Doesn't everyone? But just recently I've begun to wonder if 'ever after' really exists. I mean, maybe it should be more a case of 'happy for the moment' or 'happy until I get bored'. Or, in the case of me and my ex, 'happy till he starts shagging the girl in Marketing'. Not that I'm bitter or anything.

Violent nose-blowing zones me back in and I see Brian sniffing into his handkerchief. His eyes are all red and puffy and he's trying to focus on the bride and groom who are saying their vows. Patting him reassuringly on the back, I pass him a dry tissue and ease the camera out of his hands. I look down the lens and zoom in on the happy couple.

'Priscilla Klein, I want you to know that even though I've been married eight times before, this marriage to you will last for ever . . .'

'David Wolstenhume, I promise I will always love and honour you, even if you do have to go back inside . . .'

Which brings me on to my next wish.

- that when I get married it isn't in a pink flamenco dress. To a man who's about to go to prison.

The flash pops as I take their picture.

See? There I go again . . .

When it's all over we pack up the cameras and Brian offers me a lift to the tube. Only there are roadworks, the traffic is backed up all the way along Marylebone Road and we end up stuck in it.

Sticking my bare feet up on the dashboard, I wind down the window. Brian's driving the minivan, which has Together Forever painted down the side in swirly weddingy writing. Originally he wanted it to be on a background of confetti, but the sign painter charged by the hour and apparently confetti is fiddly and time-consuming, so he opted for a silver horseshoe and a couple of bells instead.

Brian hasn't always been a wedding photographer. He used to be a one of the big paparazzi photographers, travelling the world, snapping celebrities at flashy film premières, but the death of Princess Diana changed everything. Brian's a big royalist. He's got all the royal weddings on video, drinks tea from his beloved Silver Jubilee mug and actually cried when the Royal Yacht *Britannia* was decommissioned. When Diana died he was devastated. As part of the paparazzi he felt he was partly to blame so he jacked it all in, hung up his zoom lenses and his stepladders, and set up Together Forever.

Which was where I came in.

I'd just finished a photography course at college and I replied to his ad for an assistant. It wasn't exactly what I'd had in mind – at the time I was wearing head-to-toe black and taking moody shots of graffiti-covered walls – but I figured it would only be temporary. Just long enough to get some experience, pay back my student loans and give myself time to build up a portfolio before I turned freelance. Six years later I'm still here.

Six years! It's unbelievable. Not that I haven't applied for other jobs, but it's all about networking and contacts and getting your big break. I'm still waiting for mine. I keep telling myself it's going to happen. That one day I'm going to be the new Annie Leibovitz, that I'm going to have exhibitions in swanky galleries in Soho, that I'm going to make the front covers of magazines and newspapers . . .

Er, hello, Earth calling Heather.

'So what did you think of the wedding?' Brian is asking.

I look at him across the handbrake. Covered with confetti and puffing a cigarette, he's flicking through the *Evening Standard*, which he's strewn across the steering-wheel.

'It was interesting,' I begin cagily, a bit like you do when you first come out of the movies and you're not sure if the other person liked the film. 'What about you?'

Flicking ash out of the window, Brian nods. 'Hmmm . . . different . . .' he answers noncommittally.

'Though I wasn't sure about the dress . . .' I venture cautiously.

'I think she forgot her castanets.'

I giggle, which sets off his smoker's laugh.

'Now, come on, we're being rotten.' He tries to compose himself. 'It wasn't that bad.'

'Yes, it was.' I smile, which lets him off the hook: the floodgates open. It's a sort of a tradition of ours – like when you've been to a party with your boyfriend and you spend the journey home in the car gossiping about everyone.

'Did you see the bridesmaids? They were gorgeous.'

'Especially the little blonde one who insisted on wearing her bunny-rabbit ears.'

'But what about when the best man lost the rings? He looked gutted.'

'And broke out in that nervous rash.'

'And started scratching all over.'

'I saw him with his hands down his pants.'

'No, you did not.'

'I swear to God. I've got it on film!'

'Eugghh, that'll make a nice photo.'

Brian and I both crack up. The absurdity of our job provides us with the best in comic entertainment.

'So, what time's our job tomorrow?' I wipe my streaming eyes. 'I promise I won't be late for this one. I'm going to get myself a new alarm clock.'

'Don't worry about it. Have a lie-in. Catch up on your beauty sleep.'

I pull a face. 'But it's the weekend,' I remind him. For people in the wedding business, weekends are always manic.

'I know. And I'm giving you the day off.'

'A day off?' I repeat incredulously. 'On a Saturday?' As Brian's words register, I'm hit with the kind of high you get when you realise you don't have to go to work the next day. I can't remember the last time I had a whole weekend to myself. How fantastic. I can sleep late. I can laze around in the back garden reading trash mags. I can even spend the entire weekend in bed watching videos and eating takeout pizza . . . *By myself.*

Abruptly, my day off loses its appeal. Weekends are for couples. It's like the city suddenly turns into Noah's ark – people walking two by two round parks, sitting at tables for two in cafés, sharing buckets of popcorn at the movies. Usually my best friend Jess and I hang out together. Most of our old gang have long since paired off and as we're single we figure it's safety in numbers. But she's an air stewardess and this weekend she's on a back-to-back to Delhi.

'Are you sure? Saturdays are always our busiest days,' I start backtracking.

'Were,' corrects Brian. 'Things have been slow for a while.'

True. I'd noticed that things had eased off over the past few months but I hadn't given it much thought. Now, I see that Brian's shoulders have slumped forward and there's a big furrow running down his forehead like the Grand Canyon. Something's up.

'You're going to be having a lot more weekends off in the future,' he adds.

'The business is doing okay, isn't it?'

There's an ominous pause. 'Well, that's what I was going to talk to you about . . .' Sighing, Brian turns to me and I get a horrible sinking feeling. Something is definitely up. 'Now I don't want you to panic . . .'

I panic.

'. . . because you're a wonderful assistant and a really talented photographer . . .'

Oh, God, I'm being fired. '. . . and I've enjoyed working with you.'

Enjoyed? Did he say *enjoyed*? As in past tense? My stomach dives towards my blistered toes. Until now I've never entertained the thought of losing my job. I've been too busy complaining about it and wishing something better would come along. Now, faced with unemployment, I see all the great things about it. Going to work in floaty dresses and strappy sandals, eating smoked-salmon canapés and wedding cake for lunch, having a boss like Brian . . . 'Please don't fire me,' I blurt.

'*Fire you?*' he gasps, his voice high with astonishment. 'Lord, no! Why would I fire the best assistant I've ever had?'

'I thought . . .' I begin in confusion.

'But I might have to let you go.'

My heart sinks. Brian's doing that thing boyfriends do when they break up with you and try to make you feel better by saying it's not you, it's them. It doesn't matter how they say it, the outcome is exactly the same: you're still being dumped.

'What I'm trying to say is that I've been looking at the books. The business isn't doing very well –' He concertinas his cigarette into the ashtray and reaches into the glove compartment for a can of air-freshener. '– and, well, to be honest Heather, it might be wise to start looking for another job.' He glances at me, trying to gauge my reaction.

'It's that bad?' I say quietly.

'Worse.' He gives the van a vigorous squirt of Ocean Breeze. Satisfied, he pops the can back into the glove compartment, and turns to me. 'The bank's calling in my loan.'

Suddenly Brian looks like a man with the world on his shoulders. The bags under his eyes seem heavier, the lines etched down his cheeks are like ravines, and he has a defeated air about him that I've never seen before. 'Things might pick up.' I attempt to inject a note of optimism. I'd no idea the business was so close to bankruptcy and I feel terrible – not for me, for Brian. I might lose my job, but he stands to lose everything, including his home, which he's remortgaged for the business.

'They might,' he agrees, forcing a smile. 'Maybe by some miracle we'll get a big wedding to pay off all our debts, hey?'

'Yeah, maybe.' I smile back determinedly.

He switches on the radio and as he turns back to his paper, I let the smile drop from my face. Worry scuds like a cloud across my forehead, casting a long dark shadow over the future. Mentally I dig out my list and scribble down another wish:

- that miracles really can happen.

Chapter Three

Eventually the traffic is moving again and soon I'm standing on the pavement outside Baker Street station. 'Well, I can't let my assistant go home barefoot, can I?' Brian is saying, leaning out of the minivan, a grin on his face. 'I'll just have to give golf a miss.'

'I think, as my boss, you could have paid for a cab for me,' I grumble, gazing at my feet. Where once there'd been a pair of stylish diamanté sandals, there are now Brian's golf shoes. Caked with mud. In a size eleven.

'There's nothing wrong with catching the tube,' Brian calls, pulling away from the kerb. 'You'll be home in no time. Think about poor old me, stuck in traffic.' He hoots his horn and I watch him brake to let a group of handsome thirtysomething men cross the road. I can think of a lot of ways to describe Brian, but right at that moment, as he sits behind the wheel of his beloved minivan, his eyes flitting admiringly from one tight-T-shirted male to another, 'poor old me' isn't one of them.

As I walk on to the platform the heat hits me. It's like turning the oven up as high as it will go, opening the door and sticking your head inside. Excusing my way through the jostling scrum of pungent body odour, frayed tempers and tension headaches, I edge towards the yellow danger line.

Which reminds me of the ticket I got last week for parking on a double yellow line. I didn't actually *park* there, I just *left* my car for a few minutes in an emergency. Unfortunately the traffic warden – a man – didn't think that having to buy Feminax was an emergency (of course, he's never suffered from agonising period pains) and gave me a ticket. Which I must remember to pay. I tug a pen from my bag. My memory's like a sieve so I'm always making lists. I've got lists for everything. My fridge is covered with dozens of multi-coloured Post-it notes. The only problem is, half the time I forget to look at them. But I can't write a reminder to remind me, can I?

Scribbling 'PARKING TICKET' on my hand, I hear the distant rumble of a train approaching. I step back and watch it thunder into the station, rattling alongside the platform, the faces in the carriages blurred as if they've melted in the heat. It's packed as usual. My spirits sink. And then, like every other night of my commuting life, the same thought pops into my head: I wish there was an empty seat.

The doors slide open and, propelled forwards by the momentum of the crowd behind me, I pop, like a cork out of a bottle, into the carriage. Trying not to focus on the condensation trickling off the windows and down the other passengers' faces, I work my way through the bodies vacuum-packed into the central aisle. 'Oops, sorry . . . 'scuse me . . . sorry,' I gabble, treading on toes until the train sets off with a lurch and I have to lunge for one of the overhead handrails.

I cling on as we move out of the station, manoeuvring myself sideways so my nose isn't squashed into someone's armpit. God, I wish I could sit down. I gaze enviously at those lucky enough to have a seat, eyes passing absentmindedly across unfamiliar faces. A man with a terrible comb-over, a pretty girl with an eyebrow piercing, an old lady with salmon-pink foundation. And freeze on a man with a distinctively strong jaw, a cleft in the chin and a thatch of black hair, underneath which lurks a familiar pair of hazel-brown eyes. Oh, my God, what's *he* doing here?

My stomach does a little flip. It's my neighbour. My exceedingly *handsome* neighbour. The one I always think is a dead ringer for Brad Pitt's dark-haired younger brother. Not that I know whether Brad Pitt actually *has* a dark-haired younger brother, but if he does I'm sure he'd be just like this guy. Whatever he's called. Because although I've lived across the street from him for the past year I still don't know his name (which baffles my stepmother who takes it upon herself to know not just the names but the personal habits of every resident of Bath). That's London, though. People live in the same buildings as their neighbours for years and nod in the communal hallway, but never speak to each other.

I do, however, know everything *about* my neighbour, who from this moment onwards shall be referred to as 'him'. I know that he drives a navy blue Range Rover, shops at Waitrose for food and Joseph for clothes, and orders takeout from Shanghai Surprise, the Vietnamese restaurant on the corner, at least once a week. I also know he's a keen tennis player, has recently bought himself a white sofa and, judging by the time he opens his bedroom curtains, likes sleeping till noon at weekends.

Not that I'm *stalking* him or anything. I just happen to notice him occasionally. As he turns the page of his book I squint at the front cover to see the title. Would you believe it? It's *Life of Pi*. My own unread copy is currently doubling as a coaster on my bedside table. I make a decision to start it as soon as I get home.

For a brief moment I picture myself sitting on my front steps, bathed in the evening sunlight that photographers love to call 'the magic hour' as it makes everyone look fabulous, engrossed in a chapter, my hair tumbling seductively over my face, a Gauloise held between my fingers in an artsy French way. When I hear, 'Hey, what do you think of the book?' I look up to see my neighbour smiling at me over my hedge and throw back some witty response. Before you know it we're chatting about characters and plot and the clever use of dialogue . . .

A sudden influx of new passengers pushes me further back against the side of the carriage throwing me back to reality. In which my neighbour has never noticed me. To him I'm invisible. But perhaps that's not a bad thing, since I look ridiculous every time I see him. Hastily I try to hide my golf-shod feet behind someone's briefcase.

Take last week, for example. After jogging round the park I'd been catching my breath by the entrance, legs all wobbly, hair pasted with sweat to my forehead when who should appear jauntily round the corner all freshly shaved and *perfect*? Him, of course.

A few weeks before that I'd been unloading my shopping from the boot of my car, my arms filled with a bumper-pack of super-quilted bog roll, when he'd pulled up and reversed into the space next to me. And, of course, there was the time when I'd popped outside to put out the recycling in my bobbly old dressing gown and a self-heating face-mask – the one that turns bright blue when it's ready – and he'd just so *happened* to be at his window. Right at the very second my dressing-gown unravelled and he was treated to an impromptu full-frontal.

'Him' suddenly glances up, in the way people do when they feel someone's eyes upon them, and stares right at me. *Staring right at him*. Oh, Christ, how embarrassing. Spotting an abandoned copy of *Loot*, a free-ads paper selling everything from second-hand cars to soulmates, I grab it as if it were a life-raft and bury my burning cheeks behind a page of flatshares. Pen in hand, I go through them as if I'm really interested. Just in case he's watching. Clapham Common: cat-loving lesbian household seeks like-minded sister'; 'Earl's Court: space in three-bed flat – share with eight Aussies'; 'Shoreditch: open-minded artist wanted for funky, fashionable flatshare'.

And then my heart sinks. There it is. Right near the bottom. Just a single line: 'Little Venice: single room in flatshare, £150 a week, bills included.' I stare at it, absent-mindedly doodling a love heart round it as I think about 'him'. It has to be the most uninspiring, boring advert ever. Which was what I'd intended when I'd placed it three weeks ago.

I don't want to have to let my spare room. I don't want some stranger living in my flat, sharing my sofa, my unused set of Le Creuset pans – *my loo seat*. But I don't have much choice. When Daniel moved out he took his Bang & Olufsen TV, half of our photograph collection and his share of the flat's deposit and its profits. Leaving me with no TV, no pictures of me with dodgy blonde highlights when I was twenty-seven and huge mortgage payments. For the last nine months I've been living off my savings and now I'm stony broke. The last two months I defaulted on the mortgage and the bank are threatening me with repossession, so it's either find a flatmate or . . .

Or what? I gaze out of the window, wishing I could see an answer to all my problems, but this is the London Underground, not a crystal ball, and all I can see is my own reflection staring back at me from the darkness of the tunnel.

Chapter Four

I'd always been under the impression that by the time I hit thirty my life would be more sorted. I'd have some money in the bank, a high-flying career as a photographer, and at least one pair of designer shoes – they didn't have to be Manolo Blahniks, Kurt Geiger would do. But last year it happened – the big three-O – and I realised that while most of my friends are climbing up the ladders of life, being promoted, getting married, having their hair done at Nicky Clarke, *I* just keep sliding down the snakes.

I'm up to my overdraft limit – *whoosh*, slide down a snake. My beloved MG Midget is in the garage after the run-in with the BMW – *whoosh*, slide down another snake. As for my high-flying career as a photographer – *whooossssh*, there I go again, all the way down to the bottom.

For a while back there I thought I might have had it sussed. Meeting Daniel, falling in love, buying a flat and moving in together gave me a sense of achievement. Direction. Maturity. Suddenly I had a mortgage, life insurance, *a partner*. Even though most of the time I felt as if I was playing at being a grown-up, everyone treated me with new respect.

My wicked stepmother sent me recipe books, a mug tree and lots of Tupperware for a mysterious 'bottom drawer'; Sanjeev at the dry-cleaner's nodded politely when I dropped off Daniel's Ralph Lauren shirts along with my suede hipsters. Even the doctor at my local family-planning clinic gave me an approving smile as she wrote out my prescription for the pill.

So what if the career piece of the jigsaw was missing? All the bits for my love life were there and fitted together perfectly. Surely the rest would fall into place.

Well, no, it didn't. Instead it had all fallen apart rather dramatically when I'd borrowed Daniel's Saab and discovered condoms in the glove compartment. I know – it's such a cliché. I'd always assumed things like that only happened to characters in soaps or guests on *Jerry Springer*, but there I'd been, sitting at the lights, singing along to The White Stripes, rummaging in the glove compartment for a rogue packet of cigarettes. Publicly I'd given up months ago, but secretly I'd had a few drags now and again, and Jack White's vocals always put me in the mood for a cigarette – live fast, die young, rock'n'roll and all that. But instead of a packet of Marlboro Lights, I'd discovered a box of Durex 'assorted for maximum pleasure'.

I can remember it as if it was yesterday. My mind froze in shock for a fraction of a second as it tried to accept that not only had I just found condoms in my boyfriend's car, but a bumper pack of twelve . . . I'd tipped it upside-down and the condoms spilt into my lap. Correction: *condom*. There was just one left. And it was ribbed.

For what felt like for ever I'd stared at it resting on my denim crotch. Feeling the hairs on the back of my neck prickle. Hearing my heart thudding in my ears. I remember a bizarre urge to laugh. It was just so ludicrous. Daniel? Unfaithful? Having sex with someone else? Followed by an equally intense burst of anger. *The bastard. The two-timing bastard. How could he?* Finished off with a pathetic desire to break down into tears.

Yet I didn't do anything. I just sat numbly behind the wheel. Jack White crooning. Engine running. World turning. Until the sound of car horns had caused me to look up and see that the lights had changed. Along with everything else.

I'd confronted Daniel as soon as I got back to the flat. At first he'd tried to deny that the condoms were his. He said they belonged to his assistant – it was all a mix-up, a mistake. In fact, he came up with every excuse he could think of. Until finally he'd confessed that he'd been sleeping with someone else – but he wasn't in love with her, it was just sex. *Just sex*.

The way he had said it had been so flippant, as if it was

inconsequential, *unimportant*. Yet those two little words had impacted on my world as if they'd been an iron ball swinging from a bulldozer. Forget breaking my heart, he pretty much demolished it.

Of course I got over it. People always do. And now I'm fine. Absolutely fine. I've got my photography, my friends, my local Blockbuster for Saturday night. And there's always Billy Smith my cat, if I get a bit lonely. That's not to say I wouldn't like the odd *date* now and again, but I'm not one of those women obsessed with finding 'the one'. I mean, it's not as if I fall asleep every night wishing I could meet the perfect man who's going to fall madly, truly and deeply in love with me. Well, perhaps not *every* night. Blushing guiltily I glance at my neighbour.

He's gone.

Which is when I realise that the train has stopped and we're at a station. My station.

Beep-beep-beep-beep-beep-beep.

Oh, shit. The doors are making the high-pitched noise that means they're about to close. Frantically I begin excusing my way through the packed carriages, accidentally dropping the copy of *Loot*, which falls, scattering green newspaper pages all over the floor of the carriage. Oh, double shit. I scramble for them.

Beep-beep-beep-beep-beep-beep-beeeeeeeeeeeep.

The doors are sliding shut as I abandon the dropped pages and lunge for them. Luckily I make it on to the platform in one piece. I trudge to the escalators and glide upwards. Thank goodness the day's nearly over. A short walk along the river and I'll be at home, lying in the back garden, enjoying the sunshine. Er . . . *What sunshine?*

Greeted at the exit by dark, angry stormclouds I wish I had an umbrella. Heavy raindrops pummel the pavement, and people are rushing everywhere, holding coats above their heads, slipping in the puddles. Everyone's getting soaked. Myself included.

I try holding what's left of *Loot* over my head as I run along the high street, but within seconds it's all soggy. The electric goods page slaps me in the face and sticks, smudging print about Dualit toasters across my forehead, until the whole thing collapses like a waterlogged tent, spilling inky water down my face.

Oh, what the hell? I chuck it into a bin and continue running. The rain's bouncing up my legs and drenching my dress, turning the pale blue cotton almost transparent and making it cling to my chest as if I'm in a wet T-shirt competition – bad enough if I was in some drunken, foam-filled club in Lanzarote, but much, much worse in my local high street. Someone I know might see me – and my nipples, which are now protruding through my dress like cocktail cherries.

Just as I have that humiliating thought I spot my neighbour, completely dry under his sturdy golfing umbrella. He's a few metres ahead, waiting outside Oddbins, nonchalantly smoking a cigarette and gazing into the middle distance almost as if he hasn't noticed it's bucketing down. How does he always manage to look so damn gorgeous?

In a moment of madness I consider saying hi. After all, we are neighbours. As I near him my heart speeds up, like the beeping of a metal detector when it's found treasure. Crikey, I hadn't realised how nervous I was. Deep breaths. Deep breaths. Deep breaths.

OK, this is it. 'Hi.' I smile, and for some reason decide to raise my hand in a sort of American-Indian 'How' sign.

Only he doesn't see me, or my impression of Running Big Bear, as he's turning to a pretty brunette who's appeared at the shop doorway hugging a bottle of wine. She ducks under his umbrella, links his arm and they set off down the street together, laughing as they dodge puddles, jump across overflowing grates and pretend to splash each other. I swear to God, it's like something from a bloody Gene Kelly movie.

Deflated, I can't help wishing that it was me who was tucked under the umbrella with him, all dry and happy with a spring in my step, instead of standing here in the rain, feeling sorry for myself.

'Heather.'

A loud yell makes me spin round.

'Lucky heather.'

I see a straggle of women by the cash machine. The younger ones are dressed in tatty T-shirts and jeans faded at the knees, while their elders are wearing headscarves and holding straw baskets that are getting drenched. They're trying to approach people in the street. Unfortunately the general public dislikes people trying to sell them things – be it insurance over the phone, religion on their doorstep, or Romany good-luck charms in the street – about as much as they dislike rain, which means that this group of Irish gypsies is being ignored. Ignored, but not unnoticed.

Like everyone else, I've seen them, but I'm desperate to get home so I do what I usually do when I see market researchers with surveys, foreign students employed to give out flyers or – and I admit this with shame – the Greenpeace people who ask me if I'd like to sign up for a monthly donation. I put my head down, look straight a head, and pretend I've had a sudden loss of hearing.

'You've got a pretty face, love.' A gypsy breaks away from the others to barge in front of me like a rugby centre forward.

I try to dodge her, but she blocks my way. 'Here, take some lucky heather. Use it wisely and it will bring you your heart's desire. Good fortune will come your way . . .' She thrusts a tired sprig tied with a fraying pink ribbon into my face. 'Never underestimate the power of the lucky heather.'

'No, thanks,' I say firmly.

'Just two quid, my darlin'.'

'No, honestly.' I try to avoid her gaze, but the gypsy is grabbing my hand. It feels coarse, the skin weathered a dark tan in contrast to the pale freckliness of my own. I notice the dirty broken fingernails, the gnarled arthritic knuckles, the silver charm bracelet worn next to the pink plastic Swatch. It's jangling as she waggles the heather, billing and cooing like the pigeons on the window-ledges overhead. 'Keep it with you. Trust me, the heather will work its magic. Your luck will change. All your wishes will come true.'

Yeah, right. Do I look like a complete sucker?

But from the glint in her piercing green eyes I know she won't take no for an answer and I'm getting even more soaked standing here so, to get rid of her, I give in and stuff a couple of pound coins into her sandpapery palm. And then she disappears into the rain-soaked crowds, leaving me standing in the middle of the high street, in a downpour, clutching a sprig of white heather.

Lucky heather.

The irony isn't lost on me. Holding it between thumb and forefinger, I peer at the spindly, feathery twigs tied together with a cheap nylon ribbon. *This* is supposed to have magical powers? I consider tossing it into the bin along with the rest of the city's rubbish, but the nearest bin is across the street, so I shove it into my bag – I'll chuck it away when I get home. After I've taken off these wet clothes, cracked open a bottle of wine and climbed into a steaming hot bath.

Dreaming of poaching myself in white-musk-scented bubbles as I drink a glass of sauvignon blanc I forget about the gypsy and the lucky heather and hurry, golf shoes squelching, all the way home.

Chapter Five

Dextrously turning off the tap with my big toe, I lie back on the pillow of scented bubbles. Bliss. Sheer, unadulterated bliss. Sipping my wine I inhale the delicious aroma of vanilla and cinnamon – courtesy of the miniature bottles of Molton Brown bubble bath I found recently. They were stashed away in a wicker basket along with other souvenirs of a weekend I'd spent with Daniel in a hotel in the Lake District: a ticket stub to Wordsworth's cottage, a coffee-stained menu from a café, the little chocolates the maid had put on our pillow each night and I hadn't dared to eat for fear of my thighs. Which, I remember, with a stab of insecurity, Daniel always described as 'heavy'.

'Heavy,' I murmur, irked by my sentimentality at having kept all this rubbish and the sheer arrogance of the man in criticising my body when he sported a matching pair of back creases and receding temples (which I know is the real reason he used to shave his head, and not, as he pretended, because he wanted to look like Jason Statham).

'I'll have you know these thighs jog round the park three times a week,' I mutter slugging back an ice-cold mouthful of sauvignon blanc.' Well, perhaps only twice, and it's more of a power walk than an *actual* jog, but still . . . 'These thighs can do a hundred lunges – if they have to,' I continue. 'Thighs, goddamn it, that can wrap themselves round a lover's neck like a python!' Admittedly not something they've had much practice in recently but, hey, all they need is a bit of limbering up . . .

I balance my glass on the side of the bath, and grab the loofah and a bar of soap. Raising one pink shiny thigh out of the bubbles, I lather it like a war veteran proudly shining up his medals. Round and round in little circles, clockwise, then anti-clockwise, polishing the outer thigh first, then switching my attention to the inner. Plunging the loofah back into the water, I switch thighs. Rhythmically brushing backwards and forwards. Up and down. Side to side. Sloughing off dead skin, pounding cellulite, kneading dimples.

A thought strikes me. Why is it never like this in movies? How come every Hollywood director seems to be under the illusion that women don't lie in bubble baths pumicing the hard skin on their feet or applying thick layers of Jolen cream to bleach their moustaches? Oh no, they writhe around in masturbation heaven, soaping breasts, trickling water from flannels between their legs or rubbing a cold wine glass against their nipples. All, of course, in full makeup.

Honestly, if men knew the truth they'd be so disappointed. I pat the thick layer of cream bleach I've applied to my top lip. Nope, not ready yet – another five minutes. Discarding the loofah I reach for the razor and inspect the blade. It's stuffed full of bristles from the last time I used it. And it's the last one. Damn. I wish I had a new packet. The last time I used a blunt razor I'd cut my legs to ribbons. But what's the alternative? Spend the weekend with legs like my old German teacher?

Without further ado I give the blade a quick rinse under the tap and get to work, cutting through the lather with well-practised strokes. Shin, calf, ankle, knee. Ouch. I watch a spot of blood appear like a red bubble on my leg.

'Shit.' Grabbing the flannel I fold it into a makeshift bandage and am just pressing it to my knee when the phone rings. I listen to it echoing in the hallway. I wonder who it is. Probably Jess, I decide, then remember she's in Delhi. And it's not my father as I spoke to him earlier today. He'd just read an article about how they've started teaching yoga to cats in Hollywood, and was wondering if Billy Smith might fancy some classes for his birthday. I smile. My father's an artist and a little eccentric, but I wouldn't change him for the world. If only the same could be said for my stepmother . . .

I decide against answering it and submerge myself in the duvet of scented bubbles as I wait for the answering-machine to pick up. It's probably my stepmother calling to annoy me about something anyway. Although there is a slim possibility that it's Daniel, calling in reply to my drunken text.

As the thought occurs to me I'm unsure whether that's a good thing or a bad thing, considering the text: 'I miss you. Fancy sex with an ex?' That was the tequila talking, not me: I don't miss him, I *hate* him. And I certainly don't want to sleep with him. I hesitate. Should I make a dash for the phone?

Oh, sod it. Sliding back into the bubbles, one leg dangling out of the bath, I reach for my glass and take another mouthful of wine. Whoever it is can wait.

After what feels like forever the phone stops ringing and I hear the answering-machine click on. I wait to hear my stepmother's affected voice. Ashamed of her working-class Manchester roots, Rosemary adopts an accent not dissimilar to the Queen's.

'Hey there . . .'

Hang on a minute, since when was my stepmother a man? I feel a jolt of something – I'm not sure if it's panic or excitement. Oh, my God, it's not Daniel, is it? But then I register that this man has an American accent and I feel a flash of foolishness – and something that feels like disappointment.

'I'm calling about the ad you placed in . . . er . . . hang on . . .' There's the sound of rustling pages. 'It's called . . .'

'*Loot*,' we say in the same beat.

Shit.

I vault out of the bath and dash naked into the hallway, dripping soapy water on to the floor. Keep talking, I pray, lunging for the receiver with slippery fingers.

'Don't hang up.' I pant, tearing the phone from its cradle – then remember that if this is a prospective flatmate, I'm a prospective landlady. And I should sound like one. 'I mean, good evening,' I say, adopting my best telephone voice. My stepmother would be proud.

'Oh, hi, yeah. I was . . . er . . . calling about the ad.'

'And you are?' I demand, and then cringe. What on earth am I doing? I'm trying to rent my room. I need to sound friendly, laid-back, *cool.* 'Sorry, you caught me in the bath, I was trying to find some clothes—' I break off – I sound like one of those peak-rate 0870 numbers. 'I mean, hi, I'm Heather.'

'Oh, hi,' he says. Followed by an awkward pause. He's probably deciding whether or not to hang up, I decide, and assume I've blown it. Well, would I rent a room from me?

'I'm Gabe.'

Hmm. What an unusual name. Momentarily I wonder what Gabe looks like. Being American, he's probably tall, broad, with really good teeth – unless, with *my* luck, he's short, fat and balding. And what if he is? This is a prospective lodger, not a date.

'Right, I mean . . .' I grapple for some witty quip, then give up. 'Cool!' I blurt, closing my eyes in shame. 'Cool' is not a word you want to be saying if you still bear the remnants of a child-hood Yorkshire accent: it comes out as *koo-elle* – which is not cool.

Thankfully the stranger doesn't notice, or if he does, he doesn't comment. 'Erm . . . so I was wondering . . . about the room?'

The room. I snap back.

'Is it still available?'

'Well, there has been a lot of interest,' I lie, standing next to the window. It faces directly on to my gorgeous neighbour's and, unable to resist, I lift the edge of the blind and peek round the side to see if I can catch a glimpse of him.

'Oh, well, in that case, don't worry about it. I was only looking for something short-term.'

'Short term?' My ears prick up.

'Yeah, I'm here in London for three weeks, maybe a month.'

I like the sound of a month. It's nice and temporary. It's four weeks, which, at a hundred and fifty pounds a week, is . . . I do some mental arithmetic . . . Enough to pay off one credit card. And if I get my arse in gear it might just be long enough for me to find a job that will hopefully pay so well that I won't have to share a loo-seat with a total stranger.

'But I haven't made a decision yet so I'm still interviewing people,' I add, accidentally jerking the blind. It shoots up, leaving my window bare and exposed, not to mention myself. At the exact moment that my neighbour is drawing his curtains.

'*Agggh!*' I shriek.

There's silence at the other end of the line, and then, a few seconds later, 'Er, hi . . . Sorry, I dropped the phone . . . uhm . . . Are you still there?'

Gabe sounds tentative. No doubt it's taken him a moment to pluck up courage to pick up the receiver. 'Er . . . yes . . . I'm still here.'

'Are you OK?'

Having jumped away from the window, into the corner by the mirror, I glance sideways at my reflection. 'Yes, I'm fine,' I reply, in a strangled voice. Oh. My. God. So this is what my neighbour just saw. Boobs, streaky mascara, wet hair, a cream-bleach moustache and naked thighs. Naked *heavy* thighs.

'Are you sure?'

'Absolutely,' I reply firmly, edging forward to peer round the corner like a sniper. I glance back across the street. 'Him' is still at the window. No doubt frozen with shock. I throw myself to the ground in an army dive.

'*Agggh.*'

'Perhaps this isn't a good time . . .'

'No, now's a good time,' I pant, inching forward on my elbows as if I'm on an assault course. I wince as the sisal matting gives my nipples a nasty case of carpet burn. 'In fact . . .' Reaching the coat rack I stand upright, grabbing a jacket from a hook. I wrap it round myself protectively. 'Why don't you come along and take a look at the room, see if you like it? See if you like me.' I laugh nervously.

'When?'

'Erm, next week?' I'm playing for time. And sole usage of the Le Creuset pans.

'What about tomorrow?'

'Tomorrow?' I squeak.

'Sorry, I forgot, it's Saturday night. You've probably made plans.'

'Um . . . well, actually . . .' My voice trails off as I remember the truth. I have no plans. I'm single. I'm staying in alone. On a Saturday night.

'Sorry, am I being your typical pushy American?' His voice interrupts my awkwardness.

'Yes, I mean no, no . . . not at all,' I'm babbling. For Godsake, don't be such an idiot, Heather, think of your credit-card bills. Think of your mortgage. Think of the fact that you've been advertising your room for weeks and this is the first reply you've had. 'Tomorrow's fine,' I say quickly.

'Awesome.'

'Um . . . yep . . . awesome,' I repeat. 'Awesome' is *another* word that can only be used by those with an American accent.

There's a pause.

'I'll need your address.'

'Oh, yes, my address . . . of course.' I proceed to gabble it so quickly that he has to ask me to repeat it twice.

'Thanks. I'll see you tomorrow. Around seven?'

'Great, see you then.'

I replace the handset and lean against the wall. Reeling at the unexpected speed of events, I take a couple of deep breaths. Water from my hair trickles down my back and although it's a balmy seventy degrees in the hallway, I shiver. Sticking my hands in my pockets to pull my jacket round me I feel my fingers brush against something. Soft yet scratchy. Puzzled, I pull it out. It's that stupid lucky heather. How did that get there?

Walking to the bin I keep near the front door for junk mail, I'm about to toss it in when I notice a small package on my doormat. One of those freebies you get in the post. Only this time it isn't some hideously flavoured new Cup-a-soup, or a trial bar of soap: it's a packet of razor blades. Well, would you believe it? I pick it up. Now I won't have to go out tomorrow looking half-woman, half-beast.

Chuffed, I hurry back into the bathroom and reach for my razor to swap the blade for a new one. Which is when I see that I'm still holding the sprig of heather. For some reason, I can't get rid of it. Maybe it really is magical. *Magical?* I smile ironically. Heather Hamilton, what on earth's got into you? Of course it's not magical, it's just a plant. Or is it a flower?

Twirling it between finger and thumb I gaze at the delicate white sprigs. Superstitious nonsense or not, it's actually rather pretty. It seems a shame to throw it away. Filling the top of a deodorant can with water I place the lucky heather in its make-shift vase and pop it on the windowsill. For now, anyway.

Chapter Six

Along the banks of the River Avon a small group of art students are huddled round wooden easels. Before them rolls the Shropshire countryside, the layers of sky, fields and river the focus for their tubes of oil paint and brush-stuffed jam jars. This class is part of a summer-school programme run by Bath's local art college and the students have travelled from Texas to take advantage of it. They're being taught by Lionel, a robust, bearded man in his early sixties, who looks as if he's travelled there in a time machine from the French impressionist era. Wearing a paint-splattered smock, a neckerchief, and a beret angled sideways over thick, black curls worthy of a man half his age, he's striding round the class bellowing enthusiasm and advice.

'Fabulous use of the magenta, Sandy.'

A large-chested woman beams and continues daubing vigorously.

'Spot-on sketching, George Junior,' he growls, slapping the tiny shoulder of an elderly man in Bermuda shorts. 'Now let's see what you can do with the real stuff.' He snatches the pencil out of George Junior's fingers and replaces it with a horsehair paintbrush.

'Lionel!'

My voice catches my father by surprise and he swings round, smock billowing round him like a parachute. Waving at him from the wooden stile where I've been perched for the last five minutes, watching him proudly, I feel my heart tug. I'm very much my father's daughter. Living in London I don't get to spend as much time with him as I'd like, especially not now that he's getting older, and I miss him. A wide smile stretches across my face and I yell even louder, 'Lionel, it's me!'

Lionel peers down into his half-moon glasses and smiles back as he recognises the figure in a red T-shirt and cut-off denim shorts as his only daughter. 'Heather, darling,' he bellows, abandoning his students and striding over to greet me. 'What a wonderful surprise!' Throwing his arms round my shoulders he pulls me into a bear hug. 'Why didn't you let me know you were coming? Or did you, and I've forgotten?' He rolls his eyes dramatically. 'My memory's getting worse. Rosemary fears I'm going senile,' he confides, then laughs uproariously.

As he clucks and coos over me, I ignore his reference to my stepmother. 'I'm sorry, it was a last-minute decision. Brian gave me the day off and I just got my car back from the garage so I thought I'd come and see you.'

Well, it's partly true. Yes, it wasn't until I'd woken up this morning that I decided I needed to escape London for the day. And, yes, I had really wanted to see my dad. But not calling beforehand? That was deliberate. I hadn't wanted to let Rosemary know I was coming. If I had, she would have made some excuse about them having a prior engagement, or tell me she had one of her migraines, or suggest that perhaps another weekend might be better. This way, she can't spoil things – but then again she did that when she married Dad.

'Marvellous, marvellous,' beams Lionel, releasing me from his embrace and turning to his students, most of whom are watching our reunion with interest. 'Everyone, I'd like to introduce my beautiful daughter, Heather.'

'Howdy,' they chorus, in a strong Texas drawl.

I smile sheepishly. Dad is always showing me off like some prized possession: he even keeps a photograph of me in his wallet, which he insists on pulling out in front of complete strangers – embarrassing enough, without the fact it's a school picture of me at thirteen with braces and a custard-dip fringe.

'She's a photographer,' he continues proudly.

'Wow,' come the gasps of admiration.

Oh, no. I steel myself for the inevitable questions about supermodels and fashion shoots for *Vogue*. I always feel like such a disappointment when I have to admit the truth. People want to hear about exotic locations and the size of Kate Moss's thighs, not someone-they've-never-heard-of's wedding at Brixton town hall.

But, thankfully, I'm saved by my father's appetite. Digging out his fob-watch from the pocket of his voluminous corduroys, he flicks open the brass cover. 'Well, that's about it for today, everyone,' he declares. 'It's twelve thirty on the nose. Time for a spot of lunch.'

Lunch is back at the house. An imposing Regency building torn straight from the pages of a Jane Austen novel, it stands high on a hill in the centre of Bath, offering spectacular views of the town and surrounding villages. Built from honey-coloured stone, it boasts large sash windows that look out on to the walled garden filled with rosebushes, a gazebo and one of those vast lawns that have been mown into immaculate stripes. By anyone's standards, it's a truly beautiful house.

I, however, hate it. It belongs to Rosemary and, like its owner, it's cold and unwelcoming. Before she and Dad were married, he was living in our cosy cottage in Cornwall, with its uneven walls, tiny porthole windows and thatched roof. Now its used only for holidays and family get-togethers – Rosemary complained it was too small for her furniture.

What she'd meant was that the house reminded her of my mother.

Lionel bought it when Mum was first diagnosed. Hoping that the warmer climate and sea air might do her good, he sold our house in Yorkshire and moved the whole family hundreds of miles south to Port Isaac. Ed and I were still children, and had hated being uprooted, leaving our friends, Leeds United football team and Fred, our pet gerbil, whom we'd buried in the back garden. Our mother, however, fell in love with the place and her happiness was infectious, changing our minds but never her diagnosis. She had died less than three years later.

'So, how long are you staying?'

We're all sitting round the kitchen table. There's my dad, me and my stepmother, who'd greeted my appearance with the customary tight-lipped kiss on the cheek, then complained that they probably wouldn't have enough food as she hadn't been to the supermarket. 'I wasn't expecting guests.' She'd smiled woodenly, barely keeping the accusation out of her voice.

I turn to my father who's cutting himself a large slice of Brie, his meaty hands gripping the cheese knife like a saw.

'Just for the day,' I say. 'I've got to be back in London by tonight.'

'Tonight?' Disappointment clouds his face.

'Oh, what a shame,' coos Rosemary.

She doesn't fool me. I know she's delighted.

'Aha, I get it!' His face springs back up again and Lionel pounds his fist on the table. 'You've got a date with a young chap.'

'Not exactly,' I admit, plucking a few grapes from the bunch on the cheeseboard and popping them into my mouth one by one.

'Not still mooning over that scoundrel, are you?'

'His name's Daniel,' I remind him calmly. It's only now, a year later, that I can even say his name without that awful breathless sensation, as if I've dived into the deep end of a swimming-pool and I'm trying to swim up to the surface. 'And, no, that's all in the past.'

OK, so I sent him that text last week I remember shamefully, but I was drunk so it didn't count.

'When do we get to meet your new fella, then?'

'*Lionel*,' I gasp, suddenly feeling about thirteen again. Back then he would pick me up from the youth club and quiz me about boys as we walked back to our tiny slate-roofed cottage by the harbour. It was just after Mum had died, and suddenly he was taking me through puberty, first boyfriends, sex education. It had been a learning process for both of us.

Lionel had never been a hands-on dad – when we were little

my brother and I had learned quickly that he answered to Lionel rather than Daddy, although when he was in his studio, painting, he went for days without answering to anyone – so it had been something of an eye-opener for him to become a single parent. This was a man who'd never changed a nappy but was having to buy sanitary towels for his teenage daughter.

Somehow we got through it. As he told me when, in tears, I'd barricaded myself into the bathroom with my first trainer bra, if we could get through losing a wife and a mother, we could get through anything.

Including this lunch.

'I've been too busy working to have a boyfriend.'

'Heather's what they call "a career woman",' notes Rosemary, squeezing lemon on her smoked salmon and draping a piece over a Ryvita. I watch her taking a careful nibble. Although there's not an ounce of flesh on her bones, Rosemary's forever watching her figure. Presumably in case it should disappear.

'Your boss keeping your nose to the grindstone, hey?' mumbles Lionel through a bite of Brie.

'Something like that,' I say vaguely, deciding not to mention the possibility of losing my job. I don't want to worry him – or give Rosemary some more ammunition against me. If I hear one more time about Annabel, her daughter who's only a year older than me but is happily married to Miles, 'a high-flyer' in the City, and has two adorable children, a loft conversion and a French-speaking nanny, I'll . . . Well, I don't know what I'll do but I'm sure I'll do something.

Glancing at my stepmother, who's patting her pale yellow hair, which she's put up, as always, into an immaculate chignon, I can't help wondering what it would be like if Mum was still alive so that I could talk to her about my worries and get her advice. Ask her for a hug.

'Oh, I love weddings!' I'm distracted from my thoughts by Rosemary clasping her hands girlishly. 'I do envy you, your job must be so romantic.'

Taken aback by this uncharacteristic compliment, I'm unsure

what to say. Rosemary and I don't *do* compliments: our conversation consists of a form of jousting, each trying to knock the other off balance. It's exhausting. Sometimes I wish we could just make small-talk about *EastEnders* or discuss the new duvet cover she's bought, like Jess does with her mum. But, then, Rosemary isn't my mum.

I look at her sadly, my throat tight. And she never will be.

'Er . . . well, not really,' I begin hesitantly. 'I'm there to take the photographs, and when you've done as many weddings as I have, one is very much like another.'

'Not when it's your own,' she says pointedly, looking at Lionel like a lovestruck new bride.

I squirm. It really annoys me when Rosemary gets all soppy around Lionel. 'No, maybe not,' I agree reluctantly. To agree with Rosemary is usually tantamount to defeat, but this time I change my mind. Maybe I've been wrong about her all this time. Maybe, like Lionel says, she really does want to be friends.

'Never mind, dear.' Reaching over for the wine, she pats my arm. 'It'll be your turn one day.'

It's not as if she meant that in a bitchy way, she was just trying to be nice, right?

'More wine anyone?' she finishes topping up her glass and holds the bottle aloft.

'Mmm, yes, that would be fabulous.' Lionel beams.

'Actually I'm single out of choice, not necessity,' I point out casually. 'Plenty of men ask me out on dates.'

'I'm sure they do, a pretty girl like you,' agrees Rosemary, much to my surprise. So, she really is trying to be nice. Obviously it's just me being paranoid. 'Though it was different in my day. If you weren't married by the time you were thirty, you were considered on old maid.'

Ouch. See what happens when I let my guard down? She goes right for the jugular.

'Oh, but it's different now, my love,' replies Lionel, helping himself to potato salad and several slices of ham in ignorance of the Third World War that's currently being waged across the table between his wife and his daughter. 'Times have changed. Heather's probably beating them off like flies, hmm?' He gazes at me adoringly. As far as Lionel's concerned, I'm the most beautiful, talented, intelligent woman that's ever walked on this planet.

'OK, so perhaps "plenty" is a *slight* exaggeration,' I admit, guilted out by Lionel's devotion. 'But that's not the point.'

'It's not?' pipes up Rosemary, resting her hand on Lionel's. To anyone else that would appear to be an act of affection, but to me it looks like possession. I don't know why she doesn't wear a sign round her neck saying, 'Hands off, he's mine.'

'No, it's not the point at all,' I repeat emphatically. 'The point is . . .' I begin, and then stop. Because, you see, I'm not sure what the point *is* any more. Realising I have no hope of winning this argument I look at Rosemary's face flushed with victory, and I surrender.

For the time being.

After lunch, we go outside and have Pimm's on the lawn and a game of chess. A keen player Lionel has built a giant chessboard on the patio and when Rosemary goes inside to lie down – 'It's the heat, so incredibly tiring' – he and I pace round the board, carrying the four-foot-high polystyrene pieces on to different-coloured squares, trying to put each other in check-mate. As father and daughter we're the best of friends; as chess opponents we're sworn enemies.

'Check-mate,' I announce triumphantly, setting down my bishop.

Lionel bites down hard on the stem of his pipe. 'Poppycock!'

I fold my arms and watch as he stomps round the pieces, forehead furrowed in concentration.

'So, do you admit defeat?' I tease.

'Never!' he roars. Running his fingers through his unruly curls, he continues pacing. 'That can't be.'

'Yes, it can.' This is a well-rehearsed routine. Whenever I win a game my father's reaction is, first, disbelief, then disagreement, and finally, 'Good Lord, how did you manage that?'

He's stopped circling and is standing, hands on hips, his face incredulous.

'I had a good teacher,' I reply, as I always do.

'Aah, you're too kind,' he mutters, patting my shoulder affectionately. 'I was a terrible player until I met your mother. Did I ever tell you about the first time we played chess?'

'You were both eighteen and in your first year at Cambridge.' I know this story off by heart.

'That's right,' nods Lionel, reminiscing. 'A tutor had organised a chess tournament with one of the ladies' colleges and I nearly didn't go as it clashed with auditions for a play I wanted to be in.'

'*The Duchess of Malfi*,' I prompt.

'It was.' He's delighted that I should remember. 'But at the last minute I changed my mind and signed up for the tournament. It took place in the banqueting hall and I remember walking in and looking for my opponent. And then I saw her, sitting under a shaft of sunlight, waiting for me . . .'

'A dazzling redhead who played chess like a Russian.'

'She had me within six moves. Six moves was all it took.' Lionel shakes his head as if he still can't believe it, even after all these years.

We fall silent, drinking in the memory like vintage wine.

'I still miss her,' I say eventually.

'I know, darling.'

'I wish she was here with us right now'

'Now, that would make me a bigamist.'

I smile wryly at his feeble joke. I know he's trying to make me feel better but it still hurts. 'I just wish things were different.'

Puffing at his pipe, Lionel fixes me with his pale grey eyes. They're just like mine, almond-shaped, with tiny flecks of navy blue round the iris. 'You mustn't wish your life away, Heather.'

His face is serious but it doesn't stop me quipping, 'Why not?'

He lets a stream of smoke spiral up from the corner of his mouth. 'Because life's far too short to waste a single drop of it. Your mother taught me that.' He pauses to watch a bird hovering by the fountain, its tiny body glistening in the sunlight as it dips its beak into the water. For a moment he is lost in contemplation. 'You know I once read somewhere that yesterday is history, tomorrow is a mystery, but today is a gift. That's why we call it the present.'

Absorbing the words I'm struck by its profundity.

I wonder which philosopher came up with that. Presumably some Buddhist monk or another spiritual leader who had spent his life doing good deeds and existing on the love of others. Someone who lived without possessions. Someone who probably didn't even own a pair of shoes. Let alone a pair of overpriced sandals that ended up in the bin. Suddenly I feel ashamed. 'Who said that?' I ask, reverentially.

Having drunk its fill the bird darts away and my dad turns back to me. 'I think it was Joan Collins,' he confesses, and linking his arm through mine we begin walking slowly to the house.

Chapter Seven

The drive back to London always takes for ever. For some strange reason, never explained to me, the M4 is always 'currently undergoing roadworks', which means hours in traffic jams or crawling at 30 m.p.h. through elaborate patterns of orange cones that appear mysteriously during the night. Yet you never see any evidence of any 'works' taking place. It's one of life's mysteries.

Like crop circles, I muse, accelerating on to the motorway from the slip road and wishing there was no such thing as roadworks or traffic. Just imagine, if it was clear like this all the way I'd be home in no time.

As I speed up I increase the volume to drown the sound of the wind. In preparation for the inevitable delays I've made myself some new cassettes. I've also packed supplies in the form of a bumper bag of liquorice allsorts. Well, if I'm going to be stranded on the M4 I might as well have *The Best of Duran Duran* and my favourite pink and yellow ones with liquorice in the middle to keep me company. I pop one into my mouth and bite into the soft, sweet coconut.

But twenty minutes into the journey, I'm feeling a little disconcerted. I can't put my finger on it but something's weird. Blustering along in the fast lane with the roof down, my hair tucked tightly out of knots' way in a headscarf I feel as if something's missing. Music? Nope: Simon Le Bon's belting out 'Rio' at full volume. Food? Nope. I pick a bit of liquorice out of my back molar, then push my hand back into the bag. Headlights? It's still dusk so I only need sidelights. I check them. Nope, they're on.

Then I get it.

Orange cones. There aren't any.

And neither are there any traffic jams. Smiling in happy disbelief, I press my flip-flop against the accelerator. At this rate I'll be home in less than two hours.

Correction: one hour and forty-two minutes exactly. I know because I check my watch as I turn into my street. It has to be something of a world record. I slow down and idle along the tree-lined pavement. Leaning over the steering-wheel, top teeth over bottom lip, eyes darting from side to side, I begin my usual routine of looking for a parking space. I don't hold out much hope. In all the years I've lived at my flat I've never parked outside it.

'I wish there was a space,' I murmur, under my breath, 'just one parking space . . .'

But it's bumper-to-bumper all the way down my street. I fling myself back in my seat and put my foot down. I'll have to circle the block. Probably about a dozen times. And end up parking about a mile away. Through unlit streets that are probably swarming with muggers and rapists and . . . ohmygod!

While imagining my generally safe neighbourhood as the kind of gangland ghetto you see in Al Pacino films, I nearly drive straight into a Range Rover. Parked facing the wrong way, it's indicating right and, as it swings in front of me, I slam on the brakes.

I come to an abrupt halt, my head flung back like that of a crash-test dummy and look up at the windscreen of the Range Rover. 'Sorry,' I mouth silently at the driver.

It's him. My neighbour.

For a moment I'm not quite sure what to do so I sit there as he nods a curt response, swerves round me and roars off down the street. Leaving me sitting there like a right lemon.

I look in my rear-view mirror and watch the grey swirls of fumes round his exhaust, listening to the noise of the four-litre engine as he accelerates away. Typical! I've done it again. I've bumped into him like a complete idiot. Depressed, I slump over my steering-wheel and rest my forehead on the shiny MG badge in the centre. I close my eyes and I replay the last scene torturously in my head, with the look he gave me as he drove away – then spring up again. Hang on a minute. If he's gone, that means . . .

There, where the Range Rover was just parked, *right opposite my flat*, I see what any London resident will describe as a modern-day miracle. A parking space.

I hadn't thought much about what I was going to say to my prospective flatmate. In fact, since I'd put down the phone after our conversation yesterday evening, I hadn't given the stranger with the American accent and the funny name a second thought. I'd been too busy spending time with Lionel while trying to avoid Rosemary – never an easy task – not to mention enjoying the novelty of driving too fast on the motorway and parking outside my front door.

But now it's six o'clock. He's due to turn up in a hour. And I *am* thinking about him. I'm wondering what on earth I'm going to say, what I'm going to ask him, what rules I'm going to lay down. And, most importantly of all, as I stand in front of my wardrobe in my bobbly old dressing-gown, with a towel wrapped round my sopping hair: *what the hell am I going to wear?*

I'm no closer to answering this question thirty minutes later when every inch of my bedroom floor is covered with clothes. Denim mini-skirt? Too mini. Beach dress from last year's holiday to Ibiza? Too hippie. Off-the-shoulder Karen Millen top I've never worn? Trying too hard.

Exhausted, I perch on the edge of the bed and stare at the empty wire hangers clanging dolefully inside my wardrobe. Usually in a moment of crisis I'd ring Jess for advice, but she's in India. I pick my cuticles for a few minutes, and then, in desperation, call her anyway. It goes straight to voicemail. Bugger. I glance at my digital alarm clock: 18:50.

Oh, bugger bollocks. I've got to make a decision. OK. As usual I've got nothing to wear. OK, so I hate all my clothes. But as I have no credit cards, money or time, I either greet my possible new flatmate wearing a bobbly old dressing-gown with a tropical-fish beach towel wrapped round my head, or . . . ?

Feeling like a chef on *Ready, Steady, Cook* – faced with five minutes to make something fabulous out of a few lousy vegetables and a piece of old Cheddar – I think, Sod it, grab a few items from the bed and start to get dressed.

19.05. *He's late.* I puff nervously as a cigarette and dart up and down the living room, trying to peer out of the window without anyone seeing me. Nothing. Fiddling absentmindedly with my hair – trying to twist the damp curls into ringlets rather than the frizz that would send John Frieda and his serums into apoplexy – I blow smoke against the glass pane, then catch myself. *Jesus.* I think back to the list of house rules I came up with when I put the ad in the paper.

Number one: no smoking indoors.

I haul open a sash window, then waft my arms around manically, trying to get rid of the smoke. Before realising that I'm still holding the cigarette, which probably isn't helping. Oh, shite – I stub it out in an empty coffee cup on the mantelpiece. Oh, fuck.

Number two: no using the crockery as an ashtray.

19.12. Maybe he's got lost. Standing by the back door that opens out on to the tiny patch of grass and honeysuckle that I like to call my garden (and which Rosemary sniffily refers to as my 'yard'), I sip my drink. I've moved on to gin and tonic. Less smelly. And, anyway, I've given up smoking, remember?

As I rattle the ice-cubes in my glass, I try to imagine what an American will think of my garden. Probably that it's quaint. He's probably never been to England before: he'll think London is like something from a Richard Curtis film and that Hugh Grant lives round the corner. No doubt he'll want to ask me lots of questions about our traditions, the Royal Family and David Beckham, and it's important that I'm the perfect host: gracious, entertaining, welcoming.

19.18. *Where the fuck is he?* Having downed two gin and tonics, now I'm getting antsy. 'Don't tell me I'm being stood up,' I huff, as I stomp round my flat, feeling like a wronged girlfriend. My bladder sends me into the bathroom for a pee. 'Don't tell me I've gone to all this trouble . . .' OK, maybe that's a bit strong when I'm wearing a skirt that needs ironing, an embroidered cheesecloth top I found at the market, and a bit of lipgloss – but, still, I've made an effort of sorts. 'Which is more than he has,' I huff again, tugging at the loo roll so that it rattles loudly. '*He can't even be bothered to show up!*'

Flushing, I stand up and give the bathroom an extra squirt of air-freshener, then replace the cap. Which is when I catch sight of the lucky heather, still in its makeshift vase on the windowsill. I'd forgotten all about it, but now, reminded of the circumstances in which I was forced to buy it and irritated by my sentimentality in keeping it, I give the plastic top a quick rinse and put it back on the deodorant. The lucky heather goes into the bin.

Having emptied the bathroom bin in preparation for the American, I head for the silver one in the kitchen. But I only get half-way down the hallway when I decide to make a quick detour via the front room. The plan being I'll take a last peek through the window and then, if there's no sign of him I'll abandon the whole thing and defrost a pizza, I decide, as I lean across the back of the sofa. The plan not being to have my face squashed up against the glass like Garfield on a car window, when someone knocks on the front door.

Startled, I peel my face off the glass.

A blond stranger is standing on the doorstep, wearing a motorcycle jacket and carrying a helmet. He's checking his reflection in the brass door knocker – brushing his shaggy fringe out of his eyes, pushing his tortoiseshell glasses up his nose, lifting his chin and rubbing a rogue patch of bristles, turning his head from one side to the other side . . .

The stranger is suddenly looking right at me, his large blue eyes filled with curiosity. It throws me off balance and, giving a muffled squeak, I promptly fall down the back of the sofa.

Chapter Eight

'I'm Gabe.'

The first thing I notice are his freckles. He's got even more than me, and I'm a redhead so freckles come with the territory.

'Hi, I'm Heather.' Rubbing my elbow, I show him into the flat. 'I was, er . . . just doing a spot of housework . . . cleaning the windows.' I laugh awkwardly. 'A tidy flat makes for a tidy mind and all that . . .' Hearing my drivel, I cringe inwardly. Shut up, Heather. Just shut up.

'I'm a complete pig.'

'You are?'

'I was being ironic.' He smiles. 'Hard to believe, I know. Being American.'

'Oh, right,' I say, feeling even more of an idiot.

His attempt at breaking the ice having failed, there follows a toe-curling silence. I smile uncomfortably.

'So, can I see the room?'

'Of course,' I say hastily, and lead him down the hallway. 'This is it.' Pushing open the door I stand back. 'Not very big, I'm afraid, but it's got everything. Bed, cupboard, chest of drawers, portable TV . . .'

As I speak Gabe walks into the small, L-shaped room and regards the pale yellow walls, the polished mahogany wardrobe with its delicate inlay and curved doors that the man at Brick Lane market who sold it to me said was from the 1930s. A paper lampshade from IKEA hangs overhead, a sheepskin rug partly covers the bare wooden floor, and I've even put a couple of books on the empty shelves: the *Hip Hotel* guides, something by Salman Rushdie and Nick Hornby's *About A Boy*. Books say a lot about a person so I ignored my stack of chick-lit and *Harry Potter*, in favour of something more literary to make a good first impression. I rub my bruised elbow. Well, that was the idea.

Earlier, I opened the sash window wide to give a full view of the back garden, and now he walks over to it. With his back to me, he leans against the sill, but doesn't speak. Obviously not much of a talker, I decide, tracing the silhouette of his shoulders. He's tall – over six foot, at a guess – and much broader than I'd first thought. My eyes travel down the back of his jacket, lingering over the baggy arse of his combat trousers – well, I'm only human – to the tattered hems trailing over his flip-flops. Nope, definitely not my type. Too grungy. Too quiet as well. And when I'd caught a glimpse of his T-shirt under his jacket I could have sworn it had a photo of Mr T from the A Team on the front. I shudder.

'I'll take it.'

His voice zones me back in. 'Oh . . .' I'm not prepared for this. I'd expected lots of questions, rehearsed lots of answers, but now, faced with a *fait accompli* I'm suddenly unsure. Do I really want this stranger living in my flat? I mean, I hardly know you, pipes up a little voice inside me.

'OK, so what do you want to know about me?'

As Gabe turns I realise I spoke aloud. I blush hotly. 'Erm, well, I think we should get to know each other a bit first, you know, talk about hobbies or something . . .' *Hobbies?* As soon as the word pops out of my mouth the flush on my cheeks deepens. I sound like a twelve-year-old.

It amuses Gabe, who smiles mischievously. 'As if we're on a date?'

'No, I . . .' I falter. I know I'm being ridiculous so I try to relax. 'Sorry, I'm not used to this,' I confess. 'I've never let a room before and it just feels weird.'

'Sure, I understand.' He sits on the windowsill, pushes his hair out of his face and fixes me with a steady gaze. 'Fire away. Ask me anything you like.'

'Really?'

'Really.'

Well, in that case . . .

I disappear out of the room for a few moments and when I return with a notebook Gabe's still on the windowsill. Only he's got company in the shape of a large ginger tomcat curled up on his knee like a croissant, head tucked in one end, tail the other, purring loudly.

'Oh, you've met Billy Smith,' I say, surprised to see my cat snuggled up in his crotch. The same cat that hisses and digs his claws into anyone he doesn't know who tries so much as to stroke him. 'He normally doesn't like strangers.' Billy Smith gazes at me languidly without any sign of recognition, then closes his eyes. Traitor, I hiss silently. Who buys you Fancy Feast? Who lets you sleep in my bed in winter?

'Animals usually like me.' Gabe tickles Billy Smith between the ears. He's rewarded by an even louder purr.

I can't believe it! Even my bloody cat's cheating on me.

'It's people I have a bit of a problem with.' His face is serious, but this time I recognise the joke and smile. Despite my reservations I am warming to him. Not that that lets you off, moggy, I muse, glaring at Billy Smith who gives me a fish-breath yawn and, using his tail to wrap himself up like a parcel, turns his back on me.

Plopping down on the bed, I turn over the first page of my spiral notebook and look up at Gabe, like a secretary about to do a spot of shorthand. 'I jotted down a few things I wanted to ask you, in case I forgot,' I begin. Actually that's a lie, I didn't *jot*. 'Jot' gives the impression that I casually scribbled down a few reminders, when in fact I made one of my lists. It's three pages long and took nearly a week of countless revisions and a wastepaper bin full of scrunched-up bits of paper before it was finished. I even typed it up on the computer at work and was going to print it out and give it to prospective flatmates as a questionnaire, but Jess had advised me that that might be a bit much.

'Fire away,' he says again.

I clear my throat. 'Erm . . . do you smoke?'

'I'm trying to take it up.' He grins.

I'm not sure if he's making fun of me, but I make a note anyway. 'Well, there's no smoking indoors. By all means smoke in the garden but not using crockery, plant pots or my flower-beds as an ashtray.'

'Sure.'

'Drugs?'

'Only prescription,' he answers solemnly.

I make a scribble and move on to the next rule. 'No leaving teabags in the sink.'

'I drink coffee.'

'Oh, OK . . . Great.' I smile. *Tightly*. This isn't going to plan. If I'm honest I'd been secretly hoping my rules would deter him from wanting the room. Under my eyelashes I watch him stroke Billy Smith. He seems very pleasant and everything – if you'd bumped into him in a bar. But outside my bathroom? At seven in the morning? In his underpants?

Panic grabs me. This is never going to work. I've only ever shared this flat with one man and that was Daniel. I can't have a stranger parading around my home in his Y-fronts. I need to put him off.

'Moving on to the kitchen.' I stand up hastily. 'No leaving the dishes. I don't have a dishwasher so you'll have to wash up after every meal. And no filling a dirty pan with water and leaving it in the sink for days. Soaking is not washing-up,' I bark bossily.

Gabe gives me a mock-salute.

'As for the fridge, you can have the top shelf and if you want to put meat in there make sure it's covered. I'm a vegetarian – well, I eat fish . . .'

'So you're a pescetarian?'

I throw him a frosty look and march into the bathroom. 'I only have one bathroom so we'll have to share.' I push open the door and, as he peers inside, I start rattling through Daniel's habits which drove me mad. That should do the trick. American or British, men are men, and one thing I've learned is that they hate nothing more than a nag. So I nag: 'No taking your socks off and leaving them in little balls on the floor, no shaving and leaving your bristles all over the basin, no using all my shampoo and conditioner . . .' I pause only to draw breath – now I'm in full swing there's no stopping me. 'Oh, and no leaving the loo seat up.'

'The loo?'

'You know – the bog.'

No recognition.

'The lav?'

Not even a flicker.

'The toilet?' I try.

'Oh . . . right, yeah, of course.' He nods solemnly and rubs the end of his nose. It's a large nose and has a lump in the middle. It looks as if it's been broken. I wonder how he did it, I think, looking at him standing in my bathroom, holding my cat in his arms and gazing at me with those big blue eyes.

'Rule number ten?'

'Ten?'

'I've been counting.'

'Oh, right . . . yes.' My eyes dart back to the jotter on my lap and try to lasso my thoughts round another house rule to prevent them drifting off again. 'The TV.' I stride past him into the living room. 'I have satellite but no hogging the sports channel and watching football every night.'

'In America we call it soccer.'

'I call it boring,' I reply tartly.

'Not a big sports fan, huh?' Gabe raises his eyebrows.

'Nope.' I shake my head firmly.

Right. That must have done it. I've called football boring. He'll be out of that door in less than five seconds.

'Don't worry. I'm not a fan of watching sports either.' He runs his fingers along Billy Smith's spine. 'I prefer doing them.'

Hang on a minute. He's not moving.

'Back home I'm a big surfer,' he continues, 'but I guess I won't be doing much of that in England.'

'Actually, they have great surfing in Cornwall where I grew up,' I hear myself say eagerly. 'Every year they have this big competition in Newquay and surfers come from all over the world.' I sit down on the arm of the sofa.

'Wow, that sounds awesome. I'd love to take a trip down there some time.'

'It's really beautiful, you'd love it,' I say enthusiastically. Abruptly I'm hit with a wave of nostalgia. It's ages since I've been back – I should take a trip there, visit some of my old haunts. It would probably do me the world of good. 'You should definitely go.' I'm talking to myself as much as to him. Perhaps we can go together, share the petrol money. I watch him tickle Billy Smith's ears, like a pro. Perhaps having a flatmate won't be as bad as I've imagined. Even if it does mean sharing the Le Creuset pans. Talking of which—

'My pans are off limits.'

'Your pans?'

'My Le Creuset pans. They were a housewarming present. You use them for stews and casseroles and stuff . . .'

I can see from Gabe's dumbfounded expression that he thinks I'm some kind of loony, but he doesn't mention it. Instead he laughs and says, 'Hey, don't worry about it. I'm more of a stir-fry kind of guy. One man and his wok and all that.'

There's a pause, which Gabe breaks first. 'So, do I pass?'

I consult my notebook. Admittedly he's ticked most of the boxes. But . . . I hesitate. I'm still not sure. He seems nice but maybe I should wait. Interview more applicants. Not that there actually *are* any more applicants, but there might be if I give it a few more weeks. Wait for a non-smoking, female, tidy Japanese student who will always put the loo seat down.

'You've dropped something.' Gabe picks it up from the carpet and holds it out to me. 'Looks like some kind of buttonhole.'

I look down at the ribbon-tied sprig between his fingers. It's the lucky heather. Suddenly I have the strangest feeling. Funny how it keeps turning up. Maybe it really is lucky.

I take it from him. 'So, when do you want to move in?'

Chapter Nine

Remember the Boomtown Rats?

I don't, really, I was too young, but I remember Ed, my brother, playing their seven-inch single. He would crank up his old record-player and trampoline up and down on his bed singing along at the top of his voice to his favourite song.

'I Don't Like Mondays.'

Over and over again.

Until the divan springs broke. He spent the rest of his teenage years sleeping on a mattress on the floor. To this day he holds Bob Geldof responsible for his bad back. Suffice to say he never played the record again.

But the song's stuck with me ever since and I must say, now I'm older, I have to agree with Sir Bob on that one: I don't like Mondays much either. But this Monday morning is different. This Monday I'm in an extraordinarily good mood and the reason I've got a great big smile on my face is because . . .

'You've been shagging.'

As I push open the frosted-glass door that leads into the small office upstairs I'm accosted by a familiar East End accent.

'What?' I scoop up the pile of mail from the mat.

Brian is sitting with his feet up on the desk, munching a croissant and eyeing me. 'That smile. I'd know it anywhere. It's a shag smile.'

Rolling my eyes, I tug off my denim jacket and walk over to the old mahogany coat-stand. Every day for the past six years it's stood in the corner of the office like some kind of scarecrow, overflowing with old coats and jackets belonging to me and Brian that neither of us wants to claim. And every day for the past six years I have gone through the routine of wishing halfheartedly that there was somewhere to hang my jacket, giving up, then flinging it on top. Today's no different.

'So, come on, who's the lucky devil?'

Damn! I wish there was a free peg to hang my coat on.

'There is no lucky devil,' I retort, then fall silent. Because today, by some fluke, is different. There's an empty peg. I stare at it in disbelief. How weird. Before slipping my jacket on to it I turn back to Brian.

'You have the whole weekend off and you waltz in here with a grin the size of a ventriloquist's dummy.' He puts down his half-eaten croissant and presses his hand to his chest. 'Put your hand on your heart and tell me you haven't met a bloke.'

Honestly, Brian can be so dramatic sometimes.

'OK, so I met a man . . .' I confess. 'But before you get the wrong idea it's not like that. He's my new flatmate.'

Brian is crestfallen. 'You mean there's no gossip?

'Nope. I'm single, remember.'

'I used to watch *Sex and the City*.' He raises his eyebrows knowledgeably.

'Oh, Brian, that was a TV show.' I laugh. 'I spend most of my evenings eating TV dinners, doing my handwashing and getting into bed with a good book.'

'You and me both.' He shrugs gloomily. 'You're looking at a man who hasn't had a whiff of action since the last millennium. No, I'm serious,' he protests, before I've had a chance to disagree.

Not that I'm going to. Ever since I've known Brian he's only ever had three topics of conversation. Sex (lack of). West End musicals/Michael Crawford (a genius). And the fact he hasn't been in a relationship for seven years. Three things I can't help feeling are directly related.

'The last time I got lucky Abba were at number one with "Waterloo".' He picks up his croissant again.

'Brian, do you ever think of anything other than sex?' I tut good-naturedly, swatting his feet off the desk and plonking the mail in front of him.

'What else is there to think about?' Pastry flakes fall off the croissant and stick to his freshly shaven chin like Velcro. He dabs it with his paper napkin.

'Politics? Religion?' sniffs Maureen, appearing from the kitchen with a mop and bucket. Maureen's our cleaner. A thin, wiry woman with hair dyed the colour of pickled beetroot, she dealt with the loss of her husband last year by enrolling on a philosophy course at the local community centre.

'Oooh, thrilling,' says Brian, sarcastically.

'Actually, it can be extremely invigorating,' replies Maureen, stiffly. She throws me one of her toothy smiles, which contrasts sharply with the glower she's just bestowed on Brian. 'Morning, Heather. How was your weekend?'

'Haven't you heard? She been shagging.' Brian winks, partly because he hates being left out of the conversation, and partly because he loves winding up Maureen.

'Brian, will you stop it? I have not been . . .' I grope for a polite verb '. . . doing anything.' I give in to my hunger pangs by leaning across to take a bite out of his croissant, then remember my heavy thighs and lean back again.

'So, why are you looking so happy?'

'Haven't you read *The Road Less Travelled*?' asks Maureen, grabbing a can of Pledge furniture polish and squirting it at Brian as if it's insect repellent and he's the mosquito. 'Happiness comes from within.'

'Don't give me all that Dalai Lama claptrap.'

'It's Deepak Chopra, actually.'

'Actually, it's neither,' I interrupt their bickering. 'If you really want to know why I'm so happy it's because this morning I got a seat on the tube.'

It does the trick. Both Brian and Maureen fall silent.

'A seat on the tube?' echoes Maureen.

'That's it?' groans Brian, visibly disappointed. As the only gay man in the whole of London whose sex life went into retirement when people were still wearing leg-warmers, Brian tends to exist on whatever scraps other people throw as him from theirs. 'No hanky-panky? No kissing? Not even a little hand-holding?'

For the first time ever it seems that Brian and Maureen agree on something.

'Sorry.' I shrug, flicking on my computer. 'That's it.'

There's no point in explaining. I know Brian and Maureen are never going to understand the huge relevance of what happened to me this morning after I'd gone down the steps on to the platform and waited for the next approaching train. How everything had felt pretty much the same as always – same film poster of Kate Hudson with one front tooth blacked out, same chocolate vending machine to tempt me, same routine of watching the train pulling into the station, doors sliding open and me climbing aboard, scanning the carriage and wishing for an empty seat.

At first I hadn't been able to see a thing for jostling commuters filling the carriage, but then slowly, imperceptibly, people had shifted to the sides until, like the parting of the Red Sea, the aisle was wide open. And there, directly opposite, was – believe it or not – an empty seat.

'That's it?' repeats Brian. 'That's the reason for your good mood?'

'Yep, that's it.' Well, OK, that's not *exactly* it. I suppose it's also got *something* to do with waking up early, there being no queue in Starbucks, no traffic on my way back from Bath at the weekend, a parking space outside the flat. And then, of course, there's Gabe, my new flatmate who just so happens to be moving in today.

My stomach flutters. Not that I'm excited or anything. It's probably just hunger pangs because I haven't had any breakfast. 'Toast anyone?' Leaving Brian and Maureen staring at me, I disappear into the kitchen and dig out the bread from the fridge. Humming, I unravel the packaging, 'Hmm . . . hmm . . . hmm . . . hmmmm,' I take out two slices and suddenly realise I'm humming the Boomtown Rats. Only I'm sorry Sir Bob, I'm afraid I've changed my mind. Popping the bread into the slots I push down the lever. *I love Mondays.*

* * *

By late afternoon the phone hasn't rung once and Brian's early joviality has turned sour, a bit like a pint of milk left out in the midday sun. I know he's worried about the business and after looking at the diary, which is practically empty, I don't blame him. Taking his advice, I spend my lunch-hour updating my CV, then leave him chain-smoking in the office to make a start on developing the last wedding in the darkroom.

I usually listen to music while I work but today when I turn on the CD player I discover Brian's replaced my Gorillaz album with *Phantom of the Opera.* Much to my shame, I make the alarming discovery that it's actually rather catchy. In fact, just as I'm getting carried away thinking that maybe Michael Crawford has a better voice than Damon Albarn, I hear knocking and turn down the volume.

'Hang on a sec . . .' I finish swishing a photograph of the beaming newlyweds in a tray of fixer, then clip it to the washing-line strung over my head and open the door expecting to see Brian.

It's Jess. Air stewardess, fellow Zara-shopper and general all-round best friend. She's wearing her uniform and has her wheelie suitcase with her. 'Guess what!'

'Aren't you supposed to be in Delhi?' I usher her and her suitcase inside the tiny red-lit room. There's no need for hi-how-are-you between Jess and me. We dive straight in, change topics without warning, offer no explanation to random comments. It's like we've been having one never-ending conversation since we met. Which I suppose we have, really.

'I was. We just flew back.' She plonks herself on to a stool, turns to me excitedly – then cocks her head to one side, frowning. 'Heather, are you listening to *Phantom of the Opera*?'

I blush. 'Oh, that . . .' I turn it off. 'One of Brian's CDs,' I explain, as Jess stares at me suspiciously.

'Didn't anyone ever tell you that men and musicals don't mix?' She takes off her hat and hangs it on the back of the chair. 'Actually, correction, straight men and musicals.'

Closing the door, so as not to let in any light, I squeeze past her.

'And I should know. Every steward I fly with is in love with Michael Ball.' She sighs regretfully. 'Which is such a waste – some of them are gorgeous.'

'So, what am I supposed to be guessing?' I ask, changing the subject from men. Which, with Jess, is a bit like trying to get Jesus to talk about something other than God.

'I've got a date,' she announces.

'With Simon?' Simon is the architect Jess met on the Internet and had dinner with last week. Jess loves the Internet: when she's not flying all over the world, she's bidding for handbags on eBay and looking for love on findahusband.com, or whatever the dating site is called.

'I've already got one arsehole, I don't need another,' she deadpans.

'I'll take that as a no, then.'

'His name's Greg.'

'Who's Greg?' I find it hard to keep track of the men in Jess's life. She tends to date a few at once. It's an averages thing.

'A banker. Thirty-five. Hobbies include mountain-biking and eating sushi. Not at the same time.' She chuckles at her joke – although I fear it may have been his. 'I met him on the Internet while I was in Delhi – not that he lives in Delhi, of course. He lives here in London. Because of the time difference we've spent the last few days emailing . . .'

'But I thought you were really into Simon?' I bleat. Now I know how my dad must feel when he's watching a movie. For some reason he can never keep track of what's going on and spends the entire film asking questions and being shushed. Usually by me.

'He never called,' she says, wrinkling her nose. '*C'est la vie.*'

'I take it you're not heartbroken.'

'Honey, I'm thirty-six. I don't have time to be heartbroken.' She kicks off her shoes and rubs the heels of her stockinged feet. 'Time is men.'

Jess is remarkable. In the last few years she's taken a supremely practical approach to meeting the right guy. Forget all the stuff about fate and soulmates and butterflies, she's interested in ticking all the right boxes. For Jess, finding the right man is like finding a second-hand car. Year of make? Nice body? Number of previous owners? Reliable?

I used to think her attitude to love was *too* practical – after all, it's the heart you're dealing with, not a two-litre engine – but after my disaster with Daniel I'm beginning to think she might have the right idea. Butterflies in the stomach might feel lovely, but they're lethal – my heart was broken by those goddamn butterflies.

'And so far there's been no red flags,' she boasts proudly. 'No ex-wife, no fear of commitment, no drug problem, no deeply held religious beliefs . . .'

I take a moment to wonder if this is the time to point out that she said that about Simon. And Dennis, the advertising executive who'd turned out to be complete cokehead. And Reuben, the editor, who was Jewish and whose mother (or I should I say 'smother') insisted she convert.

'I think this could be it.'

On second thoughts, perhaps not.

'When are you meeting him?'

'Saturday. He's taking me somewhere special.'

'Where?'

'I don't know. He said it was to be a surprise.'

'A surprise?' I enthuse. 'Wow, how exciting.'

I'm lying. If there's one thing I hate it's surprises. Maybe I'm weird, maybe I'm the only person who feels like this, but I like to know what to expect so that I can be prepared. Take surprise birthday parties, for example. I can't think of anything worse than arriving home from work and someone jumping out from behind the sofa yelling, 'Surprise.' I mean, can you imagine? There you are, about to make yourself look fabulous and spend the evening at a swanky restaurant, and suddenly you've got to be all pleased and thrilled that a party's in full swing in your living room and that fifty of your nearest and dearest are crammed in spilling vodka and cranberry on your new cream carpet. Meanwhile, you're standing there with ratty hair and a spot that's crying out for cover-up, wishing you could hide in the bathroom with your hair serum and Estée Lauder Doublestay foundation.

'I just hope it's not London Zoo.' Jess's voice breaks into my thoughts.

'London Zoo?'

'Phil Toddington took me there on our first date. *Our only date*,' she adds pointedly.

'Was it that bad?'

She rolls her eyes. 'Heather, I was at the penguin enclosure for three hours. In the middle of February. In a pair of snakeskin slingbacks and my backless dress from Karen Millen. I nearly froze to death.'

'But penguins are really comical.' I smile affectionately.

'Not for three hours,' she says bitterly. 'I was bored stiff. Unlike Phil, who was transfixed. He kept going on about their funny clockwork waddle, the way they waggled their stumpy wings.' She shakes her head. 'I swear he fancied those goddamn penguins more than me.'

She looks so anguished I can't help laughing.

'And the smell . . .'

'Bad?' I venture.

'Rotten fish and penguin shit.'

'Mmm, very romantic.' I giggle, and despite herself she joins in.

'Oh, bloody hell, Heather, it was awful,' she says, between snorts of laughter. 'I remember thinking, This is it. This is my love life. Can it get any worse?'

Well, you could have fallen in love with him, bought a house together, then discovered he'd been shagging a girl at work for the past six months, I muse, as an image of Daniel pops into my head. Determinedly, I block it out.

'He could have taken you to a comedy club,' I say instead.

Immediately we stop laughing and exchange a look.

Stand-up comedy is our pet hate. That was how we met. Imprisoned in the Laugh Factory in Covent Garden by my then-boyfriend, unable to escape to the loo for fear of being picked on by the comedian on stage, I'd been bored to tears and gazing round the audience when I'd seen an attractive black girl, chin cupped in her hands, mouth wide open in a yawn. We'd caught each other's eye across the cigarette smoke and raucous laughter. I don't know which of us was more miserable, me or her, but we had both burst out laughing.

Well, something had to.

'So, how do you fancy a trip to Zara after work? Help me buy something to wear for my date?'

' 'Fraid I'm busy.'

'Too busy for Zara?' Jess is incredulous. 'But there's a sale on.'

'I know, but my new flatmate's moving in,' I explain.

'Ooh, tell me more.' Immediately perking up, she tucks tufts of short dark hair behind her ears and folds her arms, priming herself for info.

'He saw the room on Saturday and was going to move in yesterday but he had to spend the day with his uncle or something.'

'It's a he?' She raises her eyebrows with interest.

'You can't test-drive my flatmate,' I warn, stopping her in her tracks.

She looks at me indignantly. 'The thought never crossed my mind.'

Now it's my turn to raise my eyebrows.

'Oh, OK, so it crossed, but now it's crossed back again,' she protests. 'I'm going to have my hands full with Greg anyway.' She's fiddling with her rings as if they're beads on an abacus. A sure sign that something's brewing. 'So what he's like?' she asks, trying to be nonchalant. And failing.

'He's American.'

'Oooh, really?' Her eyes open wide. 'Let me guess. He's an actor.'

'Actually, I don't know,' I confess, realising I told him not to leave the loo seat up, but didn't ask him anything about himself. 'I guess I'll find out tonight.'

'Do you need me as a chaperone?'

'No, I'll be fine, thanks.' I do a mental time-check. Maybe I should skip the gym tonight and go straight home – that way I'll have time to blow-dry my hair straight. I catch myself. This isn't a date.

'Is that really safe, Heather?' warns Jess. 'He could be a crazed serial killer.'

What she really means is he could be a *single* crazed serial killer. 'I doubt it, he seems really nice,' I say, having seen right through her concerned-friend act. 'He's a bit of a hippie.'

'That's what they said about Charles Manson.'

I throw her a look.

She perseveres. 'I think I should come over, safety in numbers and all that.'

'And two's company, three's a crowd,' I add.

'Well, it's up to you. If you want to risk being chopped into little bits and pieces and buried in your geraniums . . .'

I give in. 'OK, OK. My place. Eight o'clock.'

Her face splits into a huge grin and she gives me a hug.

'But no making a fuss,' I warn, opening the door to waft her and her suitcase out of the darkroom.

'A fuss? Me?' She clutches her ample chest and looks at me in hurt astonishment. 'Trust me, Heather, you won't even know I'm there.'

Chapter Ten

'Any more wine?'

Sucking in her stomach, Jess reaches for the bottle of white she brought over. She's wearing her new black satin Alexander McQueen bustier she bought on eBay, hipster jeans and a pair of vertiginous pink stilettos, otherwise known as her 'fuck-me' shoes. When she leans over the table you can see the tattoo of a butterfly etched into the bottom of her spine, and her G-string. It's got a little diamanté heart on it. I have an urge to twang it, like a catapult.

'It's, Gabriel, isn't it? Like the angel.' She pouts, lips slick with lipgloss.

'Friends usually call me Gabe.'

'As in, rhymes with "babe"?' she teases.

'Um, I guess so.'

'Well, if you insist. Any more wine, *Gabe*?'

The three of us are outside in the garden. It's one of those rare warm summer evenings when there's not a breath of wind. The air is scented with a cocktail of jasmine, lavender and sausages from my next-door neighbour's barbecue, and Norah Jones is playing on the little portable stereo balanced on the window-ledge. I've even lit all the little tealights I got from IKEA and placed them round the shrubbery. It took for ever as they kept going out and burning my fingers, but it's worth the effort as they've transformed my garden into a fairy grotto.

I glance round it now and feel a glow of pleasure. In retrospect I don't know why I was so nervous: everything's turned out just as I wished it would.

Well, not everything.

As my eyes rest on Jess, who's wiggling round the table like a Playboy bunny, I feel a lump of irritation in my throat and flick my eyes over her shoulder – all shimmery with body glitter – and watch as my flatmate lights another cigarette.

He'd turned up with his 'things' – a motorbike helmet and one teensy-weensy rucksack that would barely accommodate my toiletries – a couple of hours ago. When he'd dumped it on his bed he'd kicked off his flip-flops and dug out a packet of American Spirit cigarettes from his biker's jacket.

'Mind if I have a smoke outside?' he'd asked, padding barefoot into the back garden.

'Er, no . . . please, make yourself at home,' I'd called after him. Somewhat redundantly: he had already stretched out on a sun-lounger, Billy Smith purring in his lap.

Well, I couldn't just leave him there, could I? As his landlady, wasn't I supposed to be welcoming him into my home and making him feel at ease? I say *supposed*, because for some reason my ability to make small-talk deserted me – I'm not used to having barefoot American men in my garden – so I'd hovered around a bit, fiddled with things that didn't need fiddling with and groped, like a man in a blindfold, for something to say.

'Wonderful weather we're having.'; 'Umm, gosh, look at my feet, I really must get a pedicure.'; 'Oh, I saw the funniest thing on *Ali G* the other night . . . erm, but I've forgotten what it was' until Jess had tottered into the garden, greeted Gabe as if he were a long-lost lover, then pulled two bottles of Pinot Grigio, a corkscrew and a Norah Jones CD out of her fake Louis Vuitton bag, and taken control of the conversation in full air stewardess mode.

'So, what brings you to London?' she's now asking flirtily. 'Business or pleasure?'

'A bit of both, actually,' he answers, in such a way that either he hasn't noticed Jess is flirting, or if he has he's politely ignoring her. 'But before I bore you with the details you'll have to excuse me a moment.' He turns to me and asks shyly, 'Heather, remind me where your bathroom is?'

'Second on the left,' chimes Jess, before I can answer.

'Thanks.'

As soon as he has disappeared, I turn on Jess. 'What are you doing?' I hiss furiously.

'Breaking the ice,' she says simply, all wide-eyed and innocent.

It doesn't fool me for a minute. 'Breaking the ice is asking someone about the weather,' I gasp. 'What happened to "Trust me, Heather, you won't even know I'm there"?'

Taking a slug of wine, she sloshes it around her mouth for a moment, swallows, then looks at me sheepishly. 'OK, so I admit I've been a bit flirty.'

'A *bit*?'

'Oh, c'mon, hon, I just thought in case Greg doesn't work out. You know, it's always a good idea to have Plan B.'

'My flatmate's Plan B?' I say indignantly, feeling suddenly protective of Gabe – and something that is weirdly like possessiveness.

'Well, why not? You don't fancy him.'

True. But—

'Oh, shit. You don't, do you, Heather?' Jess's face freezes. 'I didn't have any idea. If I'd thought for a moment—'

'No, of course I don't,' I protest hotly. 'It's just . . .' I trail off sighing, as I don't know what it just is.

She squeezes my hand. 'I know. I'm sorry. Maybe I have come on a bit strong.'

'A *bit* strong?' I grin ruefully. 'I'm surprised you didn't bring your scented candles and aromatherapy oil.'

'Who says I didn't?' She laughs and, despite myself, I can't help giggling.

'What's so funny?' Gabe reappears as Jess is topping up our glasses.

'Not Big Dave Desmond, that's for sure,' says Jess, referring to the stand-up comedian who was on stage when we first met.

Gabe is evidently confused, but she doesn't bother to explain and instead leans over to top up his glass. 'So, where in American are you from?' she asks.

OK, so the fuck-me shoes are a bit much but I'm glad Jess is here. And, I have to admit, she and Gabe seem to be getting on pretty well.

'Los Angeles.'

'Oooh,' gasps Jess. 'I've flown there a few times with work. I lurve LA.'

'Yeah, it has it's good points. I live in Venice, just a few blocks from the ocean.'

'Venice?' I repeat, my ears pricking up with interest. 'What a coincidence.'

'Yeah, I know. Weird, huh? Venice, California, to Little Venice in London.' Sipping his wine, he fixes me with those large blue eyes.

'I guess you could call it home from home,' pipes up Jess, giggling.

'Or lucky,' smiles Gabe.

'Yeah, lucky Heather.' Jess winks at me.

Now, it's not the first time I've been called that – in fact, I must have heard it a million times – but as soon as Jess says it I see an image of the gypsy outside the station, her eyes like tiny glittering emeralds, and hear her words: 'Trust me, the heather will work its magic. Your luck will change. All your wishes will come true . . .'

Slipping my hand into the back pocket of my jeans my fingers brush against a wad of notes. It's Gabe's first month's rent. A whopping six hundred pounds. I'll be able to pay the mortgage this month, maybe even make the minimum payment on my Visa bill. I feel a surge of happy relief – it's like a wish come true.

Barely has the thought popped into my head when a gust of wind appears from nowhere, rustling through the leaves of the trees and causing the flames of the tea lights to flicker and dance like tiny jewels sparkling in a sea of inky darkness. The cascade of metal discs on the windchime begin jingling, and the garden seems almost enchanted. A shiver scurries up my spine and goose bumps prickle on my arms. What the . . . ?

'More wine, Heather?'

I snap back to see Jess holding a bottle of pinot grigio and staring at me. Spooked, I fidget in my seat. 'Oh, erm, yeah, great,' I say. When I hold out my glass my hands are all trembly. 'Fill her up,' I joke and plonk it on the table.

So she does. And as I watch her I realise the wind has dropped as quickly as it blew up. That the flames of the tea lights are now as motionless as the stars in the sky and the windchime is silent. Everything is as it was before. My goosebumps have disappeared too. I feel warm. And a little ridiculous. What's got into me? Gypsies? Magic? Enchanted gardens? Honestly, Heather, you're letting your imagination run away with you. Grabbing my wine glass I take a glug. Any minute now I'll start believing wishes really can come true.

'Do you ever go to Muscle Beach?'

Twenty minutes and another bottle later, Jess is still chatting animatedly about Venice Beach. I had no idea she was such an expert.

'Oh, all the time.' Gabe pretends to flex his biceps. 'Do you think a body like this comes naturally?'

I catch him grinning at me and I can't help grinning back, unlike Jess, who's all flushed with alcohol and flirtation and misses the sarcasm. 'Oooh, no, I can tell you lift weights, not like Englishmen,' she says, wrinkling her nose. 'All they're interested in is lifting pints. Aren't they, Heather?'

'Well, not all of them,' I say loyally, trying to think of one man I know who actually *does* some form of exercise instead of lying spreadeagled on the sofa watching other people do it on telly. It's a struggle. 'What about Ed?' I suggest remembering my brother. 'He plays rugby.'

But Jess isn't listening. She's too busy reminiscing about Muscle Beach: 'Oh, Heather, you'd love it. It's this outdoor gym by the sea and you can watch all these big, bronzed bodybuilders pumping iron . . .'

As she gushes on about coconut-oiled men posing with six-packs and dumbbells I haven't the heart to tell her I can't think of anything worse. So instead I do what I usually do when I don't know what to say: I say something stupid. 'Is it true everyone in LA has fake boobs?'

Well done, Heather. Ten out of ten for tact and diplomacy.

But Gabe doesn't look offended, more amused. 'No, I wouldn't say everyone.' He tugs down his Mr T T-shirt and peers at his chest. 'Mine are real.'

'Really? Let me check.' Jess giggles and, without missing a beat, lunges for his right pec. 'Mmm, nice and firm,' she slurs approvingly, squeezing it as if it's a melon.

Oh, shit. My body stiffens. Jess, I realise with horror, is pissed. In less than a few minutes she's leapfrogged from tipsy to hammered, bypassing the middle bit. Or, to put it another way, if you're looking at a map of the world it's like going from London to LA without crossing the Atlantic.

'So, are you an actor?' I ask, trying to cause a diversion.

'I love acting,' butts in Jess, loudly. 'Maybe I should have been an actress. I was once in this play at school but I can't remember the name . . .' Her eyelids have gone all droopy and she's having difficulty keeping them open.

'Me? An actor?' Gabe gives a pretend shudder. 'No way.'

My eyes flick from Gabe to Jess and back to Gabe. As far as I can tell he doesn't seem to have noticed Jess edging towards him across her sun-lounger.

But I have. I feel a spasm of fear. She's sleepy. Drunk. And single. It's a lethal combination. Any minute now she'll be trying to spoon him.

'But my girlfriend is, and she says it's pretty tough.'

I hear a muffled mumble from the sun-lounger. '*Girlfriend?*' Enveloped in a blurry haze of alcohol, Jess might not be able to drive, operate heavy machinery, or undo her own bra strap, but she can still recognise words like—

'*Girlfriend?*' she repeats.

'Yeah, she's back in LA. She just got a small part in a movie.'

'*A movie?*' Jess sits bolt upright on the sun-lounger, like a parrot on a perch. Which isn't a bad description, considering she repeats everything Gabe says in a high-pitched squawk.

'Mmm, it's a big break for her,' enthuses Gabe. 'Mia's really talented, but so far she hasn't been in anything major. Give it time, though. One of these days I'm pretty sure we'll be seeing her nominated for an Academy Award.'

'Wow, how exciting,' I gush, attempting to cause a diversion from Jess. 'I'm really impressed.' And I am. An actress in Hollywood? It's a lot more glamorous than being a wedding photographer, isn't it? An *assistant* to a wedding photographer. Reminded of my current career status, I feel a painful stab of ambition. This happens to me a lot. For days I trundle happily along in a my little work bubble, doing my job, getting paid, not really thinking about it, and *wham* – I hear a story of someone else being incredibly successful and, *boom*, I remember I'm thirty, earning less than most graduates and my dream of a flourishing career as a freelance photographer, is just that. A dream. At which point I usually end up feeling like a great big frizzy-haired failure.

Unlike Mia, who is, no doubt, a shiny, swingy-haired success with the kind of thighs that look great in a string bikini on the beach . . .

'I think I'll catch a cab.'

My slow-motion *Baywatch* montage is interrupted by Jess standing up and hoisting her bustier under her armpits. 'Well, it was lovely meeting you.' She holds out a hand to Gabe.

'Oh, er, yeah. You too.' He's nodding, a little ruffled by her sudden departure. As am I.

'Are you sure you don't want a coffee?' I suggest. It might sober her up, although Gabe's mention of his girlfriend seems to have done that already.

'No, thanks. I'll call you tomorrow,' she says, and gives me a quick hug before she disappears through the patio doors.

'Are you sure you don't want me to phone for a minicab?' I call, hurrying after her. I hear the door slam and glance out of the window just in time to see her jump into a black cab.

* * *

'Your friend left early.'

Back in the garden I see that Gabe is gathering up the glasses. 'Erm, yeah.' I nod. 'She's tired. She has to get up early for work.'

I'm sure from his expression that he knows I'm fibbing, so, feeling awkward now that it's just the two of us, I fake a yawn. 'Talking of which, I think I'm going to go to bed too.'

'Got to get your beauty sleep, hey?' I'm not sure whether I should be pleased or offended by that comment. But before I can make up my mind he lets out a roaring yawn, so wide I can see two perfect rows of incredibly white molars. 'I know how you feel. This jet lag's killing me.'

We go inside and hover in the kitchen.

'Night, then,' I say eventually.

'Yesh, night.'

Another pause.

'You can use the bathroom first, if you like,' I offer politely.

'No, it's OK, you go ahead. Ladies before gentlemen,' he replies, equally politely.

'No, please, you're the guest,'

'Honestly, it's cool.'

Backwards and forwards it goes, like ping-pong, until finally I win and he disappears inside the bathroom with a sponge-bag no bigger than a pencil case. I go into my bedroom and start to undress, pulling off my T-shirt and jeans and tugging on my old tartan pyjamas, the ones whose elastic has perished at the waistband so my arse is all baggy and it looks as if I'm wearing a nappy. *Wearing. A. Nappy.*

On catching sight of myself in the wardrobe mirror, I freeze. Oh, my God. It's like seeing myself for the first time. What have I been thinking? Night after night I've been cheerfully putting on this outfit to potter round my flat. I spend eight hours a night sleeping in it. I sit in my garden drinking tea in it. I've even – God forbid – stood on the doorstep and signed for packages from the postman in it.

I do a slow twirl. I'm almost terrified to see the back view. Slowly . . . slowly . . . Argghh. It's worse than I thought. Folds of faded tartan hang loosely from my buttocks like two humungous saddlebags. Think M. C. Hammer. Think Gandhi.

Think new flatmate.

Stripping them off and chucking them on to the floor, I yank open my drawers and reach for my Snoopy nightie – then recoil. A Snoopy nightie? I can't wear a Snoopy nightie. I forage for another pair of pyjamas that I know are in there, but I can only find the top. Three of its buttons are missing *and* it's got a granddad collar. *A fucking granddad collar.* Why had I never noticed it before? In fact, why have I never noticed that I have appalling nightwear? What on earth did I wear when I lived with Daniel?

Nothing, I remember, thinking back to my old sexy life when I went to bed wearing eyeliner and Thierry Mugler's Angel. That was before I turned into the single, celibate thirtynothing cliché who sleeps with her cat and wears socks, big period knickers and intensive anti-wrinkle night cream.

Shuddering, I grab hold of myself. There's the nightgown that Rosemary bought me two Christmases ago, still in its Marks & Spencer carrier-bag. I hold it against my naked body. It's floor-length, decorated with rosebuds and frilly. Very, very frilly.

But I'm desperate. Next door I can hear taps being turned on and off, teeth being brushed, the loo flushing, a plug being pulled out and the basin draining. Any minute now it will be my turn. I'm going to have to try to make it from my bedroom to the bathroom without being seen. I strain for the noise of the lock. Nothing. A cough. Silence. Then I hear it. The sound of the key turning, the soft click of the door . . .

I press my cheek against the doorframe to peer through the crack between the wall and the door. I see a letterbox of light, floorboards, my fern, which needs watering. Like a learner driver I look left, right and left again. All clear. With a flush of relief, I ease open the door and tiptoe bravely into the hall. Tiptoe, tiptoe, tiptoe. I hold my breath, clutching my nightie between finger and thumb like Wee Willie Winkie. Nearly there, nearly there—

'Argggh,' I shriek.

'Wow, sorry, did I frighten you?'

Gabe is still in the bathroom. I mean, he's just standing there. On my shagpile mat. In the middle of my goddamn bathroom.

'Oh my God, yes – I mean, no – no, it's okay.' Clutching my embroidered lacy chest, I try to catch my breath. Which is when it dawns on me that (a) he's naked but for a pair of white, rather snug boxer shorts (not that I mean to look, I just can't help it), and (b) I look like someone's granny in a full-length nightgown that comes up to my neck in a fluted ruffle.

'Oh, by the way, you never did say why you're visiting,' I blurt, in an attempt at casual chit-chat. I say 'attempt', as it's not easy when he's standing there, all naked flesh and tufts of chest hair and snug white pouch.

Oh, my God, I've done it again. Eyes straight ahead, Heather. Eyes straight ahead.

'Oh, didn't I tell you?' He squeezes out a facecloth that I hadn't noticed he was holding. Just as I hadn't noticed that the bathroom is spotless. No loo seat left up, no soggy towel on the floor, no bristles on the soap. For all my good intentions, my eyes flick quickly round the avocado suite, a souvenir from the seventies that Daniel and I had planned to rip out when we did up the flat. Only he left and I tried mending a broken heart with retail therapy – which means I still have the hideous avocado suite but I also have lots of lovely candles from Diptyque. 'I'm putting on a show at the Edinburgh Festival.'

'Oh, really?' I say vaguely, throwing him my best smile of approval. I catch sight of our toothbrushes standing side by side in a mug with a tube of Colgate Extra and notice its top is firmly screwed on. I get the warm glow of satisfaction that comes with knowing I've made a right decision. We're going to get on great. 'What kind of show?'

Picking up his clothes he walks out the bathroom. Then he goes and spoils it all by telling me something I *really* don't want to hear.

Chapter Eleven

'He's a stand-up comic.'

The next morning as soon as Gabe leaves the flat I phone Jess to tell her my terrible news. Despite the hangover that's imprisoning her under the duvet with a blister-pack of ibuprofen, she summons the energy to be as horrified as I am. A sign, if ever there was one, of a true friend. 'You're joking!'

'No, he's the one joking.' I wedge the phone under my ear. With one hand I hang on to my bowl of cereal, while with the other I grab the milk from the fridge. 'He's a stand-up-bloody-comedian.'

There's muffled laughter. 'Knock knock,' she teases weakly.

'Oh, please, don't.' I plonk myself down at the kitchen table, which is littered with magazines, unopened mail and God knows what else. Balancing my bowl on top, I begin munching on a mouthful of All Bran. 'It's not funny,' I say, my voice muffled with horrid-tasting little brown sticks. God, I wish I could hurry up and lose those few pounds. I hate having to eat this stuff.

'They never are.' She laughs throatily. 'That's the problem.'

'So, is he still your Plan B?' I ask, still munching.

'No, he's not what I'm looking for.' She sounds as if she's talking about a lamp at IKEA. 'He's too American.'

'So what?'

'Heather, I'm looking for a serious boyfriend. I don't want a long-distance relationship. Haven't you seen *Green Card*?'

'But didn't Gérard Depardieu play a Frenchman in that?'

'He plays a Frenchman in every film,' yawns Jess. 'Like Hugh Grant's always a stuttering English toff. But that's not the point. The point is I'm into ticking boxes, not creating new problems like having to deal with all that immigration crap. And then there's the culture clash.'

I love Jess. Ever the romantic. 'Well, now you put it like that,' I murmur, contemplating another mouthful of cereal and wishing I could have a *pain au chocolat* instead.

'What are you going to do?' she persists.

'About what?' Curiously I eye a little leather notebook lying on the table among the mess. It looks like the one I've seen Gabe scribbling in. I wonder what's in it.

'Gabe being a stand-up comedian,' she says, barely able to keep the laughter out of her voice.

I'm beginning to think Jess is enjoying this. 'Isn't there a saying about how you've got to laugh or you'll cry?' I say absently, stretching out my arm and flicking open the notebook. Well, one little peek won't hurt.

'Absolutely,' agrees Jess, supportively. 'You've got to laugh.'

On the first page, in curly blue handwriting are the words: '*My Top Ten Mother-in-Law Jokes*'. I snatch my hand back. Actually, on second thoughts . . .

As it turns out I'm spared any mother-in-law jokes over the next few days as I barely see my new flatmate. In fact, apart from the occasional 'Hi, how's it going?' when I'm arriving and he's leaving, it's almost as if he never moved in. Almost, but not quite.

Little things begin to appear. A collection of spices in the kitchen, a carton of soya milk in the fridge, a new loofah the size of a French baguette in the shower. But there's something else – and it has nothing to do with his Wilco CD that I found by the stereo, or his brightly patterned beach towel neatly folded next to the sink. It's a feeling.

For weeks I'd been dreading the thought of having a stranger in my flat, hated the idea of a man who wasn't Daniel soaking in my bath, but all my fears were unfounded. It's fine having another person around. In fact, it's more than that: it's *nice*.

Somehow the flat feels different. *I* feel different. And not just because I no longer lie awake at night any more worrying about flat-repossession and being turfed out on the street with Billy Smith and those bloody Le Creuset pans. It's as if Gabe's presence has exorcised the ghosts of the past. Despite the shock discovery that I'm sharing my home with a stand-up comedian, I feel happier. More positive. *Thinner.*

It's Thursday evening after work and I'd popped into Boots to buy some cotton-wool balls when I noticed one of those electronic weighing machines. Impulsively I decided to weigh myself. Which is why I'm now staring at the digital display in astonishment.

No, that can't be right. I peer closer, forehead furrowing. I've lost five pounds? For the past couple of months I've been trying vaguely to shift the weight I put on at Christmas. I've been jogging – twice – I've bought a yoga video that I've got every intention of watching, and I've been sacrificing my breakfast *pain au chocolat* from the French *pâtisserie* on the corner for All Bran, which tastes like cardboard. It's hardly a major lifestyle change but now suddenly – poof – those few pounds have gone. It's amazing. Unbelievable. *Weird.*

Puzzled, I prod my stomach. I don't feel any thinner. But it's difficult to tell and, admittedly, I have been under a lot of financial pressure recently. Isn't that when you lose weight? Doesn't stress gobble up calories, a bit like Pacman in those old computer games?

I take the computerised ticket, step off the scales and walk to the cash register. For once there's no queue and, feeling a little ping of pleasure, I plop my cotton-wool balls on the counter. Yep, that must be it. I knew there'd be a sensible explanation. I mean, it's not as if weight can disappear magically overnight, is it?

Beaming at the sales assistant, I pull my purse out of my pocket. The lucky heather drops out. How did *that* get there? I'm sure I left it at home.

'That'll be one pound twenty-five,' prompts the assistant.

'Oh, yeah . . . Sorry.' Stuffing the heather back into my pocket

I happily count out my change. Whatever the explanation for my weight loss, I get my wish: no more All Bran.

Leaving Boots in a cheerful mood, I cross the main road and walk quickly through Notting Hill. I'm meeting my brother Ed at the Wolsey Castle, a gastro-type pub just round the corner, and as usual I'm late. I speed up. Ed's a real stickler for time-keeping and I don't want one of his lectures before I've even had the chance to order a gin and tonic. Though to be honest, I'm anticipating a lecture. He called me yesterday and said he wanted to 'talk about something', which, translated into Ed-speak, means *give me a talking to*, his favourite starting-point being, 'Why haven't you got a pension plan yet?' which probably gives you some idea about Ed.

But when I turn the corner into a street lined with shops and restaurants, I catch sight of something that stops me dead in my tracks. Pink, satin and with an adorable peep-toe: they are the most gorgeous pair of shoes I've ever seen, just sitting there in a window display, waiting for me to walk past.

I step back to see the name of the store – Sigerson Morrison. My heart soars. I adore this shop: it's always chock full of the most exquisite shoes. Which are completely out of your price range, Heather, pipes up a stern little voice inside me. I feel a tug of disappointment. But, still, there's no harm in looking. I lean closer. Which is when I see the sign. '75% OFF'.

My stomach somersaults. I'm not a shopaholic, although, yes, I sometimes get a physical urge to dive into the changing rooms at H&M with armfuls of clothes. And, yes, I often don't *need* to buy anything, putting it on hold is enough. It's the sense of ownership, the comfort of knowing that it's yours if you want it – without the commitment. I guess it's a bit like getting engaged.

But shoes are different. Shoes are my weakness. Clothes can make your bum look big, your boobs look small, your belly stick out, but a good pair of shoes always looks great, regardless of whether or not you've just eaten half a packet of chocolate digestives. However, there's a hitch – all of this doesn't come cheap. As Lionel says, there's no such thing as a free lunch.

But there are sales, whispers the voice inside my head. *Seventy-five-per-cent-off sales*.

I look at the time on my mobile. I'm already late. Ed will be waiting. I hesitate, then reach for the handle on the red Perspex door. Oh, what the hell? I'll only be five minutes.

Inside, it's bedlam. A scrum of women are jostling for sizes, scrabbling around on their hands and knees, snatching, grabbing, pushing, shoving. Dozens of discarded flesh-coloured pop socks lie underfoot, empty boxes are scattered randomly with their paper, harassed assistants flit between women vying for the mirrors, huffing and muttering under their breath as they're forced to wait for their turn.

Crikey! Women are so ruthless. Men might kill for their country, but a woman will kill for a pair of turquoise stilettos with a bejewelled ankle strap.

Squashing myself between the racks of shoes, I begin the hunt for those gorgeous pink satin stilettos in my size. When I finally reach the shelf marked 'Size 5', though, I see it's empty but for a lime-green Mary-Jane that won't go with anything. I feel a kick of disappointment. Especially since, over to my left, the shelf marked 'Size 7' contains a dozen pairs of the pink satin peep-toes. I pick one up, wondering if I could make it fit with an inner-sole, or maybe a couple . . .

'Can I help you, madam?'

An assistant has swooped down on me. She's one of the haughty types you get in designer shops who look you up and down and make you want to buy something, just to prove you can. Which, it suddenly occurs to me, is probably their sales tactic.

'Erm, no,' I reply, and glance down to see that not only am I cradling the shoe in the crook of my arm, but I'm also *stroking* it. 'I was just . . . er . . . looking.'

'Fabulous, aren't they?' she says conspiratorially, in a hushed voice. 'And seventy-five per cent off.' She rolls her eyes as if she can't quite believe it.

'Oh, er, yes . . . fabulous,' I agree. The shoe has now become

The Shoe, the definitive shoe, the most gorgeous, beautiful, perfect shoe you've ever seen in your life.

'Would you like me to bring you the other one so you can try them both?'

I put the shoe back on the wire shelf and smile regretfully. 'I'm afraid you don't have my size.'

'And that would be?'

As with most sales assistants on commission, she isn't giving up easily. But even she can't perform miracles, I think resignedly. 'Five.'

It's instantaneous. No sooner have I uttered the fateful number than her face crumples and her commission-hungry eyes go dull. 'Oh dear, that's our most popular size.'

'Never mind.' I shrug nonchalantly. 'It always happens.'

'But have you seen these adorable boots? We have these in a five . . .' She picks up a grotty pair of pirate boots from three seasons ago and dangles them in front of me hopefully. 'Um, no, thanks,' I say, insulted, and turn to walk out of the shop. Oh, well, it's only a pair of shoes, Heather. Reaching the door I try ignoring the window display, but at the last moment I can't help giving it one last glance and sighing wistfully.

I wish they had a pair in my size.

'Excuse me, madam.'

I spin round. It's the same assistant, but now her face is flushed with excitement. 'You're in luck. I found the very last pair. They'd been put in the wrong box.' From behind her back she produces the shoes, thrusts them at me and gasps triumphantly, 'Size five!'

'Oh, wow . . .' I splutter. I can't believe it.

But even on sale you still can't afford them, whispers that voice.

I feel a crush of disappointment. It's true. My credit card's been cut up and I've only got twenty-five pounds in cash. Damnit, I wish they were cheaper.

I'm about to give them back when I become aware of her talking in the background,

'. . . but I'm afraid there's a tiny mark on the heel, nothing anyone would notice and, rest assured, you won't see it when you're wearing them. Of course we'll discount them further . . . Another fifty per cent off from the sale price.'

Hang on a minute. Is she saying what I think she's saying? 'You mean they're only . . .'

'Twenty-four ninety-nine,' she announces breathlessly.

A few minutes later I'm standing at the cash register, watching as she wraps them in tissue paper, and overhear someone whispering, 'Oooh, the lucky thing, really wanted the shoes . . .' and feel a burst of pleasure as the assistant hands me a pink bag the size of a billboard.

'And a penny,' she trills, holding out my change.

But I'm already half-way out of the shop. And as I walk on to the street, the huge bag swinging jauntily on my shoulder and a huge smile plastered over my face, I almost have to pinch myself. I'm not superstitious, but I'm beginning to think that heather really is lucky.

Chapter Twelve

'Whoooooaaaaaaaahhhhhhhhh.'

Pushing open the door of the Wolsey Castle I'm greeted by a roar of testosterone. Talk about going from one extreme to another, I muse, remembering the frenzy of oestrogen I've just left behind in Sigerson Morrison.

I duck inside, under a builder's armpit, and head through the fog of cigarette smoke towards the bar. The place is jam-packed with men, drinks in hand, jaws open, eyes glued to the portable TV fastened to the wall in the corner. I tut loudly. Of course. I might have guessed. *Football.*

'Thought as much.'

I turn to see Ed looming down on me, all six foot five of him. Having come straight from work he's in his uniform of grey suit with pleated trousers, white shirt with button-down collars, and brown lace-up brogues. Actually, he wears that at weekends too.

'Shopping again?' Raising his thick, dark eyebrows he studies me disapprovingly, squashing my feelings of superiority. That's the problem with my brother. He likes to spoil your fun.

'Lovely to see you too.' I give him a hug.

'And you.' He kisses me formally on both cheeks. 'So, what did you buy?'

I swear, he's like a dog with a bone.

'Oh, this?' I say lightly, raising one shoulder and looking at the bag as if I've only just noticed it's there. Come on, think, Heather. I rack my brains for a feasible excuse. It's either that or a lecture on saving for the future. Honestly, my brother should have been a bank manager, not an orthodontist. 'It's a present,' I gasp, and I feel a rush of triumph. Brilliant, Heather.

'For whom?'

Now, I don't know if he's just trying to catch me out or if he's genuinely interested but, knowing my brother, I'll go with option one.

'Erm . . .' I root around in my mental address book for someone suitable. Hmm, no birthdays, no anniversaries, but there is . . . 'Rosemary.'

'Really?' Ed is suitably impressed. 'That's rather nice of you, little sis,'

I smile uncomfortably. 'Well, it's only a little something,' I say, knowing full well I'm digging a hole for myself and wondering how I'm going to get out of it.

'I'm glad you two are finally getting on better,' he continues, folding his arms and gazing at me with brotherly approval. Ed has a completely different relationship with Rosemary from the one she and I share. Partly because he's a successful orthodontist with his own business in Harley Street, which endears him to Rosemary's snobbery, and partly because he's always so busy with work that he rarely travels to Bath, and she refuses to come to London – 'filthy, overcrowded place' – so he never has to spend any time with her.

'I know Lionel will be pleased,' says Ed, and I feel a stab of guilt. The last thing I want to do is hurt my father.

'Yeah, I went up to Bath last weekend. He was on fine form,' I skirt round the issue and hope he won't notice.

'I don't suppose he's started his diet yet, has he?'

'What do you think?' I'm glad that I'm not the only one on the receiving end of Ed's sermons. Lionel is always being nagged about losing weight but, of course, he never listens.

Frowning, Ed shakes his head. 'He needs to consider cutting back on his saturated fat and going on a healthy-eating plan. I'm serious, sis.' He looks at me as if, for some bizarre reason, I should think he wasn't. When *isn't* Ed serious? 'With all the dairy products and red meat he gets through, his cholesterol must be through the roof.'

'So, how's Lou?' I change the subject to his wife. Lou is six months pregnant and really cool. On the outside she's a nursery-school teacher who wears bubblegum pink Birkenstocks and can recite *Harry Potter* from memory, but on the inside she's a reformed Goth who still has her nose pierced and loves horror movies. How my brother managed to persuade this bright, funny woman to marry him, I have no idea.

'Well, the sickness is finally over, thank goodness, but now Boris is kicking her black and blue,' he says gloomily.

'You mean you know it's going to be a boy?' I say excitedly. Then add, 'and you're going to call him *Boris*?'

'Don't be ridiculous. Of course not,' he snaps. 'We want the baby's sex to be a surprise, but Lou insists on calling it Boris – after Boris Karloff who played Frankenstein,' he explains, then sighs. 'Apparently all expectant mothers give their unborn babies a nickname, which, quite frankly, is as bad as people naming their car . . .'

Honestly, I love my brother, but sometimes I want to shoot him: he's so bloody grumpy. I know that secretly he's thrilled about the baby, but he'll never admit it. He just loves to moan.

'Drink?' I say brightly, hoping to cheer him up with the lure of a G and T.

'Huh, if you're lucky,' he grumbles, handing me a tenner. 'I've been trying to catch the barman's attention for the last twenty minutes.'

Like I was saying, a cheerful soul, my brother.

Despairing of him, I turn to the bar – I see what he means. It's at least five men deep, all holding out empty pint glasses in one hand and notes in the other. At this rate it's going to take for ever. Glumly I join the back of the queue.

After a moment a man behind me taps me on the shoulder. 'Are you being served?' he asks hopefully, waggling his empty glass at me.

'I wish,' I sigh, shaking my head.

And then the oddest thing happens.

In the middle of ringing up a round of drinks the barman turns and stares right at me. Not at the half-dozen men jostling in front of me, but *right at me.* I meet his gaze and go all goosepimply. Which is weird: he's balding, overweight and fifty if he's a day. 'Sorry to keep you waiting, what would you like?' he says.

'Erm . . .' I smile uncertainly. 'Two G and Ts with ice and lemon. Please,' I add. I can't believe my luck.

'Coming right up,' winks the barman and, grabbing two glasses, he turns to the optics.

A few minutes later when I return to Ed he's engrossed in the football match, along with every other male in the pub.

'Crikey, that was quick,' he comments approvingly, taking his glass without removing his eyes from the screen.

'You'll never guess what happened,' I hiss. 'I was served before anyone else.'

'The female touch, hey?' He sips his drink and continues to stare contentedly at the TV.

'No, it wasn't like that, it was really strange.'

'What do you mean, strange?' Scowling as the crowd shuffles to accommodate a new influx of people, he clutches his drink to his chest to avoid spilling it. 'Bloody hell, it's bedlam in here.'

I feel an elbow in my shoulder, and gasp sympathetically, 'I know. I wish there was somewhere to sit down.'

No sooner have the words left my mouth than the couple next to me start to put on their coats. *No, surely not.* I watch in astonishment as the woman drains the last of her wine and reapplies her lipgloss, while the man tucks his cigarettes into his top pocket. They can't be leaving. *Can they?*

'We're going – would you like these seats?' The man has turned to me. Not to Ed, but to me.

Suddenly I'm all light-headed.

'Er, yes, thanks.' I smile gratefully and glance at Ed, who's astounded. He claims one of the empty stools hurriedly then hitches up his suit trousers to get comfortable. 'What a stroke of luck.'

Wordlessly I slide myself on to the seat. My mind is whirling. All those niggly doubts about superstition and luck magnify as one episode after another unravels like frames on a reel of film:

the empty seat on the train, no queue at Starbucks, the packet of razor blades, the parking space, Gabe replying to my small ad in *Loot* . . . The images begin to muddle, thrown out of sequence, big things, little things . . . Driving back from Bath and there being no traffic, hanging my coat on an empty peg at work, finding my perfect pair of shoes *in my size*. And then discovering they were even further reduced. Getting served at the bar, being able to sit down . . . Faster and faster, everything blurs together until I can't stop myself blurting, 'Actually, no, it's not.' My heart is thumping like a piston. 'It's more than luck.'

I wait for him to say something, but Ed stares at me in confusion. 'I'm sorry, Heather, you've lost me,' he says eventually. 'What on earth are you talking about?'

I hesitate. Because that's the problem. I'm not really sure *what* I'm talking about. Chewing my lip, I try anyway. 'Ed, if I tell you something, promise you won't laugh?'

'Ah, now that's easy,' he quips wryly. 'I have no sense of humour, remember?' He's referring to something I said to him in an argument years ago, which he's never forgotten.

'Well, maybe this is just me being daft but—' I stop and exhale sharply. 'No, forget it, I'm being crazy.'

'My little sister? Crazy?' His eyes return to the football.

I hesitate. He's going to think I'm an idiot. But he thinks I'm an idiot anyway. 'Well, you see, the thing is . . .' I take a deep breath. Oh, sod it! Just say it, Heather. 'Everything I wish for seems to come true,' I say loudly.

But not loudly enough: my words are swallowed in another roar from the crowd that swells upwards in an arc, like a boomerang of yells, whistles and grunts, then crashes down in a groan of disappointment.

'Damn! That was close,' gasps Ed. 'We nearly scored.'

'Ed, did you hear what I just said?'

'Sorry, sis.' He places a hand apologetically on my knee. 'A momentary lapse in concentration. You were saying something about wishful thinking . . .'

I can tell he's only humouring me, but I persevere. It's a relief to tell someone, to vocalise the suspicions that have been niggling at me for days. 'No, it's not wishful thinking. It's more than that.' Saying this aloud makes it sound even more preposterous. 'Over the last few days every little thing I wish for seems to happen.'

'Well, you know what they say, don't you?' he says, draining the last of his gin and tonic.

'I do?' I ask, puzzled.

Crunching ice, Ed looks at me solemnly. 'Be careful what you wish for.'

'*Careful?*' I repeat in astonishment. The most amazing, fantastic, wonderful thing is happening and my brother is telling me to be careful? Actually, knowing him, why am I surprised?.

'Well, consider the implications. We think we know what we want, but we can never really know until we've got it. And sometimes when we have, we discover we never really wanted it in the first place – but then it's too late.' He raises a smile. 'Like, for example, I remember once wishing for some time off work when Lou and I were planning the wedding. And then I went down with flu and had to spend my week off in bed with a hot-water bottle. Not much of a wish, eh?'

'Ed, I'm being serious.' I'm perplexed as to how his example has any relevance to what's been happening to me these past couple of days. 'It's much more than that.'

He peers at me from under his dark eyebrows. 'Are you feeling all right?'

'Yes, I'm fine. And, no, it's not the flu,' I add impatiently.

He holds up his hands in surrender. 'OK, I'm sorry, but come on, how can you expect me to be serious? I mean, *really*,' he scoffs. 'Wishes coming true?'

My jaw clenches. Right, that does it. 'OK, dare me to wish for something,' I retort tartly.

'Heather, please, stop this nonsense. You're being ridiculous,' sighs Ed, who's now annoyed.

'You see? You're worried,' I snap.

'Worried?' he jeers. 'Why on earth would I be worried?

Because my sister has suddenly discovered she has magical powers?'

And as he says it he lets out a taunting little laugh. The same taunting little laugh I remember from when I was little when he would hold both my wrists in one of his hands and tickle me until I cried for mercy. And now, just as I was then, I'm infuriated.

'OK. Well, if it's so funny, play along with me then,' I demand. 'Or are you scared you'll be proved wrong?'

Now, one thing I know about my brother is how competitive he is. Years of playing Monopoly with him have taught me how much he loves to win. Probably as much as he loves to be always right. But then again, so do I.

'Well, if you insist . . .' he says immediately. Exactly as I'd thought. He thinks for a moment, then clicks his fingers. '*The match*,' he says triumphantly.

'What about it?' I ask.

'Well, at the moment the score's one–all, and there's less than five minutes to go . . .' He motions towards the TV screen. 'We need to score another goal against France to win the championship.'

'Oh, right,' I say, without a flicker of enthusiasm. 'Who's we?' Like I said, I have no clue when it comes to football. Which is the way I like it.

'England,' huffs Ed. 'Who do you think?'

'So?' I prompt.

'So if all your wishes come true, why don't you wish England scores before the final whistle?' he continues.

'Because I don't really care,' I say.

'Would you care if I said I won't mention to Rosemary that you've bought her a present . . .' He looks at me and I realise I've been busted. 'And you get to keep it yourself?'

'That's blackmail.'

'And this is madness,' he says wearily.

'OK, OK.' I turn to face the screen and try to concentrate on the men running up and down the pitch. Sorry, the teams. Screwing up my forehead, I focus on a man in a blue shirt who's got control of the ball. 'Are we in the white shirts or the blue?' I whisper.

'White,' hisses Ed, impatiently.

'Oh . . .' Disappointed, I concentrate as the French player deftly passes the ball to someone else on his team while England can only watch helplessly. He begins to charge towards the goal. I hold my breath, straining forward to see what's happening, suddenly aware of the tense atmosphere around me.

Come on, England, come on, you can do it.

I catch myself as I hear a voice inside my head. Hang on a minute, is this me? Watching a football match? In a pub? And enjoying it? I'm white-knuckling my glass – the tension is unbelievable. I can barely watch. France are going to score another goal, England are going to lose. I feel my heartbeat quicken.

'For Godsakes, come on, England, come on,' I hear Ed say.

Even though it seems hopeless, he's chanting the mantra under his breath, willing them to win. And suddenly I'm wishing the same thing. 'Come on, England,' I yell, joining in. '*Win.*'

And then, out of the blue, England intercepts and scores.

The bar erupts with shrieking, whooping, yelling, whistling. Everyone's hugging each other in celebration. A chorus of 'Would you believe it?', 'What a miracle!', 'Bloody magic!'

But I can't hear it. It's as if I'm watching a movie with the sound turned down. An unexpected blast of wind bangs the door open, and when I turn to Ed he's staring at me, jaw dropped in shock.

'Bloody hell, Heather,' he stammers, when he finds his voice. 'But that can't be . . .' He's looking backwards and forwards between me and the TV set that's showing the score: 2–1 to England. 'I mean, it's impossible . . .' He falls silent and, wordlessly, we exchange a look of amazement.

And then it hits me.

I feel a flurry of exhilaration, excitement . . .

Chapter Thirteen

Possibility.

'Excuse me, do you sell lottery tickets?' I smile broadly at Mrs Patel, who is standing behind the counter of my local corner shop stacking Marlboro Lights. Her tiny hands are heavily decorated with henna patterns.

Surprised, she stops what she's doing to stare at me. Ever since I moved to the neighbourhood I've been a regular in Mrs Patel's shop for everything ranging from my monthly PMS fix of trash mags and chocolate, to emergency loo-roll and Billy Smith's cat litter. But in all this time I've never once bought a lottery ticket.

Until now.

'Yes, of course,' she says, tossing her bright orange sari over a plump shoulder. 'By the window.' Her gold dangly earrings rattle as she motions with her head.

'Thanks.' I try to hide my flutters of excitement and hurry past her. Tucked away in the corner I find a red plastic lectern that I've never noticed before, grab the pen lying on it and I eagerly help myself to a ticket. Right, let's see. I gloss through the instructions. 'Choose six numbers and mark with a line.' Hmm, well, that bit should be easy. My age, my address . . . Merrily I cross them off. Actually, this is rather fun. Number of years I've worked at Together Forever, my mum's birthday . . .

I grind to a halt. I need two more. I fiddle with my hair and concentrate on the numbers, hoping one will jump out at me yelling 'Pick me! I'm a winner!'

A winner.

Oh, wow, can you imagine it? The only thing I've ever won is a game of chess. But the lottery? The concept makes me feel quite giddy. Winning millions and millions of pounds, being rich beyond my wildest dreams, going on a shopping spree to end all shopping sprees . . .

Automatically I make one of my wish lists:

- A house in Holland Park. One of those with large white pillars and a gorgeous terrace with a view that would put Rosemary's house to shame.
- An Italian hideaway somewhere in the Tuscan hills where I could spend lazy summers shopping for leather goods and chatting with locals.
- Through an interpreter. Preferably male, dark and clad in Prada.
- A Matisse. He's Lionel's favourite painter. Any picture will do – I'm not picky.
- Premier-league season tickets for Ed.
- A pension plan to beat all pension plans.
- A boob reduction for Jess.
- Two weeks at Chiva Som in Thailand. Actually, scrap that. A *month* at Chiva Som in Thailand.
- Highlights at Nicky Clarke, *by* Nicky Clarke.
- Shoes. Lots and lots and lots of shoes.
- And a new car so I don't have to *try* to walk anywhere in them.
- A silver Aston Martin Vanquish like the one Bond drives.
- Or maybe one of those new Mini convertibles so that when I'm in Italy buying all those shoes I can zip around the tiny alleyways.

By myself.

Abruptly I feel a familiar pang of loneliness.

'Ahem.' Someone clears their throat, interrupting my thoughts, and over my shoulder I see a queue of people waiting.

'Oh, sorry, won't be a minute. Just spending my millions,' I joke, expecting at least a glimmer of a smile from someone. Instead I can almost hear the resounding thwack as my joke falls flat on their stony expressions.

'C'mon, get a bloody move on,' I hear someone grumble under their breath. 'We haven't got all day.'

Chastised, I choose the last two numbers at random, grab my ticket and beat a retreat to the counter.

Mrs Patel is waiting for me. 'So, you're feeling lucky, eh?'

I hesitate. Now I'm standing here at eight thirty a.m., in the cold, flickering fluorescent light of the shop it does all seem rather far-fetched. Last night I'd been sure that it wasn't all coincidence. The only reason England won was because . . . Because what, Heather? Because you wished they would score a goal?

All of a sudden I realise how ridiculous I'm being. Of course it was coincidence, you idiot.

The machine whirs and spits out the printed ticket.

'Maybe,' I reply, smiling uncomfortably and trying to avoid eye-contact with Mrs Patel. Which is when I see the headline on the front page of the *Daily Mail*: 'England Magic.'

My stomach flips like a pancake. 'Maybe you could say that,' I murmur, taking the ticket. With trembling fingers, I fold it in half and tuck it carefully into my wallet.

Bloody hell, Heather.

I leave the shop in a state of nervous anticipation. Outside, the morning rush-hour is in full swing, the pavements thick with commuters in shirt-sleeves, enjoying yet another day of warm bright sunshine. But I'm so wrapped up in my own head it could have been raining Amazonian bullfrogs for all I'd notice.

I keep walking, eyes down, a million questions running around in my mind. Words like 'impossible', 'preposterous' and 'amazing' tumble over themselves as my mind wages an internal battle. On one hand the realistic, logical, sane me *knows* there has to be a rational explanation. Yet on the other, the part of me that surreptitiously reads horoscopes and avoids walking under ladders can't help getting carried away.

Leaving the traffic behind I head along beside the canal. This is one of my favourite places in the city. It's picture-postcard pretty and I never tire of looking at all the brightly painted narrow-boats, reading their weird and wonderful names, *Merlin's Sea Legs, Storm in a Teacup, Lavender Mermaid,* and wondering what it would be like to live on a boat in the centre of London. *Sod the boats, what about the wishes?* interrupts a voice in my head.

Startled, I ignore it and gaze instead at the hanging baskets spilling down the sides of the boats in an explosion of colour. Look, they're beautiful. *The dozens of little wishes I make without even realising?*

And isn't it ingenious how the owners of that barge over there have used old wellington boots as plant pots? I frown at the wooden deck where they're all lined up. They've got sunflowers growing out of them that must be about six foot tall. Squinting in the sunshine, I shade my eyes with my hand. Gosh, the sun really is bright. I wish I had my sunglasses. *Secret, silent, subconscious wishes that are part of everyday life.*

Honestly, I don't know what's wrong with me today. My mind's all over the place. I push my hands into my pockets – and stop. Hang on a minute. My fingers brush against something smooth like plastic. It can't be . . . I'm positive I left them at home. With a flutter in my stomach I tug out my sunglasses. *What would happen if those wishes suddenly started coming true?*

With trembling fingers I put them on, tinting the world a coppery hue. I take a deep breath, trying to calm myself, but it's no good. This is ridiculous. I can't focus. I need a coffee. *If everything you wished for actually happened?*

Oh, for God's sake, shut up, why don't you?

I spot a little café and abandon my tour of the canal. With my recent weight loss I can treat myself to a *pain au chocolat*. In fact, I'm toying with the idea of going a step further and making it an almond croissant when I notice a house covered with scaffolding and a skip parked outside. My heart sinks. It can only mean one thing.

Builders.

I hate builders.

Briefly I consider crossing back to the opposite side of the road and diving for cover behind a row of parked cars, but from the corner of my eye I see it's too late. Two of them are sitting on a wall drinking flasks of tea and reading the tabloids. They look up as I approach.

I've been spotted.

'Bollocks.' I lower my head, but I feel indignant. I wish they'd mind their own business and leave us women in peace. I mean, it's so unfair. I wish they knew how it felt to be leered at. Walking towards them I wait for the inevitable 'Cheer up, love, it'll never happen.'

And you know what? *It doesn't.*

They can't have noticed me, I tell myself, walking past and not hearing a single wolf-whistle. Instead there's just hammering and drilling. Puzzled, I look up, ready for eye-contact and a show-us-your-tits type greeting, but . . . there's nothing . . . Nobody's even looking in my direction.

Presuming it's too good to be true I keep walking. Waiting. Expecting. Still nothing. I feel a burgeoning sense of confidence. I slow down and strut – yes, *strut* – past a bare-chested builder mixing cement without bothering to tug down the hem of my denim miniskirt. Not even a sideways glance.

Which is when I notice the front pages of the newspapers they're reading. In large black capitals the headlines read:

SHRINKING MANHOOD:
NEW SEX SURVEY SHOWS BUILDERS HAVE SMALLEST PENISES

I clap a hand over my mouth to stifle a giggle. Then I hear that voice again in my head: *What if all your wishes were granted?*

Only this time I don't ignore it. Finally I'm convinced. As weird, inconceivable and mindboggling as it might be, that it's got to be magic. And then – I don't know what comes over me but before I know it I'm putting my fingers into my mouth and letting out a long, liberating wolf-whistle. I watch with satisfaction as a couple of bricklayers blush beetroot with embarrassment. It's abso-fucking-lutely fantastic.

* * *

And it gets better.

It's like the floodgates have opened and I spend the rest of the week in a whirl of pleasant surprises. Abandoned pots of wrinkle cream that have never before made a blind bit of difference now, on closer inspection in the mirror, actually seem to be working. Earrings I thought I'd lost, hunted for on my hands and knees, suddenly appear from out of the back of the sofa like rabbits from a magician's hat. Even my hair, which I can never do a thing with despite a daily forty-minute battle, suddenly looks glossy, kink-free and – dare I say it? – in an actual style.

One by one, the dozens of inconsequential wishes I make every day, without thinking, begin to come true. At first it's just the little things. My fake tan doesn't go streaky round my ankles. They don't sell out of my favourite sandwich at Marks & Spencer. When I flick on the TV, there's been a last-minute change and, instead of the advertised programme on turbine engines, a film I've wanted to see for ages is just starting.

But it doesn't stop there.

In fact, this is when the fun really starts. Instead of *accidentally* wishing for things, I test it out by *deliberately* wishing for all kinds of things. Nothing major – to be honest I'm a bit nervous because it's not like this sort of thing happens to me every day. I don't wish Benicio del Toro was coming round later to give me a shoulder massage (maybe I'll work up to that later), but I still get some pretty amazing results.

Take ice-cream, for example.

My whole life I've never been able to eat just one or two spoonfuls, then put the tub back into the freezer. I always polish off the lot, then wish I hadn't because I feel sick and have to undo the top button on my jeans. But yesterday, when I tried out my theory by scoffing a whole pint of Häagen Dazs Belgian Chocolate while I was watching *Breakfast at Tiffany's*, I didn't feel even a teensy bit nauseous. Furthermore, my jeans weren't tight! It was as if I'd never eaten it. It was truly astonishing.

But even more astonishing is that today, when I went to buy a fresh tub, I didn't feel like ice-cream. It's weird, but now I know that I can eat it guilt-free, it's as if the fun's gone out of it. I ended up buying some bananas instead.

Then it was the weather. Whenever I blow-dry my hair it always rains. Without fail. But not this week: this week it's been warm and dry and my hair hasn't gone frizzy once. It's looked fabulous every day.

But best of all has to be the traffic-lights. From Little Venice to Hampstead to Elephant and Castle, I haven't had a red light. For the last few days every single one has been green and I've just whizzed through them all. Driving around London has been so much fun. Well, apart from the fine I got for speeding along the Embankment (I'm used to sitting in traffic and didn't realise how fast I was going until the policeman pulled me over) but it's only three points on my licence and a sixty-pound fine . . .

'. . . and I've saved myself some money already because – would you believe it? – a traffic warden let me off a parking ticket!' I exclaim.

Jess is staring at her reflection in the mirror, pulling a face. It's Friday evening after work and we're both squashed into a changing cubicle at Zara. I was planning to go straight home and get an early night, but then I got the phone call: she was begging me to help her find an outfit for her first date with Greg tomorrow night. It's a quest that's beginning to take on epic *Lord of the Rings* proportions.

She pushes up her ample chest with her hands and frowns. 'Wouldn't it look better if I had smaller boobs?'

'You're not listening, are you?' I say sulkily. I've just spent the last hour telling Jess everything and she's not impressed. As I stand knee-deep in halter-neck tops and coat-hangers, my excitement takes a nosedive. First Ed, now Jess. Why will no one believe me?

'Yes, I am,' she protests, tugging the dress over her shoulders. 'Something about not getting a parking ticket . . .' There's a muffled grunt as she gets the waist wedged at her shoulders. And some wriggling. 'Heather, can you help? I'm stuck.'

I'm tempted to leave her there, arms flailing, head trapped inside the tulle netting, but I give in and tug sharply. There's a loud 'ow' and then her head pops out, hair all mussed up, lipgloss smeared across her face. And, no doubt, all over that dress.

'Damn, I've bust the zip.' She looks at the dress in dismay, then chucks it on to the huge pile of discarded items on the floor. 'I think Greg would have liked that dress. He said in his email he likes women to be feminine.' In her bra and knickers she rifles through the other garments she's smuggled in with her maximum of six items. She grabs a strapless boob tube.

'But that's just it! I didn't get a parking ticket,' I continue indignantly, determined not to be sidetracked. 'That's the whole point of what I'm saying. When I saw him the warden was punching all my details into one of those little computers and I was thinking, Oh, God, another fifty quid, I can't afford it, and wishing he'd let me off. And guess what? He did! He just told me to be more careful next time.' I smile triumphantly. 'Don't you think that's amazing?'

'I think it would be more amazing if Clive Owen had turned up on your doorstep, got down on one knee and proposed.' She groans. 'Just look at those mammaries, they're ginormous. I look like I'm pregnant. Jesus, I wish I had smaller boobs.'

'Clive Owen's already married,' I point out.

'You know what I mean.' She wrenches off the boob tube and stands there in her underwear. 'A football match, some builders, a set of green lights and a parking ticket is hardly exciting, is it?' she says, ticking them off on her fingers. 'What about the big stuff we all wish for? You know. Success. Happiness. *Lurve*.' Hands on her hips she gazes at me and I know what's coming.

'You've got to go out there again some time you know.'

I pick up a top and pretend to be fascinated by the embroidery on the cuffs.

'Yes, you, Heather. You've got to get back in the saddle or it's going to grow over,' she warns, gesturing down below.

'Euggh, Jess.'

'It's true,' she protests. 'I read an article about it once. Apparently the vagina . . .'

Suddenly I see that I'm wasting my time. In fact, what was I thinking of, telling Jess about the heather? She's never going to understand. This is a woman for whom falling in love isn't about magic, it's about ticking boxes.

I change the subject. 'What about this black off-the-shoulder T-shirt, and those three-quarter jeans?' I suggest, picking up two items and waggling them at her.

'Don't you think they're a bit, well, boring?'

I dangle the fashionista's carrot. 'I saw Sienna Miller in something similar.' I cross my fingers behind my back.

'Really?' She snatches the items from me and pulls on the jeans. 'Mmm, yeah, maybe if I wore them with that big low-slung belt I got in Greece – you know, the one with the amulets.' She wriggles into the top and adjusts it off the shoulder. Jess is all boobs and butt and it looks amazing. 'You're a genius, Heather!' She throws her arms round me. 'This is perfect.'

I smile modestly. Hopefully she won't find out that my inspiration wasn't Sienna Miller but the mannequin in the window display.

She pulls away and begins getting dressed in her old clothes. 'But as I was saying . . .'

Damn. I'd thought I'd got away with it.

'You've got to forget about Daniel.'

'I have forgotten,' I reply defensively.

'Denial is not a river in Egypt,' she drawls.

'I'm not in denial,' I protest.

She pulls back the curtain and turns to me. 'Well, then, what are you waiting for?'

'The perfect man,' I quip, hoping that'll shut her up. She scoops up her huge pile of clothes and dumps them on the table in front of the sales assistant, who gives me a frosty six-items-maximum look.

Jess laughs ruefully. 'I hate to be the one to break the news, honey, but he doesn't exist.'

'Maybe not.' I follow her to the cash register. 'But that doesn't mean I have to stop wishing he did.' I glance at the couple standing next to us in the queue. Arms wrapped round each other the woman is looking all doe-eyed at a man I wouldn't notice in a crowd. To me he's a balding, rather dull-looking chap who needs to buy himself a nasal-hair trimmer. But to her he's the perfect man. 'And, anyway, I think you're wrong,' I say. 'I think the perfect man does exist.'

'What happened to cynical and bitter?'

'I'm just saying—'

'That all men are bastards?' interrupts Jess, doing rather a good impression of me. After Daniel left, that was pretty much all I could say, between drags of Marlboro Lights and tequila slammers.

'I was heartbroken,' I say, in my defence. 'And, anyway, why is it that if men hate women they're called misogynists, but if women hate men we're just called bitter?'

'Or a lesbian,' says Jess, matter-of-factly.

There's a brief silence as we absorb this fact, and then, 'Bastards,' Jess announces, glaring at the male sales assistant behind the cash register, as if he's personally responsible for sexual inequality.

'Anyway, as I was saying,' I hastily change the subject, 'I think the perfect man does exist. He's just different for different people. I mean, look at Camilla Parker Bowles – sorry, Windsor.' Well, now I've started I've got to try to back up this theory. 'Her idea of the perfect man is Prince Charles.'

Jess grimaces.

'She's madly in love with him,' I add as evidence.

Jess winces. 'Oooh . . . and with those ears,' she whispers, almost as if she fears His Royal Highness might hear her.

'Exactly. It's like the woman who's married to Robin Williams. I think he's the most unfunny man alive, but she must think he's perfect.'

'Robbie Williams is married?' The teenage girl in front of us twirls round, shocked.

'No, the actor. You know. *Mrs Doubtfire, Mork and Mindy . . .*'

'Nanoo, nanoo,' mimics Jess, making me giggle.

'And what about Carrie and Mr Big?' I say, through laughter. Now I'm really getting into the swing of things. 'I never got it. She could have had Aiden!'

'Mmmm.' There's a murmur of approval from women around us.

Signing the credit card slip, Jess takes her new purchase and stuffs her receipt in her bag. 'So, c'mon, then,' she says, linking her arm through mine. 'If the perfect man is different for different people, what's yours like?' She steers me across the shop floor. 'Just in case I should bump into him.' She grins.

I play along. 'Well, he's handsome, obviously.' I chew my lip thoughtfully. 'Monogamous, of course.' I run down my list of what the ideal man would be like if you could make him up, because of course I've got a list for everything. 'He hates sport, but loves Dido . . .' I can feel myself warming up. 'He doesn't just chuck his clothes on the floor, or leave the cheese unwrapped in the fridge so it goes all cracked and hard . . .' Actually, this is rather fun. 'He's not scared of talking about his emotions, or frightened of commitment . . . or asking for directions if he's lost . . .' Everything I've ever wished for in a man comes rushing back. 'He likes holding hands and candlelit dinners. He's not just interested in getting into my knickers, he buys me flowers, and I'm not talking about those crappy bunches from the petrol station . . .' I stop to think. Is that everything? 'Oh, and he has to fall madly in love with me, of course.' We walk out into the rush of Oxford Street.

'You've forgotten the most important thing,' says Jess, making eye-contact with a guy walking in the opposite direction and throwing him a flirtatious smile.

'I have?' I ask, puzzled. 'What?'

She grins wickedly. 'A ten-inch penis.'

Chapter Fourteen

'A couple of hunters are out in the woods when one falls to the ground. He doesn't seem to be breathing and, in mad panic, the other guy whips out his cellphone and calls the emergency services . . .'

Standing in front of the full-length mirror on the back of his wardrobe door, wearing a Ramones T-shirt under a black suit jacket with an unlit cigarette wedged into the corner of his mouth, Gabe pauses to study his reflection and runs through a variety of expressions: pensive (head tilted down, brow furrowed); shocked (eyes wide, jaw thrown open); upset (eyebrows knitted together, trembly bottom lip). Sighing, his shoulders slump forward and he jabs his glasses back up his nose. 'Jeez, what a tough decision.' He scratches his head. 'What kind of look does this joke need?'

He runs through them again, then addresses his reflection: 'OK, let's imagine I'm the audience.' He points to his chest. 'And let's imagine I'm Jerry Seinfeld.' He grins sheepishly. 'No, let's say Dennis Leary.' He scowls at his reflection. 'You motherfucking fucker,' he swears, his body wound up like a spring, jaw jutting aggressively.

And then he lets out a gasp, slumping forward dispiritedly. 'C'mon, Gabe, which is funnier? None of them? All of them?' Angst-ridden, he scratches the bristles on his chin, then suddenly breaks into a huge smile. 'Jesus, that's it. *That's the look!*'

His grip tightens on the hairbrush he's holding as a microphone, he splays his legs in a sort of Elvis pose and continues: 'He gasps to the operator: "My friend is dead! What do I do?" Calmly the operator replies, "Just take it easy. I can help. First, let's make sure he's dead." ' Gabe's mouth twitches. He's trying not to laugh, but he bursts into a guffaw. Wiping his eyes, he reprimands himself: 'Gabriel Hoffman, you are seriously funny, but this is a serious business. You've gotta be angry, tortured, deadly funny. C'mon, concentrate!' He clears his throat and brushes back a chunk of sandy hair that's fallen into his eyes. 'There's silence. Then a shot is heard, and the hunter's voice comes back on the line.' After a comic pause, Gabe goes for the punchline: ' "OK, he's definitely dead. Now what?" '

Oh, my God, he's *terrible*.

Standing in the hallway, watching Gabe rehearse in his bedroom through a gap in the door, I clamp my hands over my mouth to suppress a groan.

He's going to bomb at the Edinburgh Festival. He's going to die on stage, in front of thousands of people. I mean, all that scowling and motherfucking and trying to be the angry, uptight comedian, it's just not Gabe. He's sweet and kind *and from California*. He drinks soya milk, wears flip-flops and does yoga. He's not angry, he's totally chilled out. And that outfit! A Ramones T-shirt under a suit? It's such a cliché. What's happened to his kooky shirts and flip-flops?

My heart goes out to him. I should do something. I should try to stop him. It's like sending someone into battle in a chocolate kettle, or whatever that saying is.

A floorboard creaks, and I snap to.

Oh, shit, he's going to come out of his bedroom and catch me here. *Spying*. You're not spying, Heather, you just got home from shopping with Jess and happened to be walking past, I think frantically, as I dive into the bathroom to avoid being caught.

I lock the door and turn on the taps. There must be something I can do to help. OK, so I hate stand-up comedy, but I don't hate Gabe. On the contrary, he's a really nice bloke and he even puts the top on the toothpaste, I remind myself, with satisfaction.

'Heather?' There's a polite knock on the door and Gabe's voice. 'Are you in there?'

'Erm, yes . . .' I reply, startled. 'Sorry, are you waiting? I won't be a minute.' Worried my cover's about to be blown I clank around with the soap-dish to add a bit of realism.

'No, it's fine, take your time. But when you're finished come outside to the back yard.'

'The back yard?' I mouth at my reflection, wondering what he's up to. Still, whatever it is, it can't be any worse than his jokes.

Which will teach me to jump to conclusions.

'I've gotta surprise,' he adds.

Oh, bloody hell. What was I saying about hating surprises? It's not my birthday, it's not any kind of anniversary, so what on earth can it be? I emerge tentatively from the bathroom and pad barefoot down the hallway, racking my brains for a possible answer so that I can be prepared, when I'm distracted by a funny smell. I sniff the air curiously as I walk into the kitchen. It's almost as if something's burning. As the idea strikes I hurry across the lino and glance through the patio doors at the back garden. It's full of smoke. Oh, Christ. Something *is* burning.

Panic sets in. Oh, fuck! My house is on fire! Did I remember to pay the household insurance? I know it's on my list of things to do, but . . . Frantically I start looking around the kitchen, images of wet towels being thrown on flaming chip pans flashing back from age-old commercials.

But I don't have any towels: they're all in the wash. I need something like – something like that jug. A large glass jug of lilies sits in the middle of the table. I grab it, dump the flowers in the sink and dash outside, water slopping over the edge. Grey smoke is billowing from behind the shed.

Vaulting over a flowerbed, I spin round the side of the shed, my fingers slipping on the wet glass as I swing it back with all my might. Only there aren't any flames.

Just Gabe.

'Tad-daaahhh.' He throws his arms wide and grins as he sees me, but it's too late: like a pendulum, the vase has swung. Which means it has to swing back. Oh dear.

Suddenly everything is happening at once. But it's as if someone has slowed the time right down and I'm watching it on film. The water swooshing out of the vase, soaring through the air like a huge wave, every droplet magnified as Gabe's face comes into shot and begins its journey through a remarkable range of emotions – from happiness, to confusion, to open-mouthed shock as the water hits him square in the face.

Boom. We're back in normal time and Gabe, totally drenched, is standing there dripping, blinking, gasping. 'Jeez, Heather, what's going on?'

'Oh. Shit,' I mutter, as I watch him wiping his wet hair and face with his apron. *Apron?* He's wearing my rose-festooned Cath Kidston pinny over his frilly, pistachio green shirt. At the same moment I notice he's holding tongs in one hand, a packet of veggie sausages in the other and standing in front of a shiny metal object that looks suspiciously like . . .

'*A barbecue?*' I blurt.

'It's a housewarming present – well, for my housewarming. I thought you might like it. For the yard.' As he's speaking I glance down at his feet and notice he's standing in a puddle of water. He wriggles his sunburned toes, which make a slippery squeak against his flip-flops. 'But if I'd known I was gonna get that reaction I might have stuck with a scented candle.'

'Shit.' That's all I can say. Not the best word to choose if you can only choose one but, then, saying and doing the wrong thing seem to be my specialities.

Gabe tips his head and shakes it, like a dog, spraying me with drops of water. Not on purpose I'm sure, I reason, stepping back so he doesn't drench me. 'I'm *soooo* sorry.' I try to apologise as he dabs at himself with one of Brian's Buckingham Palace tea-towels, which I stole from work. 'I thought something was burning.'

'It was the veggie sausages.' With his shirt sticking to his chest in a sodden lump, the frills all wilting and his sandy hair sticking up in peaks like a meringue, he gestures towards the barbecue, which is defiantly emitting a faint spiral of smoke.

'I bought them especially, with you not eating meat and all.' He pauses. 'Maybe this was a bad idea . . .'

'No! No!' I protest. 'It was a *great* idea – I mean, it *is* a great idea.' Enthusiastically I grab a fork and lean over him to pluck a charred object from the grill. For a moment my bravery wavers. Then I smile cheerily at Gabe. He smiles back interestedly.

Oh, fuck. You know how you feel when you've said you're going to do something and then you change your mind but you still have to do it or you know you're going to lose face and look pathetic? Well, that's me with this sausage. Backed into a corner I force myself to take a bite. 'Mmmmmm.'

Gabe watches me with what I could swear is a glimmer of amusement. 'I wasn't sure how long to cook them.'

'Mmmmm. Mmmm,' I continue as I begin to chew. Ouch. Pain shoots through a back molar as I bite down hard on a tough bit.

'Good?'

'Delicious,' I reply, covering my mouth. With great difficulty I swallow. Thank God for that. Free of my penance, I breathe a sigh of relief.

It's short-lived.

'Cool. Have another.' With the tongs Gabe pops a few more on to a plate and holds it out to me. 'There's plenty.'

'Erm, no . . . Actually, that's fine for now.'

But he's insistent. 'Hey, c'mon, it's my treat.'

Treat? This is torture. I struggle to smile as I take the plate, wondering how to distract him so I can play hide-the-sausage in the shrubbery. 'Erm, great, thanks,' I stammer.

At which point Gabe bursts out laughing. A loud belly laugh followed by a bovine snort as he takes breath.

I'm astonished. Until I twig. This is his idea of a joke and I fell right for it.

'Your face,' he doubles up, clutching his stomach, 'when you ate that sausage.'

I try not to smile but it's impossible. 'You bastard,' I mutter, mouth twitching.

'Hey, do you blame me? You threw a great big jug of foul-smelling water at me.'

At the memory I start giggling. 'You should've seen *your* face.'

He stops laughing. 'Well, I guess that just about makes us even.' He holds out his hand for a high-five.

Oh, bloody hell, I hate this bit. I always feel like such an idiot. Feebly I bring my hand down against his. 'For now,' I can't help adding.

Fortunately there are some veggie burgers lurking in the freezer and we put them on the grill, along with some corn-on-the-cob and baked potatoes wrapped in tinfoil.

After we've sorted out the food and he has changed into a T-shirt (I thought the pistachio-green shirt with the ruffle down the middle was bad, but his orange Mr T T-shirt, which I now notice has Velcro hair, is much worse), Gabe pulls out two ice-cold Sols from the fridge, carefully cuts up a lime, squeezes a sliver into each neck and offers me one. I'm much more of a wine person but I can't refuse. I don't want to look all English and uptight. Especially after the trouble he took in getting the barbecue and everything.

'. . . And I've been doing my stand-up around LA, you know, open mikes, that kinda thing, but going to the Edinburgh Festival has always been a dream so I decided this year I was gonna go for it. I booked a venue, printed up some flyers and I'm taking my show up there for a whole week. Gonna take a shot at that Perrier Award.'

I'm sipping my beer as I listen to Gabe, who's now manning the grill, flipping burgers like a pro and rearranging the tinfoil bundles.

'So you just quit your job?' I ask, from the comfort of the sun-lounger. Wow, this is the life. Having my dinner cooked, being handed beers, lying here not lifting a finger. Now I know what it must have felt like to be Daniel.

'No, a friend and I have a clothes store on Abbot Kinney – it's a street in Venice that's got some real cool shops and cafés,' he explains. 'Oh, and a great Mexican that does the most awesome chilli *rellenos*.' His eyes light up at the memory and he pauses, obviously reliving a chilli *relleno* moment. Then he realises that I don't have a clue what he's talking about. 'You've never had a chilli *relleno*?'

I shake my head.

'Jesus, you're not serious?'

' 'Fraid so.'

'Wow, Heather, you have no idea what you're missing.' He drops his spatula in horror and wipes his hands on his apron. You'd think he was about to deliver a sermon. Which he is. 'A chilli *relleno* is a feast of flavours. It's a chilli, stuffed with grated cheese, which they deep-fry, then slather in salsa and sour cream. It's awesome . . .'

'I take it you like your food?' I smile.

He's shamefaced now. 'It's a Jewish thing.'

'You're Jewish?'

He turn sideways to show me his profile and runs his finger down his nose. 'Can't you tell by the schnoz?'

'Hey, at least you have an excuse.' I turn sideways and do the same with mine. 'When I was little I used to look at drawings of princesses in fairy-tales and they all had those cute little button noses. It was the witches with the poison apples who had the big hooked ones.'

'You have a great nose,' protests Gabe. 'It's like a toucan's beak.'

'I'll take that as a compliment.' I pull a face. 'But, anyway, about your job . . .' Swiftly I move the conversation away from my nose. That's something I've learned as I've grown older: don't talk to men about the bits of your body you're unhappy with. When I was with Daniel I used to go on and on about cellulite, thrusting my buttocks into his face whenever he insisted I didn't have any. Until, eventually, I persuaded him I did have cellulite. From then on he went from thinking my bottom was like a peach to saying that, actually, I was right: it did look rather like porridge in a string bag. Well done, Heather.

'Oh, yeah, well, let's put it this way, my partner owes me a favour so he's taken the reins for a while. It's only going to be for a few weeks in any case.'

'And what about your girlfriend, Mia – doesn't she mind?'

Gabe blushes. 'Nah – too many nights spent watching me on the open mike. She probably wanted to get rid of me.' He's smiling as he says it, as only a person confident that that's not the case can. And, from what I've seen so far of Gabe Hoffman, I can't imagine his girlfriend ever wanting to get rid of him. Even if he does tell terrible jokes.

'So, what's your story?' He flips a burger and looks at me sideways, one eyebrow raised.

'My story?'

'Yeah, you know, relationship, job, family . . .'

'Oh, *that* story.' I drain the last of my beer and balance the bottle on the ledge next to me. 'I've been single since last year when I discovered my boyfriend, whom I lived with at the time, was cheating on me.'

Gabe throws me a sympathetic look but I move on swiftly. 'I've been working as a wedding photographer for the past six years but now I'm about to lose my job.'

'Aha, I wondered what the pile of résumés was doing on the kitchen table.'

'Yeah, well, I didn't exactly dream of being a wedding photographer, so let's just say I haven't had my big break as yet.'

'What about your folks?'

'I've got one older brother Ed, and he's married to Lou – they're about to have a baby – and then there's my father, Lionel, who's an artist and married to my wicked stepmother Rosemary.'

'And your mom?'

'She died when I was twelve.'

There's a pause. 'Hey, I'm sorry.'

'Me too,' I say quietly, feeling my throat tighten as it always does when I think about Mum. Even now, nearly twenty years later. 'Not much of a happy ending, I'm afraid.' I smile ruefully.

'Hang on a minute. Who's talking about endings? You know what my old grandpa used to say to me? "Son, you're still at once upon a time . . ."' He mimics a southern drawl.

'Well, you can tell your grandpa I'm thirty years old.'

'Somehow I don't think that'll wash with him. He's ninety-two.'

'Is this one of those anecdotes with a moral about how we should be grateful because there's always someone worse off in life?'

'Hey, my grandpa has a great life. He's just discovered Internet porn.'

I laugh and hoist myself up from the sun-lounger to walk over to the barbecue. 'Mmm, that smells good. I'm starving.' I look hopefully at the tinfoil bundles.

'The corn's going to be another fifteen minutes and as for the carbs . . .' He jabs a knife inside one. 'How do you like your potatoes, madam, hard or hard?'

'In that case I've got time to pop to the corner shop for a bottle of wine.'

'Beer too gassy, huh?'

I wrinkle my nose.

'I'll apologise now for later,' he says. Then, seeing my confused expression, he explains: 'We share a bathroom . . .'

'Oh . . .' There's a pause and then, 'Eeuggh,' I groan. 'Too much information.' I swat him affectionately.

'Sorry. Another Jewish trait, I'm afraid – food and bodily functions.'

Laughing, I slip on my flip-flops, scoop up my hair and tie it back in a knot. 'Won't be a minute. Red or white?'

'You choose.'

I go to leave, then stop and turn. 'Gabe?'

'Yeah?'

I look at my new flatmate, standing in my apron, which clashes terribly with his orange Mr T T-shirt, and feel an unexpected fondness for him. It's strange, but somehow I feel as if I've known him a long time. 'I love the barbecue. It was really sweet of you.'

'Hey, don't mention it.'

'And about earlier, with the water . . .'

'Is that how you English say thank you?' He gives me his big cockeyed smile.

'No. This is how we say thank you.'

Impulsively I lean over and kiss his whiskery cheek. And before either of us has time to think about what just happened, I hurry inside.

Chapter Fifteen

Barbra Streisand is wailing from the tape deck as I enter the corner shop and set off the electronic jingle. Mrs Patel looks up from the unidentifiable purple object she's knitting and squints at me over the top of her glasses with the same look she gives everyone – forehead furrowed, kohl-rimmed eyes scrunched, tiny mouth pursed in distrust. She can make her entire face pucker round the edges, as if someone was pulling a drawstring on a bag.

I smile, give a little nod, then head to the back of the shop where she keeps the wine. When I first moved into the neighbourhood, I remember thinking it was going to be a limited selection – a dusty bottle of Liebfraumilch or an overpriced Chianti in a straw basket. But I was wrong. That might be the case with most local corner shops, but this isn't just any corner shop, it's *Mrs Patel's* corner shop, and although I'd never have guessed it, this tiny Indian lady, with her brightly coloured saris and passion for Barbra Streisand and Barry Gibb, is something of a sommelier.

Now, in the depths of the shop, I ponder over a bottle of sauvignon blanc. It's always my preferred choice, but perhaps this time I should get something different. I swing back to the reds. No, too heavy, and red wine stains my teeth. I zigzag back to white. But, then, white is a bit tacky, isn't it? With its Bridget Jones overtones.

I sigh impatiently. Gosh, this is harder than I thought. I'm not normally so indecisive. I've bought wine here a hundred times and never without the slightest hesitation . . . What's different? Gabe's different, I realise, remembering the damp American back in my garden. He told me to choose, but I don't want to pick something naff. I want to make the right impression, especially after the vase incident.

I sigh despairingly. Crikey this is tough. I just can't decide. And then I have an idea.

Closing my eyes I begin muttering under my breath: 'Eeny, meeny, miny,' my eyes firmly closed I let my finger choose a wine, 'mo.' But instead of prodding a hard, cold surface, I feel something soft, warm . . . alive? My eyes snap open and I stare at my finger, which is embedded in someone's shoulder. A man's shoulder. *My neighbour's shoulder.*

Cue stomach dropping as if I'm in an aeroplane and we've just gone through clear-air turbulence and plummeted three hundred feet. I catch my breath just long enough to stammer. 'Oh . . . sorry . . .'

Think Hugh Grant on-screen. Now make him female, red-haired and thirty. Well, that's me. Only this isn't a movie, it's real life. My life. My hideously embarrassing life.

'I . . . erm . . . sorry . . . I was just . . .'

Fuck, this really is terrible. Why do I always have to look like such an idiot around him? No wonder he ignores me. I turn away and pretend to stare fixedly at the shelves. I just wish I could have a normal conversation with him for once. If only to prove I'm not a raving lunatic.

'Choosing wine is never easy, is it? You spend ages reading all the labels, and when you get it home it hardly ever tastes like you expect.'

Er, hello? Is he talking to me? My eyes travel up from his feet, past the cleft in his chin to his mouth. It's smiling at me. One of those kind, benevolent smiles you give to old people when their memory is befuddled, or children when they tell you they want to marry their hamster. It's the type of smile Meryl Streep always does so well.

My heart sinks. He probably doesn't recognise me.

'We've never been introduced. I'm James. We live opposite each other.' He holds out his hand.

'Oh, yeah . . . Hi, I'm Heather.' I try smiling back, but mine's all wobbly and nervous, like a kid on a bicycle without stabilisers. I go to shake his hand and I could swear he seems to hold mine for just a smidgen too long. But maybe that's wishful thinking.

'You know, I had a wonderful white from here a few days ago. What was it now? Oh, look, it's here.' He drops my hand and reaches for a bottle. I watch him lustfully. He's probably come here to choose some wine for him and his girlfriend to share, I muse, thinking of the pretty brunette I saw him with last week. Gosh, she's so lucky. I wish he was my boyfriend.

Suddenly aware that I'm gawping at him open-mouthed, I snatch the bottle from his hands. 'Erm, great . . . thanks for the recommendation,' I say quickly, and turn to go before I make an even bigger fool of myself.

'On the other hand there's also a great chablis . . .'

I've taken barely two steps before his firm, deep voice comes after me. I'm half tempted to keep walking, to pretend I haven't heard, but he's as irresistible as a family bag of Maltesers. You want it. You know you're going to regret it later. But you still eat the whole thing anyway.

I give in to temptation and look over my shoulder to see him holding an amber-coloured bottle. 'Maybe I can tempt you?' He smiles at me again, but this time it's not the befuddled-old-people smile, it's more like a . . . 'Listen, I'm sorry, I'm not doing this very well, am I?' *Rueful smile?* Standing there with a bottle of wine in each hand, he shrugs. 'You probably think I'm some kind of idiot going on about wine the whole time . . .' *Embarrassed smile?* '. . . when really I've been wanting to ask you . . .' *Nervous smile?* '. . . if you'd like to go out for a drink some time.' *Chatting me up smile?*

The whole time he's been speaking I've been standing still, frozen in a this-can't-be-happening to me way as his words string themselves out in front of me, one by one, like clothes on a washing-line. And now they're just hanging there, waiting for me to do something. But I can't: I'm in shock. After two and a half years of never even speaking to each other, my gorgeous, handsome neighbour, who just so happens to be the living embodiment of Mr Perfect, has asked me out on a date.

In a daze I start unpegging the words. For. A. Drink. Some. Time.

'Well?'

I zone back in: he's waiting for my answer. But isn't it obvious? Why on earth wouldn't I want to go out for a drink with him? Give me one good reason. *The brunette.*

I feel a kick of disappointment: he seems so lovely. Followed by resignation: I knew it was too good to be true. Followed swiftly by indignation: the two-timing slimeball. 'I have no respect for men who cheat on their girlfriends.'

'Excuse me?'

'My last boyfriend was unfaithful,' I explain.

I'm expecting an admission of guilt, a blush of embarrassment, but instead I get an expression of concern: 'Oh, er . . . really? I'm sorry to hear that.' There's a pause as he stares at me quizzically. 'I'm sorry, but am I missing something?'

Respect, honesty, integrity, I feel like saying, as I'm reminded of Daniel. But instead I smile tightly and say casually. 'I'm sorry, what did you say your girlfriend's name was?'

'*My* girlfriend?'

'The pretty brunette.'

'Oh, Christ.' Finally grasping that he's been rumbled, he rubs his clean-shaven chin and looks at me. Though not with the slightest guilt, I'm indignant to see, but – *could it be relief*? 'For a moment there I wondered what on earth was going on. I thought maybe you had me confused with someone else.' He smiles, then says, 'That's Bella, my little sister.'

Sister? I feel a jolt of surprise. I don't know whether to jump for joy or howl with embarrassment.

'Did you want her to come for a drink as well?' His mouth twitches with amusement.

I stifle a nervous giggle. 'No, just you is fine.'

'Great,' he replies, looking relieved. It's then that it strikes me: *he's nervous*. 'When are you free this week?'

'Erm, let me think . . .' I don't want him to know that the only date I've got lined up is with Blockbuster, do I?

'Tomorrow?' he suggests.

For a moment I consider playing it cool, which means I'll end up spending Saturday night on the sofa with a video. Then change my mind. 'Perfect,' I reply, grabbing his suggestion with both hands. Sod playing it cool. I'd rather be drinking martinis with James.

'Great,' he says again.

And then, for a moment, we just stand there, facing each other, smiling, until we're interrupted by a middle-aged man in a pinstriped suit who dashes, red-faced and gasping, into the aisle, grabs a bottle of Moët from the fridge, muttering, 'Bloody anniversary,' as he squeezes past us and hurries up to the counter.

We exchange a look.

'Of course, that's always another choice. Champagne.' James grins, finally relieving himself of the bottles. 'If you've got something to celebrate.'

Now, funny he should say that . . .

By the time I reach my flat, say goodbye to James, who's accompanied me to the doorstep and kissed my cheek, I'm walking on air. Closing my front door, I lean against it and take a couple of deep breaths. I still can't believe it. James has asked me out. James is taking me out for dinner – oh, yes, I nearly forgot: on the way back from the corner shop, it progressed from a drink to dinner. James is picking me up tomorrow at eight.

I run through every way of saying it, partly to see how it sounds, partly to allow my brain to absorb the information. And partly because I want to shout it from the rooftops.

I, Heather Hamilton, have a date.

Delighted, I kick off my flip-flops and pad down the hallway into the kitchen. 'Hey, Gabe, you'll never guess what . . .' I hurry through the patio doors and into the garden. He's not there.

'Gabe?' I glance at the empty sun-lounger, at the empty beer bottles on the wooden table, at the barbecue that looks as if it's gone out. I walk over to inspect it. The grill's bare and most of the coals have turned to powdery grey ash. Already? I check the time on my watch and do a bit of mental arithmetic. If I left at . . . and now it's . . . Crikey, I've been gone for well over an hour! Wow, talk about time flying when you're enjoying yourself.

Then, abruptly, I remember. I said I'd be a couple of minutes, that I was just popping out for a bottle of wine. I feel a stab of guilt. In all my excitement I forgot about Gabe and the barbecue we were supposed to be having. I go back inside and knock softly on the door of his room.

'Gabe? Are you there?' I can't hear anything, not even the low hum of a CD. I'm about to look out of the living-room window to see if his motorbike is still parked there when he opens the door.

'Hey.' He's holding a book entitled *How To Be Hilarious*. 'I was thinking of sending out a search party.'

'Hi . . . Look, I'm sorry,' I apologise. 'I lost track of the time . . .'

But he won't let me finish. 'Don't worry about it. I ate already, but I put your food in the oven to keep warm.'

'Actually, I'm not hungry . . .' Then I can't help blurting, 'I've just been asked out on date. It's someone I've had a bit of a crush on.' I add this hastily in case he thinks I always go out on dates with complete strangers I meet on the street.

'Oh . . . cool.'

There's a pause.

'I bought champagne instead of wine,' I say. 'Would you like a glass?'

'Thanks, but not for me. It's been a long day and I'm going to hit the sack.'

'Oh, OK . . . Look, about the barbecue.'

'Hey, forget about it.'

'Are you sure?'

'Yeah, of course.' He smiles. 'Night, Heather.'

'Right. You too, Gabe.'

Giving him a little wave goodnight with the champagne bottle, I head back into the kitchen to put it into the fridge. My thoughts turn back to James and I'm so absorbed that when, a few moments later, I hear Gabe's door click softly behind me, it occurs to me only vaguely that he must have remained standing there after I left him. But I'm too caught up by the evening's events to take much notice. Smiling happily, I pop the Moët on ice. For later.

Chapter Sixteen

Outside the ivy-clad walls of Kew Gardens, a dozen or so wedding guests are congregating. With no sign of the bride as yet, and with half an hour or so to go before the ceremony is due to start, they're taking the chance to have a last-minute cigarette and fiddle awkwardly with their outfits. They look to be mostly in their early twenties, fresh out of university judging by their woven ethnic bracelets and liquid black eyeliner, and are wearing an assortment of mismatched suits and Friday-night dresses that are too short and revealing.

And for one particular blonde way too tight, I note, and try not to stare at her black Lycra minidress, which highlights every lump and bump of her VPL as I weave my way through the guests looking for someone suitable to cadge a cigarette from. ''Scuse me, I don't suppose you've got a spare cigarette . . .' With every last drop of my female charm, I smile at a lanky twentysomething who's still sporting the remnants of teenage acne.

Clearly unused to female attention, he seems startled. 'Oh, er, yeah,' he stammers, and fumbles in the breast pocket of his jacket, which, judging by the length of the sleeves, is borrowed from a much shorter friend. 'So, um, are you part of the bride's party?' he asks self-consciously, as he pulls out a packet of Silk Cut Ultra Low.

Oh, well, anything's better than nothing. I take one. 'Oh, no. I'm here to do the photographs.'

'You're a photographer? Hey, cool,' says his friend, to whom I haven't paid much attention as he's been on his mobile with his back to me. He's incredibly handsome. And knows it. 'Maybe you could take my picture some time. I'm the lead singer in a band.' He drops in this piece of information oh-so-casually, and throws me a well-rehearsed look that's half pout, half smile.

I'm about to tell him that I'm only the assistant when the boy with the cigarettes says, 'Don't listen to Jack, he's always like this.' Then he holds out his lighter. 'I'm Francis, by the way.'

I smile appreciatively. Why is it that when men are in pairs there's always the sweet, kind one who's every girl's best friend, and the handsome bastard who gets all the girls?

'Hey, listen to you, Pizza Face,' snorts Jack, punching his shoulder as we're in the middle of shaking hands. Two spots of colour burn in Francis's cheeks, but Jack is grinning confidently, safe in his good looks. God, what a bully. I wish someone would put him in his place.

I turn to Francis. 'Thanks.' I smile, then cup my hand round his so he can light my cigarette. He strikes his lighter a couple of times and finally there's a flame. I take a drag and savour the head-rush of a retired smoker. 'Nice meeting you.'

'And you.' He smiles gratefully. Unlike Jack, who mutters something unrepeatable about me having no sense of humour and turns to the blonde girl with the VPL.

I begin to make my way back through the crowd to the Together Forever van. I hardly ever smoke, especially not on the job, but today I'm anxious. I take a puff of my cigarette. Very anxious.

I knew something wasn't right as soon as Brian picked me up this morning. Instead of the usual pre-wedding banter, we drove in silence but for the tap of Brian's signet ring as he drummed his fingers on the steering-wheel. There was something on his mind, that was for sure, but I didn't like to ask what – I'm too much of a coward. And I was too busy daydreaming about James.

But, then, just as we were pulling into the car park, his phone rang. He mumbled something about it being an important call and gestured for me to give him some privacy. It was all very cloak-and-dagger and quite unlike Brian, who usually chats away with the phone stuck under his chin as he does a million other things. Unlike most men, he's quite the multi-tasker.

But not this time. This time he's giving his full attention to whoever is on the other end of the line. He's still pacing the car park. Up and down he goes in his grey flannel suit, mobile phone wedged to his ear, face solemn. The warm breeze blows over snippets of conversation. 'Uh-huh . . . Yes . . . Absolutely . . . I completely understand . . .'

My stomach tightens. It sounds like bad news. With everything that's been happening recently I haven't brooded upon Brian's confession about how badly the business was doing, and how if we didn't get a miracle in the shape of a huge job he'd have to let me go. But now it all comes rushing back and, inside, I feel a knot the size of a fist.

'So what kind of numbers are we talking? Hm . . . Hm . . . Oh, really? As much as that?'

Oh, God. It's someone from the bank calling about the loan. I stare at his shiny black brogues as they crunch rhythmically on the gravel. I can feel the tension mounting. I wish I could conjure a great big fat wedding out of thin air.

'Heather, I need to talk to you.'

Brian's voice interrupts my panic. He's hurrying towards me, coat tails flapping. His hands are clutched to his chest as if he's holding some big news. Grinding out my cigarette under my heel, I dig in my bag for a packet of Polo mints and pop one into my mouth.

'You do?' I say, in trepidation. I smash the mint between my molars.

'I've got some good news.'

'*Good* news?' I parrot.

'Wonderful news,' he whoops, a delighted smile breaking across his face. He puts his hands on my shoulders. 'I think you should sit down.'

As he eases me on to one of the wooden benches that border the lawn I look at him in confusion. 'But I thought it was about the loan?' I gesture to his mobile phone.

'Not exactly.' He's jigging up and down on his heels. He's so twitchy he can't keep still. 'But we're talking about a lot of money here.'

'But how can that be good news?'

'It's not good news. It's wonderful news, Heather,' he reminds me. '*Wonderful* news.'

I don't believe this. My boss has gone stark raving mad. Finally I snap: 'Brian, will you please stop talking in riddles and explain why owing a lot of money is wonderful?'

'Who said anything about owing money?'

'You did. Last week. The conversation in the van about having to let me go.'

'Now, now, let's not dwell on the past,' he says dismissively, flapping his hand in the air. 'A lot can happen in a week. In a week a business can go from owing a lot of money to making a lot of money. Especially if it gets a client who just happens to be the Duke of Hurley, whose daughter just happens to be getting married—'

'You mean Lady Charlotte?' I interrupt.

'Uh-huh.'

'The blonde socialite who's always in all the magazines?'

'Uh-huh.'

'There was a picture of her only this week at some party with Paris Hilton. I swear, they're almost identical.' I shake my head.

'Lady Charlotte has much thicker ankles,' confides Brian, lowering his voice. 'Word among a few of my old *paparazzi* pals is she's got legs like a man.'

'Really?' I whisper.

'Really,' nods Brian, knowledgeably.

'But surely she can't be getting married. Isn't she only about twenty-one or something?'

'She can be sixteen for all I care, just as long as she's legal.' Suddenly the penny drops. 'What? You mean . . . we're going to cover her wedding?'

'Yep, you and me, kiddo. In three weeks!'

'Isn't that a bit short notice?' I'm so astonished it's all I can say.

'Apparently it's all very last-minute and hush-hush because they don't want the press to find out. That was the Duchess on the phone just then. She called a few days ago, completely out of the blue. Said she remembered me from the sixties.'

I pounce: 'You mean you've known about this for a few days?'

He holds up his hands in self-defence. 'I had to keep you in the dark. It wasn't definite and I didn't want to get your hopes up . . .'

'Oh, Brian, it's fantastic news!' Overcome with relief I jump off the bench and throw my arms round him.

'It's more than that – it's a bloody miracle!' he gushes, and as I hug him tight I feel a ripple of excitement.

I wished for a miracle, didn't I? And now we've got one.

A commotion interrupts my thoughts. 'Oh, look, is that the bride arriving?' I glance towards the driveway where people are circling.

Brian stands on tiptoe to see over the heads. 'No, some idiot's just had a drink thrown in his face.' He laughs derisively.

I peer over his shoulder and spot the idiot in question: it's Jack, the wannabe rock star. Only he doesn't look like one now. His face is dripping and his white shirt is soaked with what looks suspiciously like vodka cranberry, and he's spluttering with angry humiliation. I feel a glow of satisfaction. What was that about wishing someone would put him in his place?

'You two-timing creep!' I recognise the blonde girl in the tight black Lycra dress. 'Who do you think you are? Some kind of stud? I wouldn't mind, but for all the big talk, you've got a willy the size of a—'

Chapter Seventeen

'Cocktail sausage?' James guesses. He's listening to my story from the other side of the restaurant table.

Oh bloody hell, Heather.

And our first date had started so perfectly. Instead of agonising over what to wear I'd chosen the first thing I'd tried on: a dress made of plum satin that I found in a second-hand shop a few months ago that goes beautifully with my new pink satin shoes. And instead of jewellery I've clipped my hair up with all these glittery little grips I've had in my drawer for ages but never been brave enough to wear.

Normally I never attempt anything adventurous – it's always a quick blow-dry and a tonne of serum – but tonight I wanted something special. I wanted to feel different, to look into the mirror and not see jeans-'n'-T-shirt Heather, Daniel's ex with the heavy thighs and the mad curly hair that looks like a fibre-optic lamp, but knock-'em-dead Heather, James's date with the sexy dress and the sophisticated hairdo, so I copied a photograph in *Vogue* and, would you believe it?, it worked. Right down to the little tendrils at the sides of my ears.

And then, like clockwork, James picked me up at exactly eight and we drove in a cab to this gorgeous little Italian restaurant in Soho. The maître d' showed us to our candlelit table, which was tucked away from the others in a romantic corner of the courtyard, a waiter poured me a glass of perfectly chilled champagne and James told me how lovely I was looking. Then came the pause.

Now, I'm not talking a long pause, like an uncomfortable silence, more a *pregnant* pause. A pause in which we were supposed to catch each other's eye and he would smile and I would blush and it would be all wonderfully flirtatious.

Instead I did what I always do when I get all nervous and awkward: I filled the silence. Even worse, I filled it with the first thing that came into my head, which just so happened to be my anecdote about Jack the wannabe rock star. And his penis.

I look at James across the candlelit table and want to crawl underneath it. 'Erm . . . now I come to think of it, I can't actually remember . . .' I say evasively. I take a large gulp of champagne. Come on, Heather, think of something to say. Something witty. Something that shows you're not a penis-obsessed idiot. Something you're both interested in. I rack my brains. Come on, think – *think*.

Suddenly it comes to me in a blinding flash of light: 'I'm reading this wonderful book.'

He looks at me with interest. 'You are?'

'Yes. It's amazing.' I look him in the eye as I play my ace. 'It's called *Life of Pi*.' I try not to smile triumphantly, but it's hard. I'm so chuffed at my quick thinking I almost want to high-five myself.

'Oh, yeah, it's had some great reviews.' Then – to my disbelief – his nose wrinkles. 'But I couldn't get past the first couple of chapters.'

My stomach lurches. 'You couldn't?'

'No. I gave up in the end – too much of a struggle. I'm obviously a bit of a Philistine.' He reaches across the table and stokes my hand. 'So, tell me, why are you loving it so much?'

I'm in the middle of another gulp of champagne. The bubbles fizz up my nose and I hold back a sneeze. 'Erm . . .'

Oh, my God, me and my big mouth. '. . . well . . .'

I grapple for something to say. Damn. I should have stuck with penis sizes.

'. . . it's the perfect size for propping underneath my coffee-table,' I quip, 'to correct the wobble.' I laugh nervously.

James doesn't. Laugh, that is. In fact, there's not a flicker of a smile. 'Oh, right.' He seems puzzled. Then there's another pause. Only this time it's definitely awkward. And this time I definitely don't try to fill it.

Fortunately a waiter does it for me by arriving to take our order and reeling off a list of specials. There's chicken, beef, rabbit, pastas, risottos, a dozen different types of salad . . .

'Mmm, it all sounds good,' murmurs James. 'What do you feel like, darling?'

Darling?

He says it casually, so naturally, so affectionately, it's as if he's unaware he's even said it.

Except he did say it.

All my earlier embarrassment vanishes. I can't believe it. A term of endearment. Women can wait years for this level of intimacy from a man, and yet here's James, calling me 'darling' on our first date. 'It all sounds great,' I reply, as if nothing out of the ordinary has just happened when in reality I want to dash to the loo and call Jess on my mobile. But she's on her own first date with Greg. And even if she wasn't, I'm thirty years old, and supposed to be a sophisticated, mature adult.

I sit up straight in my chair and throw James what I hope is a sophisticated smile. 'But I'm actually a vegetarian,' I say coolly. 'Well, according to my flatmate, I'm technically a pescetarian as I eat fish—'

'Are you serious?' interrupts James, all wide-eyed. And I'm just wondering what I've said now when he clinks his champagne glass against mine. 'I'm a vegetarian too.'

'What a coincidence.' Wow, he really is my perfect man, I tell myself. He's looking at me in a way that makes me feel intoxicated – and it's got nothing to do with the champagne.

'So tell me, are you a mohair-sweater-wearing-lentils-and-nut-roast-vegetarian? Or the microwaveable-macaroni-and-cheese type?'

'Oh, definitely the second.' I smile. 'I hate nuts – I'm allergic to them.'

'No way! So am I!'

'Really?'

'No, not really.' Smiling, he shakes his head. 'But I can be if you want me to.'

'No, it's OK.' I laugh. 'You seem fine the way you are.'

Reaching across the table he brushes my fingers, which are entwined round my wine glass, with his thumb. Now it's his turn. 'Really?' he asks quietly.

I look down at his hand, that's now covering my own, and feel a delicious tingle run all the way up from my groin. 'Really.'

The waiter coughs to attract our attention. 'Have you decided?' he asks patiently.

James closes his menu but keeps hold of my hand. And, turning to the waiter with his lovely, lazy grin, asks, 'Would it be possible to make two macaroni cheese?'

The evening gets better and better. After dinner, which James insists on paying for, we drink lattes and share a tiramisu at Bar Italia, a pavement café in Soho, then grab a cab back to our flats. That's one good thing about dating your neighbour: you get to go home together.

En route, James entertains me with stories – about how his sister regularly beats him at Scrabble, he can cook a mean porcini-mushroom risotto, and the scar on his wrist is the result of falling off his sledge when he was six years old. Most intriguing of all is the story of how he's been plucking up courage to ask me out for months. 'There was never a right time. We kept bumping into each other but I was scared of looking like an idiot . . .'

'You were scared?' I repeat in disbelief.

'Well, yeah,' he says, amazed, apparently, that I could challenge such a statement. 'Whenever we saw each other you ignored me – I got the impression you weren't interested . . .'

Close your mouth, Heather.

'. . . but yesterday when I saw you in Mrs Patel's, I just thought, What the hell. Ask her out, James – she can only say no.'

I don't believe I'm hearing this. It must be a dream and I'm going to wake up, like Bobby Ewing in the shower.

'Sorry, am I freaking you out telling you all this?'

'No, no . . .' *Yes. Yes.*

'I just wanted to tell you how I feel.'

By now the cab has dropped us off at the top of our street and we're walking along the pavement together, ducking under low-hanging branches. 'I've never been into playing games,' James confesses quietly. 'I'm not interested in all those rules about waiting three days before calling. If you like someone, why can't you call straight away? Why can't you be honest and say how you feel?'

I look at him suspiciously and am just at the point of thinking that all this seems too good to be true when he does something completely unexpected. He holds my hand. In public. Without being asked. Now, this might not sound like much to most people, but to me it's a minor miracle. I'm used to men who grumble about PDA (public displays of affection) and hold my hand stiffly under duress for five minutes, then pretend they have to scratch their nose or something in order to let go. But not James. He squeezes his fingers tightly round mine as if he *never* wants to let go.

'Well, here we are.' I stop outside my flat reluctantly. It's in darkness. Gabe must still be out, I think, as James wraps his arms round my waist and pulls me towards him, saying, 'I've had a wonderful evening.'

Bathed in the golden light from the streetlamp, I feel a warm, happy glow. 'Me too,' I murmur, gazing into his dark eyes.

'And I was wondering . . .'

'Yes?' I wait expectantly. Although my dating experience is limited, I do know this is the part where he comes in for coffee. And I do know that 'coffee' is a euphemism for all kinds of things. None of which have anything remotely to do with Nescafé.

'Can I see you again?'

Having been debating how far I should go (kissing is fine for the first date, but if he wants to stay the night I have to be firm and say no) I hadn't anticipated this question. 'Oh . . . yes . . . of course,' I reply, feeling a surge of delight – but disappointed that this is where our date ends.

'What about the cinema tomorrow night?' he suggests.

I consider pretending I've got to check my diary first, not because I might be doing something (I know I'm not) but out of habit. And then I remember: James doesn't play games so I don't have to either. 'Sure.' I smile. Wow, it's so refreshing to meet a man who's not trying to play it cool. And what a relief. Now I won't have to occupy the next few days with the will-he-won't-he-call-me scenario.

'How about I pick you up around seven? We can go for a drink beforehand.'

'Great.'

Smiling sexily, he leans closer. 'Goodnight, Heather.'

So this is it. *The kiss.* I feel a delicious fizz of anticipation. I've been wanting to kiss James from the moment I first laid eyes on him. Closing my eyes, I lift my face towards his expectantly.

So I'm unprepared when I feel his lips brush my cheek and he says, 'Thanks for a lovely evening.'

My eyes snap open. *Is that it?* I give it a few moments, half expecting a follow-up, but when there's no sequel I say briskly, 'Right. Goodnight, James,' in the hope he won't notice my embarrassment. 'See you tomorrow.'

He waits dutifully until I find my keys and let myself in, then walks across the street to his own flat.

In my hallway I watch his retreating figure, listening to the sharp click of his heels against the Tarmac, thinking about our date and how James is everything I've always wished for in a man – handsome, kind and a real gentleman, not one of those guys who are just interested in getting you into bed. And I'm not disappointed that he didn't want to come in for coffee. Or try to kiss me. It means he wants to get to know me as a person first.

Distracted by a loud miaowing, I look down to see Billy Smith appearing from the shadows. No, I'm not disappointed at all. And scooping up my cat I nuzzle his soft orange fur, then close the door behind me.

Chapter Eighteen

'Wow, this place is so quaint.'

It's Sunday morning and Gabe and I are having breakfast at a busy pavement café in Hampstead. Despite the bright sunshine a chilly breeze is ruffling the stack of half-read papers. Pulling my cardigan tightly round me, I laugh, 'You sound like such a tourist.'

'That's because I am a tourist,' he smiles, putting down his knife and fork and taking a slurp of cappuccino. I follow his gaze past the Tudor-style pub, with its ye-olde-English sign, the traditional red phone box on the corner, the narrow cobbled street lined on either side with neat Victorian houses, and out towards the Heath. I must admit, it's so picture-postcard pretty it's like a set from a Richard Curtis film.

'So, is that a park?'

'No, it's Hampstead Heath. It's very famous.'

'Why's it famous? What do you do there?'

Actually that's a good question. 'Oh, you know,' I say vaguely, 'you go for walks, fly kites . . .'

'Fly kites?'

'Uh-huh.' I nod, amused by his expression.

'You Brits and your weird traditions.'

'What weird traditions?'

He rolls his eyes as if there are too many to mention. 'Well, for a start, driving on the left.'

'Driving on the left's not weird. You're weird for driving on the right.'

'Along with the rest of the world,' he points out.

'What about Australia?' I argue 'Or India or New Zealand

or . . .' Actually, now I come to think about it, I can't think of anywhere else. '. . . loads of other places,' I mutter weakly, as he looks at me, eyebrows raised.

'And then there's going to the *loo*,' he persists. 'Your bars – sorry, I mean *pubs* – are filled with guys and there's barely a woman in sight. Strangers tell you it's gonna be a lovely day when it's raining and freezing cold in the middle of July . . .'

He has a point there.

'*Queuing!*'

'It's polite,' I say defensively.

'It's nuts,' he retorts. 'You stand in line and if someone walks straight to the front no one says anything.' Shaking his head, he picks up his knife and prods at his food. 'And as for your love of these funny beans in ketchup . . .'

Until now I've taken it all pretty much on the chin, but now he's gone too far. 'Heinz baked beans?' I say defensively. 'You don't like them?'

'Are you kidding me?' He snorts and pulls a face.

On impulse I lean across the table, scoop up a forkful from his plate and stuff them into my mouth. 'Mmmm,' I moan, doing my impression of Sally faking orgasm in *When Harry Met Sally*. 'Mmmmmm.'

'Oh, and one last thing.'

'What?'

'The British women – or should I say birds?'

'What about them?'

He picks up a section of the newspaper and disappears behind it. 'Crazy. All of 'em.'

It has to be one of the most amazing things about life that within a couple of weeks you can go from not knowing a person even exists to sharing your home, the TV remote and the Sunday papers with them. Gabe and I are like an old married couple – him with the sports section, me with the *Style* magazine – who would have thought it?

It's amazing for anyone, but for me especially, as I'm very protective of my Sunday-morning ritual. There's nothing I love more than sitting in a café, reading the *Style* magazine over a plate of fluffy, yellow scrambled eggs and – unlike most people, who see it as a couple activity – I love to do it alone.

OK, maybe I'm weird, but it's a thing of mine. I love the fact that I don't have to fight over sections of the paper, or read one that's already been creased. I love being able to spread out on the table without worrying that the *Travel* section might end up in someone else's fried mushrooms. And more than anything, I love not being distracted by conversation, that I can sit in perfect silence, happily engrossed in whatever article takes my fancy. It's one of the few pleasures in life.

But on this particular Sunday morning I bumped into Gabe in the kitchen, pacing around in his Tibetan slipper-socks somewhat at a loss. And felt guilty. There he was, a stranger in a foreign country, and I hadn't once offered to show him the neighbourhood. OK, so it's not as if he doesn't know anyone. He has an uncle here – but, as Ed always says, relatives are like Christmas: they should only come once a year.

So, I made the ultimate sacrifice and invited him for breakfast.

Finishing my scrambled eggs I watch Gabe stroking his whiskery chin absentmindedly as he studies the sport. Eventually he sits back and puts down the paper. 'So,' he says, 'you haven't mentioned how your date went last night.'

I blush, I don't know why.

'That good, huh?' He laughs.

'Yeah, I guess you could say that.' Unexpectedly self-conscious, I look down at my plate and begin to sweep the crumbs into a little pile with my fork. 'Anyway, how did you know my date was last night?' I ask casually.

'I'm psychic.'

'*You are?*' I ask, then realise that of course he isn't, he's trying to be funny.

'No, not really. I was in my room and heard him come pick you up.'

'Oh . . . right.'

'Eight o'clock on the dot.'

I smile bashfully. 'Well, it's rude to keep a lady waiting.'

'That's what Mia's always telling me, but I have a mental block when it comes to the time. I'm always late.'

At the mention of his girlfriend, I smile sympathetically. 'You must really miss her.'

'Yeah.'

He doesn't elaborate and I get the vague sense that he doesn't want to talk about it. So, of course, I blunder on: 'How's her movie going?' I ask, which is really code for 'What's going on with you two?'

'OK.' He shrugs, and then, running his fingertips along his burgeoning moustache, adds, 'At least, I think so.'

Like I thought. Something's definitely up.

'I haven't spoken to her in a while. It's difficult for her to call from the set.' He scrapes the cappuccino foam from round his cup and licks it off the spoon. 'And the time difference doesn't help.'

He's obviously making excuses for her, I decide, feeling suddenly protective of him and disliking Mia, with her swingy hair and perfect teeth. 'Long-distance relationships, hey?' I say.

He nods, then changes the subject. 'So, you like this new guy? What did you say his name was?'

'I didn't.' I smile. 'It's James. And, yeah, I like him.'

I catch myself. That, Heather Hamilton, has to be the understatement of the year. 'The funny thing is, apparently he's been wanting to ask me out for ages but thought I wasn't interested.'

'When are you seeing him again?'

'Tonight,' I reply casually, taking a sip of my latte.

At least, I try to say it casually, but Gabe sees right through me. 'Two nights in a row?' He nudges me under the table with a knee.

'I know,' I admit, trying to suppress my excitement. James is so gorgeous I'm scared of jinxing things by getting too carried away.

Gabe, however, has no such worries.

'Wow,' he drawls. 'Has he got the hots for you, girlfriend.' Grinning, he bites into his toast and chews with his mouth open. A habit that in anyone else would be revolting but in Gabe is somehow endearing.

'Oh, I don't know about that . . .' I say modestly, but Gabe stops me.

'Heather, listen to me.' Pausing to noisily suck up the remnants of his orange juice through a straw, he eyes me seriously. 'You've liked this guy for ages, and after what you told me he said last night it's pretty obvious he's liked *you* for ages – so where's the problem?'

'OK, OK, you're right. There isn't a problem . . . *that's the problem.*'

Gabe looks at me with amusement, 'Are you sure you're not Jewish?'

I have to say, that when Gabe isn't in stand-up comedy mode, he can be rather funny and I'm swatting him playfully with the *Style* section when someone bangs into the back of my chair, knocking my coffee, which slops into my lap. 'Hey! Can't you watch where you're going?' I yelp as I jump back in my seat.

'Sorreee!' There's a chorus of yelling from a crowd of boys as they rush past down the high street.

'You OK?' Gabe asks, passing me a napkin.

'Fine.' I begin to blot my lap.

'The youth of today, huh?'

There's a pause as I continue rubbing at my clothes, and Gabe digs into the paper, pulls out the magazine and flicks straight to the back. The actions of a seasoned horoscope reader. 'Shall I read you your horoscope?' he asks brightly.

'Oh, those things are a load of nonsense,' I say dismissively, and put the soggy napkin on the table.

'OK, suit yourself.' Gabe shrugs and begins to read to himself.

For a moment I sit there, watching him absorbed in Jonathan Cainer, but then I'm curious. I crick my neck and try to read upside-down. I wonder if mine will say anything about new relationships. Damn it's useless. I can't see a bloody thing. 'Oh, go on, then,' I say, as if he's been twisting my arm for the past ten minutes. 'I'm Pisces,' I add, after a beat.

'Pisces, huh?' Gabe raises his eyebrows, as if this means something significant, but I resist asking. After all, it's nonsense, right?

' "With all your planets aligning this is an important time for Pisceans in the areas of your career, family and love. Major changes will be happening. You're on a winning streak, so watch out for a sudden windfall." ' He looks up. 'Wow! Sounds like you're going to win the lottery.'

'Me? I never win anything,' I laugh, then suddenly remember my lottery ticket. My heart starts to beat very, very quickly. 'Quick, Gabe, pass me the papers. I want to see something.'

'Don't you want to hear the rest of your stars?'

'In a sec.' I fumble with the different sections until I find the one I need, and start flicking through it. No, not there . . . My eyes scan the pages. Then I see them: last night's lottery numbers.

I zoom in for a close-up.

They look familiar.

I take a moment to remember to breathe. 30 my age; 14, my address; 6, number of years I've been working at Together Forever. Cautiously I edge my eyes along the page: 27, Mum's birthday was 27 April . . . I try to remember the last two numbers I chose hastily at random. I'm pretty sure one was 13 . . . Bloody hell! Sure enough, it's there in black and white. My stomach flips, half excitement, half terror. Now for the last one. It's 41 – did I pick 41? I rack my brains. Come on, Heather, think, think—

'Heather?'

I jump. I'd forgotten about Gabe.

'Are you sure you're OK?'

'Fine . . .' I'm trying to calm my jittery nerves.

Oh, my God, I think I've won the lottery.

'That's a very serious look you've got on your face,' he says, peering at me as if I'm an exhibit in a museum.

'Really?' Unscrewing my forehead, I force a smile.

And it's a rollover week.

'You don't look too good. You've gone pale.'

'Honestly, it's nothing.'

I'm going to be a millionaire.

'Maybe we should go home. I'll get the check.' He beckons the waiter.

'Wait a mo. I just want to check my lottery ticket.'

'So, horoscopes are a pile of nonsense, are they?' he laughs, waving his arm in the air.

I reach feverishly for my bag. Wow, can you imagine how exciting it's going to be? What everyone's going to say? Though perhaps I should be anonymous, refuse the publicity – I don't want loads of begging letters and people trying to kidnap me for a huge ransom.

Er, hang on a minute. I run my hand along the back of my chair, feeling for the leather strap. A tiny flame of panic ignites in me and I glance over my shoulder to where I'd slung my bag earlier.

It's not there.

'It's been stolen,' I whisper, almost frozen with shock.

''Scuse me?' I hear Gabe's voice but it doesn't register.

'It's gone.' As the reality kicks in, I jump up in horror, eyes darting under the table, around the side of the chair, along the pavement.

'Hey, what's up?'

'My bag!' I wail desperately, wondering how on earth it had happened. Then I remember the gang of boys banging into my chair. Realisation dawns as anger surfaces. With them and myself. Jesus, Heather, it's the oldest trick in the book. 'Those kids must have stolen it,' I jabber wildly, still looking up and down the pavement as if a brown leather bag from Nine West is going to jump out from behind a chair leg. 'I've been robbed.'

'Oh, Jeez.' Gabe stands up and begins to look with me. 'Was everything in it?'

I feel tears prickling. 'My phone, house keys, wallet . . .'

'Did you have a lot of cash?'

Even under the circumstances, the idea that I might have lots of cash in my wallet is vaguely amusing. 'Not much, maybe a tenner,' I murmur, and slump back into my chair. 'But that's not important.'

'Hey, I know, it's the sentimental stuff.'

'No, it's not that . . .' I begin to sniff, then stop. I can't tell him about the significance of the lottery ticket, can I? It would mean launching into the whole story about the gypsy, the lucky heather and how all my wishes have been coming true. He'll think he's sharing a flat with a fruit loop.

'Is it the shock?' Gabe squeezes my hand.

I nod mutely. Shocked? I'm bloody mortified.

One minute, there I was in my Holland Park pad, with my Italian villa and my new Aston Martin, and now – *poof* – it's all gone. Along with my wallet, keys, mobile, Filofax – which has my address in it, which means I'll have to change the locks. At this rate that ticket is going to end up *costing* me a fortune . . .

'I know it sucks,' Gabe is saying, 'but there's not much we can do here. We should head back to the flat, report it stolen to the cops.'

'Actually, I might as well go straight to the police station,' I say, trying not to think about how much I wanted to go for a walk on the Heath with Gabe and how it's all been spoiled. 'But you don't have to come with me.'

'Hey, of course I will.'

'No, honestly, it's fine. Enjoy the rest of the day, go fly a kite,' I tease weakly, gesturing towards the Heath.

'Well, if you're sure . . .'

'I'm sure,' I say firmly. 'The bank will need a crime reference number so I'll have to fill in a report – might as well get the boring paperwork over with now.' Great. Just how I wanted to spend my Sunday afternoon.

'Oh, OK . . .' There's a pause, and then he adds shyly, 'Look, I don't know if you're interested, but I'm meeting my uncle later at some comedy club he knows about. It's open mike tonight and

I could use a little practice . . . you're more than welcome to join us?'

I'm flattered by his invitation, but the words 'open mike' are enough to bring me out in hives. Thankfully, however, I already have an excuse. 'Thanks, but I'm seeing James,' I remind him.

'Oh, yeah, I forgot – *duh* . . .' For a second I swear I see a flash of disappointment in his eyes, but now he's smiling and saying, 'Maybe next time, huh?'

'Yeah, next time.' I nod, trying not to think of how I'm going to get out of it.

'Well, I guess I'll see you later.' Gabe moves towards me and, presuming he's going to kiss my cheek I move my face to one side. Only it goes wrong and, bumping noses, our lips collide. We jump back as if we've been stung.

'Oops! Sorry about that.' I laugh uncomfortably.

'Don't worry, it's the big schnoz.' Gabe grins, but I'm sure he's as embarrassed as I am.

'Well, 'bye then,' I say briskly.

'Er, yeah . . . 'bye.' He waves awkwardly.

Left behind on the pavement, I watch him striding out towards the Heath, mingling among the dozens of people heading for a lazy afternoon lying on the grass. Feeling a stab of envy, I curse the thieves who stole my bag. And then, completely out of the blue, I remember something Ed said that night in the pub: *Be careful what you wish for*. His words make me strangely uneasy. Did wishing I could win the lottery somehow cause my bag to be stolen? Was it because the ticket was in my wallet?

Or because my wish was about simply *winning* the lottery, not about *keeping* it?

As the thought strikes I feel a spark of panic. Of responsibility. Fear. But then I catch myself. Honestly, Heather, since when did you ever listen to anything your brother said? And feeling foolish for even considering his words, I march resignedly to the tube.

Chapter Nineteen

'So, what did you think of the film?'

It's later that evening and James and I have just been on our second date – to the cinema – and are driving back in his Range Rover, him at the wheel, me in the leather passenger seat trying not to stare at his broad linen-coated shoulders, perfect Roman nose and a jawline that any leading man would kill for.

'I really enjoyed it,' he replies, taking his eyes off the road and catching me staring.

Damn.

'I thought Renée was really funny, and that bit with the adorable little girl . . .' He laughs faintly. 'Hilarious.'

I feel like the cat that's got the cream. Not only is this man drop-dead gorgeous he also loves romantic comedies. Can you believe it? A man who likes romantic comedies? *And he's not gay*. Vague memories of Daniel and me arguing over *Bridget Jones* versus *The Thin Red Line* in Blockbuster begin to stir . . .

'What about you, darling?' James is saying, as he indicates left, then drives down our street. 'What do you think?'

That we're outside your flat and I'm wondering if you're going to invite me in for coffee, I think lustfully. But instead I reply, 'It was great.'

He swings into a parking space, switches off the engine and turns to me. It's quiet now, without the radio or the noise of the four-cylinder engine, and I feel a flutter of anticipation. But instead of kissing me he says, 'I'm afraid I've got a confession.'

'Oh.'

'Uh-huh.' He's holding my gaze. 'I don't have any coffee.'

'Oh.' The man has reduced me to monosyllables.

'So I don't have any excuse to invite you up.'

I feel crushing disappointment. Followed by tingles all through my body as he strokes the side of my face. I can feel his breath on my cheek and then, before I know what's happening, he's kissing me. Light feathery kisses behind my earlobe, along my collarbone, the nape of my neck . . .

'Do I need one?'

He pulls away and my breath catches in the back of my throat. Struggling to find my voice, I smile shyly. And only then do I finally manage to squeak, 'No.'

Which, of course, means yes to everything else. Yes, to kissing in his hallway, yes, to his hands running up the back of my T-shirt, yes, to him pushing me against the radiator and grinding his hard-on into my pelvis . . .

Well, it *would* be yes if any of this was happening.

But it's not – unless you count my imagination. Instead he unlocks the door to his flat, takes my coat politely and offers me a nightcap.

'Cheers.' He passes me a glass of champagne and clinks his glass against mine. We're standing by the fireplace in his living room, which I've glimpsed dozens of times from my bedroom across the street. Only this time I'm on the inside.

Surprisingly, his flat isn't anything like I imagined. Instead of being modern, it's traditional, with old-style standard lamps, floor-to-ceiling bookshelves and a gilt-edged mirror hanging over the fireplace. It's also immaculate. I feel secretly pleased. I've always wished I could meet a man who's neat and tidy. And, hey presto, here he is.

'Cheers.'

I go to take a sip when James stops me with a hand on my arm. 'You didn't look me in the eye,' he protests.

'I didn't?' I presume he's joking, then realise he's serious.

'No,' he says, looking at me intently. 'We'll have to do it again.'

This time I meet his gaze and he holds it for just a moment longer than necessary, which, of course, is incredibly sexy, before we clink glasses and I take a gulp of champagne. To be honest, I'd have preferred coffee, but this is all very romantic, isn't it? I watch James walk over to his rack of neatly stacked CDs.

'What do you feel like listening to?' he asks.

'Whatcha got?' I quip.

'Is that a band or an album?'

'Oh, no, I meant . . .' I start to explain, then decide against it. 'What about The White Stripes?' I suggest.

He looks at me doubtfully. 'Actually I don't think I have anything of theirs,' he says, running his finger along the spines of his CDs – in alphabetical order I notice, unlike mine, which are piled in a messy jumble on the shelves, minus their cases.

'Oh . . . well, why don't you choose something?' I say brightly.

'OK, let's see . . .' He begins to throw out names: 'Billie Holiday, Bob Dylan, David Bowie, Coldplay, Sting, Madonna . . .' As he reels off one name after another he could almost be reading out my own CD collection, minus the White Stripes and a few quirky entries such as my beloved Billie Jo Spears album. Mum adored her. I remember her singing along to 'Blanket On The Ground' at the top of her voice while she was doing the ironing. The memory gets me right in the throat, like a boxer's jab, and I have to swallow to stop my eyes watering. It's always the silly little things that remind me. Everyone assumes its birthdays and Christmas, but it's in the everyday details that I miss her most.

'. . . Roxy Music, *The Best of Spandau Ballet* . . .' James glances sideways at me, and I quickly fight down the lump in my throat. 'OK, I'd better confess my guilty secret.'

James has a guilty secret?

'I used to be a New Romantic. If you want to leave now and never see me again I'll understand.'

'What a coincidence. I was Duran Duran's biggest fan.' I grin.

He laughs and I feel a buzz of happiness. I've always wished I could meet a man who shared my taste in music but most of my old boyfriends liked completely different bands from me. There was John who loved punk, Marcus who was into jazz, and then there was Daniel. I have a flashback of us driving to Cornwall, arguing over whether we'd listen to his Snoop Dogg CD, or my Norah Jones.

'What about Dido?'

'Perfect.' I beam.

James looks relieved.

He's adorable when his face is all scrunched up with worry, and I resist the urge to go over and kiss him. It's not easy.

He slides open the CD drive, opens the case and frowns. 'Damn. After all that there's a different CD in here.'

His expression is so hangdog I start to laugh. 'Oh, don't worry, that happens to me all the time.'

'Well, it doesn't happen to me,' he grumbles, staring at the disk in confusion.

'Perhaps you put it back in the wrong case by accident,' I suggest.

'But that's impossible,' he protests. 'I'd never do that.'

My smile fades. Surely one CD in the wrong case isn't going to throw him into a bad mood? 'Why don't we listen to that CD anyway?' I say. I'm fast regretting wishing he could be neat and tidy.

He glares accusingly at the silver disk in his hand as he puts it into the player. 'This should be interesting . . .'

From concealed speakers swell the opening chords of a guitar, and a woman's voice, soft and sexy. She's singing in French. 'Who's this?'

James's face is flooded with recognition. 'Emmanuelle. She's an old friend of mine – she used to play in clubs in Paris. Crikey, I'd forgotten I had this.'

'You lived in Paris?'

'For a couple of years after university.' The memory seems to make him forget his annoyance and re-embrace our earlier flirtation. 'A long time ago.' Slipping his fingers through mine, he leads me over to the large suede sofa.

'Wow, how exciting,' I blurt, more out of nerves than anything else as now we're sitting on the sofa and he's slipping his arm around my shoulders and pulling me towards him. I inhale the scent of his faded aftershave, butter popcorn and underarm deodorant. It's unbelievably erotic.

'So do you speak French?' I ask, trying to steer my thoughts away from X-rated ones.

James lifts my chin with a finger and gabbles something that I, at rusty O-level standard, can make no sense of whatsoever. 'Do you want me to translate?' he murmurs softly.

No, not really. I'm content to listen to his sexy French accent and not understand what he's saying. I open my mouth to reply. But then, when I'm least expecting it, he kisses me full on the lips.

Wow. Me likee this translation. Me want you to translate a bit more, I muse, kissing him back. It's been so long since I've been kissed by someone I've forgotten how thrilling it is, and for the next few moments I don't ever want this to stop.

Only my bladder's got other ideas.

It twinges. I try to ignore it and not to think about the litre of Diet Pepsi I drank in the cinema. Instead I cross my legs and concentrate on James's tongue, his hands, which are wandering round my ribcage and, hopefully, any time soon, up my T-shirt . . .

But it's no good. My bladder feels as if it's about to burst. 'Where's your bathroom?' I ask, pulling away reluctantly.

'On the right, through the bedroom – it's *en suite*.' He smiles up at me, untangling his hand from behind my neck as I stand up.

'Won't be a minute,' I whisper, and attempt a flirtatious smile as I sashay across the living room.

Once out of sight in the hallway I make a mad dash for the bedroom. Like the rest of his flat, it's immaculate. No over-flowing drawers, no clothes or shoes strewn on the floor, which is sort of how I left my own. And then I notice the bed: with crisp cotton bed linen that looks suspiciously as if it might have been ironed, and pillows that have been plumped to an inch of their lives, it stares up at me from the middle of the room.

Despite my bladder, I stare back approvingly. In my limited experience single men and beds do not go together. More often than not it's just a mattress on the floor, and as for the bed linen . . . it's either something horribly frilly their mother bought for them or some tattered remnants from their student days. And they never change it. In fact, most single men have no idea that a bad bed can make or break a budding relationship. But then, James isn't most men.

Feeling a tingle of excitement as I imagine us in his bed later, I hurry through to the bathroom and flick on the light. Aaaah, the relief. With my jeans round my ankles, I glance idly at the clawfoot bath, shiny round silver wash-basin, magazines stacked neatly in the rack next to me. I have a quick rifle through – *Investment Today*, a *Relais Châteaux* brochure, *Toilet Humour*, which is one of those cartoon books you always find in bathrooms – and then, satisfied that I haven't found anything dodgy, like a dog-eared porno mag, I flush the loo and go to wash my hands.

As I turn on the taps, I check my reflection in the mirror of the bathroom cabinet.

The bathroom cabinet.

Curiosity prickles. But I resist. I can't possibly look inside his bathroom cabinet. That's snooping. Who knows what I'll find?

No sooner has that thought popped into my head than I remember Jess telling me about the time she 'just-so-happened' to look under the basin of a man she was dating and found a violet lace bra stuffed next to the spare bog rolls. She was devastated. Not because he was cheating on her with a pretentious wannabe novelist called Sabrina but because Sabrina was a pert little B cup.

And then I have another thought; only this time it's me and I'm rummaging through Daniel's glove compartment and finding the packet of condoms . . .

Actually, on second thoughts, maybe I should take a quick look – just as a safeguard.

Opening the door I glance inside. I'm relieved to see it's all perfectly normal and innocent. Toothpaste, dental floss, Band-aids . . . Oh, hang on, what's that? Spying a tube at the back I reach for it, and knock over a bottle of aspirin. It crashes into the basin. Oh, shit! I stuff it back on the shelf and glance at the tube in my hand – vitamin E cream.

Which is when I feel guilty. What am I doing? I shouldn't be rifling through James's toiletries. I wouldn't want him looking through my bathroom cabinet, discovering my secret box of Jolen bleach, the emergency tube of Canesten, or the big, unsexy sanitary towels I wear to bed during my period. Shuddering, I shut the door and busily apply a fresh coat of lipgloss. Anyway, why am I bothering about what's in his bathroom cabinet when he's out there waiting for me? And blotting my lips with a tissue I hurriedly turn off the light.

I walk back into the living room with an empty bladder and a pair of lips all pink and glossy and ready to be kissed. The sofa is empty.

Oh.

Standing alone in the living room I feel a twang of disappointment, then notice a light in the small office at the end of the hallway. I wander in and find James bent over his laptop, his fingers flying over the keyboard. He looks up. 'Just dealing with a few emails.' He extends a hand towards me. 'I've got a client in Sydney, a very impatient client,' he adds, interlacing his fingers with mine and pulling me towards him.

I plop on to his lap and curl an arm round his shoulders in no doubt that this impatient client is going to have to wait. In fact, my mind is already fast-forwarding and I'm debating whether or not I should stay with him tonight or if he'll respect me more if I go home, when he says, 'Darling, would you mind if we leave tonight to be continued?' I'm obviously looking as confused as I feel because he adds, 'Australia's nine hours ahead. If I wait until tomorrow morning it will be too late – I'm afraid I really need to work on this tonight.'

Ha, ha, very funny. I search his eyes for a dart of humour, but all I see is his laptop screen reflected back at me. Which is when I know he's not joking. I'm disappointed and frustrated all at once. 'Yeah . . . of course,' I say. 'That's fine.' I force a smile and try not to think of how excited I was about tonight, about all the effort I've gone to: shaving my legs, waxing my bikini line, putting on my sexiest underwear *just in case*. But I can't help it. I'm miffed. And bloody uncomfortable. Wriggling on James's knee I try to free my lacy G-string, which has trapped itself up my bottom, but it remains wedged. 'Actually, I could do with an early night anyway,' I lie, pretending to yawn.

Brushing my hair out of my eyes, he smiles. 'So, are you free tomorrow night?'

'Sorry, I'm busy.' I'm about to explain that Lionel and I are going to see a new art exhibition in Kensington then decide not to. Childish, I know, but I can't help feeling a little indignant that James is sending me home and not even *trying* to persuade me to stay. Honestly, sometimes you can be too much of a perfect gentleman.

'What about the night after?'

'I have to work.'

He raises his eyebrows with interest.

'A mock-Tudor wedding at Hampton Court,' I elaborate, stiffly.

'Oh, right,' he nods seriously, his mouth twitching with amusement. 'Well, unfortunately I have to go to Zürich on Wednesday for a couple of days.' He's looking at me as if he's weighing up what my reaction will be when he says, 'What about Friday?'

'Maybe.' I attempt to appear elusive.

'In that case, *maybe* I'd like to cook you dinner.'

I look up at him. Into his dark irises with the tiny flecks of grey. And remember the months I've spent wishing he would notice me. Now here *I* am sitting on his knee, and here *he* is wanting to cook me a romantic candlelit dinner.

I grab hold of myself. Honestly, Heather, you really are an

ungrateful old cow. 'That would be lovely,' I murmur, tilting my face to kiss him.

I mean, for goodness' sake, what more could I possibly wish for?

Chapter Twenty

Arriving at the Serpentine Gallery in Hyde Park the following evening, I discover a hive of activity. Strobe lights illuminate the dusky sky overhead, a string quartet is playing a funky classical mix, and a large crowd has spilled outside on to the grass, filling the balmy evening air with a cacophony of chatter, laughter and air-kissing.

I'm early, thanks to the lucky heather, which I tucked into my new purse before I left the house (just as I thought, it's cost me a small fortune to replace everything that was stolen). Usually I have to wait at the bus stop for ages, wishing for a bus to turn up, but tonight a number twenty-eight appeared immediately. Then, instead of sitting in traffic wishing the bus would hurry up, all the lights were green and I was whisked here in no time. It was amazing. Even Lionel hasn't arrived yet, I muse happily, enjoying the novelty of being early by diving straight for the complimentary apple martinis and killing time by observing the crowd.

It's an eclectic mix – tall, skinny model types wearing those shapeless vintage dresses that wouldn't flatter anyone, distinguished grey-haired men smelling of aftershave and lots of older women in sequins. Nibbling on canapés and drinking cocktails they're mingling around the artwork. Although from where I'm standing most people seem more interested in the free booze and spotting celebrities than they do in 'Installation: Global Urbanisation and the Search for the Self'.

'Good Lord, I never thought I'd see the day.'

Lionel is bearing down on me, a smile plastered across his bearded face. He's wearing his favourite suit, which he had made for him in Morocco back in the early seventies. Aubergine velvet with brown leather elbow patches, that I remember mum sewing on for him, he refuses to throw it away although it is far too tight. As it strains across his belly, I swear I can almost hear the cotton on the seams creaking

'*Good Lord, is it really you?*'

Heads turn at the sound of his thunderous baritone and I brace myself. 'Hi, Lionel.'

'My daughter? *On time?*' He throws his arms round me in the customary bear hug and succeeds in spilling my drink all over my pink satin shoes.

'When have I ever kept you waiting?' I protest, lifting each foot and shaking it hastily.

'When haven't you?' he roars good-naturedly. 'You were over two weeks late when you were born.' He releases me from his embrace and steps back to admire me as if I was one of his paintings. 'My, my, don't you look grand!' he declares, somewhat loudly. Honestly, he can be so embarrassing.

I link my arm through his and steer him to the drinks. 'Have a martini, they're delicious,' I coo, pointing at the waitress with her tray.

'Haven't they got any wine?' He frowns as he's handed a green cocktail. 'A nice merlot or a pinot noir?'

'And these smoked salmon thingies are yummy.' I try to distract him with his other passion in life apart from art: food.

'Mmm, yes, I see what you mean, darling,' he says, through a mouthful of crumbs. 'Rather smashing. I think I'll have a couple more.' He beams appreciatively at the waitress as he piles a few into a napkin. She giggles and a mild flirtation ensues, even though she's only in her early twenties.

I watch with amused affection. It never ceases to amaze me how people love Lionel. For me it's understandable – he's my father – but he has this magical effect on everyone he meets. Over the years I've lost count of the number of my girlfriends who've had crushes on him, boyfriends who've wanted to be him, students who've idolised him. And I'm not just talking about those who know him but about shop assistants, traffic wardens and this waitress who's now blushing and gazing at him adoringly.

'Aren't you having anything?' Lionel has noticed that I'm not eating and frowns. 'I hope you're not going to turn into one of those dyslexics.'

'You mean anorexics,' I whisper, as a couple of incredibly thin models waft past and shoot us both a glance. 'And, no, I'm not. But talking of weight, Ed thinks *you* could do with losing a few pounds . . .'

'Oh what does he know,' pooh-poohs Lionel. Defiantly reaching for a mini-quiche he looks at me from beneath his bushy eyebrows. 'Honestly – you should try one of these. They're delicious.'

As he tries to sidestep the subject, I'm half tempted not to let him. Maybe Ed's right: Lionel does seen to be carrying a little more weight than usual, and maybe he should cut back on his wine. I watch him quaffing his merlot, which the 'nice waitress' got for him. But then again, he is enjoying himself. I decide against it. Sod it. Let him have his fun. I'll talk to him about it later, but in the meantime—

'I thought we were here for the exhibition, not the food,' I point out.

'So we are, so we are.' He throws the waitress an apologetic look and flicks open his pamphlet like a Spanish dancer opening a fan. 'Righty-ho, then . . .' He steals another mini-quiche from the tray, pops it into his mouth and throws a huge arm round my shoulders. 'Let's go look at some art.'

It turns out to be quite an interesting exhibition and for the next half an hour or so we walk round the different 'installations' while Lionel tries valiantly to explain to me the symbolisation of a washing-machine that's been taken apart and strewn all over a roll of dirty shagpile carpet.

I don't get it. I'm a complete heathen when it comes to that sort of thing. Not that I haven't tried. I'm a fully paid-up member of Tate Modern, and I've been to the Saatchi Gallery a few times, but I'm just not inspired by a cow in formaldehyde – unlike Turner's 'storm' at the National: I can stand in front of that picture for hours, mesmerised by the sheer emotional force of the colours and textures.

Ironically, I blame my bias on Lionel. Growing up with a father who cocooned himself in his studio made me believe from an early age that there was something magical about painting. Sometimes as a treat Ed and I were allowed to enter his secret world before we went to bed. We'd sit on his oil-splattered lap, inhaling the smell of turpentine as he told us weird and wonderful stories about painters who had cut off their ears or made telephones out of lobsters. We loved all that gory stuff, and adored Lionel's bedtime stories.

But we also knew they were our little secret. Mum would have killed him if she'd ever found out it wasn't his rendition of *Cinderella* that made us go to bed so quietly and wide-eyed.

'So, how are things?' he says, noticing my glazed expression and abandoning his explanation of how the washing-machine is a metaphor for global warming spinning out of control.

'Pretty good, actually.' I'm happy that, for once, I mean it, and am not simply saying it to ease his fatherly concern. 'We're booked to do a huge society wedding in a few weeks which is great for business. Jess has met a man she seems really into. I'm renting out my spare room to an American for a few weeks to help with the bills . . .' I look sideways at his face, trying to gauge how he will react to my next bit of news. 'And I've met someone.'

Without flinching Lionel continues to gaze at the installation. 'Would that someone be a fellow?'

'His name's James,' I say, trying to sound normal and act as if it's no big deal, while I'm struggling to stop the smile that's threatening to take over my face, which is what happens every time I think of him. Which is every few seconds. 'He seems really nice.'

Nice?' repeats Lionel. 'Nice is such a wishy-washy adjective. If it were a colour it would be a pastel.'

We played this game as children: Ed and I have always associated words, numbers, objects and even people with colours – probably something to do with having an artist for a father. Unsurprisingly, considering our personalities, it was always different for each of us and we would argue about it furiously.

'OK, in that case . . .' I'd planned to play down my feelings for James, but now I change my mind. 'What about "wonderful"?'

'Aha, now you're talking,' Lionel looks at me approvingly. ' "Wonderful" is about as bold an adjective as you can get. As a colour it's bright red.'

'You mean green.'

'Nonsense! I can see it now, written in vermilion.'

'No way. It's more a British racing green,' I argue, thinking about the colour and realising it's a lot like James. 'Classic, sophisticated, understated.'

The middle-aged couple next to us throw Lionel and me a puzzled glance and I notice we're now standing in front of a huge purple sculpture.

'*Green?*' Lionel shakes his head. 'Never!'

'Well, it's definitely not red.'

Gesticulating widely, my father gasps with exasperation. 'How on earth can you possibly think that wonderful . . .' He trails off and stares at me as if he's seen a ghost. 'Did you say *wonderful?*'

'Uh-huh,' I nod.

'Oh, my goodness . . .' A wide smile breaks across his face. 'Heather darling, that's marvellous news.' In a celebratory mood he grabs two more martinis from a passing tray, passes me one and demands, 'You must tell me all about him.'

Which, of course, is what I've been dying to do all evening. Without further prompting, I take a gulp of my cocktail to grease my vocal cords, and describe how James and I met, how I'd secretly fancied him for ages and been delighted when I discovered he'd been secretly fancying me too. How he used to work in the City but left five years ago to establish a property business with clients as far afield as Australia, and his plans to set up an office in America in a few years' time. This is all business-type stuff that I would never dream of boring my friends with, but which greatly interests my father who, despite his Bohemian outlook on life, can be incredibly traditional when it comes to the type of man he wants to date his daughter.

I also tell him James is handsome, funny and incredibly well-mannered, that we've already been on a couple of dates and that he's going to cook me dinner later this week. I tell him practically everything. Well, nearly everything. I don't tell him that I keep wondering why James didn't ask me to stay over last night. How the kiss on the sofa was lovely but left me wanting more, and that although I've spent months wishing I could meet a man who was interested in my brain, not just my body, I'm now having doubts.

'Hmmm, he seems like a great chap,' says Lionel, as I draw breath, and we move in front of a sculpture of a naked torso made of knitting needles. 'However, one thing concerns me.'

I guess immediately what it is. 'Oh, no, you don't have to worry.' I remember my father's horror when Daniel wouldn't have a sherry with him before lunch. 'He's not AA. In fact, he's quite the sommelier.' Turning my attention back to the sculpture I can't help noticing how the artist has made full use of differently sized needles. Absentmindedly I think of Rosemary, an avid knitter, and wonder what she'd make of it.

'I'm not talking about wine, darling, I'm talking about sex.'

I blush hotly. '*Lionel*,' I groan, and glance around to make sure no one overheard.

As I expected, he ignores me. 'You haven't mentioned it,' he persists, without the teeniest smidgen of embarrassment. 'And that worries me.' Parental concern is etched on his face. 'Well?'

Now, I know this is highly unusual. Most fathers hate to think that their little girl has grown up and I've heard countless stories from female friends about their jealous fathers threatening to beat up any boy they found in their bedroom. But my father isn't like most fathers. As an artist he has a very open attitude to the human body.

'Is everything all right?'

'Yes, it's fine. He's being the perfect gentleman,' I say briskly. And somewhat defensively. 'Which, after Daniel . . .' I allow my voice to trail off pointedly. Lionel knows all about Daniel. After we broke up I'd spent hours on the phone, crying mostly, yet Lionel refused to judge him. Instead he listened tirelessly until one night when he told me gently, 'Life is full of experiences, Heather. One has finished, but that only means another is about to begin.'

I'd wanted to sob, 'Is that how it was with you after Mum died? Is that why you married Rosemary?' but I'd choked back my angry tears and tried to appreciate what he was telling me. After all, it wasn't Lionel who'd betrayed me, it was Daniel. Right?

'Ah, yes, of course.' Lionel is nodding understandingly. 'You don't want another cad, do you?'

'Cad' conjures up images of Nigel Havers in a pin-striped suit being all charming, and I can't help smiling. 'Two-timing bastard is how I usually refer to him.'

Lionel lets out a roar of approval. 'And so you should,' he declared abandoning his neutral status for once. 'In my day if you were found cheating on a girl the father would have gone after you with a shotgun.' Draining his glass, he shakes his head. 'But it was all very different then. There was an unspoken code of behaviour we had to follow. When I met your mother, I had to ask her father's permission to court her.'

'Were you nervous?'

'Dreadfully. I shook like a lily.'

I try to imagine this bear of a man shaking with nerves, but it's impossible.

'Your grandfather was frightening,' he goes on. 'Many suitors had fallen by the wayside before I came along, I can tell you.'

'You must have been in love.' I laugh.

'From the moment I saw her,' he says quietly, squeezing my arm and looking at me in the way he does sometimes when we talk about her.

We fall silent and move to the last exhibit, a series of black and white cubes. But I don't really see them. I'm still thinking about my parents, trying to picture them in their early twenties when they first met. Lionel's right: it *was* different back then, but there's something about my relationship with James that feels like theirs. It's almost as if he's courting me. First our date at the restaurant, then the cinema, and now his promise to cook me dinner. Yet we've still only kissed. Today it seems unusually chaste, but back then it was obviously normal to take things slowly. And so much more romantic, I decide. Mum and Dad would have fallen in love long before they fell into bed.

Reassured by this thought, I turn to Lionel and, unable to resist, ask, 'Tell me, how long did you and Mum wait? You know, before . . .'

'Wait?' He looks at me in astonishment, then guffaws.

'Oh, my word, no. Your mother and I were at it like rabbits on our first date.'

Bzzzzzzzzz.

Forty-five minutes later I'm standing on James's doorstep, finger on the doorbell, stiletto heel tapping agitatedly.

That's it, I've had enough.

Or, to be more precise, I haven't had any. Not even a whiff. Unlike my parents. I mean, *please*. You know there's something horribly wrong when you're having less sex than your parents.

Bzzzzzzz.

'Hello?' Finally I hear James's voice on the intercom. He sounds sleepy. I look at my watch: it's late. He was probably already in bed. 'Who is it?' He yawns.

'It's me, Heather,' I say. So what if he's sleepy? I've made a decision. Sod waiting. Sod getting to know each other. And sod him respecting me in the morning.

'I thought you were doing something tonight.'

'I've done it.'

There's a pause, before: 'Is everything OK?'

'Yeah, fine,' I fib. Well, you can hardly call abandoning your father at an exhibition, jumping into a cab and turning up at your boyfriend's house in a sexual frenzy fine, can you? 'Can I come up?' I demand forthrightly. And a bit drunkenly. Maybe those apple martinis were stronger than I thought.

'Of course.' There's the sound of the door being released. I push it open and flick the light switch. A large brass chandelier illuminates the hallway and I dive for the stairs, taking two at a time. My heart's thumping and I can feel the blood rushing through my veins, my eyes dilating, head spinning, groin aching.

Turning the bend I see James waiting for me in his doorway, a vision in a white waffle robe, the kind you get in swanky hotels. He frowns when he sees me. 'Heather, what's wrong? You seem—'

I silence him by sticking my tongue down his throat. He doesn't try to resist. It would have been useless, anyway. I'm drunk. I'm horny. I haven't had sex in nearly a year. The poor bloke doesn't stand a chance.

Chapter Twenty-one

'And then he said to me, "Jessica, you make me want to be a better man." '

The next morning I'm in a yoga class with Jess. After a seemingly never-ending and – for someone who needs a half-hour's stretching before touching their toes – torturous round of sun salutations I'm resting in what the instructor describes as 'child's pose'. In other words, I'm face down on a mat.

I take a deep breath. It's so hot; sweat is sticking my forehead to the mat. I close my eyes and try to imagine I'm on a beach in Goa, or lying in the garden in Cornwall – or anywhere but here, packed like a sardine among dozens of sweaty bodies at the Sacred Movement Centre in Notting Hill, listening to Jess. 'Isn't that a line from a movie?' I hear myself ask.

When Jess called earlier, announcing that she was back from her trip to Sydney and reminding me that I've been promising for weeks to go with her to Bikram yoga – 'it's amazing, they heat up the room to about ninety degrees so you can reach these really deep poses' – I felt my *chakras* tie themselves up in a knot. Exercising? In ninety-degree heat? For two hours? I felt exhausted just thinking about it. 'Sorry, but I've got a mock-Tudor wedding at Hampton Court that starts at three,' I replied, relieved that I was booked to take photographs of a bride and groom dressed up like Henry VIII and Anne Boleyn. Which shows how much I hate yoga.

But Jess wasn't taking no for an answer and so, reluctantly, I met her before work for an early class. Only when I arrived I discovered she had an ulterior motive for seeing me, which had nothing to with Bikram yoga.

And everything to do with Greg.

'Heather, do you always have to be so cynical?' she grumbles. For the last forty-five minutes she's been all dreamy-eyed in her blow-by-blow account of Greg and his amazing technicolour life – how he's training for a triathlon, just got back from climbing Machu Picchu and is fluent in five languages. But now she's scowling at me from her mat.

'I'm not being cynical,' I protest hotly. 'I was just saying—' *Damn, what was the title of that movie?* It's niggling me now.

'Well, don't,' she interrupts crossly. 'OK, I admit in the past I've kissed a lot of men I thought were princes who turned into frogs, but Greg's different.' At the mention of his name she gets that dreamy-eyed look again. 'He seems really genuine and honest. *And* he's got a perfect record when it come to relationships. Never been married, several girlfriends but no one special . . .' she's counting off the points on her fingers '. . . wants to settle down and have children.'

'Jack Nicholson,' I blurt triumphantly. '*As Good As It Gets.*'

'What?'

'That's the line from the movie. Jack Nicholson says it to Helen Hunt.'

Jess glowers. Oh, shit, why did I just say that?

'*. . . and so, bringing ourselves up to a standing position, let's take some deep breaths . . .*'

'It's a great movie,' I add feebly.

Jess presses her thumb against one nostril and begins doing her yogic breathing. Dressed in all the latest yoga gear she bought on eBay and able to fold her body in half, she's the kind of person whom beginners like me dread getting stuck to next to. I, on the other hand, in my ratty old T-shirt and shorts, am a beginner's dream. I'd make your granny look supple.

'Greg sounds great,' I enthuse, trying to make amends.

'He is,' she says curtly, switching nostrils and inhaling deeply. 'Really fit.'

And exhaling.

'A triathlete. Wow,' I persist.

Nothing. She just stands there, inhaling and exhaling. Inhaling. Exhaling. Only it's not a deep, relaxing, get-in-tune-with-my-inner-peace kind of a breathing, it's more of an angry, I-hate-my-friend-Heather snorting.

Fearing she might soon explode as the veins on her forehead are bulging, I make one last attempt at the peace process. 'I've had sex.'

It's like an Exocet missile, obliterating all her earlier thoughts of being offended.

'*Sex?*' She's stopped snorting. 'With whom?'

'Well, you're never going to believe this . . .'

'Who? Who? Tell me who.'

'My gorgeous neighbour.'

Jess's eyes grow saucer-wide. 'You're serious?'

'Deadly.'

'Fuck.'

The woman next to us, in a leotard that looks as if it belongs to her daughter, stares at us.

Jess clutches at my arm in excitement. 'I can't believe it.'

'*. . . and now move slowly into Warrior One . . .*'

She drops my arm and we move into position – Jess with the graceful ease of someone who did childhood gymnastics, I with the crunching of knees that makes both me and the woman next to me wince.

'I want dates, times, places, size,' she demands.

I smile coyly. 'His name's James and we've already been on two dates.'

'*. . . and carry through into Warrior Two . . .*'

The woman next to me sighs loudly. 'Do you mind? I'm trying to find inner peace.'

'Oh, fuck your inner peace.' Jess moves into warrior pose.

Startled, the woman reddens.

'I go away for a few days and it's Bombshell City!' continues Jess.

'*. . . and now bending your right knee and shifting your hips forward carry through to triangle . . .*'

I try to lean forwards, then remember I have the special kind of body. The one that won't bend.

'So, come on, spill the beans – tell me all about him.'

'*Breathing deeply, let's move to the balancing pose . . .*'

Standing on one leg, Jess brings her hands smoothly to her chest as if she's praying.

'He's great.' I get a flashback of last night, all tangled up in James's sheets. His naked body. Him kissing every single bit of me, starting at my toes and working his way up to . . .

'*. . . it's important to keep yourself focused . . .*'

The memory throws me off balance and I wobble over. 'Amazing, actually,' I whisper, trying to steady myself.

'That's fantastic.' Jess grins with delight, then gets down to business. 'What age bracket is he in?'

Trust Jess. She's not interested in how James makes my stomach flip over, his lazy smile, or the way he calls me 'honey'. She's interested in make, model and income.

'He's thirty-six,' I say, trying to focus on my yoga pose.

'Excellent.' She nods knowledgeably. 'The twenty-six to thirty-five bracket are too immature, the forty-one to forty-five are fortysomething fuck-ups, but the thirty-six to forty guys are ripe for commitment. She leans closer as if telling me a secret, 'Take it from me, if you're lucky enough to find one, hang on to them like a rat to a meat cage.'

I recoil at the analogy. 'What are you saying? That I'm a rat?' Any hope of finding inner peace has vanished.

'*And . . . Swan dive . . .*'

Smoothly touching her toes Jess ignores my last comment and moves swiftly on: 'Does he have a clean relationship record?'

'Clean?' I repeat dubiously, swan-diving for my toes but unable to get any further than my knees. I strain as hard as I can.

'You know – ever been married?'

'Nope.' Ouch. The backs of my knees are killing me.

Obviously this is a good answer: she looks pleased. 'Lived with someone?'

'Jess,' I plead, 'I like him, he likes me. It's that simple.'

'It's never that simple,' she warns solemnly. 'You need to be aware of any red flags.'

Honestly, what *is* she going on about now?

'You don't go swimming if there's a red flag, do you?'

I crumple: her logic makes no sense to me, but it's easier to give in and comply. 'He mentioned something about a girlfriend from South Africa. . .' I say vaguely.

'Why did they break up?'

'. . . *hands touching the floor once more into plank* . . .'

Relieved to move poses, I lower myself on to the floor. My arms are shaking. 'Erm, I think she moved back to Cape Town,' I grunt. Crikey, this is a lot harder than I thought.

'Sense of humour?'

'. . . *and let's see if we can hold this position for three minutes* . . .'

I glare at the instructor. Three minutes? Is he mad? Sweat drips on to my outstretched fingers and my chest feels as if it's about to burst. I glance at Jess. She's not even broken a sheen. 'Uh . . . well . . . he can be a bit serious sometimes . . .' I need to lie down.

'Serious is good. You don't want a joker.'

It has to be three minutes by now. It just has to.

'Annoying habits?'

'Nugghhh.' I groan, wishing this class was over.

'*And now it's time to relax. Lie down on your mats and close your eyes* . . .'

With relief I do as I'm told. This is great. I'm getting used to all my little wishes coming true.

'Bank balance?' Jess's voice snaps me back.

I groan, 'Oh, God! I don't know and I don't care.'

'You won't be saying that when you're turning right on an aeroplane,' she warns, in stewardess mode. 'Like my mother's always told me, there's nothing romantic about being poor.'

'But your mother's not poor!' I protest impatiently. Jess's parents are super-wealthy and live in a million-pound house in Muswell Hill.

'Exactly,' she says evenly. 'She's not stupid.'

'. . . *allow yourself to float away* . . .'

I love this. We're at the bit where we get to nod off for ten minutes.

'So that only leaves one thing,' Jess is saying triumphantly.

I'm so knackered I really don't want to ask, but unfortunately I'm too curious not to: 'What?'

'Sex.'

An image of me jumping on James springs to mind. 'Let's just say you can definitely put a tick in that box.'

'Really?'

'Uh-huh.' Satisfied that I've appeased her, I settle and close my eyes.

'What about foreplay?'

The woman in the leotard huffs.

'Please, Jess.' I'm squirming with embarrassment.

But she persists. 'I need to know these things. It's important. You've been out of the dating game for years. Trust me, I'm a professional at this.'

I open one eye to glower at her.

'You don't need to tell me the details,' she placates. 'Just nod or shake your head.'

I really want to ignore her but when she leans closer and asks, 'Less than ten minutes,' I can't help shaking my head.

'More than ten minutes?'

I nod more than a little proudly.

'More than twenty?

I nod again, reliving last night for the umpteenth time. As a lover James was so – how shall I put it? – *unselfish*, and afterwards he'd hugged me close, kissing my eyelids and telling me how beautiful I was until I'd fallen asleep.

'Thirty?'

'A whole half-hour,' I confess. 'All to myself.'

'Wow! So your wish really did come true.'

'My wish?' I repeat, trying to sound casual as a now familiar tingling erupts in my toes and whooshes up through my fingertips. I feel excited and scared all at the same time, like when I was a child on fairground rides.

'Yeah. Don't you remember wishing for a perfect man?'

Until this moment it hasn't occurred to me, but now I realise she's right. James is everything I ever wished for in a man. He even offered to run to the corner shop to buy me Tampax this morning when I complained of stomach ache. As it turns out it was just gas from all the champagne last night, but even so – *he offered to buy me Tampax.* Those words should be inscribed on a tablet of stone.

'*Clear your mind and let it drift away.*'

A pair of feet belonging to the instructor appears alongside us and saves me from answering Jess. I'm more than relieved. My head is spinning, and as the instructor gives me a little shoulder massage, I try to do what he says. Stop thinking about James. Imagine my mind is a helium balloon, drifting away . . .

I close my eyes and fall asleep.

Chapter Twenty-two

Fast forward to Friday morning, eight a.m., and I'm standing on the doorstep in my dressing-gown, thanking the man from Interflora and staring down in amazement at the huge Cellophane bundle in my arms. Tied with a big, shiny pink ribbon, a dozen perfect red roses gaze up at me lovingly. Plucking out the little white card that nestles next to the sachet of flower food, I quickly read the message. 'Just because you're beautiful – James'

My stomach flips. Wow, how romantic. This kind of stuff never happens to me. I often see the little Interflora vans zipping around and wish they'd stop at my address with a delivery. But they never do.

Never *did*.

Since Wednesday morning that little van has stopped outside my flat, not once, not twice, but three times! I still can't believe it. Some people might think it's a bit over the top, but isn't it what every girl dreams of? A man who sends you flowers and romantic little cards that say, 'Can't stop thinking about you' and 'I miss you already', which, I know might sound soppy, but are actually really sweet. When Daniel and I were together I was always wishing he could be more thoughtful, but James couldn't be *more* thoughtful: he's always calling and text-messaging me . . . which admittedly might feel a bit suffocating if it was anyone else, but with James it's different.

Hugging my bouquet to my chest, I turn to go back inside but it's so cumbersome to hold and hard to see over the top. I try to manoeuvre into the hallway but the roses and I get squashed between the doorframe and the wall. I tug at the Cellophane and accidentally break a couple of stalks.

Damn.

The scarlet heads of the roses droop, necks broken. Dismayed, I poke my fingers through the wrapping, trying to straighten them. A thorn pricks my finger, which starts bleeding. Ouch. I suck it. That bloody hurts.

I glare accusingly at the roses. I haven't actually told James, but I'm not a big fan of red roses. I think they're a bit corny – in fact, to be honest, I'm not really into cut flowers at all. They remind me of hospitals, of being a child and visiting Mum when she was ill. She was always surrounded by vases of her favourite pink carnations and I remember sitting at the bottom of her bed, feeling sad that something so pretty was going to die in a few days, and wishing they could live for ever.

But I don't want to sound ungrateful. It's the thought that counts, isn't it? And the roses are beautiful, in a flawless, ideal, traditional way. Well, apart from the broken ones but I'll throw those away. No one's going to count them, are they?

As I walk down the hallway I push my nose into the petals, breathing in their perfume. Mmm, they have such a strong scent. I take a deep breath. Mmm . . . Oh . . . I feel a tickle in my nostrils – hang on, it's my hay-fever – all these flowers have brought on an attack. It's really weird, I haven't suffered from it for years, in fact I thought I'd grown out of it, but all these roses have . . . ooh, I think I'm going to . . . Throwing back my head I let out a violent sneeze.

It reverberates through my body at what feels like a hundred miles an hour and then – ooh – it's gone. I open my watering eyes and sniff. Euggh, how disgusting. My beautiful bouquet is now sprayed with little flecks of snot. Hastily I wipe the Cellophane with my sleeve, but that's even more disgusting.

Yuk. I'd better get a dishcloth.

I walk into the kitchen and see Gabe in a crumpled white T-shirt and Paisley boxers. He's hunched over the toaster with a chopstick, poking around for something that's got stuck and is emitting a strange smell. Almost like burning strawberries.

'Lost something?'

'Another darn Pop-Tart,' he mutters, pushing his glasses up his nose. His face lights up when he sees me. 'Secret admirer?'

Realising the bouquet, not me, is the reason for his smile, I feel curiously deflated. 'Actually he's not so secret.'

We exchange a look and suddenly I'm self-conscious.

'Wow, that guy's got a real habit.' Gabe scratches his head, and his hair sticks up vertically in sandy tufts. 'He needs Red Roses Anonymous.'

'You're not funny.' I fish for my nasal spray in the pockets of my dressing-gown, then inhale deeply. With all these flowers I've spent a fortune in Boots this week – eyedrops, sprays, two boxes of antihistamine pills, and masses of tissues. Still, it's worth it.

'I'm not funny?' Gabe is looking at me with genuine concern.

Of course I can't go around telling stand-up comedians they're not funny – even if it does happen to be true. 'I was joking, silly,' I lie hastily. 'You're hilarious.' I rest the bouquet on the draining-board and start opening and closing cupboard doors to find something to put the roses in.

'Are you looking for a vaize?' he says, after a moment.

'A what?' I ask, crouching to bury my head among the saucepans.

'A vaize,' he repeats, only louder.

I reappear empty-handed from the cupboard under the sink and look at him in confusion. 'What's a vaize?'

'You know, they're made of glass or ceramic. They're for flowers?'

'Oh, you mean a *vase*.'

'No, I mean a *vaize*.'

I laugh. 'Now you're just being stubborn.'

'So are you.'

'Well, I'm a Piscean. We're meant to be stubborn,' I say self-righteously.

He eyes me with amusement. 'That's Taureans, actually. And I thought you didn't believe in astrology.'

I feel myself redden. 'I don't. But in England it's pronounced vase.'

'Well, in America it's a vaize.'

'But you're in England,' I insist.

Somehow, and I'm not sure how, I've found myself in the middle of an argument – which I'm determined to win.

'So? I'm American.'

'So are you going to go around calling pavements sidewalks, the tube the subway, dressing-gowns robes—' I break off as I flail around desperately for something much more – I've got it. 'Or bottoms fannies?'

Ha! That's shut him up. Feeling very told-you-so I continue my search *for a vase*.

'You mean your fanny isn't your ass?' he asks, after a pause.

'No, of course not.' I laugh, examining an old jug.

'So what is your fanny?'

'My fanny?' I echo distractedly. *Hmm, I wonder if I could squash a dozen roses in there or if the jug would topple over.* 'Well, that's easy. It's—' Oh, fuck. I stop dead – like one of those cartoon characters who keep running even though the ground has disappeared beneath their feet until they stop to look down. And then they plummet to their doom. I can feel myself plummeting.

'Erm, well . . .' As blotches of colour prickle on my chest I pull my towelling dressing-gown closer. Now, come on, Heather, don't be so ridiculous. You're both adults, there's no need to be embarrassed. 'My fa—' I begin, and grind to a halt

I'm sorry, but I can't do it. Call me a prude, but this is my vagina we're talking about. Or not. I cross my legs.

'You were saying?' he asks evenly.

Honestly, I'm a dreadful loser but now, looking into Gabe's blue eyes, magnified behind his glasses, I can't help wishing this was one argument I *had* lost.

'Oh, nothing,' I say, and hurriedly change the subject to cover my embarrassment and the fact that, actually, I *have* lost this argument. 'Can I ask you a favour? As you're much taller than me, will you look on top of that cupboard?' I gesture above the oven. '*For a vaize,*' I add pointedly – surrendering.

A wicked grin threatens to spread across his cheeks and Gabe shrugs. 'Sure,' he says, standing on tiptoe. But that's not good enough with my eleven-foot-high Victorian ceilings so he climbs on to the counter. After a few minutes' rummaging, he says, 'What about this?' He's holding an empty spaghetti jar.

'Nope.' I shake my head. 'Too skinny.'

He puts it back and grabs the next object: the glass jug from the coffee percolator I never use – which is next to the blender, the ice-cream maker, the pop-corn popper and the pasta-machine that I never use either. 'Or this?'

I look up, almost cricking my neck. 'Nah. Too small.' Shrugging, he roots around until finally he finds 'This?'

'Oh, wow! I've been looking for that everywhere.' He's holding out the orange plastic watering-can I bought in IKEA months ago. 'But no,' I add, taking it from him and setting it on the counter, 'it'll clash with the red of the roses. Anyway, it's too big.'

'Jeez, who are you? Goldilocks?' he grumbles.

I watch him grope around on top of the cupboard until my neck aches and I look down. And come face-to-face with his hairy calf muscles splayed on the counter. I'd never noticed them before but Gabe has really nice calves. They're covered with pale brown hair and from a distance they seem really tanned, but if I peer closer – I move my face so that my nose is just inches away – I can see that they're covered with millions of tiny freckles that have sort of joined up to give the impression of a tan. It's a bit like squashing your face against a TV screen and seeing the picture disintegrate into tiny little dots.

'*Awesome.*'

Brandishing a filthy object, Gabe is looking down over his shoulder at me. 'Guess what I . . .'

Which is when I realise my head is stuck between his legs and jump back.

'. . . found.'

Oh, shite.

Trying to appear innocent and not like a pervy old landlady, I reach up to take it from him. It's an ugly ceramic vase Rosemary once gave me and which I've kept stuffed in the cupboard ever since. Still, beggars can't be choosers. 'Great, thanks,' I gush enthusiastically, hot with embarrassment. I dunk it in the washing-up bowl and try to look all busy, busy, busy – turning on the tap, grabbing a pair of yellow Marigolds from under the sink, squeezing Fairy Liquid in frantic, green wiggles.

'Hey, I can do that. You'll be late for work.'

'No, it's OK,' I cut him off. 'It's my day off.' I grab the cloth and lather the vase.

'Cool,' he says cheerfully, and for a joyful moment I think he's going to leave the kitchen.

Instead he loiters behind me.

Out of the corner of my eye I see him turn back to the toaster. This time he succeeds in spearing an unrecognisable charred object on the chopstick. He takes a bite and chews thoughtfully as he walks across the kitchen. 'By the way, about your fanny,' he says matter-of-factly, pausing by the doorway.

I freeze. 'Er, yes?'

Our eyes meet, and just as I feel myself teeter on the edge of humiliation, he winks. 'I was just kidding with you.'

He grabs his Marlboros and, as I watch him disappear into the garden for his morning cigarette, a thought strikes me—

I got my wish. Without a doubt, this was one argument I definitely lost.

Chapter Twenty-three

OK, now what?

After I've chucked away the broken roses, stuck the rest on the windowsill, made myself another cup of instant coffee and finished off what's left of a packet of liquorice allsorts for breakfast, I sit down at the kitchen table and wonder what to do with the rest of my day off. Normally I like to lie in till noon, but I'm already up and wide awake, courtesy of my new alarm: the man from Interflora. I drum my fingers on my mug.

I know! I'll watch a bit of morning telly.

I feel a rush of joy. I love morning telly: it's such a guilty pleasure, like wearing big knickers or fancying Enrique Iglesias. Gleefully I reach over to flick on the portable TV stuffed next to the microwave and happen to glance at the digital clock. My heart sinks. It's not even nine a.m. *Trisha*'s not on for ages.

Thwarted, I drain my coffee and wonder what Gabe's up to. I pinch open the slats of the window blind and peer out into the garden. Surrounded by piles of joke books, he's lying belly down on a sun-lounger, scribbling into the notepad he takes everywhere with him. Better not disturb him: he looks busy.

Which is what I should be, I tell myself guiltily, letting the blind snap back. There's a million things that need doing.

No sooner has the thought popped into my head than I glance at the fridge door, which is wallpapered with Post-it notes, bills that need paying, and a pair of tickets for *The Rocky Horror Show* on Monday night. I'd forgotten about that. Jess arranged it with a bunch of her gay steward friends and I've got a ticket for James. Though I'm not sure if suspenders are his thing, I muse, grabbing a pen and a notepad and sitting down at the kitchen table.

OK. I need to write a list. I flick open the pad to find a dozen lists I've already made and forgotten about.

OK, I need to write a *new* list.

Friday – My List of Things to Do.

- Ring James.

Well, that's easy. I dial his number but he's not there so I leave a message thanking him for the roses and telling him how lovely they are.

- Handwashing.

One of the downsides of having sex. Before James, I wore comfy old knickers that I could throw in the washing machine, but now it's all about scraps of frilly lingerie that don't fulfil any of the roles of underwear (support, comfort, protection) but act simply as decoration. Expensive, uncomfortable decoration that's a complete faff to wash.

- Get a high-flying job as a photographer.

Fuck.

Initially I think of skipping this one and going straight to 'Buy a new shower curtain' as I quite fancy a trip to IKEA, but I can't ignore it. Not only have I just underlined it twice, but it's made the top five on my list for the past six years, and while everything else gets crossed off eventually, it stays there. Staring at me. *Taunting me.*

Which is why, hours later, I'm sitting at my computer Googling 'photography jobs'.

'Hey, how's it going?'

Gabe has stuck his head round my bedroom door with two steaming mugs of peppermint tea and a fresh bag of liquorice allsorts.

'Wonderful,' I say dolefully, as I take a mug. Blowing on it I take a large slurp. 'I've spent nearly four hours and so far the only thing I've found is an ad for a staff photographer on *Farm Machinery Monthly*.' I shuffle through the stuff I've printed out 'Here it is.' I clear my throat and I read, 'Exciting opportunity for an experienced photographer. Knowledge of tractors and silage equipment an advantage. Must like cattle and being outdoors in all-weather conditions . . .'

Gabe throws me a puzzled look and offers me a liquorice allsort.

'I'm trying to find a job,' I explain, nibbling off the yellow fondant.

Propping his bum on the edge of my unmade bed, Gabe chews slowly as he strokes Billy Smith who's curled up on the duvet. 'But I thought you said your job was safe now you've got this fancy royal wedding.'

I smile, despite my gloom. 'It's not a royal wedding. It's the daughter of the Duke and Duchess of Hurley,' I explain, entertained by Gabe's confusion. 'Which means she isn't a princess, just a lady.'

'Not necessarily,' he quips.

'I know it's all rubbish,' I admit, smiling weakly, 'but it's good for business. They're paying my boss a fortune, and one of the big celebrity magazines has offered to buy our pictures, which means we'll be credited as photographers.' I pause.

'But?' Gabe has sensed I'm unhappy about something.

I'm about to pretend there isn't a but, that everything's fine, then change my mind. He looks genuinely concerned.

'But when I dreamed of having my photographs published, it wasn't in a magazine with Jade from *Big Brother*,' I confess.

'Who's Jade from *Big Brother*?'

'Exactly.'

Unfazed, he waggles the bag of liquorice allsorts at me. 'You've got me addicted to these things,' he confesses. 'Especially the blue and pink jelly ones.'

'Yuk. They're my least favourite.'

He's astounded. 'Jeez, I can't get enough of them. It's the coconut ones I hate.'

As he speaks, I pluck one out and wave it at him teasingly. 'Mmm, my favourite,'

'I guess that makes us the perfect people to share a bag of these, then?'

Chewing, I nod happily. 'I guess so.'

We smile at each other for a moment, my bad mood forgotten. That's the annoying thing about Gabe: he'll never let me wallow in a bit of self-pity, or dissatisfaction, or good old-fashioned British negativity. He's always so positive. Must be something to do with being American and having a nice day and all that.

'So what's this dream of yours, then?' he says. 'Where do you want to get your photographs published?'

I blush. No one's every asked me that before.

'Well?' he pesters.

It's been my dream ever since I was a teenager, but I feel awkward about admitting it to someone. 'The *Sunday Herald*'s magazine,' I blurt shyly. And then, when I see he's not laughing at me, I grow bolder. 'I want my photographs to be on the front cover,' I continue, my mind flicking back to Sunday mornings in Cornwall, Lionel hogging the arts section, Ed buried behind the business pages and me leafing through the magazine.

'So why don't you go and work for them?' Gabe says it as if it's the most obvious thing in the world.

'Have you any idea how hard it is to get a job there? Every photographer in the world wants to work for them. I've been trying for years.'

'So why don't you give it another try?' persists Gabe, hugging Billy Smith who's now curled on his lap, purring contentedly.

I feel a prickle of impatience. As an American, Gabe obviously has no clue about how hard it is even to get an interview at the *Sunday Herald*, let alone a job. 'What's the point? I'll only get a rejection letter.'

'Not necessarily. Maybe this time will be different. Maybe you'll get lucky.'

I'm looking at Gabe as he says this and I don't know if it's something in his voice or in his expression, but it's as though someone's flicked on a light inside me. Of course. This time *is* different. This time why don't I try *wishing* for a job?

As soon as the thought pops into my head, I notice the lucky heather lying next to my computer. How strange, I'm sure it wasn't there before. But then I forget about it as I'm hit with a surge of excitement. Of course. Why on earth didn't I think of it before? If I can wish for little things like parking spaces and designer shoe sales and they can come true, why don't I try wishing for something big and important? For something I've dreamed about since I was a little girl? *Like being a photographer for the* Sunday Herald*?*

'OK. What shall I put?' I open a word document and bash away at the keyboard. 'Dear Sir/Madam . . .'

Gabe grins at my new-found enthusiasm. 'Say you're a wonderful photographer and they'd be crazy not to hire you immediately.'

'I can't put *that*.'

'Hey, there's no room for modesty in this business.' He wafts his hand for me to continue typing. 'I'll dictate . . .'

And he does exactly that. Walking backwards and forwards he rubs his stubbly chin while I sit hunched over my computer transcribing. Until I finish up with a letter whose tone, I argue, sounds as if I'm 'blowing my own trumpet', but which Gabe insists is 'just selling yourself'.

We're in the middle of bickering about it when the doorbell rings.

'Expecting anyone?' Nudging his glasses over the bump on his nose, Gabe peers towards the front door as if somehow he can see through walls.

'No, I don't think so,' I say, getting up.

But Gabe stops me. 'No, print off the letter and sign it. I'll get it.' Putting his mug down he hugs Billy Smith to his chest and pads barefoot into the hallway. As I turn back to my computer screen I hear him shout, 'It's probably more flowers,' and laughing as he opens the door. I don't pay much attention. The cursor's winking at me tantalisingly and, filled with confidence, I concentrate on finishing the letter. Is it 'faithfully' or 'sincerely'? I never can remember. I take a guess and am watching it spool out of the printer when I hear, 'Heather?'

James is standing in my bedroom doorway, dark eyebrows knitted, eyes searching mine as if he wants an explanation.

'James? What are you doing here?' I begin, then suddenly remember. *Our romantic dinner*. My stomach drops into my sheepskin slippers. How could I forget?

'I waited for you. I was getting really worried,' he's saying, sounding all wounded as I sit motionless in my seat, shocked into silence by his appearance. Swiftly followed by the recollection that I'm still wearing my fleecy tartan pyjamas and my hair's scraped up on top of my head like a pineapple. Mortified, I jump up.

'I'm sorry, I was just . . .' I begin to tell James about my job search, then change my mind. 'Oh, nothing, it doesn't matter.' I shut my laptop and smile apologetically. 'Please, make yourself at home. I'll just go and freshen up.' Trying not to make eye-contact as I'm not wearing a scrap of makeup, I gesture round my room. A room that, until a moment ago, was perfectly fine – but which now, seen through James's immaculately tidy eyes, suddenly looks – I realise, with horror – like a pigsty.

'Erm . . .' He smiles uncertainly, but doesn't move – apart from his eyes, which dart about and finally come to rest on his feet. And yesterday's G-string, discarded on the floor, all rolled up, crotch facing upwards as if to greet him. Triggering two thoughts: (a) Damn, I missed that. I've already done my handwashing; and (b) *I want to die*.

For a moment I'm so mortified that I can't think of a decent thing to say. There's James sending me bouquets of roses and offering to cook me a romantic candlelit dinner, and there's me offering him dirty knickers and a terrible memory. I look at him. All shaved and polished and smelling divine. He's looking as handsome as always in a pale blue shirt and jeans.

While I'm a complete mess. I just don't measure up. He's so considerate, kind and sensitive, and just *so* perfect that, next to him, I feel selfish, ungrateful and *un*perfect. This man has no faults.

I, on the other hand, have a long list:

- My life's chaotic.
- I forget things, even little things, and have to write myself reminders on dozens of multi-coloured Post-it notes. Which I forget to look at.
- I leave dirty laundry on the floor.
- My sofa's covered in cat hair.
- I don't floss.
- My toothbrush isn't a super flashy Sonic-electric one.
- And I forget to change it every six months so that the bristles stick out at right angles and it's flat in the middle.
- I have no pension plan and zero savings.
- But I do have an unhealthy obsession with gossip magazines.
- And secretly fancy Ant and Dec.
- Sometimes I don't feel like making love, I just fancy a quick shag.
- I slurp my tea.
- And leave rings all over my coffee-table as I don't own any coasters.
- I'm not really this delicious golden tan. Once a month I go to a little tanning salon in Hammersmith and pay twenty-five pounds to stand naked in a booth wearing paper knickers and a shower cap and have it sprayed on. Yes, that's right. *Sprayed on.*
- I am a terrible drunk.
- And I'm even worse at karaoke.
- My fridge hasn't been defrosted for over a year and I have an iceberg growing out of my freezer compartment that could have sunk the *Titanic.*
- I have no idea what you do with flavoured olive oils and the ones gathering dust next to the cooker are simply for decoration.

- My culinary expertise consists of sliding M&S meals out of their cardboard packets, pricking the Cellophane with a fork and popping them into the microwave.
- Mould is growing out of a mug next to my bed that resembles a Portobello mushroom.
- Sometimes between waxes I have to pick out ingrowing pubic hairs with my eyebrow tweezers.
- One chocolate Hobnob is never enough. I have been known to polish off the whole packet. Make that two packets.
- I can't park. There - I've said it. May feminism strike me down.
- I don't really wear scraps of lacy lingerie. I wear unidentifiable grey objects with perished elastic.
- I have unpaid parking tickets. Lots of them.
- I rarely go to the gym, and when I do I usually just end up in the sauna with a face mask and a copy of *Now*.

And last but not least my most shameful confession of all:

- I have been known to pick my nose. And eat it.

'Actually, maybe I should get back, check on the food.'

I tune back in to see James backing out of the door. I feel a crash of disappointment. Christ, you're such an idiot, Heather.

And then, just as I'm thinking how completely I've blown it, he steps on Billy Smith's tail.

There's an ear-splitting screech. My cat rears up, his jaws wide, and sinks his claws into James's leg. At which point everything speeds up, like a video being fast-forwarded. James lets out a howl and hops around in the hallway while I flap around him asking if he's OK. Then Gabe appears with a tube of antiseptic and checks to see if he's bleeding. It's like something from a comedy sketch, only it's not remotely funny.

Thankfully, ten minutes later everything has calmed down and on closer inspection it turns out to be just a scratch. James, however, is a bit embarrassed because of the fuss he made but, like Gabe says, it was probably shock rather than the pain that made him yell. 'Anyway, I'm just relieved you're OK,' I say, pouring him a glass of wine as we cluster in my living room.

James takes a sip. 'Luckily, yes. But those claws were pretty sharp. Haven't you thought of getting him declawed?'

I freeze mid-mouthful. '*De-clawed?*'

'Mmm,' nods James, seemingly oblivious to my horrified expression.

'But that's so cruel,' I protest, snatching up Billy Smith and hugging him to me. I suddenly feel incredibly protective.

'You've got to be cruel to be kind,' he says simply.

'Kind to whom?' I ask.

'Well, your furniture for a start,' he says, gesturing towards my sofa, whose legs have been shredded over the years into tiny ribbons. 'He's ruining it.'

Staring helplessly at my sofa, I can feel my fantasy of James and I living together happily ever after fading fast. 'Oh, I don't care, it's old,' I say breezily.

'I can see.' He laughs as he sits down and brushes off the cat hairs that cling to his trouser legs – like iron filings to a magnet.

'I take it you're not a cat person,' comments Gabe, squatting down and rubbing his fingers together. Immediately Billy Smith leaps from my arms and pads over to him.

'Oh, no, I love animals,' disagrees James, 'and animals usually love me.' He smiles flirtily at me. 'Your cat's probably just jealous of another male vying for your attention.'

Unexpectedly embarrassed by the compliment in front of Gabe, I smile back awkwardly. This is the first time Gabe and James have met and things feel a little cool between them. But maybe I'm imagining things.

'And I don't blame him,' adds James, reaching out a hand and pulling me on to his knee. I feel a flicker of something from James that might be mistaken for possessiveness. Not that I'd ever mistake it, of course.

'Hey, I'm gonna go out. Do you want me to post those letters for you?' Gabe stands up, eyebrows raised questioningly.

'Oh, yeah . . . thanks.'

'Letters?' asks James, with interest.

'Just bills and crap,' I say dismissively, then wonder why I didn't tell him the truth. After all, we shouldn't be keeping secrets from each other, should we? But then again, I haven't really talked to James about my job or confessed to him my ambitions. Not that he hasn't shown an interest. On the contrary. It's just that when he asked me, I felt so intimidated by how successful he is in his career that I glossed over it.

'Hang on a sec. The letter's in my bedroom, I'll just fetch it.' I jump up from James's lap and pad into my room, grab the letter, stuff it into an envelope, scribble on the address and hurry into the hallway, where Gabe's waiting for me. 'Thanks,' I whisper, passing him the envelope.

'No problem.'

'Heather?' James pops his head out of the door and his eyes flit between us. 'Shall we go?'

I redden. I don't know why, but I feel as if I've been caught doing something I shouldn't. 'Oh . . . yes! Look at the time,' I fluster.

'Well, have a great evening, you guys.' Gabe pulls open the front door. 'Nice to meet you, James.'

'And you, Dave.'

'It's Gabe,' I correct him.

'Sorry, Gabe,' apologises James, curling his arm round my waist as Gabe disappears. I eye him suspiciously. Did he do that on purpose?

'Aren't you going to change?' James glances down and I remember I'm still in my pyjamas. 'Oh, yeah . . .' Honestly, I don't know what's wrong with me. My mind's all over the place. 'I won't be a minute,' I add hastily. Damn, I wish I'd got time to get in the shower and wash my hair. I'm such a mess.

'Don't worry, I don't mind waiting,' says James, pleasantly.

'But I thought—'

'Take as long as you want.' He kisses my cheek and returns to the living room.

Take as long as I want? I stare after him in disbelief. That's got to be every woman's dream. And, dismissing any worries I might have had, I head to the bathroom to shower and get ready. After all, I have a romantic dinner to go to, remember?

Chapter Twenty-four

I arrive at James's flat to find it candlelit, the large oak dining-table set for two, and an ice bucket with champagne already chilling. It's so romantic it's almost textbook in its perfection. As he takes my coat, pulls out a chair and cracks open the Veuve Clicquot I feel a little overwhelmed.

'A toast,' says James, passing me a flute of champagne.

Smoothing the bit of my dress that I forgot to iron, I look at James. He clinks his glass against mine, gazing at me intently, and I know I should be feeling all – well – romantic. 'To us,' he says, his voice heavy with implication.

But instead I feel faintly ridiculous. 'To us,' I whisper. Out of nowhere I have an urge to giggle. To crack some stupid joke that's not even funny. Like Gabe kept doing the other night when I was watching *Love Actually* on DVD, and I kept having to shush him by hitting him with a cushion.

'So,' James is saying, touching my cheek, 'did you like the roses?'

'They were beautiful,' I say, banishing all thoughts of Gabe and his terrible jokes, which seem to haunt me. 'I left you a message. Didn't you get it?'

'Yes,' he smiles, 'but I wanted to make sure.' He begins to nuzzle my neck.

'Oh, really?' I whisper, standing still, the urge to giggle vanishing. To give James his due, he has an amazing knack of kissing me right where . . . Oooh. As his mouth circles the soft flesh under my chin I abandon any self-consciousness and tilt my head back with pleasure.

'Because I couldn't help noticing . . .'

Enjoying the heady sensation of champagne bubbles fizzing on my tongue and his lips moving delicately across my cheeks with soft, feathery kisses. I close my eyes and feel myself letting go.

'. . . they only sent nine roses.'

I snap my eyes wide open.

'Didn't you notice?' he says, looking at me now with concern.

I can't believe it. *He noticed.* 'Erm . . . no, I don't think so,' I say.

Head tilted back I stare at the cornice.

'Yes, there were definitely only nine,' says James, kissing my neck again, only now it's irritating rather than sexy. 'I counted them while you were changing. I'll call the florist tomorrow.'

'No, don't. Honestly, it's fine, it doesn't matter.' I don't know which I'm more alarmed by: that he might call the florist, or that he counted them. Pulling away I reach for the champagne bottle to top up my drink, only I do it too quickly and the bubbles overflow down the side of the glass.

'But I asked for a dozen red roses,' he continues, quickly grabbing a napkin and pressing it around the side of my glass to blot up the excess.

'Don't worry, I have plenty.' I squeeze his arm.

'I know, but that's not the point,' he says, dropping to the floor and feverishly dabbing at the rug, although I'm sure I didn't spill that much. It was only a dribble. 'You can't send nine,' he mutters.

'Why not?' I tease, half joking, half serious. Taking another elaborately folded napkin from the dining table I go to help him but he shoos me away, telling me I'm the guest. A vague feeling of unease descends on me, and before I know it I say, 'Who made the rule that it has to be a dozen roses? What's wrong with nine?'

'Because you just can't,' he says, perplexed, as if I'm challenging a universal truth, like saying the earth's flat or men are great at multi-tasking. 'That's not how it works.'

How what works? *Romance?*

As I gaze down at him squatting on the floor I suddenly feel my whole belief system being shaken. I've spent my whole life dating unromantic men when I wanted to be sent flowers and treated to candlelit dinners and now – I glance at the candles on the table, the champagne chilling, the glasses with not so much as a smudged fingerprint – instead of being romantic, all the rules and this formality feel a bit contrived.

'Hey, let's forget about it, shall we?' I smile lightly, taking the napkin from his hand and replacing it with his refilled champagne glass. 'Don't let it spoil tonight.'

'You're right. I'm sorry, darling.' He stands up and strokes the hair off my forehead. 'I just wanted everything to be perfect for you.'

'Everything is perfect,' I say reassuringly, putting my arms round him. He looks so crestfallen I try to cheer him up. 'Hey, I'm going to go down to Cornwall tomorrow. It's my family's annual get-together and, well, I was wondering if you'd like to come with me.'

A family get-together may be viewed as a nightmare by some men, but not James: his face immediately brightens.

'We own a little cottage in Port Isaac, it's nothing fancy but really pretty. It's called Bluffers Cove as it's set right on top of a hill.'

'That sounds great! I can't wait.' He hugs me, then looks serious. 'So this is where I get to meet your parents?'

'Oh, don't worry, it's very casual,' I reassure him. I don't want to frighten him off.

But I've obviously misinterpreted him: this seems to make him even more keen. 'No, I'd love to meet your parents,' he says, kissing the tip of my nose.

'You would?' Wow, this is amazing.

'Of course. And mine are dying to meet you.'

'*They are?*'

'Absolutely. I've told them all about you. Maybe we can drive to Kent and visit them next weekend?'

I hesitate. Gosh this is all very serious. *And very soon*, pipes up a warning voice.

'Well, what do you think?'

'Yeah,' I'm suddenly nervous at the thought of meeting his parents, but I take a large glug of champagne and swallow my fears. 'That sounds great!'

The rest of the evening slips past in a hazy blur of food, alcohol and music. James is a terrific cook, and we eat oysters, pumpkin risotto and the most delicious passion-fruit sorbet that he had made himself, all washed down with three different types of wine. In fact, by the time we've finished eating and he asks me to dance I'm a little drunk.

I giggle tipsily. 'But we need some music.'

Picking up the remote he points it towards the stereo. 'Your wish is my command,' he murmurs. There's a faint whir as the disk inside begins to spin and pulling me to my feet he wraps his arm tightly around my waist. Now *this* is what I call romantic.

Interlacing my fingers through his I rest my head dreamily against his chest, waiting to hear what music he's chosen. It's probably something soft and sensitive like Simon and Garfunkel, or classically romantic such as 'Something', by George Harrison, my absolute favourite.

A song begins and I close my eyes. I recognise the opening chords. They sound familiar, like . . .

I stiffen. No. It can't be.

But it is.

Wet, Wet, Wet.

As James waltzes me round the living room I listen with horror as he sings along about feeling it in his fingers and toes. This has to be a joke.

'I love the lyrics don't you?'

Is he insane? I open my eyes to see James gazing at me earnestly. 'Mmm . . .' I nod. Honestly, what can I say? That they're corny? An image of Marti Pellow grinning flashes into my mind.

'I thought you'd love it,' James is saying, 'that perhaps this could be our song.'

Oh. My. God. I'm cringing with embarrassment and my feet move like lumps of lead. The song seems to go on for ever and I can feel the earlier mood of seduction fast disappearing. Much longer and it will be totally ruined.

As we continue slow-dancing round the living room I wait hopefully for James to make the next move. Dinner, champagne, music . . . Surely by the rules of romance the next on the list should be the bedroom? I wait in anticipation. And desperation. Until I can't stand any more Marti Pellow and decide to make the first move by steering James into the bedroom and unbuttoning his shirt.

Thankfully he gets the hint and we take it in turns to remove each other's clothes until I'm lying naked on his super-king bed and James is . . . Where is James?

I open my eyes woozily and take a few seconds to adjust to the darkness. And then I see him. Standing at the foot of the bed. With a hard-on. *Folding our clothes.*

'James, do you have to do that now?' I ask, sitting upright.

'It will only take a moment darling.'

I stare at him indignantly. I'm lying here. Naked. Ripe. And up for it. And my boyfriend is putting his socks into little balls. Insulted, I cover my breasts with my hands and watch as he picks up my dress, which I chucked with abandon on to the floor, and puts it on a hanger. Honestly. Neat and tidy is one thing – but this?

'There, all done.'

He strides over to the bed, slides his naked body next to mine and curls his arm round my waist. 'Now, where were we?'

I'm tempted to sulk – after all, it's not exactly flattering to come second place to someone's underpants – but it's hard to stay mad while James is kissing those deliciously erogenous zones behind my ears, slowly, gently, delicately. I let out an involuntary moan. Mmm, this is amazing – I wish it would go on for ever.

Abandoning myself to the feeling of his lips against my neck, I close my eyes. I swear I've died and gone to foreplay heaven.

Feeling him hard against my thigh, I reach down but he pushes me away and circumnavigates my belly-button with tiny kisses.

I smile at his teasing and wait. After a moment, I let my hand wander back. 'What's the rush?' he whispers, pushing it away again, only this time with a lot more determination.

Oh, OK. Feeling a little redundant, I lie there as he continues to run his hands over my body and kiss my nipples. Wow, this is incredible . . . It's phenomenal . . . It's . . . I stifle a yawn . . .

A bit boring.

No sooner has the thought appeared than I'm shocked. I never thought it was possible to have too much foreplay. But you can, I realise, fidgeting to hurry him up. Steadfastly ignoring me, he's now doing feathery kisses down the side of my face.

I take matters into my own hands: 'Erm, do we have any condoms?' I mumble, as James buries his face in my chest. Not exactly subtle, I know, but hey, what's a girl got to do to get a bit of nookie around here?

But instead of taking the hint, James merely murmurs, 'Sssh,' and begins doing this funny thing with his eyelashes against my nipples.

Over his shoulder I catch sight of the digital alarm clock, the time illuminated in the dark. It's nearly two in the morning. *We've been in the bedroom for over an hour.*

'Mmmm, you smell amazing,' groans James, his voice muffled by my hair as he hugs me to him.

'Mmm, so do you,' I groan back. *So now can we have sex, please?* begs a silent voice inside me as I press myself closer. I try wriggling my hips. Usually this works a treat, but James merely hugs me and for a while we just lie there like that. Hugging.

I try looking on the bright side. It's so rare to find a man who likes cuddling: normally they get a hard-on and it's just wham, bam, thank you, ma'am. But not James. James lurves to hug. Last time we slept together he spooned me all night long. Admittedly it was a bit hard to sleep as I like sleeping face down, limbs spread starfish wide, and the next day I was so knackered I kept nodding off at work, but it was very romantic.

Waking up in your lover's arms. Your hair and makeup all perfect. Well, it's the stuff of movies, isn't it?

Not that my makeup was perfect. In fact, when I woke up my mascara had smudged all over his three-hundred thread count pillowcases.

'Heather?' In the far distance I can vaguely hear James's voice, 'Are you asleep?' I shake my head dreamily. Then it goes quiet and just as I'm drifting off I hear his voice again: 'I love you.'

I turn my head sharply to him. I feel a twinge of panic. Just a twinge, nothing major, and I'm sure that's a completely normal reaction as I'm not used to men telling me they love me first. I tend to go for emotional cripples who have difficulty expressing their feelings.

Yes, that must be it. That's why I feel a little freaked. And a bit claustrophobic – but I'm sure that's because, with the heat of the duvet and James, it's actually getting a bit difficult to breathe.

I fidget in his embrace, pushing the goosedown away from me to get a little air. Ah, that's better. I stop wriggling and smile flirtily at James, only he doesn't smile back.

And then I realise: he's waiting for an answer.

Oh, fuck. Here's me wanting a bit of good old-fashioned nookie, and here's James wanting to declare his undying love. By rights, I should be delighted. Filled with joy. Over the moon. After all, it's something I've dreamed of and wished for. Only the funny thing is, I'm not. Instead I feel cornered. I really, really like James. Honestly I do. He's so sweet and kind, and the last thing in the world I want to do is hurt his feelings.

But?

But you don't love him, Heather.

The voice inside my head startles me. No, that's not true. James is everything I've ever wished for in a boyfriend. So what if it's only been . . . Hurriedly I work out the days in my head. *A week?*

Seconds, that's all it takes, from him uttering those three words, to me now lying here in his arms feeling confused and overwhelmed.

Like eyes in a haunted-house painting I peer sideways and see him gazing lovingly at me from across the pillow, his perfect olive skin, his chocolate brown eyes, his strong square jaw. I feel myself melt. Oh, for Godsakes, Heather, just look at him. He's perfect. You must love him. I mean, what's not to love?

And so I say it. 'Me too,' I whisper.

He breaks into a grin and grabs hold of me and—

Well, put it this way. I get my wish.

Chapter Twenty-five

'Whereabouts are you?'

Ed's voice nags at me from my mobile, which I've wedged under my chin, 'Ummm, not far . . .' I reply evasively.

Sitting bleary-eyed on my bed I continue stuffing things randomly into a leather holdall. It's Saturday and James and I were supposed to be leaving bright and early this morning to drive down to Cornwall for my family get-together, the plan being we'd arrive – oooh. I peer at my watch. Ten minutes ago.

Fuck.

My hangover thumps dully and, cradling my throbbing head in my hands, I take a few deep breaths. I say *supposed* because we slept past the alarm and now it's already lunchtime.

'Can't you be more specific?' Ed is demanding impatiently.

'Oh, you know me,' I laugh lightly in a ooh-silly-me kind of way. 'I'm terrible with directions.'

Actually, that's not true. I have an inbuilt compass, but I can't tell Ed my real whereabouts, can I? He's assuming I'm somewhere on the M4, not crawling around on my hands and knees on my bedroom floor hunting for my hairdryer.

'What's the nearest town?'

'Erm . . . Brighton.' It's the first place that pops into my head.

'*Brighton?* But that's miles away!' Ed's bleating. 'What have you been doing all this time?'

Shagging, I'm tempted to say, but instead I spot my hairdryer under the wardrobe and drop the phone, grunting, 'Hang on, I need to change gear.' Lying flat on my stomach I reach under the wardrobe and resurface to hear him complaining at the other end of the line, his voice muffled by my duvet: '. . . you're talking and driving at the same time? Don't you have a hands-free? Surely you know it's illegal to use your mobile in the car . . .'

As he launches into one of his lectures I have a quick root through the tangled mess that it my underwear drawer, then give up. Sod it. Too hung over to attempt to find anything that matches I pull out the drawer and tip the whole lot into the holdall.

'. . . the police are really cracking down on offenders and it's a large fine, and points on your licence, and I really don't think . . .'

In the background I can hear Ed getting himself all worked up. I decide to put him out of his misery. And mine. 'OK, OK, Ed, calm down,' I say picking up the phone. 'You don't have to worry. I'm not really driving.'

'Is this your idea of a joke?' he gasps. 'Are you on a train?'

Oh dear, I should never have started with these stupid fibs. Fibbing only gets you into trouble, Heather, warns a voice in my head. I get a flashback of last night. In bed with James. Telling him I loved him. Regret grips me like a vice. Oh, God, I wish I hadn't said that. But I did, and I can't wish for something to *un*happen – *can I*?

'No, I haven't left yet,' I confess.

It takes a moment to sink in. And then: 'I can't believe it,' he thunders. 'You haven't left yet? But it's nearly two in the afternoon! You know you're going to hit appalling traffic now, don't you?'

'I know,' I murmur, feeling suitably chastised and peering at the piles of clothes that still surround me. I wonder if I should take my bikini or if it's going to rain. Maybe I should, just in case.

'And you'll miss dinner. Rosemary's going to be very upset.'

Oh, I very much doubt it, I think grimly, imagining her delight when she discovers I'm not going to be there to spoil her hostess-with-the-mostest routine. 'I'll buy her some flowers on the way,' I say, to appease him. Now, what about another pair of jeans? I grab another pair from the pile. Just in case.

'Just in case' is the curse of packing. It's the reason why I always end up going away with far too much stuff that I don't wear and why on the last three occasions I've flown I've had to pay excess baggage. I should learn from Jess and 'capsule pack'. As a stewardess she's a professional at it. Apparently all you need are two white T-shirts and a pair of black drawstring pants.

Despairingly I look at my overflowing suitcase. I'm only going for the weekend and I've already packed a dozen tops and four pairs of trousers. Oh, and my baby blue cords, combats and a pair of white jeans that I've never worn as I'm not sure they're particularly flattering. I try to shoehorn them into the tiny space left in the corner next to my sponge bag. Hmmm, I haven't quite got the hang of it yet.

'. . . and I hope you're going to hire a car and not take your own. It's completely unreliable, Heather. Why don't you just be sensible and sell it? I mean, why you need a sports car in London when you can manage perfectly well on the bus, I have no idea . . .'

'Actually, I'm going in my boyfriend's car,' I interrupt, before I can stop myself. Gosh, how weird. It's the first time I've referred to James as my boyfriend and it feels a bit strange – like new shoes the first time you put them on. But I'm sure I'll get used to it. I mean, look at the satin stilettos. Now the novelty's worn off, they're just like a pair of old slippers.

In the middle of this train of thought it suddenly occurs to me that instead of this idea being a comfort to me, it's actually worrying to know that I'll soon be thinking of James as a pair of old slippers – and that it's a good thing.

'And we're going to share the driving,' I add hastily. Straddling the battered old holdall I bounce up and down to squash everything in. 'And it's not a sports car, it's a very reliable Range Rover.'

I wait for his reaction, but there's complete silence at the other end of the line. 'Ed, are you still there?'

I can hear a muffled whispering at the other end of the line. I can see him now, breaking the news to my family, who are gathered around, waiting to hear what crazy mess Heather has got herself into now. I feel myself prickle with annoyance. I can't quite catch what he's saying but no doubt it's something along the lines of: 'NEWSFLASH: Sister – single, feared spinster – has been found alive with boyfriend and top-of-the-range vehicle . . .'

'Ahem, yes, we're all here,' he says hurriedly.

Just as I'd thought.

'Well, I'm afraid I'm not,' I say breezily, putting my feet into my glittery flip-flops. 'Which is why I can't stand here chatting to you all day, now can I Ed? Otherwise I'll never get there.' And grinning smugly because, for once, I've actually managed to get in the last word with my brother, I hang up.

Ten minutes later I'm not feeling so cocky. 'You can't come?' I wail, as James tells me he's discovered he has to fly to Paris for crisis talks with some big client and there's no way he can get out of it.

'I know. I'm disappointed too, darling,' he says. 'I was really looking forward to meeting your family.'

My family.

As he reminds me my heart sinks. Oh, God, my brother's going to be insufferable all weekend. And as for Rosemary. I say goodbye to James and reach resignedly for the keys to the MG, which are lying on the windowsill, next to the sprig of lucky heather.

My gaze falls upon it, and I pause for a moment, my spirits lifting as I marvel at the shaft of sunlight coming through the wooden blinds, bathing the tiny white flowers in a bright light. It's quite incredible how long it's lasted. It might just be down to me looking after it – it's in an eggcup now, which I refill with fresh water – but since every spider plant I touch turns brown and crispy and I murdered my orchid by placing it in direct sunlight, it's evident that a stronger force is at work here than my not-so-green fingers.

Some might call it luck.

But I like to call it magic.

No sooner do I think this than the weirdest thing happens. I've been standing in a little spot of sunlight on the kitchen lino, enjoying its gentle warmth, when it suddenly intensifies into a searing heat and floods through me. And I get the strangest feeling. It's almost as if . . . I'm being watched.

Automatically I glance up at the window, fully expecting it to be empty and to feel like an idiot. But there, peering through the slats in the blind, a pair of emerald eyes glitter hypnotically. I feel a jolt of shock. Swiftly followed by recognition. No – it can't be.

It's the old gypsy woman.

'Heather?'

My heart nearly jumps out of my chest. With a sharp intake of breath I twirl round to see someone standing in the doorway. For a second I'm so startled that I barely register it's Gabe. He's wearing another of his strange wardrobe manifestations – a bright orange boiler suit and flip-flops. 'Oh . . . hi.' My mind is falling around all over itself, desperse to make sense of what just happened. Was that . . .? Could it have been . . .? Struggling to grasp the incredible, I glance back nervously at the window. I hear a miaow and catch a streak of ginger as Billy Smith jumps from the ledge. Or was it just a trick of the light?

'Going away from the weekend?' Gabe is saying, as he pads over to the kettle and flicks it on.

'We are going to Cornwall, to see my family,' I murmur, feeling dizzy. Tucking my hair firmly behind my ears I try to concentrate. 'I mean I am.' I sit down at the kitchen table, resting my hands on its scratched wooden surface. It feels warm and solid beneath my fingers. 'James was supposed to be coming with me,' I say. 'But he had a meeting.'

'Oh.' Gabe studies me for a moment, then asks, 'Are you OK with that?'

I'd thought I wasn't but now, thinking about it, my initial disappointment seems to have disappeared and it's occurring to me that, actually, I'm fine with it. In fact, to tell the truth, the more I think about it the more I'm relieved that James and I are going to have a break from each other. Last night was lovely, but it's left me uneasy.

'Yeah, it's just a long drive. And with the traffic . . .' I add, and then, realising I sound exactly like my brother, joke feebly, 'I'll just have to make sure I take lots of chocolate to keep me company.'

'You could always take me.' He's laughing when he says it but I'm so taken by surprise I don't say anything. 'I don't have any plans for this weekend and you were saying the surf's pretty good down there . . .' He keeps talking, shuffling awkwardly and scratching his nose '. . . so I was kind of thinking . . .' He trails off and waits for my reaction.

Only I'm not sure what it is.

Gabe? Spend the weekend with my family in Cornwall? I'm sure they won't mind, but what about James? Well, what about him? Gabe and I are platonic, and he'll love it there. He'll be able to surf, eat Cornish cream teas and be a complete tourist. I mean, if he thinks Hampstead's quaint, he'll go nuts over Port Isaac.

But what about you, Heather? Forget everyone else. *What do you want?*

I pause to think about it. Not because I need to, but because I think I ought to. I know the answer, though – I'd known it before I went through all this in my head. I want him to come with me.

'The surf's great.' I smile shyly.

'Awesome!' he whoops, holding out his hand to high-five me. Feebly I high-five him back. Damn, I hate that bit.

'Now can I make a suggestion?'

He lassoes his fingers through my car keys and drops them on the table. 'Forget sitting in traffic. We're gonna take the bike.'

Chapter Twenty-six

I'm going to die. Frozen with terror, I cling to Gabe's leather jacket for dear life. We're going to crash! We're going to end up in some horrible, gruesome wreckage! We're going to be so mangled up they'll have to identify us by our dental records!

Racing down the M4, I squeeze my eyes shut inside my full-face helmet and tighten my already vice-like grip round Gabe's waist. When we first set off he told me to hang on – so I threw my arms round his neck (well, he told me to hang on) – but when we stopped for petrol he said I'd probably find it more comfortable if I held on to the little metal thing at the back of the seat.

I ignored him. More comfortable? Is he mad? Forget trying to get comfortable – I'm travelling at nearly a hundred m.p.h. with no seat-belt, balancing on a skinny little leather seat and *trying to stay alive.*

Alive but deaf, I scream silently, with the thundering roar of the engine blasting into my eardrums, making them ring painfully. This is sheer torture. I feel sick. My head's spinning. My body's jolting. My nerves are raw. This is terrifying. Petrifying.

Gabe revs the engine and we overtake a Jaguar in the fast lane. *Totally exhilarating.*

And then I hear a siren.

I glance back over my shoulder and see a police car racing up behind us with its lights flashing. Oh, fuck. He's pulling us over for speeding.

Gabe drives on to the hard shoulder and, we climb off. A grave-faced policeman clambers out of his Range Rover and stalks towards us. 'Do you know what speed you were doing, young man?' He glares at Gabe.

'Hey, I'm really sorry, Officer. I'm visiting from California . . .' Gabe begins his innocent-tourist act.

Unfortunately it's not going to wash with a member of the UK traffic police, whose face sets even harder. 'Well, in California, do they let you drive at ninety miles per hour? I think not.' He raises an eyebrow. 'Can I see your licence and insurance documents, please?'

Dutifully Gabe passes him his licence. 'But I haven't got my paperwork with me. You see, I've only had the bike a couple of weeks.'

The policeman's expression is one of triumph. 'Well, in that case I'll have to ask you to follow me to the station.'

My heart sinks. Oh, Christ, a ticket would have been bad but this is worse. At this rate we're never going to get to Cornwall.

Gabe gives me a woeful shrug, then turns back to the police officer, who switches on his radio.

I stare at the officer, wishing he'd let us off with just a caution.

'Mr Gabriel Jefferson?'

'Yes, sir?'

The officer is giving Gabe back his licence. 'This time I'm going to let you off with a caution. In future, keep to our speed limits.'

'Thank you, Officer,' says Gabe, throwing me a sideways look of astonishment. I feign surprise. 'I heard the British cops were somethin' else and it's true.'

The policeman walks back to his car, looking as if he's about to burst with pride. Then he turns. 'Are you one of them Hollywood actors? You look familiar.' I stifle a giggle as Gabe reddens.

'No, I'm afraid not,' he shakes his head.

'Hmmm,' he shrugs. And looking unconvinced, the sergeant gives us a curt nod and climbs back into his car.

It's early evening by the time we reach the turning for Port Isaac. Pulling off the motorway Gabe shifts down a gear and slows the bike to a leisurely purr along the winding country lanes. I slide open my visor and take a deep lungful of Cornish air. Mmmm, delicious. It smells of salt, surf and wood smoke and, as always, I'm hit by nostalgia. This is the smell of my childhood. Of days spent on the beach collecting seashells and writing my name in the damp yellow sand. Of walks along the clifftop, holding hands with my parents, who swung me high into the air as I squealed with laughter and begged for more. Of playing hide and seek in the wooden fishing-boats tied up in the harbour, and fighting with Ed when he threatened to tell on me.

The exhaust is reverberating loudly now as we weave along the narrow lanes, past the patchwork of fields dotted with grazing sheep who raise their heads to acknowledge us as we pass. I smile at them and they stare back with bored, unblinking expressions, quite unimpressed by the sight of a motorbike being driven by an American tourist with a red-haired local girl riding pillion.

Gradually the green meadows give way to rows of stone cottages, and as we whiz past them up the hill I feel a tingle of anticipation. I love this part of the journey. It's like unwrapping a gift, waiting for the moment when you get to see what's inside. Because in just a second I know we're going to get our first glimpse of the sea. I hug Gabe tightly. I'm bursting to point over his shoulder and yell at him to watch out for it. But I resist with difficulty. I don't want to spoil the surprise.

And now we're flying over the brow of the hill and it's there. A silvery blue streak clinging to the horizon.

'Wooo-hooo,' howls Gabe into the wind.

The sea stretches out in front of us, like the cinema screen before a movie. Wider and wider, until it's filling the entire horizon, the frothy peaks of the waves turning pink, red and orange in the setting sun.

Gabe pulls over to the side of the road and turns off the engine. The bike splutters into silence, and yanking off my helmet, I shake out my hair. My ears are buzzing. It seems so quiet after the noise of the engine.

'Wow.'

I watch Gabe walk to the cliff edge and stare out at the

horizon. I climb stiffly off the bike and go to join him. He's standing there, completely still, and when I reach him he doesn't move, just gazes straight ahead. I follow his eyes, watching the sun sink slowly into the sea, and for a moment we stay like that. Side by side. Silhouetted against the sky, changing from orange, to red, to purple. Listening to the faint rhythm of the waves lapping against the deserted beach.

Then, out of the corner of my eye, I see him turn to me. I hold my breath tight inside me. Is he going to do what I think he's going to do? The air between us seems charged. I lift my face towards his and shyly meet his eyes. *Is he going to do what I want him to do?*

'Shall we go?'

His voice brings me crashing to earth. Embarrassment washes over me like the waves on the shore below.

'Erm . . . yeah . . .' I fluster. It was all that damn sunset's fault. I misread the signs and got carried away. Deserted clifftop, beautiful scenery, attractive man by my side—

Who isn't your boyfriend.

'By the way, I must warn you about my stepmother,' I say.

'Why? Does she bite?'

Despite myself, I giggle.

Gabe watches me thoughtfully. 'Do you know? That's the first time I've ever seen you laugh at one of my jokes,' he says.

Abruptly, I stop. 'I laugh at you all the time,' I protest defensively.

'At me, but not my jokes,' he says, pretending to be offended.

At least, I think he's pretending but I can't be certain. I feel myself sliding into an awkward situation. I can't admit to hating stand-up comedy, that my idea of hell is listening to a man on stage making unfunny observations about his girlfriend, and I'm certainly not going to confess about the time I heard him practising and thought he was terrible.

The wind whips at my coat, like a child tugging at its mother for attention, and all at once I notice how dark and cold it's become. I glance at my watch. 'It's getting late, we should go.'

This is true, but it's also an excellent way to create a diversion. 'They'll be waiting for us back at the cottage,' I add for emphasis.

Gabe pulls a face and, with his hands still in their big leather gloves, pretends to bite his nails.

'Don't worry, you'll be fine,' I reassure him, and link my arm through his to walk back to the bike. So what if I misread the signs? I didn't want him to kiss me anyway.

Chapter Twenty-seven

As it turns out Gabe is an instant hit with my family, including Rosemary who, from the moment he walks into the kitchen and shakes her rubber-gloved hand – 'Stepmother? No way! You look like sisters' – is eating out of his hand. Blushing like a teenager she pours him sherry in one of her best Waterford crystal glasses and never once tells him to take his shoes off, while the rest of my family crowd round him, shaking hands or, in the case of my father, slapping him vigorously on the shoulder as if beating dust from a carpet.

Meanwhile I'm left to pour my own sherry and not allowed off the doormat until I've removed my boots. Honestly, everyone makes such a fuss of him that I almost feel miffed.

'So, what happened to the muzzle?' I whisper, once the introductions are over and we're squashing ourselves round the dining-table, which is laden with a glistening roast and all the trimmings.

'She seems pretty cool . . .' shrugs Gabe, shuffling past Ed's wife Lou, who's listening politely to Rosemary's daughter Annabel and her husband Miles explaining how they've decided to go for laminate flooring rather than carpet 'because of the twins'. '. . . although she did give me some of that funny brown stuff to drink.'

'Sherry,' I inform him, then notice he's about to walk straight into an exposed beam and yell, 'Watch out.'

But it's too late.

He bangs his head hard and grimaces. 'Ouch. Jesus, that hurt!'

'Oh, yes, mind your head,' pipes up Ed. Ed being one of those annoying people who take pleasure in warning you after the event. 'Those old beams can be very dangerous.'

'Yeah, you're not kidding me.' Gabe forces a smile, while he rubs his temple. Pulling up a chair, he tries cramming his long legs under the table. He's still wearing his orange boiler suit but my family are pretending not to notice. 'The people who built this place must have been tiny.'

'Indeed,' nods Ed, gravely, his six foot five frame stooping low over the table. 'Their poor diet stunted their growth.'

'Wow that's terrible.' Concern flashes across Gabe's face. 'You knew them?'

A bellow of raucous laughter erupts from Lionel as he sweeps into the room with a handful of wine glasses and two dusty bottles of cabernet sauvignon he's raided from his cellar. 'Dear boy, this cottage was built in 1642. It's over three hundred and fifty years old.'

There's a pause, and just as I'm worrying that Gabe is offended by my father's brusqueness, he replies good-naturedly, 'Hey, what can I say? I'm American and the oldest thing we have is Joan Rivers.' Which, as Gabe's jokes go, isn't bad at all. But there's just silence and looks of confusion around the table.

'Joan who?' asks Annabel, politely, tucking her neat blonde bob behind her ears.

'She's kind of a comedian,' explains Gabe, 'and she's gotta be nearly a hundred but the woman's had so much surgery . . .'

I look at the blank faces around the table. They don't have a clue what he's going on about. Unlike me, my family are not on first-name terms with celebrities.

'Oh, I know the one! Her face makes her look like she's in a wind-tunnel,' says a voice from the hallway.

Startled I look up to see . . . *Rosemary*. Appearing through the door with a jug of iced water she pops it in the middle of the table. 'There was an "At Home" spread about her in one of my magazines.'

I look at her with surprise, and, I have to admit a certain grudging respect.

'In the *Lady*?' asks Annabel, frowning.

Last year Annabel bought Rosemary a year's subscription to

the *Lady* for Christmas, and whenever I go to Bath, copies are always spread out like a fan on the glass coffee-table, filled with riveting articles on needlepoint and how to deal with wayward nannies. Rosemary hides her secret stash of *OK!* and *Hello!* in the pantry. Now, caught out, she stutters incomprehensibly, her middle-class cover threatening to crack under Annabel's glare.

Around the table we're preparing ourselves for one of their arguments to erupt when Lou deftly changes the conversation, 'So, Gabriel, what brings you to England?' she asks, throwing him a friendly smile and passing him a bowl of buttered Brussels sprouts. He looks at them for a moment with absolutely no clue what they are, before tentatively taking a spoonful. 'The Edinburgh Festival,' he says, then bites into one suspiciously. 'I'm going up there in a couple of weeks to put on a show.'

A couple of weeks? I feel a jolt of surprise. The time has passed so quickly. He'll be gone in no time. I snatch a sideways glance at him, feeling vaguely troubled.

'Oh, bravo, a theatre man!' Lionel bellows, from across the table where he's carving. He's thrilled: my father lurves the *thee-at-re.*

'No, actually, comedy's my thing,' corrects Gabe, swallowing with what appears to be great difficulty. When he thinks no ones looking, he surreptitiously slides the remainder of the sprout off his fork. 'Stand-up.'

'So how did you two meet?' asks Rosemary, dabbing the corners of her mouth daintily.

'Through an ad,' says Gabe, and then, realising how that sounded, smiles. 'Not that kind of ad, Mrs Hamilton. Heather was advertising for a roommate, and I needed a place for a few weeks.'

'So you're not Heather's new boyfriend?' demands Ed.

'With the Range Rover,' accuses Rosemary, in a tone that tells me she doesn't believe a word of it. I glare at her as my cheeks redden.

'Nope, that's not me,' says Gabe, good-naturedly.

'So, where is your new boyfriend, Heather?'

Rosemary says 'new boyfriend' as if she's putting inverted commas round the words and it's only now I realise the table has suddenly gone quiet.

'You mean James?' I wonder why I feel as if I'm facing a jury. A jury consisting of seven pairs of eyes – six belonging to couples. 'He had to work,' I explain.

'On a Saturday?' pipes up Annabel.

'It was really important,' I protest, which is true. So why do I feel as if I'm making all this up, as if I'm trying to defend him?

'Well, it would have to be,' Rosemary murmurs, spooning a tiny portion of glazed carrots on to her plate, 'for him to let you down at the last minute.' She says this in such a way that I might think she was being genuinely sympathetic – if I didn't know her better.

'Yes, but did she tell you about the bouquets?' interrupts Gabe, squeezing my hand supportively under the table. I throw him a look of gratitude. What a star.

'*Bouquets?*' repeats Lou, dark eyes sparkling. 'Ooh Heather, how romantic. The most I ever get is a bunch of daffs.' Turning to Ed, she pouts playfully while he looks all affronted and indignant.

'Yep, he sent three separate bouquets – a dozen red roses in each,' continues Gabe, laying it on thick. 'The guy's crazy about her.'

'And who can blame him?' booms Lionel, with fatherly pride. 'Wouldn't you say, Rosemary?'

Rosemary has fallen unusually quiet. Silenced, no doubt, by the astonishing fact that I actually have a man sending me flowers and, no, I haven't made him up. 'Yes, absolutely,' she says tightly. 'More Brussels, anyone?'

After dinner everyone heads off to bed, until it's just me and the boys in the front room, eating second helpings of apple crumble and custard and talking about – yes, you've guessed it – football.

'Are you a soccer fan?' Gabe is asking, prodding doubtfully at his custard. I made it earlier to show I'm not completely crap in the kitchen, although admittedly it did come from a packet.

'Absolutely,' says Ed proudly.

'Yes old son,' says Miles, slapping Ed's arm. 'An amazing win we had the other week. A real stroke of luck. The papers described it as a miracle.'

Ed and I exchange a look. 'Uhm . . . yes, so they did,' he says, and fills his mouth with apple crumble. It's been a few weeks since that strange night at the pub, and although Ed and I have spoken on the phone, he hasn't referred to it. Not that I'm surprised. Ed's way of dealing with anything he doesn't understand is simply to ignore it.

'I heard England won a big game,' says Gabe. 'Awesome.'

'Well, we've got some really good players, so I'm hoping for big things from them . . .' grins Ed, delighted to be talking about his beloved football. 'With any luck I'm pretty much going to be glued to the box these days. Thank goodness for Sky Sport, hey?'

'I bet the missus isn't too happy about that,' grins Miles, nudging Ed knowingly.

Ed smiles uncomfortably and I get the feeling that Miles might have touched on a sore subject there. Oh dear, I hope I haven't caused any trouble with that silly wish of mine.

'Erm, Heather?' Gabe is looking at me with a nervous expression. 'About this custard stuff you all love . . .'

I glance at his bowl. His spoon is standing upright.

'I don't suppose you'd have any ice-cream,' he asks apologetically.

'Is it that bad?' Shit, I really must be an awful cook. I can't even make custard from a packet.

'Worse,' he confesses, trying not to a smile.

'There might be some Häagen Dazs left from when I was last here,' I whisper, not wanting Miles and Ed to hear me and want some too. Not that they're listening. Their conversation has moved on to the housing market. 'I'll go and look in the freezer.' Then I lean close to his ear: 'Meet me upstairs in the bedroom in five minutes.'

As soon as I've said it I realise how it sounds. 'So we don't have to share the ice-cream,' I explain hastily, indicating Ed and Miles who are also prodding warily at their custard.

But if Gabe notices my embarrassment, he doesn't show it. 'Which is our bedroom?' he asks.

'Up the stairs, first door on the right,'

'Cool.'

'I don't think you'll be saying that when you see the flowery wallpaper.' I smile ruefully and, taking his bowl of uneaten custard from him, I leave on my quest for double chocolate chip.

'Do you want to go on top or underneath?' One tub of ice-cream later, Gabe is looking at me with one eyebrow raised.

'Hmmm.' I pretend to think about it for a moment.

'Well?'

'I always like to go on top,' I confess, sticking the spoon back in the tub of Häagen Dazs and passing it to him.

He digs for chocolate chunks, then finds a large cluster. 'Well, that's lucky.' He stuffs the spoon into his mouth and chews with his mouth open, letting the ice-cream dribble down his chin. 'I prefer underneath.'

For the last five minutes Gabe and I have been standing at the doorway of my old bedroom, eating ice-cream and staring at the wooden bunk beds we're going to sleep in tonight. When I was ten years old bunk beds were cute and fun. Twenty years later things are rather different.

Fortunately, however, Gabe isn't unnerved by it and instead finds it amusing. Hence our *double-entendre*-laden conversation. Which is fun.

That's not fun, Heather. That's flirting.

Oh, my God, so it is. What am I doing? I have a boyfriend. A perfectly lovely boyfriend.

'I'm sorry – I'm a pig. I've finished it,' he says remorsefully, as he scrapes the bottom of the tub.

And Gabe has a girlfriend, I remind myself. A beautiful

Hollywood-actress-type girlfriend. 'Don't worry, I've had enough,' I say, suddenly uncomfortable.

'Oh, OK.' A little confused by this change in my mood, Gabe stops fooling around and puts down the empty tub. 'So, what now? Bed?'

It's an innocent enough question, but now I'm feeling so self-conscious that everything seems laden with innuendo. 'Yes, definitely. We'll need to get up early if you want to surf.' And then, just to make sure there is no room for misunderstanding, I throw in a yawn for good measure. 'And I'm exhausted.'

'Well, if you want to use the bathroom first . . .'

'No, it's fine.' I say briskly. Grabbing hold of a pillow I begin to plump it vigorously for want of something else to do. All this standing around in my bedroom is making me jumpy. 'I'll go after you. It's at the end of the corridor.'

'Well, if you're sure . . .'

'I'm sure.'

He bends down and rummages in his rucksack for his toothbrush. Out of the corner of my eye I can see him pushing up his glasses, which keep sliding down his nose, and try not to think how sweet he looks when he does it. No doubt he pushed his glasses up his nose yesterday, and the day before that, and the day before that. So why am I noticing it now? And why am I thinking it makes him look utterly adorable?

'Back in five.' He pulls out a toothbrush and some toothpaste, turns to leave, then pops his head round the door. 'In case I forget, I wanted to say your family are awesome. I had a great time tonight.'

'Me too.' I feel guilty for my earlier grumpiness.

'But there's something else . . . something I should've told you before . . .'

I stiffen. Crikey, what on earth's he going to say?

Taking a deep breath he makes his confession: 'I snore.'

Chapter Twenty-eight

The next morning dawns another beautiful August day. Like a cat basking in the sunshine, Port Isaac stretches out, its cobbled streets and whitewashed cottages gleaming in the bright sunlight. It's early and most of the village is still dozing. Down by the harbour, the wooden fishing-boats huddle quietly together, and around the cove, at the bottom of the steep grassy cliffs, the horseshoe shaped beach lies empty.

It's the same all along the rocky coastline to Newquay. The day-trippers haven't yet arrived, and for miles there's just the frothy white waves rolling in and out like big wet butter curls and the distant squawking of a flock of seagulls circling overhead.

But not everyone is a sleep. Further out from the shore, where the light is dancing on the waves like liquid diamonds, a dozen or so shapes bob up and down on the water. With their shiny black bodies they could easily be mistaken for seals, but if you look closer you'll see they're surfers waiting, watching for their next wave. Most are local men who rise at dawn every day – summer or winter – and rush down to the beach for a precious few hours.

And then there is Gabe.

Straddling the board he rented early this morning, he brushes wet, salty hair out of his eyes and concentrates on the horizon. He's been like that for the last few minutes, waiting for a set to come in. So far there have been a couple of meagre waves, nothing to get excited about, but now he sees something better.

Throwing his body flat on the board he begins paddling furiously. His hands are like mini-propellers, cutting through the water. It's all about timing. Co-ordination. Skill. Like a hunter chasing its prey, he focuses on the wave in the distance, moving closer and closer until, nimbly lifting his muscular body high into the air, Gabe plants his feet firmly on the board, his arms stretching outwards like a tightrope walker's as he catches the cusp.

He keeps his balance seemingly effortlessly, zigzagging backwards and forwards, faster and faster, swooping and dipping as the wave arches its back beneath him, trying to throw him off like a wild horse.

Click.

As the shutter of my camera releases I feel the glow of satisfaction. For the last hour or so I've been waiting for that exact shot. Sitting on this hillside running alongside the beach, I've been watching Gabe through the lens of my Nikon, trying to capture in one image the true emotion of surfing.

I'd forgotten how difficult, time-consuming and thrilling photography can be. When I first left college I was always taking photographs – it was like breathing, I had to do it every day – but in recent years I've stopped doing my own stuff. I tell myself it's because I'm busy taking photographs for a living but if I'm honest it's because it hurts too much: it's a painful reminder of all the hopes and dreams I had, and how I haven't achieved any of them.

Yet. I feel a tingle of excitement as I think about my letter to the *Sunday Herald.* Gabe posted it for me on Friday, so with any luck – I catch myself – with *my* luck, maybe I'll get a reply this week.

I feel a rush of positivity – the same positivity that prompted me to take my camera from the bedside cabinet where it had lain for months, clean the dust from the lens and bring it with me to Cornwall. The same positivity that woke me up early this morning full of anticipation for the photographs I would take.

I focus once more. Gabe is still riding the wave, but he's blurry now and I zoom in closer to catch the concentration on his face. His jaw is clenched and the sea sprays him with a salty film. I even catch a flash of his eyes, half hidden beneath the shaggy eyebrows. They seem to stare straight at me and then—

Crash. He's in the water.

Startled, I glance up from my camera and look out to sea. Without the magnification of my lens the rest of the surfers are now just tiny figures in the water. I scan backwards and forwards across the waves, glittering in the bright sunlight. But there's no sign of him.

'Gabe!' I yell, standing up on the hillside and waving my hands high above my head to make it easier for him to see me. Not that I'm worried or anything because I know he's a good swimmer. He's lived near the ocean all his life, he told me, and is practically a fish in water. But the currents are pretty strong around here, and if you're not used to them you could easily get caught up in one and dragged down under the water and . . . My mind spirals.

'Gabe!' I shout louder this time. Shit, if anything's happened to him I'll never forgive myself. I should've told him to be careful, warned him about the undertow, taken more responsibility . . . I click on the lens cap, I take the camera from round my neck and hold it as I make my way down the hillside, tripping on tufts of grass.

It seems to take for ever, but eventually I reach the car park at the bottom and look again at the beach. There's still no sign of him.

Now I'm fretting. Something's wrong. Tugging off my socks and trainers I discard them by the bike and jump over the wall. My bare feet land on the soft, damp sand and I run into the sea. Breathlessly I scan the water. I can see lots of other surfers but no Gabe. Where the fuck is he?

Panic takes a stranglehold. What if he's hit his head and is lying unconscious in the water, or badly hurt or—

I've got to do something – alert the lifeguard or ring 999 or . . . A sob escapes. I so wish he was here.

'*Boo!*'

I almost jump out of my skin and swing round, clutching my chest.

Gabe is standing behind me holding his board, with a grin spread across his face.

I feel a burst of heady relief – followed swiftly by fury.

'What the fuck?' I yell. 'You nearly frightened me to death.'

'Hey, c'mon, it was a joke.'

'A joke?' I shriek. 'I thought you'd drowned!'

'I wiped out and when I came to the surface I was on the other side of the cove.'

'But I was looking for you and shouting—' I break off, furious that tears are pricking my eyes.

'You know you're cute when you're angry.'

I throw him an evil glare. 'You are *so* not funny.'

'Of course I'm funny. It's my business to be funny.' He laughs with mock-indignation. 'I'm a stand-up comedian, remember?'

Now this is the point where I probably ought to keep my mouth shut . . . 'Well, that's another thing.'

Except I don't.

'I hate stand-up comedy.'

No sooner have the words flown out of my mouth than I want to stuff them back in.

For a moment there's silence and then, 'You hate stand-up?' Gabe is staring at me in astonishment. 'And you don't think I'm funny?'

Oh, fuck. I consider bluffing briefly, but realise it's no use and shake my head meekly.

'*At all?*'

I move my head just a twitch, hardly daring to look him in the eye, but when I do I see his solemn blue eyes filled with hurt. I wince. Me and my bloody big mouth. What did I have to go and say that for? I'm such a stupid idiot.

And then when I'm in the middle of beating myself up, Gabe throws back his head and roars with laughter. Literally *roars*, his jaws so wide I can see every single one of his gleaming white molars.

Confused, I watch him until he grabs my hands and snorts, 'I might not be funny but, goddamn it, you are, Heather Hamilton.'

I'm bewildered and humiliated. 'I thought you were dead,' I protest.

He smiles sheepishly. 'I know and I'm sorry. I shouldn't laugh.' He picks up his board, tucks it under his arm, and we start to make our way up the beach towards the car park. We walk in silence, until Gabe turns to me, eyebrows raised. 'So, c'mon, the suspense is killing me, why don't you think I'm funny?'

I squirm. He is never going to let this drop, is he? But maybe he should know, constructive criticism and all that. Maybe he'll even thank me for it. 'I saw you rehearsing and I just don't think you should pretend to be someone you're not,' I blurt finally.

'What do you mean?' Gabe seems more than a little offended and I regret my bold honesty-is-the-best-policy strategy.

'You know, being *angst*-ridden, chain-smoking, all those stupid voices and daft jokes, all that anger and negativity.' In for a penny, in for a pound.

'Comedians are *supposed* to be angry and negative,' points out Gabe.

'But you're not,' I say simply. 'You're easy-going and laid-back, and most of the time you're pretty happy.' I allow myself a smile. 'You're American – what do you expect? You're from the world that has a nice day.'

'But it's part of the act,' he protests, pushing back his wet hair.

'But that's just it. It's an act. Why can't you be yourself?'

'I've spent thousands asking my shrink the same question,' he wisecracks.

There's a pause.

'Oh, I dunno.' Suddenly serious, Gabe glances at me sideways, and I see that he's using flippancy to cover something that's a big deal for him. 'I guess I've never thought about it before but maybe I don't think I'm funny as plain old me.'

'But you're much funnier when you're being plain old you. Forget the jokes and talk about you.'

'But is anyone going to want to hear about me?'

'Try it and see.'

At the bike, Gabe digs out the towel he's packed under the seat, and sits on the wall to dry his hair. 'For someone who hates stand-up, you've sure got a lot of opinions on it,' he says.

I shrug. 'I'm sorry, I've got a big mouth. Next time tell me to shut up.'

He laughs. 'So, what now?'

'What do you feel like doing?'

'I'm easy,' he says, unzipping his wetsuit.

I resist the urge to make a *double-entendre*. 'Well, how about I give you a guided tour of the village before lunch?' I suggest.

'Great. You mean I get to be a real American tourist?'

'You *are* a real American tourist,' I remind him teasingly.

He screws up the towel and chucks it at me. 'Shut up, Heather.'

Chapter Twenty-nine

'This is my old school.'

'Wow, it's so cute,' marvels Gabe, peering at the small stone building tucked away at the end of the street. 'Like a little doll's house.'

'You're just used to everything in the States being so big.' I grin good-naturedly. 'Don't tell me, your school was the size of a football pitch?'

'No, I went to Venice High. Remember *Grease*, the movie?'

'That was your school?'

'Yep.'

'Crikey, how glamorous.'

Gabe bursts out laughing.

'What's so funny?'

'Believe me, Venice High is anything but glamorous.'

We continue up the steep hill and pass the post office, ablaze with hanging baskets. 'You mean Port Isaac is more exciting than Hollywood?' I gesture to a sleepy tabby cat on the window-ledge and a little old lady hobbling out clutching her shopping basket.

'You'll have to come visit some time, see for yourself. I have a spare room.'

'Don't tempt me.'

'But I'll need to make up some house rules . . .' He grins and I blush, remembering my own list, which was several pages long.

'And this is where I had my first kiss,' I announce, gesturing to a spreading oak tree, tucked away at the edge of a field. 'His name was Seb Roberts and I was thirteen.'

'What an awesome place for a first kiss. Mine was in the den at home and my mom caught me. There I was with my hands up Hopey Smith's T-shirt, feeling up her trainer bra. Boy, I have never been so embarrassed.'

I laugh, then feel a twinge of sadness. 'I remember wanting to run home and tell Mum all about Seb, but she'd died the year before . . .'

Gabe reaches out and squeezes my hand. 'Hey, I'm sorry, I didn't think.'

'It's fine, honestly,' I reassure him. 'It's just the little things that make you remember.'

We stare at the oak tree, its mighty trunk all knotted and twisted. It's been there for years and it will remain there for years.

'But I had my father instead. He was my surrogate mum. Growing up I confided everything in him, I still do. That's why we're so close.'

'Is that why things are difficult with your stepmom?'

We've started walking down the hill.

'What do you mean?'

'Two's company, three's a crowd . . .'

'No, it's not that. She's just not a particularly nice person. She's really cold, always has been. We've never got on.'

'But your father must like her.'

'I guess so. I don't know why. Mum was so full of life, always laughing and fun. Rosemary is serious, nagging him to do this and that. It drives me crazy.'

'Maybe that's her way of caring.'

'Well, its a funny one,' I grumble. 'But less about Rosemary.' I stop in front of the Badgers Arms. 'Have you worked up an appetite yet with all this sightseeing?'

'As if you have to ask. I could eat a horse.'

'I don't know about that,' I laugh, 'but what about a ploughman's?'

'What the hell's that?'

'Aha.' Pushing open the door to the pub I hold it open for him to pass. 'That's for me to know and you to find out.'

* * *

After placing our order, we carry two pints of cider into the garden where we find my family clustered round a wooden table eating lunch.

'We were wondering where you two had got to,' booms Lionel, through a mouthful of Cheddar cheese and Branston. Ripping off a chunk of bread he beams at us jovially.

'We got up early so Gabe could surf.' I plonk down my cider and kiss Lionel's cheek.

'How does it match up to California?' asks Ed, surfacing from beneath the *Sunday Times* sports section, which, according to the headline, appears to be devoted to the England football team.

'Yeah, it was awesome.'

'Good waves, huh?' chimes in Miles, trying to sound knowledgeable when I know he hasn't a clue. He's sitting next to Annabel and they're each holding a twin's reins and looking harassed as usual.

'Come on, budge up, everyone,' instructs Lionel, who has noticed us hovering.

'No, it's OK, we can sit over there.' I gesture over to where a couple are leaving the next table.

'Nonsense,' says Lionel. 'A family that eats together stays together.'

Everyone shuffles up obligingly and a gap opens next to Rosemary. I glance at it with dismay. She's the last person I want to sit next to. Fortunately Gabe slides along the bench first, and I throw him a grateful smile.

'You know, we've got to stop meeting like this,' he quips lightheartedly and Rosemary blushes like a schoolgirl, and dabs her frosted-pink mouth with a napkin.

'Two Cheddar-cheese ploughmans,' hollers a voice, and we look up to see a ruddy-faced member of staff carrying two large plates. We wave her over and she puts them down before us.

Gabe stares at his, bemused. 'What's this?' he asks, spearing a pickled onion with his fork.

'Try it. You'll love it.'

Bravely he takes a bite and the whole table falls quiet as we wait for his reaction. There's the sound of crunching and then, 'Eugggh, you eat these for pleasure?'

Everyone laughs. Honestly, his expression is priceless. In fact, I'm laughing so much I reach for a napkin to wipe my eyes when I hear a voice: 'Heather?'

And get the shock of my life.

'James?'

The laughter dies in my throat. 'What on earth are you doing here?' I gasp, then add quickly, 'I thought you were in Paris?'

'I managed to fly back early.'

'But how . . .'

'I had your address so I drove straight to the cottage. When you weren't there I guessed you might be at the pub, Sunday lunchtime and all that . . .'

The table has fallen silent again but I can feel looks flying around. Which is when I realise how this must seem. Gabe and I and my family, all together, all laughing, all very cosy. Abruptly it dawns on me that I shouldn't still be sitting on the other side of the table from James. I should be jumping up to give him a hug. I should be delighted he's made such an effort in coming all this way to see me. I should be introducing him excitedly to my family.

I leap up and throw my arms round him. 'Everyone, this is James. My boyfriend,' I add in explanation. As I say the word 'boyfriend' I catch Gabe's eye and look away, feeling awkward.

There's a murmur of 'Pleased to meet you' but none, I have to say, with the same enthusiasm that greeted Gabe. Even Rosemary, whom I'd thought would be firing questions, is now so taken with Gabe she barely gives James a second glance.

'Do you want to order some food?' I try to make amends, but James shakes his head.

'No, thanks, I've already eaten. I'll just grab myself a drink at the bar. Would anyone else like one?'

'Another glass of merlot,' says Lionel, jovially.

'I'll come with you,' I offer.

'No, it's fine, you carry on with your lunch.' He says it without a hint of sarcasm, but it still stings.

'Well, if you're sure . . .'

'Positive,' he says, and turning, he walks stiffly across the grass and disappears inside the pub.

'I can't believe you didn't tell me you were coming.' Holding my hair back against the wind, I turn to James. We've left everyone at the pub and are walking hand in hand along the rocky clifftop that fringes the beach. The same beach where only a few hours ago I'd been with Gabe.

'I wanted it to be a surprise.'

It was certainly that.

'I felt terrible cancelling at the last minute.'

'It's OK. Don't worry about it. I got a lift with Gabe.'

'I noticed,' he says evenly, and I can tell from his expression that he's not exactly happy I rode pillion on my flatmate's motorbike.

'Well, I thought with him being Californian he'd like to surf, and he's never been to Cornwall before and—' I stop trying to justify myself. 'Though it was a bit scary on the bike,' I admit.

'I can imagine.' His face softens. 'But don't worry, you'll be in the Range Rover on the way home. Heated seats and all.'

I feel a twinge of disappointment. The bike might have been terrifying, but it was also an incredible thrill.

'And I brought along some brochures on Tuscan villas you might want to look at on the ride back. I remember you saying you've always wished you could own one, and I know it's not the same but I thought maybe we could rent one this summer.'

I gaze at him in amazement. He thinks of everything. I can't remember mentioning it to him, but I suppose I must have. He pulls me close and wraps his arms round me. 'I've provisionally booked one in Florence that I think you'll love.'

Despite his good intentions, I can't help feeling annoyed. Suddenly my fantasy of lazing around a villa in Tuscany doesn't belong to me any more: it belongs to James and his brochures. 'Are you sure you're OK to drive back tonight?' I ask, changing the subject. 'It's just that I've got this meeting tomorrow morning with Lady Charlotte so I have to go home.' I roll my eyes. 'This wedding's a bit of a nightmare.'

'Hey, it's fine. I've got work too. I just wanted to come down and meet your family.'

'But I feel terrible you had to drive all this way.'

'A promise is a promise,' he says quietly, silencing me with a kiss. 'And, anyway, I missed you.'

Only now, hearing those words, does it occur to me that, actually, I haven't missed him at all. In fact, until he appeared I'd forgotten about him. But that's only because I've been so busy with my family and Gabe and . . . well, everything, I tell myself firmly. And banishing my doubts, I kiss him back. 'I missed you too.'

'You're leaving already?' It's late afternoon and Lionel is hugging me goodbye on the little patch of front lawn, 'Can't you stay a bit longer? It's quiz night this evening at the Forrester's. What do you say we go down and clean the place up, hey?' he says hopefully. Squeezing him tightly, I smile apologetically.

'Sounds great, but I've got to get back to London. *Work*,' I add, pulling a face.

'It was lovely to meet you, Mr Hamilton.' James holds out his hand formally.

Lionel ignores him. 'I've got a lovely ripe Brie and a bottle of shiraz I've been saving,' he continues, pretending he hasn't heard what I said. He always does this when people say something he doesn't want to hear. Usually it's when Ed's nagging at him to go on a diet and do more exercise. 'We can have it later to celebrate our win.'

'*Lionel*,' Rosemary reprimands him, placing a bony hand on his flannel bicep as if to hold him back, 'didn't you hear what Heather said? She has to go to work tomorrow. People don't just stop getting married because you've got a lovely Brie.' She smiles at James and takes his hand. 'So lovely to meet you at last, James. We were beginning to wonder if you were a figment of Heather's overactive imagination.'

I roll my eyes but James smiles, says he'll wait for me in the car, then strides across the gravel to where the Range Rover's parked, and Gabe is packing his stuff into the little panniers on the sides of the bike. He looks up and throws me a look of sympathy.

'Actually, no one's getting married tomorrow. It's in a couple of weeks, a huge society wedding,' I say proudly, to Rosemary. I know it's supposed to be a secret, but I can't resist: 'The daughter of the Duke and Duchess of Hurley.'

'You mean Lady Charlotte?' asks Rosemary, visibly impressed. 'She was in *OK!* last week doing a fashion shoot.'

'Don't you mean the *Lady*?' asks Annabel, crossly.

'Oh, yes, of course, dear,' says Rosemary, meekly.

'Well, it's been a pleasure, you guys.'

In his leathers, Gabe is giving everyone bear-hugs, even Ed. Annabel and the twins run towards him, arms outstretched. 'I'll see you back at the apartment,' he says, when he gets to me.

'Flat,' I correct him, giving him a hug.

'Apartment,' he repeats stubbornly.

He strides off towards his bike, and I turn to Lionel. 'James is waiting. I'd better go.' I wrap my arms round him again and kiss his cheek. 'But I'll see you soon.'

'Righty-ho.' He smiles, but his eyes are glistening and he's fiddling with his neckerchief, as he always does when he's upset. 'Rosemary and I are thinking of staying here the rest of the week, but I'll call you.'

James pulls up next to us in the Range Rover and I climb into the passenger seat and slide down the window, while my father, who swore to Ed and me when mum died that he would never say goodbye to us, waves me off as he always does.

'See you later, alligator,' he says softly.

'In a while, crocodile,' I reply as always.

Fastening my seatbelt, I wave as hard as I can out of the car window as we race down the driveway in a cloud of dust and fumes. I keep waving until my wrist hurts.

Chapter Thirty

'Absolutely no shots of your cankles . . . I mean ankles?' I repeat. 'Er . . . yes, I'm sure that can be arranged.'

It's early the next morning and I'm in the office on the telephone to Lady Charlotte, who rang the moment I walked through the door. Usually Brian likes to answer the phone in the morning, while I sort out the mail and make coffee, but today he fled into the kitchen cooing 'Fancy a Nescafe Gold Blend?' Which is what I'd call passing the buck.

Or, in this case, the bride.

I open the large leatherbound diary we keep on the desk and turn to the date of her wedding. Already it's filled with dozens of notes. Resignedly I grab a pen. Although it's amazing for business that we're doing her wedding, the woman is an unbelievable nightmare. Even more unbelievable is that someone wants to marry her. Although he's probably one of those chinless Hooray Henry types she's always being photographed with, I tell myself consolingly. 'Don't worry, your ankles will be . . . er . . . strictly off limits,' I say, as she continues ranting in my ear. 'Oh, OK. Instead, you want lots of . . .' Surely she didn't just say what I thought she just said. *Did she?* 'I'm sorry, could you repeat that?' I ask gingerly.

Brian appears and hangs over my shoulder to see what I've just written. 'Tits?' he says loudly

Flapping my hand at him to be quiet, I strain to hear what she's saying, which isn't easy as she has a nasal sort of voice.

'Mummy and Daddy have just spent a fortune on my breast augmentation – it's their wedding present to us. As I said to my fiancé, Daniel, which would you prefer? Dreary old china or perfect titties?'

'Daniel?' I repeat, before I can stop myself. After all this time that name still gives me a twinge.

'Yes, Daniel Dabrowski. He's a sculptor.'

It's as if someone's kicked me hard in the stomach.

'He's from Russia,' she continues.

'Actually he's Polish,' I say before I can stop myself. It's too much of a coincidence. There can't be two Daniel Dabrowskis who are sculptors. 'He was born in Krakow.'

'What?'

The indignation in her voice is like a slap in the face, and I pull myself together. I *can't* endanger this wedding. 'I once saw an exhibition of his . . .' I fib, voice wavering, 'and there was some information about him.'

How can I tell her that he's my ex-boyfriend and I know every last thing about him? Or I did, I think, as his fiancée snappily informs me that her manicurist has arrived and rudely hangs up. Because now, I realise, I know nothing about him.

'So,' says Brian, reappearing with two steaming mugs of instant coffee and a couple of berry bran muffins from the deli round the corner. They're my favourite, but my appetite has now deserted me. 'What did Bridezilla want this time?' Perching on a stool and crossing his legs, he eyes me with a mixture of sympathy and amusement.

I gulp some coffee. 'It's all written down in the book,' I say, passing it to him. It's the shock more than anything. Daniel? Getting married? And not to just anyone but to a twenty-one-year-old heiress?

'What is this? A wedding or a glamour shoot?' grumbles Brian, tearing off a piece of muffin.

I can't believe it. I wished for a miracle to get the business out of trouble and we got one. But I never wanted that miracle to be my ex-boyfriend's wedding.

'Heather? Are you OK? You've gone white.'

'Me, yeah, I'm fine.' I force myself to tune back in, but it's a struggle.

'I was saying, what will she think of next time?'

'You mean there's going to be a next time?' For a split second I consider explaining to Brian that I can't do this, but then I see the post lying on the side. Bills, bills and more bills. I file them with the rest in the overflowing tray next to the computer. I can't tell Brian. I've got to do this.

'Of course,' Brian is saying, as he glances over my shoulder at the clock on the wall. It's an official Prince Charles and Lady Di wedding souvenir and has a painted portrait of them on the face and the words '*A Fairytale Romance*'. 'And I'd say, in less than an hour.'

'I heard her leave two messages on the machine before either of you arrived,' chimes in Maureen, the cleaner, appearing from the kitchen in her checked overalls and brandishing her beloved Dustamatic. She flicks the switch with her trigger finger and hoovers round the windowsill. 'If you ask me, she sounds like a right madam.'

'Nobody did ask you, Maureen,' mutters Brian, into his coffee.

Fortunately she can't hear him over the noise of the vacuum.

'Well, this time it's your turn to answer the phone. I'm going into the darkroom. There's a dozen rolls of film from the mock-Tudor wedding that still need developing.' I head into the back. I need time and space to collect my thoughts.

'Actually, I might have to pop out.'

'Pop out?' I stop dead in my tracks.

'Only for half an hour,' he protests. 'I need to sort out my costume for tonight.'

Of course. Tonight's *The Rocky Horror Show*. I'd forgotten. Unlike Brian, who's been looking forward to it for months.

'You know what it's like,' Brian is saying. 'I've got absolutely nothing to wear . . .'

'Hark at him,' snorts Maureen, nudging me with a bony elbow.

'Well, some of us like to make a bit of an effort,' barks Brian, then jumps backwards as Maureen lunges at him with the Dustamatic. Only it's not a big enough jump and the nozzle attaches itself to his jacket. A small – yet aggressive – battle ensues between him and our cleaner.

'Brian . . .' I plead, but he's busy freeing his gilt buttons from the machine's powerful suction, then making for the door.

'Don't worry, I'll be back in a jiffy,' he says, lying blatantly. I know Brian. He does nothing in a jiffy. Everything takes hours of indecision.

'Well, in that case I'll leave the answering-machine on,' I threaten, playing him at his own game. 'That way you can call her when you get back.' Pleased with my quick thinking, I lean back against the filing cabinet.

'Oh, didn't I tell you? I gave her your mobile number, just in case.'

He ducks as I throw a muffin at him, but I've got a pretty good aim. It hits the back of his head, showering him with a confetti of berry bran crumbs as he dives, laughing, out of the door.

Several minutes later I'm in the darkroom, tugging the cord that switches on the special developing light. Immediately, I'm bathed in a crimson glow and flop on to a stool to absorb the shock of discovering that Daniel is soon to marry Lady Charlotte.

After a moment, I pull myself together. OK, so he's getting married. So bloody what? If he got down on one knee and asked you to marry him right this minute, Heather, would you? No, you wouldn't. And why not? Because he's a liar and a cheat, because you have a perfectly lovely new boyfriend called James and because . . .

Well, just because. I stand up and turn my attention to the mess that is our darkroom filing system. From now on I'm going to block Daniel out of my mind. Now where did I put those films?

After a good fifteen minutes I unearth them and flick on the CD player. This time it's *Chess* and, glad of the distraction, I hum along as I prepare the developing trays. I'm getting to like these musicals and feel a little burst of happiness as I recognise the opening chords of the duet between Elaine Page and Barbara Dickson. I lean over to turn up the volume and hear the jingling ring of my mobile.

My heart sinks. Lady Charlotte? *Already?*

I pick up my phone and stare at the caller ID. 'Private Caller.' Usually I don't answer withheld numbers: they're either credit-card companies demanding money or Blockbuster wanting to know the whereabouts of *Swept Away*. But now all that's changed. I made the minimum payments this month and the video appeared a few days ago on top of the telly, completely out of the blue.

Well, not completely, I correct myself, thinking about the lucky heather with a sense of satisfaction. These days, things have a habit of happening to me out of the blue.

'Hello?' Wondering what Lady Charlotte is going to demand this time, I grab a piece of paper, then rummage around for a pen.

'Hi, is it possible to speak to Heather Hamilton?'

I'm surprised to hear a male voice, oldish-sounding and very well spoken. Probably the butler.

'Speaking,' I grunt, tugging out a drawer and rifling through it. Bloody hell, how am I supposed to find anything in this mess?

'Oh, hello, Ms Hamilton, this is—'

'Sorry, can you hang on a minute.' I press my shoulder against the drawer, reach deep inside, right up to my armpit, and grope around. God, you'd think there'd be a biro in here somewhere!

'If this isn't a good time . . .' In the background I can hear the voice on the phone still talking.

Damnit. I give up. I'll have to use my eyeliner.

'. . . perhaps I can call back later.'

I bring my hand out of the drawer and stare at the mouthpiece. Did he say *later*?

A wicked thought pops into my head. Well, it *is* Brian's turn, I tell myself, sorely tempted to tell the butler to call the office later.

But then the sensible assistant takes over. Lady Charlotte might be Bridezilla, and she might be marrying my ex, but her wedding is bringing Together Forever back from the brink of bankruptcy. And saving my job.

'No, now's fine,' I say resignedly, pulling my kohl pencil out of my makeup bag. 'OK, so what are Charlotte's latest demands . . . I mean, thoughts?'

'Charlotte?' repeats the voice at the other end of the line. It sounds rather snappy.

'Sorry, *Lady* Charlotte,' I correct myself quickly. Honestly, all this title business is ridiculous. I'm reminded of Gabe's comment about her not necessarily being a lady, and smile.

'Look, I think there's been some mistake,' says the voice. Now I detect the faint drawl of an American accent and feel a prickle of doubt. Perhaps it isn't Lady Charlotte's butler. In which case it must be someone from one of the credit-card companies after all.

Like American Express.

No sooner has the thought popped into my head than footage of me buying up half of Knickerbox begins playing in my mind like film from a CCTV camera. Oh dear, I'd forgotten about that. It was all the new sexy underwear I bought last week. 'I'm sorry – is this about the three hundred pounds I spent on lingerie?'

'No, it isn't,' says the voice impatiently. 'It's about a job vacancy.'

'At American Express?' I frown. How strange. It must be some weird promotion thingy they're doing.

'No, at the *Sunday Herald*.'

It's a moment before the words register.

'Did you just say the *Sunday Herald*?' I whisper.

'That's right.'

My chest tightens a notch, as if I've fastened a button on my cardigan. 'And you are?'

'Victor Maxfield, the editor.'

'Oh, my Lord, it is. It really is. I'm speaking to the editor of the

Sunday Herald. Right now. On my mobile. And any minute now I'm going to pass out from lack of oxygen, I realise, as it dawns on me that I'm holding my breath. Crumpling on to a stool I inhale deeply. 'Gosh, I wasn't expecting this. You see, I thought you were somebody else.'

'So it seems,' says the voice, and although I can't see Victor Maxfield, I could swear he's smiling now. 'But I wanted to call as I'm going to be out of the office from Wednesday. It's my annual fishing trip up to Scotland, a little place called Loch Kulloch . . .'

As I listen to him I almost have to pinch myself – it's so surreal.

'Have you ever been to Scotland, Miss Hamilton?'

'No, never . . .' I stammer.

'Well, you should, my dear. It's a remarkable place. I'm American and we've got some beautiful scenery in the States, but having moved to this little island of yours over twenty years ago, I have to say Scotland beats it all, what with the mountains and the moors and, of course, your namesake.'

'Sorry?'

'Heather!' he exclaims. 'The moors are covered with it. Purple and white heather – as far as the eye can see.'

His deep voice resonates in my ear and I feel a tingle all over. Heather. Lucky heather. My lucky heather. All at once I get a dizzy sensation, as if I've been spun round quickly and made to open my eyes, and the room is swaying and blurring in the crimson light. I grip the stool to regain my balance but all I'm aware of is my heart beating in my chest, my ribcage moving up and down, a strange buzzing in my ears. It could be just nervousness, surprise or faintness, but it feels like something more. Like all my dreams are running up through my toes to my fingertips, and down the phone line. All the way to Victor Maxfield, the man with the power to make them come true.

'So, are you free tomorrow morning for an interview? I know it's a bit short notice, but no time like the present, hey?'

'Yes, of course. Tomorrow sounds great.'

'Grand. I'll see you around nine, then. You know our address, I take it?'

'Yes, thanks.' How could I not? It's imprinted on my brain.

And then he hangs up. An interview. At the *Sunday Herald*. It's just like Gabe said. It's just what I wished for.

'Heather?'

A firm rap at the door startles me, and I jump. It's Brian, back already.

'Er, yes, hang on a minute.' I stand up quickly, and stuff my phone into my bag. I feel guilty about my conversation with Victor Maxfield, as if I'm somehow being unfaithful to Brian, even though he's always encouraging me to follow my dreams.

I flick open the lock and reach for the door handle. On second thoughts perhaps it's best to be honest and tell him now about the interview. I don't like keeping secrets from him and he'll probably be delighted for me anyway. 'Hey, Brian, guess what? . . .' I open the door.

'Ta-dah.'

My mouth opens and closes.

It's Cher.

'So, what do you think?'

Standing in the doorway is a vision in suspenders, fishnet stockings and a long curly black wig. 'I'm a *trrrransexual* from Transylvania,' pouts Brian, kicking his leg menacingly.

I stare at him wordlessly. I have to admit, Brian has exceedingly good legs.

Dropping the act, he smiles sheepishly. 'Sorry, I was getting a bit carried away there. What were you saying?'

'Oh, nothing,' I say causally. Now no longer seems the right time to tell him about the interview. I reach out and twang a suspender. 'I'll tell you later.'

Chapter Thirty-one

A white minivan honks loudly, the driver hanging out of the window to shout something I can't quite catch – and having seen what he's doing with his tongue, I don't want to.

As I walk through the grey concrete jungle of Hammersmith with Brian, I keep my head down and my eyes focused on the chewing-gum spotted pavement. Anything to avoid the gawps. It's been like this all the way from the office: slack-jawed pensioners freezing with their shopping outside Marks & Spencer, groups of snickering teenagers elbowing each other furiously, boozy businessmen in the etched window of the Rat and Parrot draining their pints in silent disbelief. Earlier, some Japanese tourists even asked us for a picture. You'd think no one has ever seen a sixtysomething man in suspenders, a PVC basque and four-inch stilettos before.

It's just after seven and Brian and I are making our way to the nearby Apollo Theatre to see *The Rocky Horror Show*.

'Perhaps we should have taken a cab,' Brian complains as he stops yet again to do up one of his suspenders. Tutting impatiently, he fumbles with the fasteners, his slim hands, so dexterous when it comes to the intricate workings of a Hasselblad camera, now a pair of clumsy ornaments. 'Jesus, how do you birds cope?'

'Birds have feathers, Brian,' I point out stonily. '*Women don't.*' Folding my arms across my pink cardiganed chest, I catch my reflection in the window of Starbucks. I'm wearing a pleated pink skirt, American tan tights and a pair of lace-up shoes I've had since I was seventeen when I worked as a Saturday sales assistant at Dolcis.

The outfit was Jess's idea. She's one of those huge fans who've seen the show about a hundred times and know all the steps to the Time Warp. She organised the whole thing, ringing the tickets hotline months ago, lending me her spare costume and excitedly telling me I'd make 'the perfect Janet'. Her enthusiasm was so infectious I felt quite chuffed by the compliment. Only the problem with Jess is she does tend to go over the top. I stare doubtfully at my frumpy reflection. Think Doris Day in Hush Puppies.

Honestly, I don't want to sound like a spoilsport, but when people say fancy dress is fun, *who* exactly is it supposed to be fun *for*?

By the time we reach the theatre it's nudging dusk. Purplish grey smudges of clouds are hanging above the trees, like big fat bruises, providing a backdrop for *The Rocky Horror Show*, which is illuminated in shimmering white lights on the theatre. Crowds of outrageously dressed people are milling around outside, practising their steps to the Time Warp and comparing costumes. Scanning the throng for James, who said he'd meet me here, and Jess, who was coming along with a crowd of air stewards, I squeeze past a giant of a man covered with tattoos and sporting fishnets and black suspenders like Brian's. It's perturbing at first, but I'm getting used it. Everyone – I repeat, *everyone* – is wearing fishnets.

Brian leads the way and I follow him into the foyer. Which is when I hear a peal of throaty laughter, shooting like an arrow above the chattering buzz. It's immediately recognisable.

'Jess!' I yell, and spot her surrounded by a group of handsome men with buffed arms. Obviously the air stewards. She throws her arms round me and gives me a hug. 'You look fantastic,' I gasp.

'You think so?' she says, and does a little twirl. She's wearing the obligatory basque, fishnets and stilettos, but all that Bikram yoga has paid off. I make a mental note to attempt a few sun salutations next time and not spend the whole lesson in a child's pose pretending I'm on my 'cycle'.

'So do you.' Her brow furrows. 'Hey, are you OK?'

Trust Jess. Only a best friend would notice I've got something on my mind. Momentarily I toy with not telling her, then realise how ridiculous that would be: I tell Jess everything. 'I just found out Daniel's getting married,' I say matter-of-factly.

She shuffles me into a corner. 'Married?' she hisses disbelievingly. 'To whom?'

'Well, you're never going to believe this . . .'

'Who?' she demands.

'Lady Charlotte.'

Jess's jaw drops. 'You're serious?'

'Deadly.'

'Bloody hell, Heather. How are you feeling?'

I shrug. 'You know.' She nods understandingly. 'But what's worse . . .'

'*There's worse?*' For Jess, this is an impossibility. To her, marriage is a race and you have to beat your ex to the finishing line. The other way round is the ultimate shame.

'Brian and I are the official wedding photographers.'

In a rare occurrence, Jess is rendered speechless. Then she finds her voice: 'Well, you're far nicer than her anyway. She's got cankles.'

Despite myself I have to smile: Lady Charlotte's cankles are obviously infamous.

'And as for that two-timing toad Daniel, you've met someone much nicer now. You said yourself, James is perfect.'

'You're right. I'm fine, honestly . . .'

'Oy, slut.'

Someone jeers as they walk past and I twirl round to see who's being shouted at. Then realise, with a shock, that it's me. 'Did you hear what he just called me?' I gasp, affronted.

'Get used to it, honey,' giggles one of Jess's stewards, who introduces himself as Neil and offers me honey-roasted peanuts. 'It's all part of the show. Whenever you see Brad on stage you shout, "Arsehole," and for Janet you shout, "Slut" ' He winks at Brian, who blushes and accepts a peanut. Strange, I could have sworn he told me he was allergic.

I turn back to Jess and put my hands on my hips in mock-offence. 'Are you trying to tell me something?' I pout good-naturedly.

She ignores me and grabs the elbow of a big, muscular man who's got his back to me. 'I want you to meet someone,' she says, unable to keep the pride out of her voice. 'Heather, this is Greg.'

He turns now and bats his false eyelashes at me. 'A pleasure,' he says, and smiles. And it's the smile I notice: crinkling up his mouth it stretches out a pale silvery scar that runs up through his Cupid's bow. It seems vaguely familiar.

'You too,' I smile back, trying to place him. Not easy when a man's wearing false eyelashes and women's lingerie. 'Have we met before?' I ask.

'Oh, no,' he says. 'I'd definitely remember you.' And he looks at me in a way that, if he wasn't with my best friend Jess, I'd think was flirting.

'So, where's your man?' asks Jess.

'Oh, Gabe mentioned something about going to his uncle's for dinner.' It's still niggling at me: where have I seen Greg before? It's like when you see a film and can't remember the name of an actor.

'I meant James,' she says pointedly.

'Oh, right, of course.' Why did I think she was talking about Gabe? 'He should be here in a minute – he's probably stuck in traffic.'

'Hey, the show's about to start. We should go in,' interrupts a steward, rescuing me.

'Yeah, come on, let's find our seats.' Jess links arms with Greg.

Everyone starts filtering off, leaving me in a rapidly emptying foyer waiting for James. It's getting really late. Where can he be?

'Excuse me, miss,' I feel a tap on my shoulder and turn round to see a uniformed attendant. 'You'll have to take your seat now or I can't let you in.'

The swirly carpet of the foyer is now empty, but for a few ticket stubs and scattered popcorn. Perhaps I missed his call in all the noise and confusion. I dig around in my bag and find my mobile, only to discovers there's no reception.

'Miss?'

The attendant is still waiting patiently.

'Oh, sorry.' I give the door a last hopeful glance, then reluctantly hand him my ticket. He tears off the stub and gives it back to me, then stands aside as I go into the theatre. I pause. 'If a tall, dark-haired man should arrive . . .' I hold out James's ticket.

'Of course.' He tucks it into his breast pocket. And, as he gives me a look that's so sympathetic it's obvious he thinks I've been stood up, I turn and hurry inside.

Chapter Thirty-two

The squeaking of the orchestra tuning up signals that the show's about to start and I quickly try finding my seat in the packed theatre. No doubt I'll be right at the back, slap-bang in the middle of a row as usual and I'll have to do the shuffling-along thing, apologising and trying not to trip over people's feet. I squint at the row numbers and glance wistfully to the front. There's a couple of empty seats right at the end of the row. Gosh, I wonder who's got those. I wish it was me.

Hang on a minute . . . In all the anxiety over James's no-show, I hadn't paid much attention to the row number on my ticket, but now . . . I double-check – that is me! A front-row seat! For once I'll be able to see everything rather than the back of someone's head. Cheered, I peer behind me at the rest of the theatre and spot Jess. She's waving at me and mouthing, 'Where's James?' I shrug a 'Don't know,' look, peer once more at my watch, then sit down next to Brian.

Only it's not Brian, I realise, as I turn to whisper in his ear. Brian has switched to sit next to Neil, leaving me beside a stranger. Which is fine, of course. I'm a big girl.

It's just that James's empty seat is on the other side of me. Staring at its big, velvet emptiness I feel a bit sorry for myself. And then, just as the novelty of feeling like a VIP in a front-row seat is wearing off and I'm spiralling into a host of anxieties about how I've been stood up, I'm going to have a horrible night and I might as well go home now, the orchestra strikes up, the curtains pull back and *The Rocky Horror Show* begins.

For the next hour I'm transported into an outrageously camp world of transsexuals from the planet Transvestite. The rest of the audience seems to know the entire script off by heart, erupting into greetings of 'arsehole' and 'slut' whenever Brad and Janet appear on stage and waving torches over their heads. Most of the time I'm at a loss as to what's going on and try to pick things up as the show progresses.

Which isn't easy, especially when someone passes me a newspaper for no apparent reason. What am I supposed to do with it? Not read it, that's for sure, I tell myself, looking at it distractedly and noticing it's the *Evening Standard*. Suddenly I get that weird sensation again, vibrating up through my finger-tips, which are smudged with ink from fingering the headline: 'LOTTERY JACKPOT STILL UNCLAIMED. WINNING TICKET FROM WEST LONDON.'

Oh, my goodness! It must be my stolen ticket!

I stare hard at the headline, my mind whirling, but now I'm being dragged to my feet to do the Time Warp and everyone's hands-on-hipping and I don't have time to think about anything but having stupid, ridiculous, outrageous fun.

'So, what did you think?'

The show's over and we're inching our way towards the exit through the crush of the crowds leaving the theatre. I grin at Jess, who's wrapped round Greg like a feather boa. 'It was great, really great,' I say, as I find myself still humming the Time Warp – God, that song's catchy.

'Even better than *Phantom*,' gushes Neil, and I see Brian glow with shiny-cheeked happiness – even though his face has swollen and gone all blotchy. See? I *knew* he had a nut allergy.

'Is anyone hungry? I know a place that does the best chicken tikka,' says one of the stewards, whose name I wish I could remember.

And then, of course, it comes to me in a flash: Rick.

'Nah, not for me, mate,' mutters Greg, who seems a little agitated. 'I've got to head back to Kent. Early start,' he explains, and throws an arm round a visibly dismayed Jess.

As we spill out into the cool evening darkness of the street I contemplate them together for a moment, a vague unease clinging to me. I try to put my finger on it, but I can't. Maybe it's nothing. Maybe I'm just being over-protective. After all, Jess seems to adore him.

'Heather? Is that you?'

A voice distracts me and I see a man walking towards me, dressed in black trousers, a checked jacket and a pair of thick-rimmed glasses.

'James?' I ask doubtfully.

'Yep, it's me,' he says, with a self-conscious smile.

'Hey, look, it's Brad,' whoops Rick. '*Arsehole.*' He's about to burst into hysterical laughter when he senses from my glower that perhaps this isn't the right time and quickly shrinks back.

'Sorry I was late. The show had already started. I tried calling you . . .'

'There was no reception in the theatre,' I explain. 'Have you been waiting long?'

'I had a drink at the pub and watched a bit of the rugby.' He gestures across the road. 'Though in this outfit I got some funny looks.' He runs his fingers over his shoulder-wide lapels.

My mouth twitches into a smile. 'You didn't have to wait for me, you know.'

'I know.' He pauses and we look at each other across the steps. Maybe I'm imagining it, but I can feel awkwardness between us. 'Do you want a lift home? My car's parked just over there.'

'Sure.' I realise that's an expression I've picked up from Gabe and add, 'That would be great, thanks.'

I turn to launch into a round of goodbyes, but everyone's arguing over whether to go for an Indian or Chinese and I change my mind. Better just to slip quietly away, I decide. Whispering to Brian that I'm leaving I hurry back to James before Jess sees him. I know she's dying to meet him and if she spots him, that will be it: interrogation time.

'So, how was the show?' asks James, as we walk towards the car.

'Great,' I say. 'But completely crazy.' I can't help noticing he's not holding my hand. Something's definitely up.

'Good,' he says evenly.

The conversation peters out and we fall silent.

We reach the car, James beeps the alarm and we climb inside. I sink back into the squashy leather seat and look out of the window as James pulls into the traffic. And then neither of us speaks for ages. Well, actually it's less than two minutes – I sneak a glance at the digital clock on the dashboard – but it *feels* likes ages. It's one of *those* silences. In the past I've heard couples talk about comfortable silences, as if it's something to aspire to, something to boast about, and I could never understand why. Now, sitting in James's Range Rover in a silence so claustrophobic I feel as if it's suffocating me, I understand perfectly.

'I wasn't waiting for you, I was waiting for me.'

For a moment I think he's talking to himself. But then he addresses me directly. 'Tonight. I waited for you because I needed to talk to you. We need to talk.'

At once I feel both relieved and apprehensive. Translated, I know this means *James* needs *me* to talk. I know this because I used to shout the same thing at Daniel because he would never open up to me. James, on the other hand, couldn't be more open: he's always wanting us to talk about things. So much so that it's exhausting.

Watching James raking his fingernails through his hair I begin hastily preparing a speech in my head about how much I like him but how things have been moving a little too fast.

'You're not in love with me, are you?'

Out of the blue, his words disarm me. 'Erm, well . . .' I abandon my gloriously inadequate speech. My knee-jerk reaction is to deny it, to persuade him otherwise. But what's the point? says a voice inside me. Why try to convince him *when you can't convince yourself*?

'No, I'm not,' I confess. 'I love everything about you, but I'm not in love with you.' As the words tumble out I feel an unexpected release. 'I'm sorry.'

'It's OK. I already knew,' replies James, and throws me a small smile as if to show that he's not angry with me. 'That night after dinner when we were in bed and I told you I loved you, I hoped you'd tell me you loved me . . .'

I feel a clench of regret.

'. . . but you didn't.'

'I didn't? But I thought . . .' I break off. My memory's a little blurry due to all that champagne, but I'm sure I told him I loved him. I just wish I hadn't, I think regretfully.

'You said, "Me too,"' says James, quietly. He pulls up at the traffic-lights. 'And we both know that's not the same as saying, "I love you."'

He's right. I didn't fool anyone. Not myself. And certainly not James. Meeting his gaze it occurs to me suddenly that I got my wish after all. Yet instead of relief, I feel only sadness.

'You said it to not hurt my feelings, and I appreciate that,' James is saying, 'but it's not enough. I want all of someone or nothing.'

Unexpectedly I feel horribly inadequate. 'I'm sorry, I don't know what's wrong with me.'

'There's nothing wrong with you, Heather.' He reaches across and slides his thumb down my cheek. 'But it might have helped if you weren't in love with another man.'

Incredulity stabs me.

'You mean my ex? No, you've got it all wrong,' I cry, animated in my denial. OK, I was shocked to hear he was getting married, but I'm not in love with Daniel any more.

'I'm not talking about your ex.'

I frown in confusion.

'I'm talking about your flatmate.'

'You think I'm in love with *Gabe*?' His words send me reeling, but for the briefest, most fleeting moment I dare to wonder if he's right. Is that why I hadn't fallen in love with James? But no sooner has the thought brushed my consciousness than I dismiss it. 'That's ridiculous,' I say indignantly.

'I saw you together in Cornwall,' he counters.

'But nothing happened. We're just friends.'

'I believe you,' he continues, 'but that doesn't mean the feelings aren't there.' He pauses, then says kindly, 'You might not be able to see it, Heather, but I can.'

The lights change and as we head up Ladbroke Grove towards Little Venice, I look across at James. Despite my indignation, I'm filled with a fondness for him. He's still being lovely even though we're breaking up and he thinks, wrongly or rightly, that I'm in love with another man. It makes me doubt my sanity. I mean, we've never had an argument, he's honest and romantic and amazing at foreplay – a bit *too* amazing. The man has no faults. He really is the perfect boyfriend.

And then it dawns on me. 'You really are the perfect man, James,' I say quietly. 'You're just too perfect for me.'

He looks bewildered.

'It's true. We never row, you like the same music, you love romantic comedies, you're a vegetarian, you buy me Tampax, you know how to find the G-spot without having to ask for directions . . . How *do* you do that?'

'Confidential information.' He taps his nose.

'And you even dressed as Brad for my Janet without me telling you.' I slump in my seat. 'Trust you. I mean you're so damn perfect I feel like a complete mess.'

'Yes, well, your bedroom was a bit—' He grimaces.

I blush with embarrassment as we turn into our street. He pulls up outside my flat, but keeps the engine running. 'Got to go find a space,' he explains ruefully. 'You know how it is.'

Actually, no. Since I got the lucky heather I always find a space when I wish for one. But I nod anyway. And then we just sort of look at each other.

'Well, I guess this is it,' he says after a moment.

'I guess so,' I agree, not quite sure what happens now. I'm used to break-ups that involve tears, arguments and emotions flying all over the place, but this is so amicable it's ridiculous. I lean across the handbrake and kiss his cheek. ''Bye, James.'

''Bye, Heather,' he says pleasantly, and returns the kiss.

I climb out of the car.

'Look after yourself. And no more flashing at me through the blinds or I'll have to ring the police,' he calls after me, as I climb the steps to my front door.

I twirl round. 'You *saw* me?'

'Not just me. I was having a dinner party,' he says, lips twitching. 'Great tits.' He winks and buzzes up his window.

Standing outside my flat, I watch as he accelerates out of my life. He was everything I wished for in a boyfriend, but in the same way that 'You can't buy love' I've learned you can't wish for it either. And, with a pang of sadness, I open the front door and go inside.

Chapter Thirty-three

That night I have the weirdest dream. I'm wearing a suit and walking through the revolving doors of the the *Sunday Herald* building. Ahead is an office with EDITOR etched on the door and on entering I see Victor Maxfield behind his desk. But when he stands up to shake my hand he's wearing suspenders and a basque, and we're not in his office any more, we're at a wedding and he's doing the Time Warp and Brian is photographing him and I'm throwing confetti.

Except it's not confetti: it's millions of tiny scraps of newspaper. And it's started raining and the tiny scraps have joined up to make one big newspaper – the *Sunday Herald* – and it's got my photograph on the front and I'm holding it over my head and running home in the storm. Then I see the old gypsy woman and gaze into her eyes, which glitter like tiny emeralds, and I watch them change into lapis-lazuli and suddenly I'm not looking into her eyes any more but Gabe's.

And he's laughing and laughing, only it doesn't sound like laughter, it sounds almost like a siren. And even though I'm covering my ears and trying to run away, it's getting louder and louder and louder—

I wake up with a start. Next to me on my bedside table my radio-alarm is wailing. I slam my hand on the snooze button and am just submerging beneath the covers again when I remember: I have my interview today.

I sit up on full alert, swing my legs over the side and sink my toes into my Ugg boots, which have been relegated to being a rather expensive pair of slippers – such is the fickleness of fashion. Hoisting myself out of bed, I tug on my dressing-gown and open my bedroom door.

The faint sound of the radio is wafting down the hallway, intermingled with a sickly sweet artificial smell. I've grown to recognise it these past few weeks: Pop-Tarts.

'Morning,' I say automatically, padding into the kitchen in the knowledge that I'm going to find Gabe curled over the toaster with a chopstick in his hand. And, sure enough, there he is, curled over the toaster with a chopstick in his hand, like a spear fisherman waiting for the moment to strike. But this morning he's so engrossed in singing along to Eddie Bedder on the radio that he doesn't hear me and I'm treated to an impromptu display of ball-scratching. It's almost as if he's playing an imaginary bass guitar, only *this* Fendi is in his Paisley-printed boxer shorts. Up and down, up and down goes his slow hand, his bony foot with the funny-shaped hammer toe tap-tapping along to Pearl Jam, the back of his hair all knotted up to resemble a sort of sandy Brillo pad.

Transfixed in the doorway I hear James, like a voiceover in my head: '. . . but it might have helped if you weren't in love with another man . . . your flatmate . . .'

Righteousness grips. I mean, honestly. What was James thinking? Me? In love with *that*?

In the middle of yawning like a hippopotamus, all flared nostrils, hundreds of big white molars and loud grunting, Gabe turns and sees me. His jaws snap shut. 'Oh, wow, Heather.' Like a thief who's been caught with his hands, quite literally, on the Crown Jewels, he yanks one free of his boxer shorts and pushes his glasses up his nose. 'I didn't see you there.'

'Uh-huh. So I gather.' I smile sweetly, flicking on the kettle and taking a mug from the cupboard. Feeling his embarrassment radiating like warmth from a storage heater, I innocently continue unwrapping a teabag, adding a teaspoon of sugar and grabbing a new carton of milk from the fridge as if nothing has happened.

'So, how was last night?' asks Gabe, trying to be nonchalant.

Crossing his legs and leaning back against the kitchen worktops, he tugs at his Mr-T T-shirt.

'You mean *The Rocky Horror Show*?' I say, trying to undo the milk carton. I've bent back the wings, like it says in the little diagram on the side, and I'm now pushing them forward to create a spout. Damn, I can never do it properly. In frustration, I tear a hole with my finger like I always do. 'Or the part where James dumped me?'

Gabe is staring at me blankly. 'Are you serious?' he asks.

'Uh-huh.' The kettle clicks off and I fill my mug.

He sucks his teeth, then exhales for a very long time. 'Shit,' he says eventually. 'I mean, I'm sorry. That sucks.'

'It's OK,' I shrug, pouring milk into my tea and dribbling all over the counter. Tearing off a paper towel I begin wiping up the spilt milk. It's true. I do feel completely OK about James because I realised last night that I was never in love with him. I was in love with the *idea* of him. 'It was very amicable,' I add.

I catch Gabe's eye and he looks down at his feet uncomfortably, as if he's afraid I'm going to start talking about feelings. But while normally this would have annoyed me, I'm delighted now by such good old-fashioned male avoidance. After my relationship with James I'm relieved *not* to have to talk about my feelings.

Fortunately we're distracted by the catflap and Billy Smith, who appears looking somewhat bedraggled. He miaows loudly.

'Someone's hungry for his breakfast.' I stroke his soft fur as he weaves round my ankles.

'I'm not surprised. He was pretty busy last night. Man, that kitty gets all the booty calls.'

'Booty calls?'

'You know, those phone calls late at night from some old boyfriend or a girl you had a fling with, calling you up and inviting you over for sex.'

'No, I don't know.' I pretend to be shocked.

And try not to think about that two a.m. text message I sent to Daniel a few months ago.

'Well, Billy Smith sure does.' Gabe is laughing now. 'I woke in the night to find a couple of stray cats sneaking through that kittyflap.'

I laugh too – it's impossible not to – and grab a tin of Fancy Feast to scoop it into a bowl while Billy Smith circles me like a shark. I put it on the floor and watch him pounce. His little pink raspy tongue devours it ravenously.

'Are you sure you're OK?' Gabe is watching me thoughtfully.

'I'm fine. Just a bit nervous.' I'm thinking of my imminent interview. I've been waiting for the right moment to tell him, and now I can't wait any longer. 'I . . .'

But he interrupts: 'Hey, don't worry. You're gonna be fine,' he rests his hand gently on my bare forearm. 'You've got Billy Smith and me . . .' He looks at me so intently that I feel a bit weird.

'No, I'm not nervous about being single,' I correct hurriedly.

Instantly his face colours and he moves away his hand. 'Oh, I misunderstood, I thought—'

'I'm nervous about my job interview,' I cut him off.

He looks astounded.

'At the *Sunday Herald*,' I add shyly.

'Whoo-hoo!' He throws his arms round me. 'That's awesome.'

I'm scooped into the air and twirled round, laughing with embarrassment. 'Hey, it's only an interview,' I protest, but his enthusiasm is infectious and by the time he's plonked me back on the lino I'm wearing a huge smile. Which freezes as Gabe goes to high-five me. Oh, no, not that again . . .

'Well, whatever.' He laughs, shrugging off my limp response and rubbing the back of his neck self-consciously. Then, refusing to let the American dream be dampened by English realism, he adds confidently, 'I know you'll get the job.'

Cradling my mug, I sink into a chair and take a sip of tea. My legs feel a bit wobbly and it's not from being twirled round. 'You think so?' I say, trying to sound cool and casual but failing. Hope is so audible in my voice it's doing a solo.

'*I know so*,' replies Gabe, fixing me with that look you see on the author photographs of self-help books. You know – the you-can-do-it-even-if-you-think-you're-crap look.

'Thanks for the vote of confidence, but—'

'But nothing. Why does there always have to be a but?'

'Because there always is.'

'Jeez, Heather.' Gabe sighs in frustration. 'You're so goddamn pessimistic. Stop thinking your glass is half empty. This interview is amazing – can't you be excited?'

'I *am* excited,' I protest hotly, and then, narrowing my eyes, I drawl, 'It's awesome.' It's a dreadful impression of him but he chortles.

'Much better. Believe me, you're gonna get this job. They'd be crazy not to give it to you. When they see how awesome and talented and cute . . .'

Blushing, I roll my eyes at the outpouring of compliments. God, what is he like? '. . . your roommate is.'

'Oy!' I snatch up the teaspoon, which still has a wet teabag stuck to it, and flick it at him.

'Hey.' He yelps as it hits him, splat, in the chest.

'Bull's-eye,' I cry, and we both crack up as the damp splodge of PG Tips spreads out across Mr T's face.

Then noticing the time on the microwave, I catch myself. 'Shit, it's getting late. I'd better jump in the shower.'

'Sure you don't want to join me for breakfast?' He spears a charred lump from the toaster and waves it at me in what I assume is meant to be an enticing manner. His eyes are twinkling.

'Mmm, tempting,' I concede, playing along as I meet his gaze.

And then, unexpectedly, my stomach flutters.

What the . . . ? Looking into his big blue eyes I don't know what comes over me. Suddenly he's not my flatmate in his underpants, he's this flirty, half-naked American who's actually quite sexy . . . *Heather Hamilton, what's got into you?*

I snap out of my daze. Christ, I must be having withdrawal symptoms from James. I don't fancy Gabe. Our relationship is purely platonic. And, anyway, he goes out with Mia, his model-Hollywood-actress girlfriend. He's hardly going to be attracted to me with my terry-towelling bathrobe and eyebrows that need plucking, is he?

I look at Gabe who's grinning at me but suddenly I'm feeling quite indignant towards him. 'Maybe some other time,' I say stiffly, and do my best model strut out of the kitchen.

Half an hour later, I'm in my bedroom. Showered, blow-dried and deodorised, I open the wardrobe door.

Right. Operation Interview. I begin flicking through the row of hangers dismissively. No, no, no, no . . . *maybe.* I pause on a pink mohair skirt that cost a fortune in some fancy little boutique, but it's one of those things that look lovely on the hanger and dreadful on me. In fact, I've got loads of stuff like that. There's this beautiful lace vintage top, which makes me look like someone's granny, and a gorgeous embroidered jacket from India with all these mirrored bits, which must have taken someone ages to sew on – and which Jess says makes me look like a student bedspread. Honestly, I should start framing some of these clothes and hanging them on the walls instead of pictures.

No, I need a suit. Everyone wears a suit for an interview. And I once had a lovely suit. I wish I still had it . . .

A prickle of static electricity surges through my fingertips, making me jump. What was that? I peer into the wardrobe and see that they brushed the shoulder pads of a jacket. *My suit jacket.* Aha! I knew I couldn't have thrown it away. I got it from Jigsaw in the sale, and even then it cost a small fortune. I unearth it from the back of the wardrobe. Just as I remember. Dark grey with a faint pinstripe. Very *Great Gatsby*. Very hip-professional-photographer. Very *Sunday Herald.*

Bubbling with optimism, I unhook the jacket and slip it over my naked arms. Hurrah, it still fits. Which is doubly great as it means I'm the same size as I was when I was . . . I attempt a bit of mental arithmetic . . . Well, I'm not sure exactly, but clogs were in fashion so it *must* have been a long time ago.

Buoyed up by the success with the jacket, I unhook the trousers. Yippee! This is going to be a great look, I just know it. I can team it with that lovely white shirt Jess gave me and maybe my brogues and go for a Diane Keaton in *Annie Hall* vibe, or maybe I should do T-shirt and Pumas and do that whole androgynous Jude Law thing . . . Carried away by the host of possibilities I step into the trousers and pull them up.

And up. And up. *And up.*

Shit.

I fasten the button and look at my reflection.

Two words spring to mind. Simon and Cowell.

No, this can't be. I've been thinking hipsters, bootcut, flattering. Not a waistband that's so high it's nudging my nipples. Plus – and, believe me, this isn't a plus – *they're pleated.*

I'm aghast. I don't need Trinny and Susannah to point out the fashion disaster: it's right there before my eyes. I do a nervous twirl and catch sight of my bottom. At least, I *think* it's my bottom. Lost under swathes of gathering it appears to stretch from my ribcage to the backs of my knees. I shudder. This has to be the most unflattering pair of trousers I've ever seen. *Ever*. Did I really wear these? *In public?*

I could go on for ever, but I'm running out of time. My interview's at nine and I've got to go straight to the office afterwards. Which means, I decide, tugging off my suit and chucking it on to the bedroom floor, it's time for Plan B. Delving back into the wardrobe I start rifling through the hangers. Now, where was that pink mohair skirt and lacy top?

Two squirts of perfume later I'm all set. Grabbing my black leather portfolio I start a hunt for my keys and mobile. Where are they? I'm going to be late. I dash into the kitchen and sort through piles of magazines and newspapers on the table, then upturn a fruit bowl that's home to loose change. Damnit. I wish I could find them.

Hang on, what's this?

I spot my sparkly key-ring under a tea-towel. Fantastic. Now what about my . . . I do a double-take: there, in the fruit bowl, is my mobile phone. But how can that be? I only looked there a second ago. Amazed, I scoop it out and pop it into my bag. Wow, thank goodness for the lucky heather. What would I do without it? I take a deep breath. Now, have I got everything for the interview?

Quickly running through the list in my head, I glance round the kitchen and notice that Gabe's trainers have disappeared. He must have gone for a run, I muse, and feel a bit guilty for being short with him earlier. Then I notice that he's left the window open and go over to close it.

Which is when I spot the lucky heather on the windowsill. Gosh, how could I forget that? I pluck it from its vase and hold it tight. Almost instantly I feel myself grow calmer. Gabe's right. I'll be fine. Actually, no, I'll be more than fine, I'll be awesome. I'm going to wow Victor Maxfield with my skill as a photographer and he's going to ask me to work for them. *Beg* me to work for them, I tell myself, enjoying a splurge of confidence as I entertain this happy thought.

Followed by another: telling my family about my super-duper new job. Dad will be delighted as he knows it's what I've always wanted. Ed will be amazed. As for Rosemary, she'll never be able to boast about Annabel again. Because I'll have something much better than an all-weather conservatory and a French-speaking nanny. I'll have a high-flying career!

I catch my breath. My childhood dream is so close I can almost touch it. I pop the lucky heather into my pocket, sling my portfolio over my shoulder and hurry down the hallway towards it. Just think. Me. Heather Hamilton. The *Sunday Herald* photographer. And pulling open the front door with both hands, I take one small step for mankind and one giant step into my new life.

Chapter Thirty-four

I *think I'm going to be sick*

Behind his desk, in one of those chunky high-backed leather chairs that big-shot people spend their days swivelling in, Victor Maxfield is telling me what makes the *Sunday Herald* the best-selling weekend newspaper in the UK. Sitting opposite him in his large corner office, which has huge glass windows with an amazing view of the London Eye, I'm doing everything those how-to-win-the-job articles always say you should do in interviews. I'm making eye-contact, appearing interested and enthusiastic with occasional nods, cocking my head to the side and murmuring, 'Really?' and 'Absolutely,' and laughing in all the right places at his jokes – even though secretly I don't really think they're *that* funny. But I'm so nervous I still feel as if I'm going to throw up.

Honestly, I had no idea it was going to be so bad. When I arrived fifteen minutes ago and was told to wait in Reception I felt relatively calm. I sipped some water from the dispenser in the corner and flicked through a few magazines. When Margot, Victor Maxfield's secretary, came to take me up to his office, I made easy chit-chat in the lift about the weather, thinking, Look at me, I'm mature and confident and not in the least bit nervous. It was as if I was the one putting *her* at ease.

In fact, I was even OK following Margot through the busy open-plan office, although I do admit I had to stare at the carpet the whole time as otherwise it might have been a bit intimidating. But still. I was fine. I was taking it all in my stride, flicking my hair, swinging my portfolio, thinking of how, finally, in the Snakes and Ladders of life, I was climbing up the ladder.

Then I saw it. A door with EDITOR across it in shiny silver letters. Just like in my dream.

And that was when I lost it.

'. . . and so when our circulation figures surpassed that of every other leading newspaper I went home to my wife and told her the good news. And she said, "Well done, that deserves a nice cup of tea." '

'Really?' I smile.

I'm sweating. I can feel dampness mushrooming out under my lacy armpits, two revoltingly sticky patches. I wriggle self-consciously, making sure to keep my arms clamped firmly by my sides. Ugh.

'. . . I've lived here nearly twenty years but it must be a British thing, hmm?' He laughs amiably.

'Absolutely.' My bladder twinges painfully. Damn, why did I have that second cup of coffee? I cross my legs, squeeze my thighs together and smile tightly.

'. . . But enough about me and the paper. We're here to talk about you . . .'

I can hear Victor Maxfield's voice in the background but I'm distracted by someone else walking past the office and peering in at me.

'So tell me, what made you want to be a photographer, Heather?'

I knew I shouldn't have worn this stupid mohair skirt and the lacy granny blouse. Everyone's in jeans and T-shirts, all cool and funky, like real journalists and photographers. Not impostors like me. A lowly assistant to a wedding photographer. Oh, God, what on earth was I thinking? I don't belong here. I'm way out of my league.

'Heather?'

With a start I snap back from Planet Failure, and see that Victor Maxfield is waiting for what the interview-technique books call 'input'.

'Oh, absolutely.' I adopt a confident look. Which freezes to my face like a mask as I see his expression change from expectation to confusion. 'I mean . . . I think . . . I'm sorry, what was that again?' My voice comes out much higher than usual.

'I was wondering what sparked your interest in photography,' says Victor Maxfield, patiently, but I know his easy manner camouflages a steely demeanour.

I sit up straight in my chair and pretend to give the question some serious thought (tip number two: never rush an answer) but again I'm distracted by someone walking past the office and peering in. Honestly, I wish people wouldn't stare at me.

'Don't worry, he's not staring at you,'

I jump as Victor Maxfield gestures to the man outside. 'He's looking at himself. Vain bunch, my staff.' He chuckles. 'I don't know if you noticed before you came in but my window's a mirror,' he explains.

'Really?' I laugh pleasantly. Now I feel like even more of an idiot. All this time I've thought they were staring at me when in fact they've been checking their appearance.

'So?' Victor Maxfield steeples his fingers and rests his chin on them. He seems to be pondering me and I can feel my chances, *whichwerethisclose*, slipping away.

Spiralling downwards into a pit of insecurity I glance at him from under my eyelashes. Victor Maxfield is an imposing figure. Even though he must be nudging sixty, he's still attractive. His tanned, freckly face has the well-worn furrows and lines that on men are called 'rugged', and on women are the reason plastic surgeons drive around in top-of-the-range Mercedes. His hair is still thick, albeit sprinkled with grey. But it's the eyes I notice most. Partly hidden by his baggy eyelids, they match the faded blue of his Ralph Lauren shirt, and briefly I'm reminded of Gabe's and how, when I looked into them this morning, they were filled with his belief that I can do this.

'I was eight,' I begin quietly, 'and my family and I were moving from Yorkshire to Cornwall.' It all comes flooding back as if it were yesterday. 'We were saying goodbye to all our friends and neighbours. I remember seeing all these faces and expressions and wanting to capture them for ever. There was Mrs Bird who lived next door and never put her teeth in and little Andrea swinging on the gatepost. Buster the Alsatian was barking and wagging his tail. I didn't want to forget any of them.'

Snapshots of their faces come alive in my mind, and even though I'm sitting in a high-rise office on the banks of the river Thames, I'm right back in Yorkshire again. 'I asked my father if I could borrow his camera,' I continue. 'It was an old Leica, big, black and heavy, and he'd never let me use it before. But today was special, so he showed me where to look, what to press and how to focus.

'It was incredible, all this life, all these memories, all this emotion, and as I clicked away it was as if I was soaking it all up, like a sponge. I knew I'd be able to keep it for ever.' My voice falters when my mind flicks to Mum – as it so often does. 'I don't like saying goodbye and I knew this way I wasn't really saying goodbye because I was taking those people with me.'

I look at Victor Maxfield, who's been listening quietly all the time. 'I still have them today, Andrea, Mrs Bird and Buster.'

'Can I see them?' asks Victor Maxfield.

'I'm afraid they're a little blurred,' I laugh, 'and there's a lot of my thumb.'

He laughs too and I'm buoyed up. 'But I do have lots of other pictures,' I say eagerly, pulling out my portfolio from under my chair, 'if you'd like to have a look.'

'Please.' He pats his desk.

I place the large black case on it, unzip it and, lay it open. Like myself, I think, feeling suddenly vulnerable as Victor Maxfield undoes his cufflinks, and, rolling up sleeves, says, 'Let's get down to business, shall we?'

For the next thirty minutes Victor Maxfield studies my photographs, nods admiringly and asks dozens of questions. I can't quite believe it. The editor. Of the *Sunday Herald*. Looking at *my* pictures.

But as I talk about my photography, my nerves disappear. My voice becomes steady and confident, I stop fiddling with my clothes and use my hands to gesticulate depth and perspective. I even forget that I need a pee.

Engrossed in describing the different inspiration for each subject, I sneak sideways looks at Victor Maxfield and, although I barely dare to believe it, he seems impressed. One moment he's nodding approval, the next he's raising his eyebrows with interest or laughing at an over-processed image of one of Ed's patients – a boy of about nine with his mouth full of braces and chewing-gum. When he comes upon one image he falls quiet and I watch him studying it, his forehead furrowed in contemplation. 'Who's this?' he asks.

He's holding a black and white photograph of my mother. Wearing a headscarf, she has her face tilted to the sunshine and a faint smile playing on her lips. She has a luminous quality. So luminous, in fact, that you might not notice she has no eyebrows, or that no tendrils of hair are escaping from beneath the scarf. She died just a few weeks after it was taken.

'My inspiration,' I say quietly.

'She's a beautiful woman.' Victor Maxfield talks in the present tense.

'I know,' I agree. Because in this photograph she is alive.

There's a pause as we gaze at the picture. 'Well, I've very much enjoyed your portfolio,' Victor Maxfield is saying, as he eases himself back into his chair. He rolls down his sleeves, deftly replaces his cufflinks and fixes me with a thoughtful look. 'Do you have an extra five minutes? I'd like you to meet our picture editor.'

'Of course.' Like he has to ask.

Picking up the phone he presses a button. The person at the other end answers immediately. 'Yvonne? Hi, it's Victor. Are you free? There's a photographer I'd like you to meet.' Without waiting for a response he hangs up with the confidence of a man for whom questions are merely rhetorical.

'Well, that's settled.' Seeming rather pleased he stands up and, taking this as my cue, so do I. He walks out from behind his desk and holds out his hand. 'Heather, it was a pleasure to meet you.'

So this is it. The interview's over. 'You too,' I say, shaking his hand and feeling a mixture of relief and sadness that perhaps this is the closest I'm ever going to get to my dream.

We're interrupted by a knock at the door and a curly-haired woman with large dangly earrings puts her head round the door.

'Ah, Yvonne, this is Heather, the photographer I was telling you about.'

She smiles energetically and the rest of her appears. 'Hi,' she says briskly, then pumps my hand and bobs back out of the office. 'This way.' She beckons.

I pick up my portfolio and glance back at Victor Maxfield. Arms folded, leaning back, he's watching me intently, as if he's deep in thought. Is that good or bad? I can't work it out and, making a mental note to look it up in my interview book, I hurry after Yvonne.

Chapter Thirty-five

Yvonne turns out to be scary but friendly. She shows me briskly round the picture desk, introduces me to her assistant, whose name I've forgotten already, and flirts aggressively with a floppy-haired freelance photographer looking for work ('Never be afraid to abuse your power,' she advises, after commissioning him for a shoot), shakes my hand, shows me to the lift and disappears 'for a fag'.

I think about her the whole tube journey to work. Well, not Yvonne specifically, but in context with the *Sunday Herald*, Victor Maxfield and my interview. Excitement bubbles. If I get the job my whole life will change. Daydreaming, I close my eyes and allow the Piccadilly line to transport me out of my imaginary future and back to reality.

When I arrive at work I'm surprised to discover that the building is still locked up. Where's Brian? I check my watch – it's nearly eleven. Puzzled, I let myself in with my keys, turn off the alarm and pull up the blinds. Sunlight streams into the office, illuminating the dust particles swirling in the air like confetti, and scooping up the mail from the mat, I walk over to the front counter.

As usual its mostly bills, but while a few weeks ago we'd had no hope of paying them off, now with Lady Charlotte's wedding we needn't worry. Which is great, I muse, wandering into the little kitchen to make myself some coffee. Just not so great for me. A knot of dread tightens in my stomach as the day looms closer.

Trying not to think about it I'm spooning Nescafé into my mug when I hear the electronic jingle of the door. That must be Brian. 'So, what time do you call this?' I shout.

'I beg your pardon?'

I put my head round the door and the grin freezes on my face. It's not Brian. Instead, it's a reed-thin blonde. With a suspiciously large cleavage. She stalks towards me, kitten heels clicking loudly on the laminate flooring. 'I'm looking for Brian Williams,' she demands, in a high-pitched whinny.

My stomach drops. I don't need any introductions to know who this is – Lady Charlotte. 'I'm afraid he's not here yet,' I reply, moving behind the front counter where she's rested her Mulberry tote.

She pushes her black Chanel sunglasses on to her forehead and fixes me with a haughty stare. I stare back. There's love-at-first-sight, but this is hate-at-first-sight. 'Not here?' she repeats indignantly.

Tread on eggshells, Heather, warns the voice in my head. Tread on eggshells.

'Perhaps I can help,' I venture carefully. I mustn't let my personal feelings get in the way. I have to be totally professional about this.

'Perhaps.' She sniffs and it's apparent from the look she gives me that 'Perhaps *not*' is what she means. However, with the absence of anyone else, she's got little choice. 'I think we may have spoken once on the phone.'

Once? More like fifty times, I want to cry. Instead I bite my tongue and concentrate on remaining friendly and smily. *Friendly and smiley. Friendly and smiley.* Repeating it in my head, like a mantra, I shuffle a few papers on the counter in an attempt to give myself an air of authority.

'I've come about my wedding.'

'You must be excited,' I enthuse.

'Very,' she says, in a voice that couldn't have sounded less excited. 'But, quite frankly, I'll be glad when it's all over. Organising a wedding for five hundred people is so completely stressful. What with the string quartet flying in from Prague, Harrods saying they won't have time to gold-leaf the cake and my makeup artist breaking her wrist . . .' She rolls her eyes dramatically. 'But, then, that's me. Always taking on far too much. My doctor's warned me I've got to be careful otherwise I'll find myself in hospital with exhaustion. But I told him, "No, Doctor. This is my wedding day and if I have to apply my own eyeliner, then I'll jolly well do it."'

'Good for you,' I say encouragingly. Er, hello? Is this woman for real? I'm almost tempted to ask her if she'll have the strength to apply her own mascara too, but I'm distracted by her handbag – it's wriggling.

'Jesus.' I jump away from the counter. 'Something's alive in there!' The bag wriggles again and a black nose pokes out of a corner. 'Oh, my God, it's a rat!'

The first genuine smile I've seen appears on Lady Charlotte's face and scooping out the tiniest, baldest, ugliest dog I've ever seen she begins scratching its tiny ratty head, cooing, 'Oooh, did the big horrible woman frighten you, Poo-poo?'

Poo-poo?

'This is Pollyanna, my chihuahua,' she says, looking at me crossly.

'Gosh, I'm sorry. I thought . . . she's got those little beady eyes and I thought . . . well—' I'm interrupted by the electronic jingle of the door and Brian appears.

'Good morning.' Bounding into the office with a tray from the little café on the corner and more energy than I've seen in him for ages, he takes a drag of his cigarette and smiles broadly at us both. 'Isn't it a glorious day?'

Behind him, out of the window, the skies are still overcast and threatening rain.

'I bought you a double cappuccino, no foam, just how you like it,' he says merrily, passing me a Styrofoam cup, 'and a *pain au chocolat*. I know they're your favourite.'

As I silently accept them I peer at him suspiciously. Hang on a minute. Is this the same Brian I find slumped each morning at his desk, smoking cigarettes and making bitchy comments about whoever's on the front of the *Daily Mail*? Who refuses to pay two pounds fifty for a takeout coffee, calling it 'daylight robbery' and insists on drinking instant? Even if it means taking a flask when we're on a job?

'I must say you're looking very chi-chi this morning. What's the special occasion?'

'Erm . . .' I'd been planning to tell him about my interview when he arrived, but with Lady Charlotte here it's impossible.

'Don't tell me!' He slams his cup on the counter, takes a drag of his cigarette and peers at me through narrowed eyes. 'You and James have got engaged.'

'Not exactly.' I smile uncomfortably, then, trying to quickly steer him off the subject of James, say brightly, 'Have you met Lady Charlotte?'

It seems a shame to spoil his extraordinary good mood, but she's standing there like a lemon. Or should that be looking like she just sucked one.

'Delighted,' she mutters, offering a limp hand.

I expect Brian to look sickened, but he's unfazed. 'Lady Charlotte! What a surprise. I've been so much looking forward to meeting you.' Clasping his hands in delight, he beams at her like a politician. Actually, he's not unfazed, he's unhinged, I decide, and watch an unsavoury bout of air-kissing.

Then I spot a crimson splodge on his neck.

Like a line of dominoes, everything falls into place. Last night. *The Rocky Horror Show*. Neil, the good-looking air steward. This morning. Late for work. Ridiculously good mood. *Lovebite*.

I catch his eye over Ladys Charlotte's shoulder, smile knowingly and give him the thumbs-up.

He reddens and focuses his attention on Lady Charlotte as she whinges on about how her bouquet is going to clash with her complexion and make her look ghastly in the photographs. 'Well, we need to get this matter sorted immediately. Ideally, we should go to the florist and take some Polaroids . . .' He tries to ignore me.

'Oh, could you? Could you really?' pleads Lady Charlotte, her voice husky with hopeful gratitude.

Hopeful gratitude? Lady Charlotte? I'm amazed: Brian works his magic like a sorcerer.

'But that would mean me cancelling appointments.'

'Well, of course I'll reimburse you.'

'Which would incur considerable costs.'

'Whatever. I've got access to Daddy's Coutts account. I'll write you a cheque right now.' She scrabbles for a pen.

'No, I'm afraid I can't accept that. It could reach into thousands.' He holds up his hands as if he needs to defend himself from a Coutts cheque.

At which point I gaze at him in awe. This man is a genius. With an empty diary and a pile of bills, we're looking at making the grand total of zero today.

'Will this cover it?' begs Lady Charlotte, brandishing a cheque.

Brian looks at it, then hesitates for dramatic effect. Furrowing his brow, he sucks his teeth and then, in what is truly a superb move, finally looks over at me and asks, 'Heather, do you think you'll be able to clear the diary?'

Honestly, the man should get an Academy Award.

I play along: I adopt a solemn expression and open the diary. Blank pages stare back at me. 'It won't be easy, but I'll do my best,' I say gravely.

'Oh, marvellous!' Whooping with relief, Lady Charlotte clasps her hands together. 'How can I ever repay you?'

'Please, don't mention it,' protests Brian. 'Here, at Together Forever, we go that extra smile.' Beaming at his play on words, he tucks the cheque into his breast pocket and, putting his arm round her trim little waist, ushers Lady Charlotte out.

Half an hour later, having eaten half of my *pain au chocolat* and realised that I'd prefer a bowl of cereal today, I'm toying with the idea of popping out to buy some All Bran when the phone rings. It's one of our customers calling about extra prints of their wedding, which took place a few months ago.

Yes, of course, we have them on file, I assure them, abandoning my breakfast run. I go into the little back room where I survey the overflowing cabinets, shelves cluttered with different folders and jumbled boxes of film. *This* is Brian's idea of a filing system. Sighing, I make my usual vow that one day I'm going to reorganise it and, flicking on the CD player, roll up my lacy sleeves and get stuck in.

Mr and Mrs K. Peck. Nope, that's not them. I reach for another folder on which is scribbled STAR . . . something. I struggle to decipher Brian's handwriting. STAR T-R-E . . . Oh, it's the *Star Trek* couple who said their vows in Klingon. I glance at a photograph of a portly middle-aged groom in a Starship *Enterprise* crew outfit, then stuff the file back into the cabinet and pull out a different wedding.

Oh, this is the one where the bride wore black, and this was on the London Eye . . . and they were a lovely couple. I spot an elaborately dressed Indian bride and groom, and drift off into a memory of a red and gold-embroidered sari, beating drums, tables piled with the most delicious food. But that's not the couple I'm looking for. I rummage through a tray of contact sheets with no luck.

I flop dispiritedly on to a stool and chew my fingernails until my eye falls on a packet marked 'June 2005'. Pulling out a wad of photographs I angle them to the light.

My heart skips a beat.

No, surely not, it can't be . . .

With Michael Crawford reaching a crescendo on the CD player I stare at the photograph in horror. My eyes absorb the happy couple, the bride smiling at the camera, the groom smiling at her, rubbing his nose against hers. I glance again at the date: 8 June. Barely two months ago. I hesitate, not sure what to do. And then realise there's only one thing I *can* do.

I pick up the telephone and start dialling.

Chapter Thirty-six

'He's married?'

Sitting in a hotel bar near Heathrow airport, I look at Jess in her uniform. She's got a cigarette in one hand and in the other a black-and-white photograph of a smiling bride and groom: Mr and Mrs Gregory de Souza. Otherwise known as—

'*Greg?*' repeats Jess. 'Greg is married?'

It's nearly seven p.m. After discovering the photograph this morning, I called her saying I needed to see her, but she was with Greg, having breakfast in some little café, and said she was flying out to Cape Town this evening on a two-week trip. Couldn't it wait till she got back?

No, it couldn't. But I so wanted it to.

I wanted it to wait for ever. I wanted never to have found that photograph, recognised the pale silvery scar running up through the groom's Cupid's bow and realised that was why Greg's smile had been so familiar. And I wanted never to have to tell her that the man she'd been busy falling in love with is married and that I had photographed his white wedding less than two months ago.

But I had to. So I spent the whole day wrestling with my conscience, working out how to break it to her. In the end, however, I just passed her the photograph. After all, a picture says a thousand words. Or in this case, just one.

'Bastard.'

I flinch. 'Maybe there's been some mistake . . .' But, of course, there's no mistake. It's there in black and white.

Jess's jaw is rigid and I brace myself for an outburst. But then it seems to just dissolve away, as if the effort is too much for her.

Slumping forward over the bar she puts her head into her hands. 'I just can't believe it.'

I watch her helplessly. I've never seen Jess so broken and upset. 'Maybe it's been annulled,' I venture hopefully.

She lifts her head and shoots me a sideways look.

'OK, maybe not.'

There's a tense silence as she puffs her cigarette, then exhales two streams of smoke from her nostrils. 'I thought this was a real relationship, but for him I was obviously just an affair. A sordid little extramarital affair.' She grinds out her cigarette in the ashtray and takes a slug of red wine. 'Christ, I've been sleeping with someone's husband.'

I stir the ice in my gin and tonic wordlessly. I can't think of a thing to say.

She misinterprets my silence for condemnation: 'And don't look at me like that.'

'What? I wasn't.'

'I might have slept with a few men – OK, a lot of men . . .'

Across from us a middle-aged couple with suitcases, sipping coffee at the bar and waiting for the shuttle to take them to the airport, glance round. When they see a furious air stewardess chain-smoking and knocking back red wine, they look anxious.

'. . . but I don't sleep with married men,' Jess is protesting loudly. 'That's my one rule, Heather, my one rule.' She slams a hand on the bar and curls her fingers round a paper coaster. Crumpling it in her fist, she sniffs furiously. Her eyes are brimming with tears. 'My one rule,' she repeats, as a tear dribbles down her cheek and splashes on to the bar.

'Oh, Jess, come here.' Putting my arm round her shoulders, I pull her close. As I listen to her muffled sobs it occurs to me that I haven't shed one tear over my break-up with James.

'I feel like such a fool,' she says eventually, sniffing into my lace blouse. I can feel the wetness of her tears on my shoulder. When she surfaces, she sweeps her index fingers under her eyes to wipe off her smudged eyeliner. 'I thought I'd got it right this time. I was so careful. I made sure he ticked all the right boxes.'

'That's no guarantee,' I say quietly, thinking of James.

'I know that now.' She lifts her glass to her lips. Swallowing another mouthful of wine, she stares into the middle distance, then says softly, 'I never talk about my father, do I?' But it's as if she's asking herself the question, not me, so I just listen as she talks.

'That's because I never knew him. I've seen a couple of pictures. He was a sax player in a band and really handsome. Mum said she fell in love with him the moment she laid eyes on him. He told her it was the same for him too.' She pauses to light another cigarette. 'He told her lots of things. That he was going to buy a house, and they were going to get married, and he was going to be the best husband and father in the whole wide world.' She flicks ash and blows out smoke.

'He left before I was even born. Just split. Did a runner. Never contacted her again. She was eighteen and six months pregnant. He broke my mum's heart and I don't think it's ever really mended.' Jess sniffs, and I think she's going to cry again, but she smiles. 'She's a survivor, my mum. Being single, unmarried and a teenager – well, you can imagine the stigma in the sixties. *And* she was black. My mum's had pretty much every insult you can imagine thrown at her at one time or another.'

She traces a pattern on her glass, and I can see her mind spooling backwards. 'It was a struggle and she took on two jobs at a time, but she did it. She brought me up single-handedly. Honestly, she's amazing, my mum. I never went without. OK, so we didn't live in a big house, or have a car, or go on holidays abroad—' She looks down at her uniform ruefully. 'That's why I took this job. When I was little I used to dream of growing up and seeing the world.' Jess smiles, almost embarrassed at her confession, and takes a sip of wine. 'And I swore that when I did I was never going to fall in love and let some lousy guy hurt me, like my dad hurt my mum.'

Her jaw set, Jess faces me. 'I'm not like you, Heather. I'm not looking for butterflies in my stomach. I don't want them. They're dangerous. I want security, commitment, financial stability. Oh, and great sex,' she quips as an afterthought. 'Tell me. Why is it that the bastards are always great in bed?'

I smile despite myself. 'But without those butterflies your mum wouldn't have had you,' I point out. 'I bet if you ask she doesn't regret a thing.'

'But what about you and Daniel? You were heartbroken.'

'It doesn't mean I don't want to fall in love again,' I say evenly.

'*Why?*' Jess gasps.

'Because it's the most amazing feeling in the world. You'll risk everything for it. Nothing comes close.'

'But you're so vulnerable.'

'True,' I agree. 'It's as scary as hell.'

'I guess I'm not brave enough.'

I pause. I'd never thought of it like that, but maybe she's right. 'What's that saying? "Better to have loved and lost than never to have loved at all." '

'Where did you get those pearls of wisdom? A fortune cookie?'

'I dunno,' I confess.

Jess smiles then shakes her head and wails in frustration, 'Fuck! What's wrong with me, Heather?'

'Nothing.'

But Jess is hell-bent on beating herself up and, ignoring me, she starts shredding the coaster. 'Yes, there is. Look at me, I'm thirty-six and still single. I've never been in love. I've never lived with anyone for longer than six weeks. And now I'm dating married men.' Her dark eyes flash. 'Believe me, when I was ticking those boxes one of them wasn't "already has a wife".' She glances at the photograph on the bar and puts down her wine glass on it. 'Everyone else manages to hold down a successful relationship. I mean, look at you and James . . .'

'We broke up.'

She stops tearing up the coaster. 'You've broken up with James?'

'He broke up with me,' I correct her.

Her amazement morphs into pity. 'Crikey, Heather,' she

whispers. 'I'm so sorry. Here's me going on about stupid Greg and all the time—'

'No, honestly, I'm OK,' I say quickly.

'If I hadn't kept on at you about how you had to get over Daniel and start dating again . . .' She's stricken. 'Oh, my God, I feel so responsible. It's all my fault . . . you've lost weight, haven't you?'

'I have?' I say, delighted that she's noticed, despite the circumstances.

'Yes – around the face. You look drawn. And your boobs are smaller,' she says decisively.

I frown. When I wished I could lose a few pounds, that wasn't what I'd had in mind. 'Jess, I'm fine,' I repeat firmly.

'You are?' she says doubtfully, as it dawns on her that perhaps I'm not just putting on a brave face. '*Seriously?*'

'Seriously. No butterflies,' I add in explanation.

'Are they really as good as you say they are?'

'Better.' I smile.

She slides her elbow on to the bar and, resting her chin in the palm of her hand, tilts her glass and drains the last mouthful of wine.

The middle-aged couple stalk past with their luggage and throw her a couple of appalled glances.

'She'd better not be on our flight, Margaret.'

'I think she's drunk, Leonard. I saw her smoking.'

Jess and I giggle.

'I hope you're not going to get into trouble.'

'I'll drink some coffee.'

'But what if they're on your flight?'

Jess waves dismissively. 'I'll keep the seatbelt sign on. They'll be no trouble.'

'You can do that?'

'We do it all the time. Stops the passengers wandering around and annoying us when we want a bit of peace and quiet at the back.' She catches my astonishment. 'Aw, c'mon, Heather, you didn't really believe all that stuff about clear-air turbulence?'

I stare at her speechlessly. I feel like someone's just played a dirty trick on me.

'Maybe I'll try it some time,' she says, after a pause.

'What? Clear-air turbulence?' I scowl. When I think of all the times I've sat there obediently, dying to use the loo but unable to move because the seatbelt sign's on.

'No, you dope.' She frowns. 'Butterflies.'

She says it with such hope that I can't help smiling. 'I'll drink to that,' I agree and lifting my glass I clink it against hers. 'To butterflies.'

Chapter Thirty-seven

The next day at lunchtime I'm standing in a queue with Brian in the little pavement café on the corner when I discover Jess and I aren't the only ones with butterflies in mind. But while we're chasing them, Brian has definitely caught them.

'I think I'm in love,' he confesses.

'Love?' I echo, as my stomach rumbles. C'mon, I wish we could hurry up and get served.

'At first I thought it was just going to be a sex thing, but it's much more than that.'

There's a loud snort and a middle-aged woman swings round, her face flushed beetroot. 'Can't you keep your filthy talk to yourself? Some of us are trying to eat lunch.' She throws us a filthy look. 'Come on, Carol, come on, Louise.' With her two friends she marches out of the shop. Leaving us at the front of the queue. And all eyes in the café upon us.

I swallow hard. Maria, the matronly shop owner, is staring at us with her mouth wide open.

'Erm, a grilled chicken and pesto panini, and a toasted mozzarella and tomato ciabatta. Please,' I add awkwardly. Honestly, not having to wait in line is great, but sometimes a wish coming true isn't all it's cracked up to be.

Thankfully, Maria is quick with our order. A few minutes later she hands us our sandwiches, and Brian gives her a tenner. 'I wasn't going to say anything because of you and your fella,' he says, a reference to my break-up with James, the details of which I had told him earlier, 'but I just had to talk to someone.' He drops his loose change into the tip basket on the counter. 'I haven't felt like this for years,' he adds quietly, so this time no one overhears.

'But that's great.' I grab our sandwiches. It feels rather claustrophobic in the little café, and as I excuse my way past the queue trailing out of the door, I'm relieved to step out into the bright sunshine. 'I take it this is Neil we're talking about.'

'How do you know?' he asks, surprised.

We cross the street and walk towards the office.

'A wild guess. Or maybe it could have something to do with swapping seats at *The Rocky Horror Show*, then coming in late the next day, the lovebite . . .' He blushes. 'He seemed really nice,' I reassure him. I check to see which sandwich is which, and pass him the chicken.

'Oh, he is,' agrees Brian, as if he still can't believe it. Unwrapping his panini he takes a bite and chews pensively. 'But there's a bit of an age gap.'

'How old is he?' I ask, slipping on my sunglasses.

'Thirty-two,' admits Brian. 'Half my age.'

'Oooh, a toyboy.'

'That's what I'm worried about. People will laugh.'

'No, they won't. Look at Michael Douglas and Catherine Zeta-Jones.'

'Exactly,' Brian retorts gloomily, 'He looks like her father.'

'Or her grandfather,' I quip, then seeing his stricken expression say quickly, 'Hey, stop worrying. You're very handsome for an older man. And your legs are amazing in fishnets.' I nudge him affectionately.

He laughs and clamps his jaws round the rest of his sandwich as I take the first bite of my own. I usually go to M&S for lunch, but often my favourite sandwich is sold out. However, these past few weeks I've been able to get it every lunchtime, and now I've actually grown rather sick of it. Which is why today I decided to get one from the local café instead.

For a moment everything is quiet, but for the sound of our footsteps. Then I hear a muffled jingle. With my free hand I dig my mobile out of my bag and glance at the screen. No number.

Probably Jess from the hotel in Cape Town, I think, and press the little green button.

'Hello, is that Heather?'

Only it's not Jess, and my mouth is stuffed with melted cheese, tomato and bread.

'This is Yvonne from the *Sunday Herald*.'

I stop abruptly as I make the mental leap from gossip-with-best-friend to terrifying-every-word-counts-conversation-that-could-change-my-life.

'Victor left for his annual fishing trip this morning but he asked me to call you . . .' She continues briskly, obviously so busy she doesn't notice I haven't yet said a word. '. . . as he was very impressed by your interview.'

She pauses momentarily, and I know this is my cue to say something but I'm still chewing frantically. God, what is it with this ciabatta? It's swelling up in my mouth like a sponge. I swallow hard.

'He'd like to offer you the job of staff photographer.'

And nearly choke.

'He would?' I gasp between coughs.

Brian holds out his bottle of Evian and I take a grateful glug. 'Thank you,' I say.

'Don't mention it,' stereo Yvonne and Brian.

'You'll be receiving a formal letter of confirmation in the post from our human-resources department,' she continues. 'You know, the usual thing. Employment contract – holiday entitlement, salary.' Then, 'Did you discuss salary?' she demands.

'I'm not sure . . .' I look uncomfortably at Brian, who's striding alongside me, monitoring shop windows. Suddenly I feel horribly deceitful.

'It says here thirty-five thousand.'

My stomach flips. 'It does?' I whisper. *Thirty-five thousand!* That's nearly – bloody hell – loads more than I'm earning now.

'With a review after six months.'

'Hmm.' I make a noise as if I'm giving this serious thought, but mentally I'm already spinning round with shopping bags, like

Julia Roberts in *Pretty Woman*. Imagine! I'll be able to afford a holiday, and some new clothes, and that gorgeous silver necklace with the little teardrops made of garnet that I saw in the window of Dinny Hall on the way to the gym.

'There's just one thing.'

Yvonne's voice stops me in mid-spin. 'Yes?' I say, my mind still whirling.

'Victor wants you to start on Monday. Will that be OK?'

I feel my delight wither like fruit on a time-release film. *Monday?* I glance at Brian. He's lit a cigarette and is puffing away, enjoying the sunshine and the novelty of being in love. I can't give him only two days' notice. Although business *is* slow . . .

And then I remember. *Lady Charlotte's wedding.* It's next weekend.

That's it. I have to say no. 'Well, you see—' I begin, but Yvonne interrupts.

'Good. I didn't think it would be a problem. What Victor Maxfield wants Victor Maxfield gets, hey?' She gives a short, sarcastic laugh. 'Right, that's sorted then. See you on Monday – shall we say around ten?' and before I can interrupt she's hung up.

'Good news?' Brian raises his eyebrows.

Everything's happening so fast that I'm not sure. 'Er, yes. It's good news.' Oh, bloody hell, how am I going to tell him? 'You see, the thing is . . .' I think of all the different ways to break it to him, but none is right. There's no easy way out of this.

We're outside the office now and, as Brian unlocks the front door and I follow him inside, it hits me. Wanting a high-flying career and getting one, I now know, are two completely different things.

'I've got a new job. It's with the *Sunday Herald.* They want me to start on Monday,' I blurt.

Brian's face drops with shock – blink, and I'd have missed it – but he recovers immediately. 'Heather, that's fantastic.' He pins a wide smile on his face. Well done.' He'd sat down, but he jumps up again to give me a hug. 'I'm really proud of you.'

'But what about Lady Charlotte's wedding?' I urge.

'What about it?' He pulls a face. 'I can find someone to give me a hand. After all, it's only a wedding.'

I smile gratefully. Brian's such a superstar. 'I can't let you down at such short notice. Not after all this preparation. Maybe I can explain to them,' I suggest. 'I mean, I should really give you a month's notice.' Now it's actually happening, I discover I'm not so desperate to leave after all.

'Heather, *please*. What's all this notice bollocks? I know I'm your boss . . .' he looks at me kindly '. . . but I'm your friend first and foremost. Take the rest of the week off. Have a few days' holiday. Believe me, you'll be thankful for it once you start working for a newspaper.' He smiles at his memories.

'Well, if you're sure . . .' I say doubtfully.

'Listen, I've had my career. Now it's your turn. Go and be a photographer for the *Sunday Herald*. Go and take some amazing shots that don't involve confetti.' He clicks his tongue. 'Bloody hell, girl, sod Bridezilla. This is your wish come true.'

He's right. This *is* my wish come true. But as I glance around the office of Together Forever, the familiar walls filled with framed photos of newlyweds, the Charles and Di wedding clock, a black-and-white picture of Brian in his heyday, it occurs to me that I've been so busy wishing I could move on in my career that I've never stopped to appreciate this place.

'Now I know most people get a gold watch when they leave a job . . .'

I zone back in to see Brian opening a drawer in his desk: 'Isn't that when you retire?' I say.

But Brian's in mid-flow. '. . . but I thought you might prefer this.' He holds out a CD.

'What is it?' I say. And then I realise.

'A little memento,' he says quietly.

I turn the plastic case in my hand. 'Andrew Lloyd Webber's *Phantom of the Opera*.' Tears prickle.

'It's my autographed copy,' he adds, the pride audible in his voice as he points at the felt-tip scribble: Michael Crawford.

I'm touched. I know how much it means to him. 'I'll treasure it,' I say, and kiss his cheek.

'I should bloody well hope so. I stood in the rain for two hours to get it.' His voice is thick with emotion.

'Well, I'll start packing my things.' I force a smile.

'Rightly-ho.' Brian picks up the paper and pretends to read it.

A lump forms in my throat and I walk into the little back room. This isn't how I imagined it would be. Blinking back tears, I tug open a drawer. It's filled with my stuff, and as I grab a bin-liner and begin to clear it out, I can't help wondering; if this is something I've wished for my whole life, why do I feel so bloody miserable?

Chapter Thirty-eight

At six o'clock Brian and I say our final goodbyes, both of us hiding behind brave faces as we crack feeble jokes and promise to keep in touch. Then it's time for me to go home. I've spent the afternoon gathering up everything I've accumulated these past six years and filled two large carrier-bags, but when he offers me a lift I fib and say I'm fine, they're actually quite light and I'm meeting Jess for a drink to celebrate.

None of which is true.

Struggling out of the tube station, the bags clanking against my shins and leaving little red marks, which I just know are going to turn into big purple bruises, I begin traipsing down the high street towards my flat. It's rush-hour and, as usual, it's swarming with noise and activity, exhaust fumes and cigarette smoke, but I barely notice it. Snippets of my conversation with Yvonne, flashbacks of Brian's reaction, stills from the interview with Victor Maxfield, a jumble of memories from six years at Together Forever – they're all edited into a montage that's spooling round and round in my mind.

I've heard about people going into shock after an accident or other traumatic experience, but after they've been offered their dream job? I'm pondering this when I notice I've reached the corner of my street and catch sight of a slouching figure in the window of Mrs Patel's. *It's me.*

I stop dead in the middle of the pavement. Honestly, Heather, what's wrong with you? Take that sorry expression off your face. Anyone would think you'd just *lost* your job. You should be over the moon. You should be rushing home to ring Lionel and Ed and break the fantastic news. You should be celebrating with champagne and getting merrily plastered and telling everyone how much you love them in a very slurred voice.

Well, OK, maybe not that bit.

I throw back my shoulders and smile unnaturally, like you do when you're being photographed and it's taking too long. C'mon, Heather. Just think. No more sniggering at parties when someone asks you what you do. No more comparing yourself to all your peers on Friends Reunited and feeling like a big, fat failure. No more looking down the lens and wishing you were photographing something other than a rosy-cheeked bride in butterscotch satin. This is it! You've done it! You're a success!

Looking past the pyramid of Batchelor's Cup-a-soups on special offer in the window, I stare hard at my reflection. Funny, but I always thought a success would look different somehow.

When I arrive at the flat, I dump my bags in the kitchen and decide to celebrate my good news by unhooking the phone from its cradle and start dialling. For the next half an hour I yabber away excitedly about my new job to Lionel, Jess's voicemail, and Lou, as I discover Ed's in Las Vegas at an orthodontists' convention, which 'is the best place for him as all we do when he's at home is row about football,' she huffs angrily. And then, once I've rung everyone, been congratulated and told to 'have a drink on me', I hang up and stare blankly round the kitchen.

OK, now what?

Drumming my fingers on the table I glance at the clock on the microwave: 19.03. Hmm, I wonder where Gabe is. At the thought of him I feel a tingle of excitement. I can't call him as he doesn't have a mobile, but I can't wait to share my news. He's going to be so excited – after all, it was his idea.

I tug open the fridge and peer inside. The bottle of champagne I bought when Gabe first moved in is still chilling, just waiting for a special occasion. And now I've got one. Excitedly I clasp my fingers round its gold tinfoil neck, set it down carefully on the table and grab two champagne flutes.

My mouth waters. The Moët's ice cold. Condensation clings

frostily to the dark glass and for a moment I stand there, staring at it, as if I was eyeing someone up in a bar. No, Heather, I tell myself sternly. You have to wait for Gabe.

I glance at the clock again: 19.07. He'll be home in a minute. I set about distracting myself: feeding Billy Smith, giving the hob a once-over, rearranging the fridge magnets.

Perhaps one little glass won't hurt.

Heather. Nobody drinks champagne by themselves. You have to drink it *with* someone. Idly I pick up a satsuma and peel it, concentrating on stripping the stringy threads of pith off each segment, before savouring the little bursts of sweet juice as I pop them into my mouth one by one.

Which takes up about three minutes.

Not even just one teensy-weensy drop?

I eyeball the Moët lustfully. I can feel my resolve weakening. After all, why shouldn't I drink champagne alone? Why should society dictate that it's a couple activity? I grab the bottle and rip off the tinfoil. Anyway, it's not like I'm going to drink the whole *bottle*. I just want a taste. Squeezing the cork with my thumb, it explodes with a loud pop, and grabbing my glass I hold it underneath to catch the froth of amber liquid.

Three glasses later, I'm tipsy. Duetting with Michael Crawford, I pirouette round the kitchen in my satin stilettos, flinging out my arms and closing my eyes as we reach the crescendo. I feel exhilarated. Alive. So happy I'm going to burst. I take in a deep lungful of air, throw back my head and really go for it. You know, I have to say I think I've got a really good voice. I'm a natural. I should have been on the stage. With a bit of training, I'd make a great dancer. I mean, look at Catherine Zeta-Jones. All it takes is practice and a pair of fishnets. And I'd end up with amazing thighs from all that high kicking.

Just like this . . . Champagne slops over the edge of my glass as I thrust my leg into the air – Tad-daah! My stiletto heel skids on the wet lino and I land with a crash on my bottom. *Ouch.* Well, obviously I'd need to practise a bit.

Dragging myself shakily to my feet, I limp to a stool and pour myself another glass of champagne. Wincing, I sip it medicinally. Fuck, I could murder a cigarette. I consider running to the corner shop for a packet of Marlboro Lights, but my ankle gives a painful twinge. Oh, well, scrap that idea. I take a consolatory swig of champagne.

But it's no good.

I really wish I had a cigarette.

Then I remember. Gabe smokes.

Joyfully, I limp into the hallway and head for his room. I'm sure he won't mind, smoker in need and all that. I go to push open the door when something in the nook under the stairs catches my attention. It's the little green light on the answering-machine, tucked away behind a vase of wilting red roses. It's blinking to tell me I've got a message. What with everything going on, I forgot to check it when I came in.

Hobbling over I glance at the display. Three messages. I press the play and wait expectantly. It beeps. '*Hello, don't hang up. This is IPC Finance and we can save you thousands on your mortgage . . .*' I hit delete impatiently and the machine beeps to signal the next. '*Hey, honey, it's me and I'm lying by the pool . . .*'

Jess! Cheered, I listen to her nattering on about how she's having a good time in Cape Town and how she's decided to lay off men for a while. I can hear her puffing away at a cigarette, which reminds me of my craving. I push open Gabe's door.

'*. . . so I thought to myself, You know what Jess? If it happens it happens . . .*'

I can hear her chattering away in the background an I scan the room for the familiar sight of a red and white packet. My eyes come to rest on the bookshelf in the corner. Aha. Triumphantly I pounce on twenty Marlboros and pull out a cigarette.

'*. . . because you're right, better to have loved and lost than— Beeeeep.*

The answering-machine cuts her off in mid-sentence. Trust Jess, I don't think she's ever left a succinct message. Unlike the owner of the next voice, which sounds short and efficient, as if they're in a hurry.

'*Hi, Gabe . . .*'

I feel a ping of disappointment. Damnit, I was hoping it was going to *be* Gabe.

'*It's your uncle . . .*'

Huh, so this is the uncle he's always talking about. I help myself to a lighter and turn to leave. I should've known. He's got an American accent, but it's much milder than Gabe's. In fact, it's really funny but he sounds just like . . .

'. . . *Victor*,' says the voice on the telephone.

Maxfield, finishes the voice inside my head.

I freeze. Victor Maxfield is Gabe's uncle? My flatmate is the nephew of my new boss? For an instant I'm numb. Then, like a ten-tonne truck, it hits me.

That's why I got the job.

The message keeps playing, something about changing the restaurant they were meeting in tonight, but I'm no longer listening as my mind's gone into freefall. That's why Gabe suggested applying to the *Sunday Herald*. That's how come I got the interview. That's why after six years of getting absolutely nowhere . . . Suddenly I feel sick. I clamp my hand across my mouth and sink to my knees.

Fuck.

'Hey, where are you?'

I'm not sure how long I've been sitting on the rug, deafened by the sounds of my dreams crashing around me, when I hear the voice. Dazed, I look up and focus on the figure in front of me. It's Gabe. Standing in the doorway in his motorcycle jacket, he's staring at me in confusion.

And, staring right back at him, I feel my shock and hurt mutate into anger.

'*You bastard*.'

Chapter Thirty-nine

Gabe pales. 'What's going on?' he whispers, his eyes searching mine.

'You know exactly what's going on,' I sneer, hauling myself off the carpet. Everything is piecing together like some hideous, hideous jigsaw puzzle: Gabe dictating my application, his unerring optimism, Victor Maxfield's enthusiasm . . . A flashback of me in his office, showing him photographs, the feeling of pride when he complimented me on them. 'God, I'm such a fucking idiot.' I can't remember ever feeling so angry.

'Hey c'mon, calm down . . .' he begins placatingly.

'Calm down?' I know I'm shouting, but I can't stop. The alcohol is pumping through my veins, mixed with adrenaline and fury. It's a lethal combination. 'How dare you tell me to calm down, after everything you've done?'

'Done? What have I done?' he stares at me in bewilderment. Scraping his fingers through his hair, he waits for me to say something. Until gasping with impatience, he turns and drops his helmet on his bed. 'For Chrissakes,' he mutters, taking off his glasses wearily and pinching the bridge of his nose. 'I walk in here and the first thing you do is call me a bastard, and you're not even going to explain why.'

'Victor Maxfield,' I say simply.

I see his back stiffen, a slight hesitation. Then he looks at me brazenly. 'What about him?' He shrugs, but there's no mistaking the guilt in his eyes.

'Don't lie to me,' I snap.

'When have I ever lied?'

From the rug I glare up at him, hostility oozing from my pores. 'He's your uncle, Gabe,' I say flatly. My words strike him like an archer's arrow, and I see the flash of understanding in his eyes. 'I heard his message on the machine about the restaurant. The game's up,' I quip cuttingly.

'It was never a game—' he protests, steadfastness crumbling.

'Oh, yeah?' I interrupt. 'Pretending to come up with the idea, faking surprise when I got an interview. You should be the actor, not Mia.' All that champagne has magnified my emotions and loosened my tongue. I'm ripe for a huge row.

But Gabe's refusing to give me one. Jaw clenched, he's staring into the middle distance, shaking his head, as if determined not to believe what he's hearing.

'Don't you have anything to say?' I press, infuriated by his silence.

He turns away from the window to me. 'Look, I can see why you'd be a little annoyed but you're making too big a deal out of this.' He tries to smile, but suddenly I feel as if I'm just one big joke to him.

'Stop patronising me!' I yell, as tears of frustration squeeze out of the corners of my eyes. I blink them back determinedly. 'How dare you say I'm making a big deal out of this? It is a fucking big deal to me.'

'It doesn't have to be,' he tries again quietly.

'Says who? *You*? Just who the fuck do you think you are? What do you think gives you the right to play God with my life? Don't you understand? This was my big dream.'

'And I *know* that,' protests Gabe, suddenly vehement. 'That's *why* I did it. I knew it was what you'd always wanted.'

'But not like this,' I wail. 'Don't you understand? I wanted to get it on my own merit. I wanted Victor Maxfield to give me this job because he thinks I'm a great photographer—'

'But you *are* a great photographer!'

There's a pause.

'I didn't want you to find out,' he says quietly.

'Why? Because I'd react like this?' My voice is thick with

anger. What was I thinking? How could I have believed I got the job on my own talents?

'No,' Gabe is saying evenly, and I can see he's struggling to remain calm. 'Because you've got real talent, Heather. You've shown me your stuff and you just needed a break . . . like we all need breaks,' he falters, his Adam's apple bobbing up and down furiously. 'And that day when you said it was your childhood dream to work at the *Sunday Hearld*, and my uncle's the editor, it was such a coincidence. I mean, what are the chances of that happening?' For a moment his eyes seem filled with wonderment. 'It was like fate.'

'Fate?' My voice comes out all high-pitched. 'It's not fate. *It's cheating*.'

Gabe turns ashen.

'You even dictated that stupid letter,' I continue. 'Was this one of your jokes?' Even as I'm saying it I know I'm being cruel but I don't care. 'Because if it is it's not fucking funny.'

Gabe's expression hardens and I feel a sudden shift.

'Well, it wouldn't be, would it?' Bitterness is audible in his voice. 'Because I'm not funny, am I? What was it you said on the beach? My jokes are crap. I'm a crap comedian.'

I flinch. Did I really say that? It sounds so harsh. 'No I didn't say it like that—'

He cuts me off. 'Yes, you did. So now who's the fucking liar, Heather?'

I'm shocked into silence. All the colour has drained from Gabe's face but for two red blotches high on his cheeks. 'And, yes, you're right, I'm going to go up to Edinburgh and probably die a fucking death up there.'

Like a river that's burst its banks, the argument has changed direction and is rushing furiously out of control.

'That's not true, I . . .'

But Gabe's not listening to me and all at once I feel dizzy and sick. *How did we get here?* Heart thumping, I look fearfully at Gabe. His blue eyes are hard and angry and I want more than anything to make it stop. To rewind. To go back to how we were before.

'You're not the only one with dreams, Heather,' he says, tugging me back into what we've become.

'I know that,' I whisper. Oh, God, this is awful. Why did I have to hear that message? Why did I drink all that stupid champagne? A wave of nausea hits me and I steel myself.

'I should go.'

I look up. Gabe's face is grim. My chest tightens. 'What do you mean?'

'I'll pack my stuff.' His eyes are filled with hurt. 'I was leaving next weekend anyway.'

I hesitate for a second. I know that if I apologise right now I can probably persuade him to say, that if he leaves I'm going to regret it for ever, that if I don't say something within the next breath Gabe is going to walk out of my life and I'll never see him again.

But I'm just too pissed off, too proud, too angry and too goddamn hurt to care. 'Good,' I say flatly.

For a second I think I see a flash of disappointment, then it vanishes. 'Fine,' He nods. 'I'll leave first thing in the morning.'

Our eyes meet, but it's as if we don't see each other any more.

I get up shakily and turn to leave.

'You're right . . .'

I glance back.

Gabe's still staring after me, but instead of sadness in his face there's something horribly like contempt. 'I made a big mistake.' He speaks quietly, but his voice is hard and I know he's not referring to the interview.

I swallow hard, pride sticking in my throat. I am not going to let him see I'm upset. 'Yeah, me too,' I reply defiantly, and holding on to my resolve as tightly as I can, I walk out of the door.

Chapter Forty

A shaft of sunlight pokes its way through a gap in the blinds, stabbing my eyelids with urgent brightness. I let out a piteous moan. 'Urrrgggh.'

Billy Smith miaows in alarm and jumps off the duvet.

I haven't had a hangover like this for years. What was I drinking? My brain whirls groggily, and then, like a fruit machine, clicks into place. Champagne. Champagne. Champagne.

Oh, fuck. *Gabe.*

Remembering our argument I sit upright, which induces a spinning sensation, then lurch unsteadily out of bed. I reach for my dressing-gown, my feet tangling in the clothes that are strewn across the floor, and pull it tight round my naked body. I catch sight of my puffy, blotchy face in the wardrobe mirror. So much for waterproof mascara.

Last night comes back to me. Listening to the message on the answering-machine, realising that Victor Maxfield was Gabe's uncle, yelling at him '*You bastard.*' Flinching, I pad into the hallway, head thumping.

'*What was it you said on the beach? My jokes are crap. I'm a crap comedian . . .*' His bedroom door is ajar and I push it open with trepidation.

'*I'll leave first thing in the morning.*'

I stand motionless in the doorway, the shaft of sunlight on the hallway carpet growing wider as my worst fears are confirmed. His room is empty. Shelves once filled with joke books are now bare. Above the little wooden desk, the corkboard that had been covered with a clutter of photographs is blank but for a scattering of drawing-pins. There's a space in the corner where his guitar used to be propped – I only heard him play it once. Badly, I remember, smiling at the memory of him sitting in the garden clumsily trying to pick out the chords to Bowie's 'Life On Mars'.

I glance at the bed and the smile fades. The bedclothes are piled neatly on the mattress, and perching on the edge I hug my knees to my towelling chest. I begin to think of all the silly little things I'm going to miss about Gabe – walking into the kitchen in the morning and seeing him bent over the toaster, pretending not to listen while he reads me my daily horoscope, hitching a ride down to Cornwall on the back of his bike.

Remembering our weekend together, I sigh heavily. God, I miss him already. It's only been a few weeks since he moved in, but now the flat seems so empty without him, *without his energy*. I catch myself. I'm beginning to sound like him. It's *so* LA. But that's exactly what he has. A positive energy that, like a new lens on a camera, makes me look at my life in a different, brighter way.

And now he's gone.

A furry ginger head appears round the door and Billy Smith pads in. He sniffs round the empty room and miaows accusingly at me. As if I don't feel guilty enough. Now my cat is blaming me for getting rid of the nice man with the warm lap and fingers that tickled his ears for hours. 'Sssh, Billy Smith . . .' I reach out to stroke him but he darts away, knocking over the wastepaper basket as he jumps on to the window-ledge. He can't leave fast enough. But I have the same effect on everyone don't I? First Daniel, then Gabe, now my cat . . .

Dismayed, I watch him disappear into the garden, then crouch down to pick up the rubbish that's spilled on to the carpet. Old cigarette packets, empty Coke cans, an old copy of *Loot* . . .

My stomach flips.

It's the issue from a few weeks ago, the one with my ad for the flatshare – but that's not what makes me freeze. It's the small black biro heart that's been drawn round it. *By me.*

I'd forgotten all about it, but now I remember that evening

riding home on the tube, dashing off the train, dropping *Loot* in the rush and scrabbling to pick up all the pages. Gabe must have found the ones I'd left behind, noticed the love heart round my ad and called me. Coincidence after coincidence after coincidence. Or is it?

Suddenly I have a flashback: being squashed up on the tube, feeling sad and broke and lonely, staring out into the darkness of the tunnel, wishing I could find an answer to all my problems.

Followed by another: running home in the thunderstorm and meeting the gypsy with the lucky heather who promised me my luck would change and all my wishes would come true.

And then – *poof* – Gabe shows up on my doorstep like my fairy godmother with his magic wand, keeping the credit card companies at bay with his rent, inspiring me to start taking photographs again, being related to the editor of the *Sunday Herald*.

A shudder runs up my spine and I pull my dressing-gown round me. Is that why I got that job? Not because of Gabe *but because I wished it*?

Sinking to the floor, I stare at the pages in my hands. Until a few weeks ago I would have dismissed it as ridiculous, but a lot's happened in those few weeks and now the idea is exploding like a firework in my mind, showering me with questions. Is this all my fault? Am I the one to blame? Did I make this happen? Gabe might have pulled the strings, but ultimately he pulled those strings because of me – because *I* wished for that job. If I hadn't, none of this would have happened.

None of this would have happened. As the voice repeats inside my head I'm reminded of Ed's warning, 'Be careful what you wish for,' but this time I'm not dismissing him as a spoilsport. I'm finally listening to my big brother. And for once – just this once – I'm realising he was right. Be careful what you wish for – *because it might just come true.*

And it has all come true, hasn't it? But whereas a few weeks ago being offered my dream job, a huge salary and the kudos I've always dreamed of would have made me the happiest girl in the world, now I don't want it. I don't want any of it. It doesn't mean anything. I didn't get the job because of my talent, so I don't deserve it. It's an empty triumph that has cost me my friendship with Gabe. The realisation is like a kick in my stomach. What have you done, Heather? What *have* you gone and done?

Crouching on the floor, I close my eyes, trying to block everything out, but it's like I've opened a door and all the wishes from the past weeks rush back to me. Little boomerangs of hopeful energy that I've chucked out into the universe to be granted, some big, some small, but they form into a long list. I try ignoring it, but I can't. I've spent the last weeks on an amazing fun-filled shopping spree, wishing for this, that and the other, indulging my every whim, never stopping to think of the consequences. Now it's time to face up to them: now I have to pay for it all.

Filled with apprehension, I work my way through the list.

I wished . . .

- for the perfect man.

As I think about James my stomach lurches. I wished for him when I was with Jess in the changing room at Zara, and then – abracadabra – there he was, waiting for me in the wine section of Mrs Patel's a few hours later. A romantic-comedy-loving, Dido-listening, three-hundred-thread-count-bedlinen-owning male, whose hobbies included foreplay, romance and talking about his feelings. And the icing on this perfect thirty-six-year-old man? Telling me he loved me. Only I didn't love him.

- for a miracle to get Together Forever out of debt.

And, boy, did we get one. A huge society wedding that will put the business firmly back in the black. Only it just so happens to be my ex-boyfriend's.

- to win the lottery.

It hurts even to think about this one as I'm pretty certain I did get all six numbers, but I wish I hadn't. It makes getting my bag stolen with the ticket inside even worse. One minute there I was, spending my millions, living in a mansion, driving around in an Aston Martin, and the next it had all been snatched away and I had to spend the afternoon in a police station, instead of with Gabe on Hampstead Heath.

- England would win against France.

Yes, their spectacular final goal made sporting history and put a permanent smile on my brother's face, but it's also thrown his marriage into jeopardy. Instead of focusing on Lou and the baby he spends all his time glued to the TV watching football on SKY Sport. So much so that I'm worried my little niece or nephew is going to end up with divorced parents. And it's all going to be Auntie Heather's fault.

- for no traffic on the roads.

It was fantastic until I got a speeding ticket, three points on my licence and a sixty-pound fine – which I keep forgetting to pay.

Wretched, I haul myself to my feet and walk over to the window. Resting my elbows on the ledge I gaze out into the sunshine-filled garden. Which brings me on to the next wish on my list:

- that it would be sunny every day.

A bumble bee buzzes past and I watch him bounce from one flower to the next, trying to gather pollen. Except Mr Bumble Bee can't find enough because all the plants are wilting – we haven't had a drop of rain. Guilt stabs. Now I feel like a bumble-bee murderer.

- for those pink satin stilettos in a size five.

If I hadn't been wearing them last night I wouldn't have slipped on the kitchen floor and hurt myself. Right on cue my swollen ankle twinges painfully and I rub it gingerly.

- that I could lose those stubborn few pounds.

I thought I'd be really happy but it's very disappointing. Only Jess has commented – but she said my boobs were looking a bit smaller and my face was drawn . . .

And it's the same with *all* of my wishes, I realise suddenly. Yes, I got the perfect boyfriend, the dream job, the size ten figure and all the empty tube seats, front-of-queues, parking spaces and *pain-au-chocolats* I could ever wish for. But sitting here, with just a thudding hangover and a raw sense of regret to keep me company, all the gloss, fun and excitement of the last weeks have disappeared. And I'm left with the harsh truth.

None of my wishes have made me happy.

I bury my head in my hands. I don't know what to do. It's all such a mess. I want it all to go away, for everything to be how it was before, but how?

Then it comes to me in a flash.

Of course – the lucky heather.

Before, it seemed like a blessing, but now it's like a curse. If I can find it and throw it away, everything will be OK. I can put everything back to how it was.

I jump to my feet. The last time I had it was at my interview – I put it in my pocket for good luck. The irony isn't lost on me and I rush into the hallway, unearth my cream jacket from the layers of coats hanging by the door and thrust my hand into the pocket.

But it's not there. I check the other side. Empty. I feel a pang of alarm. I can't have lost it. I look on the floor in case it's fallen out somewhere – and then notice something lying on the mat. A letter.

Distractedly I pick it up.

The Sunday Herald,
45 Kings Way
London W1 5OY

34 Spring Street
Flat B
Little Venice
London W9 7PG

Dear Miss Hamilton,

Further to our recent interview, I have great pleasure in offering you the position of staff photographer with the

Sunday Herald. Salary will start at £35,000 with a review after six months. Monica Hodgekins in Human Resources will be in touch to confirm your start date and provide details of our private health plan and pension scheme. If you have any queries in the meantime please contact her on ext. 435.

Yours sincerely,

Victor Maxfield

Victor Maxfield

I take a moment to absorb each word, to savour every syllable. Except whereas once I would have been over the moon to open this letter, now I feel only bitterness and regret.

And so for the next twenty minutes I do one of the hardest things I've ever done. I write a letter I never imagined I would write, turning down Victor Maxfield's offer. In it I explain why: about Gabe, how I can't take a job I don't deserve, and how I still respect him as an editor. Then I fold it neatly into three, slide it into an envelope, and seal it and my fate. I feel a wave of relief. Now I can put it behind me like one of those mistakes I'm supposed to learn by. I can forget all about it. I can forget about Gabe.

Without washing my face, I pull on an old tracksuit and my Uggs and, with my sore ankle, trudge to the postbox on the corner. For once I don't have to wish for a stamp: I have one in my purse. I stick it on to the letter and shove it through the slot. But I can't let go. For a moment my resolve wavers. Then I open my fingers and hear it drop softly inside.

There. It's over.

The burble of my mobile interrupts my mood. I reach into my pocket and glance at the display. Briefly, I hope it's Gabe, but it's my father. A warm glow engulfs me. If anyone can make me feel better, it's Lionel.

'Hi there,' I say, feeling a rush of love for him.

'Heather, it's Rosemary.'

I feel a stab of disappointment, followed by irritation. What's she bothering me for?

'Something's happened.'

An icy hand grasps my heart. 'What is it?'

There's silence, then—

'Your father's had a heart-attack.'

And the bottom falls out of my world.

Chapter Forty-one

I don't remember what happened next. My mind simply shut down.

To most people the thought of losing a parent is inconceivable – you can't imagine it, you don't want to imagine it. As they grow older you might think about it sometimes, but only briefly, and then you push it from your mind. But when it's happened to you, it's all too real. It can happen. It does happen.

It happened to me.

My mother, a vibrant redhead with a laugh that made you feel as if you'd been dipped in melted happiness, isn't here to laugh any more. She's gone, her life rubbed out like a child's pencil drawing. And now the prospect that Lionel might—

Fear stops the word forming in my mind. I cling to the steering-wheel of my MG and force myself to stay focused on the car ahead.

I'm on the M4 on my way to Cornwall. I'm not sure how long I've been driving. Two, maybe three hours. Everything's a blur, – vague memories of going back to the flat, asking a neighbour to feed Billy Smith, throwing some stuff into a bag. I glance into the rear-view mirror and catch sight of my haggard face, the deep crease etched between my eyebrows. I'm still wearing my ratty old tracksuit, and I think Lou must have called me as I know Ed's on a flight back from the States, but I don't remember speaking to her. In fact, I don't remember much at all about the last few hours, except Rosemary urging, 'Get here soon, Heather, you must get here soon,' her voice filled with foreboding.

Pressing the accelerator pedal to the floor, I pull out to

overtake the car in front of me. There's a blasting horn, and I swerve sharply, narrowly missing a silver BMW I hadn't noticed alongside me in the next lane. The driver races past, giving me the finger. Before, I would have yelled some obscenity, but now it barely registers. Instead I stare fixedly ahead, concentrating on making it to the hospital in time.

In time.

In time for what?

Until now I've been too afraid to acknowledge the unspoken fear, but huddled in my car on the stretch of grey motorway, I face up to it. I'm trying to make it to the hospital in time to say goodbye.

The journey from London to Cornwall is the longest, scariest one of my life. It's late afternoon when I reach Newquay and see the signs for St Luke's Royal Infirmary. But it's not until my first glimpse of the hospital that I recognise it: this was where Mum had her chemo. Pulling into the car park, I gaze up at the ugly concrete building, a casualty of sixties architecture. I haven't been here for nearly twenty years, yet I remember it as if it were yesterday.

I find what seems like the last space and, ignoring the 'Pay & Display' signs, I run across the hot Tarmac, weaving through row upon row of cars, the bright sun glinting off their bonnets. Indignation bites. How can the sun be shining when inside that building my father is fighting for his life? The sky should be grey and there should be a fine, persistent drizzle that will dampen my clothes and make me feel wretched. Instead of just numb.

I hurry towards the automatic doors – then falter. Visitors are arriving with flowers and the obligatory grapes, and I move sideways so that they can enter. I need to go in too, but it's as if I'm twelve, visiting Mum – so scared that I've started wetting the bed again.

'Y'okay, love?' One of the visitors, a middle-aged lady with a bunch of pink chrysanthemums, is looking at me with concern and I see that I'm white-knuckling the railing.

'Er, yeah, I'm fine – thank you. I just needed a bit of fresh air.'

'It'll be all right,' she murmurs, giving my arm a supportive pat, before turning away. I watch as she disappears through the doors and drawing strength from this stranger's gesture, I release my hand from the railing. Dad made a promise never to say goodbye and neither will I. Gathering my courage, I go inside.

The hospital is a labyrinth of wards and corridors, but finally I'm directed to the intensive-care unit and find Rosemary sitting on a plastic seat in the corridor. Handbag in her lap, she's staring straight ahead, mouth pursed, jaw tight, face devoid of emotion. She turns as she hears my footsteps.

'Heather, you're here – finally.' I'm struck by how everything she says sounds like an accusation. Still clutching her handbag, she stands up, then hesitates, as if unsure how to greet me. Eventually she kisses my cheek awkwardly. She smells artificial, like air-freshener, and I stand stiffly, my hands clenched into fists. I dig my fingernails deep into the palms of my hands, but I can't feel anything.

'Where's my dad?' I don't want to call him Lionel. He's my dad. My flesh and blood. Mine, not yours, I think, staring defiantly at Rosemary.

'He's in Intensive Care.'

'I want to see him.'

'We can't just yet. The doctors—'

'Doctors? What do the doctors know?' Memories of my mother flood back.

Rosemary is horrified. 'Heather, please.' She shushes me. 'Your father's had a massive coronary.'

My throat tightens, and suddenly all the love I have for him mutates into anger for her. 'How?' I gasp accusingly. 'How did this happen? You live with him, you're supposed to look after him!' Even as I'm saying it, I know I'm being a bitch. It's not her fault – it's not anyone's fault. But I can't stop myself: it's as if all the hurt and resentment of the past years are rising to the surface like bubbles.

But Rosemary doesn't react. Her face, with its rouged cheeks and powdered nose, remains impassive. 'Heather, you're upset,' she says stiffly, smoothing her skirt before she sits down again. 'I did everything I could. As soon as it happened I called for an ambulance. The paramedics were so very good . . .'

As she talks I feel as if a huge weight is crushing me and have to sit down – if I don't I might fall down.

'. . . but he arrested twice in the ambulance. They had to rush him straight into theatre . . .' She leaves the sentence hanging as if she's too afraid to finish it, and clutches her bag tighter in her lap.

And then neither of us speaks.

The terrible thing that should have brought us closer together is pushing us further apart. Instead of comforting each other, we sit silently side by side, staring at the mustard-coloured walls, our weary bodies folded uncomfortably into hard, plastic chairs. Two people, one fear and a million insurmountable miles between them.

A few moments later the clanging of the fire doors causes me to turn my head sharply. An older man in a green surgeon's gown and cap is walking towards us.

'Mrs Hamilton?' He looks at us both, his expression grave.

So, this is it. Fear crushes the breath out of my body. 'I'm Miss Hamilton, his daughter,' I manage.

He holds out his hand. 'I'm Mr Bradley. I performed your father's angioplasty.'

As he speaks his voice seems to be fading, as if he's moving down a long tunnel. All I can hear is my own breath, rushing in and rushing out, like the waves on the beach less than a mile away. And now I'm remembering Lionel teaching me how to swim in the sea, my arms flailing in bright orange armbands, his strong hands holding me under my tummy. 'I won't let you go, Heather, I won't let you go,' he booms, over and over again. But, of course he does and, kicking my legs and arms as hard as I can, I manage to stay afloat.

Just like I'll stay afloat now, I tell myself, forcing myself back to hear Rosemary ask the question I'm too afraid to. 'How is he?'

I brace myself.

'The operation went well . . .'

Like a drowning man, I come up gasping for air. Relief is flooding me.

'We had to perform an angioplasty to remove the blockage in the coronary artery . . .'

Rosemary clasps her hands beneath her chin as if in prayer.

'. . . which is entirely normal in these situations,' continues the surgeon, his deep voice reassuring. 'We've done an ECG and other tests to confirm the diagnosis, and at the moment he's heavily sedated and in recovery . . .'

As he's speaking I'm standing statue-still, anaesthetised by the shock of everything that's been happening.

Unlike Rosemary who breaks down and sobs almost hysterically. 'Oh, thank you, Doctor, thank you, thank you . . .'

The surgeon glances at me. I know he's expecting me to comfort her, but I don't move – I can't. I've never seen Rosemary betray emotion before and stare at her blankly.

There's an awkward pause.

'Now I know this has been a tremendous shock . . .' The surgeon puts his arm round Rosemary's shoulders, easing her gently into her chair. He beckons a passing nurse. '. . . and I know this is hard, but you must try to be strong. I'm afraid I must warn you that your husband isn't out of danger yet. The first forty-eight hours after a heart-attack are critical and he will need you to be there for him.'

As the nurse arrives, he gestures for her to take over and I watch her crouch to offer Rosemary tissues and words of compassion.

'Miss Hamilton?' The doctor's grey eyes are searching my face, and for a moment I think he's judging me. But then he smiles kindly. 'Would you like to see your father?' and I realise the only person judging me is myself.

The room is quiet, but for the faint beeping of the heart monitor. After the starkness of the corridor outside, it seems strangely calming. In the corner, a bed is surrounded by a cluster of machines and monitors attached to the network of wires, tubes and drips that are keeping my father alive.

I creep up quietly and gaze down at his ashen face. My legs buckle and I have to cling to the side of the bed for support.

This isn't my dad. My dad is a giant of a man who could pick up Ed and me together as children and swing us round until we yelled for mercy. Who greets me with a bearhug so strong he almost cracks my ribs. Who loves food, art and life with a burning passion. Who, from the moment I was born, has wrapped me in a blanket of unconditional love that makes me feel safe and protected.

In his place is a pale, shrunken figure, lying on a bed, chest slowly rising and falling. All his strength has disappeared. He looks weak, vulnerable, *fragile*. 'I'm here, Dad,' I whisper, slipping my fingers round his hand and holding it.

And as I do, my whole world melts away. All those stupid lists of things I need to do. All those trivial worries about cellulite and what to wear, or finding Mr Right. All my dissatisfaction and the things I want to change, like getting a better job, more money, firmer thighs. None of it matters any more.

Squeezing hard, I stare at his face. I've been so stupid and selfish, wasting all this time wishing for things I didn't have, all this . . . I think back over all the hundreds of trivial, irrelevant, unimportant wishes . . . *all this stuff*. Stuff that I don't want, need or care about now that I have it. I took everything for granted – I didn't appreciate what I had. And now I'm in danger of losing it all.

I press my lips tenderly to my dad's forehead. Until now, wishing for things has been just a part of everyday life. But I was wrong. Wishes are sacred. They're about magic. It's just as the old gypsy woman said when she gave me the lucky heather: *Use it wisely and it will bring you your heart's desire*.

A lone tear splashes on my hand like a drop of rain. Then another, and another. Great big fat tears that spill down my cheeks, blurring my eyes and soaking my face, until I'm sobbing so hard my body's shaking. Because now I know what the old gypsy woman was trying to tell me. But I haven't been wise at all: I've been careless, irresponsible and so bloody foolish.

Well, I'm not going to be any more.

And it's here, in a tiny room in Intensive Care, with the sound of the heart monitor keeping beat in the background, and my father's hand in mine, that I make my final wish – and it's the only wish that's ever mattered.

I wish for my father to live.

I'm not sure how long I stand here holding my father's hand, but the next thing I know the doctor arrives, and gently unlacing my fingers, tells me to go home, to get some sleep: my father needs to rest.

'I'm fine.'

'You look exhausted.'

I shake my head firmly. 'I'm not going home. I'm not leaving him.'

'Your stepmother said exactly the same thing,' he says, gesturing outside to the corridor where she's still waiting.

'She did?' I feel a jolt of surprise. I had assumed Rosemary would want to spend the night at home. She likes her comforts.

'Lionel's a very lucky man to have both of you,' he smiles kindly, 'and you're lucky to have each other. Family is very important at a time like this.'

I've never considered Rosemary part of my family before: she's always been a usurper, an outsider, someone who doesn't belong. And for the first time it occurs to me that she might have felt like that too. 'Thanks, Doctor.'

'My pleasure.' He leads me across the room to the door. 'Just don't say I didn't warn you about the appalling coffee.'

Chapter Forty-two

'Shall I get us some coffee?'

Rosemary looks up from the scuffed linoleum floor as she hears my voice. Her eyes are red from crying.

'The doctor says it's not very good, though,' I add, smiling nervously.

We look at each other for a moment and it's as if a few bricks in that invisible wall between us dissolve. Not many, just enough for us to see each other for the first time.

She smiles tentatively. 'That would be lovely. Do you need money?' She reaches for her handbag but I stop her.

'My wallet's in here somewhere.' I rummage through all the rubbish in my bag and locate it, only to discover that the coin compartment is empty. 'Can you change a tenner?' I pull one out and waggle it hopefully.

'Take my purse,' says Rosemary, holding it out to me. 'There's change in the side pocket.'

'Are you sure? Maybe I could ask someone else . . .'

'I might be a pensioner, but I can still afford to buy you a cup of coffee,' she says. 'And, anyway, if it's as bad as the doctor said we won't be needing to buy another.'

Smiling, I give in, take her purse and walk down the corridor in search of a vending machine. After a few minutes I discover one in a waiting room filled with tired, frightened-looking people, some huddling close to each other in tiny groups, others flicking through out-of-date copies of women's weeklies and nursing plastic coffee cups. Then there are those, like the old man in the corner, who are sitting alone staring blankly at nothing. I notice his fingers. Bent out of shape with arthritis, they're twisting his gold wedding band round and round and round.

I look away. It dawns on me just how lucky I am that I'm not alone, that I've got Rosemary, that we've got each other. I glance at the clock on the wall. It's going to be a long night.

I begin feeding ten-pence pieces into the slot. There's a whir and a plastic cup appears, and begins to fill with powder and water. I retrieve it and balance it on top of the machine, then scrabble around for more change for the second cup. Some of the coins are wedged into the corner, and I'm tilting the purse to get at them when something falls out on to the floor.

I pick it up. It's a photograph, small with a white border, a picture of Rosemary and Lionel, but they both look younger. Lionel's wearing a flamboyant peacock green suit and Rosemary's in a tasteful cream frock coat with a pillbox hat perched on her chignon. Absently I flick it over. On the back there's an inscription in my father's handwriting:

For my wonderful wife on our wedding day,
Thank you for making me happy again.
All my love
Lionel

Of course. This is a photograph of their wedding ten years ago. It was on a cruise ship, just the two of them. Ed and I couldn't go. Didn't want to go, I correct myself. I've never even asked to see their wedding album, though I remember Rosemary wanting to show it to me when I came home from university. I made up some excuse about being too busy. Too busy. I pause to let the words register. I've been too busy for the last ten years.

I feel a stab of guilt. All this time I've been resenting Rosemary but now, seeing this inscription, I realise I'm indebted to her. Somehow, over the years, I've blocked out the memories of how devastated Dad was when Mum died, how for years afterwards when he smiled there was always a lost, haunted look in his eyes, and how when he met Rosemary it went away.

''Scuse me, have you finished?'

A young guy in a beanie hat is gesturing at the machine with a handful of change.

'Oh, sorry I won't be a minute.' I slip the photograph back into the purse, stuff it into my pocket and quickly feed more money into the vending machine. The plastic cup fills quickly and I grab it along with my own. There's something I need to do and it's long overdue.

'I'm sorry.'

'I beg your pardon?' Rosemary's brow furrows as I hand her a plastic cup of coffee. Then comprehension floods her face. 'Oh, I see. Is it really that bad?' She peers suspiciously at the brown liquid that's masquerading as coffee.

I stand in front of her awkwardly. 'No, it's not that.' This is much harder than I imagined.

'Heather, sit down.' Rosemary pats the chair next to hers.

I do as she says and take a gulp of coffee. Yuk, it really is as foul as it looks. I glance at Rosemary. 'I want to apologise,' I blurt out. 'I've been a total bitch. All that stuff I said before—'

'It's OK,' she interrupts, laying a hand on my arm. 'I understand.'

'No, you don't.' I gather the courage to meet her eyes. 'I want to apologise for the way I've behaved over all these years, for resenting you for taking Mum's place, for wishing you weren't part of our lives . . .'

There. I've finally admitted it. 'I'm so sorry, Rosemary. I've been such an idiot.' I swallow hard. She's going to hate me now, and I don't blame her. I hate myself too.

There's a pause while she absorbs what I've said. 'Thank you, Heather, I appreciate that,' she says quietly, after a moment. 'You have no idea how much it means to me.'

Her graciousness catches me by surprise.

'But I need to apologise to you too.'

She's gazing at her coffee, deep in thought. 'I'm guilty too. I've been jealous of the close relationship you have with Lionel. I don't have that with my children. Annabel and I—' She runs her top teeth over her bottom lip, which still bears the traces of frosted-pink lipstick. 'Well, let's just say we don't understand each other like you two do.'

We both smile, despite ourselves.

'And I'm jealous that you remind him of Julia . . .'

'Mum?' I whisper quietly.

'I know it's wicked of me,' she confesses, 'to be envious of my husband's daughter because she looks like her mother, to feel threatened because she's a constant reminder of his first wife . . .' Her eyes fill and she looks up at me, her face white and pinched. 'I'm a bad person.'

I've never thought of it from her perspective, but now suddenly I'm seeing just how difficult it's been for her. Instinctively I reach out and squeeze her hand, and it occurs to me that this is the first time I've ever touched her with affection. 'You're a good person, Rosemary, a really good one,' I say reassuringly. And I'm not just saying it. I mean it. She is. All these years and I just never realised it.

'Am I?' A tear rolls down the side of her nose and splashes into her coffee.

'Well, either that or we're both horrible.' I shrug, and a smile breaks through her tears.

'I never tried to replace Julia,' she says quietly.

'I know,' I nod, wondering why we didn't have this conversation a long time ago.

'I never could and I never wanted to. Just like Lionel could never replace Lawrence, my first husband.' She looks at me, and for the first time I see real fear. 'I couldn't bear to lose someone so dear to me again. I love your father so much, Heather. I don't know what I'd do without him.' Her voice trembles and bowing her head she breaks down and sobs.

And now it's up to me to be strong, I tell myself, because even though I echo that same thought in my mind, I know Lionel wouldn't want us to cry for him. If he were here now he'd wrap us both in his arms and make us feel better. But he can't at the moment so it's my turn.

I hold Rosemary close – because that's what dad would want . . . and I want it too.

It's a long night. Eventually Rosemary drifts off but I can't sleep and just sit there, drinking coffee and flicking through old magazines.

After a few hours I need to stretch my legs and go outside. It's still warm, and there's a stillness you don't get in London. A calm that makes you believe everyone and everything is sleeping and you're the only person awake in the whole world. In the car park, I see a couple of people huddled close, smoking. It's a few of the nurses and I hesitate for a moment. Under the circumstances, I shouldn't even be thinking of it, but I walk up to them anyway: 'Would you have a spare cigarette?'

They stop talking, and one of the nurses looks at me sympathetically. I haven't seen a mirror, but I must look like I feel. 'I shouldn't really . . .' She offers me a Silk Cut Ultra Low. 'Just don't tell anyone.'

'I won't, promise.' Smiling gratefully I accept a light and walk to where the car park meets open fields. I take a drag of the cigarette and tilt my face up to the sky. There's a full moon, glowing milky white in the darkness. I gaze at it and can't help wondering if Gabe is looking at it too. In Edinburgh. I let out a deep sigh. I want to call him and tell him what's happened with my father.

But I can't.

Sadness aches and dropping the unsmoked cigarette on the ground I squash it with my boot. It tasted horrible anyway.

I don't know how long I stay outside – I lose track of time – but when I go back in Rosemary is still dozing. Curled up across three plastic chairs, she's using her handbag as a pillow. I spread her jacket over her as a makeshift blanket. I'm tired too now. I sit on the last remaining seat next to her, lean my head against the fire extinguisher and think about my father, just a few metres away. I tell myself that he's going to make a full recovery and live to be a hundred, but it's hard. Like the doctor said, he's not out of danger yet.

Rosemary lets out a quiet moan, and I glance down at her. For the first time I feel bonded to her by our love for Lionel. It brings a strange comfort. Because, as hard and painful as it is to think about it, if we have to say goodbye, at least we'll say it together. And with my eyelids weighing heavy, I close my eyes and surrender myself to sleep.

Chapter Forty-three

I wake up with a start. Where am I? I sit bolt upright. Then it punches me like a fist in the stomach. *Dad.*

Rosemary is still asleep, as I stagger to my feet. What time is it? The clock on the wall reads just after six. I've been asleep for hours.

The hospital is still quiet and, as I hurry down the corridor towards Intensive Care, I don't see anyone. Even the nurses who were sitting outside on Reception have gone. I glance at the windows, but I can't see through the blinds. With no one around to stop me, I push open the door.

Inside, the room's dimly lit and silent but for the sound of the heart monitor beeping rhythmically. A wave of relief sweeps over me.

He's still alive.

Honestly, it's as basic as that.

Breathing deeply, I approach the bed quietly so as not to wake him. I reach out to stroke his hand, then snatch mine away.

It's not my father.

My stomach freefalls. A much younger man is lying in my father's bed. I notice the thick blue tattoo of a bird etched on the side of his neck, a pulse beating, the pallor of his skin. All in a fraction of a second as the ground tips under me.

'Excuse me, but you can't be in here.'

I whirl round to see two nurses.

'Where's my dad?' I cry desperately. 'What's happened to him? What have you done with him?' My mind's spinning, and as they rush towards me I'm gasping for breath. Now they're holding me and trying to comfort me but I can't hear what they're saying. I can't hear anything but the howl inside my head. Because I know.

'He's dead, isn't he?' I gasp. 'He's dead . . . he's dead . . .'

They lead me, stumbling, out of the room, supporting me as I flop like a rag doll.

'Miss Hamilton, it's Mr Bradley . . . Miss Hamilton, you have to listen to me . . .'

A man in a white coat looms over me but I can't focus. Darkness is closing in from around the edges and everything is receding.

'We needed the bed for an emergency in the middle of the night. Your father has been moved to the coronary unit. He's doing fine. He's awake and asking for you . . .'

And then everything goes black.

'Did I give you two a bit of a shock?'

It's later. Rosemary and I are sitting at either side of Lionel's bed each holding one of his hands.

'I think it was Heather who gave us a shock.' Rosemary smiles. My cheeks redden. How embarrassing – flipping out like that and fainting at Mr Bradley's feet. I feel like a complete moron.

Then I look at my father. Never forget, Heather. You came this close – *this close* – to losing him.

Apparently Lionel can't remember anything after the first heart-attack and it's been something of a shock for him to discover that not only is he in hospital, but that he's undergone heart surgery. Much less dramatic, but momentous in its own way, is the change in the relationship between Rosemary and me.

'Just look, here I am with the two beautiful women in my life.' He smiles approvingly. 'I'll have to do this again.'

'Oh, no, you won't,' scolds Rosemary. 'And to make sure, Ed is going to be staying with us. I just had a message. He's arriving this afternoon.'

'With a nutritionist friend from LA,' I add.

Lionel manages a grimace.

'You heard what the doctor said. It's very important you stick to this diet. No cheese, no wine . . .'

'No fun,' he whimpers.

'Lionel, you're not going to make me a widow for the second time,' warns Rosemary, in a voice that makes even me a little scared.

'Me? Disobey doctor's orders? I wouldn't dream of it.' He puckers his lips for a kiss.

'You've had a heart-attack, you need to rest.'

'I want a kiss, my dear, not a sexual marathon.'

Rosemary blushes, and I stand up. 'I'll leave you two lovebirds to it.' Once I would have felt resentful, but now I feel a warm sense of contentment and pressing my lips lightly to my father's whiskery cheek, I whisper. 'See you later, alligator.'

And, smiling, he whispers right back, 'In a while, crocodile.'

I spend the next few days at the cottage. Ed duly arrives with his nutritionist friend, a woman named Miranda whom he met at university and who now runs successful practices in London and Los Angeles. She's here for a whirlwind twenty-four hours, meeting Lionel and his doctors, drawing up detailed diet plans and nutritious low-fat recipes, which she pins all over the small oak kitchen as if she's wallpapering a room.

Lionel is discharged at the weekend. I can call him Lionel again now, as he's definitely back to being Lionel. Bushy-faced, loud-voiced and larger than life – though soon to be sixty pounds lighter, if Miranda has anything to do with it. And I think he will be. Despite his jokes and bravado, he's had a shock. Every so often I hear a tremble in his voice and when Rosemary orders him to eat up his grilled chicken breast and steamed curly kale, he gets on with it like an obedient child, without so much as a whinge for a glass of pinot noir.

I'm more than happy. And it's on afternoons sitting outside on the lawn with Lionel, Ed and Rosemary, laughing at some crappy joke or other, I think of how I got my wish – and with it, much more than I could have ever imagined.

'So, how's that young American chap getting on?'

We've just finished another healthy picnic lunch when Lionel brings up the subject of Gabe. Honestly, I swear my father's a bloody mind-reader.

'Er, he's moved out,' I say, as casually as I can, but it's as if I've been stung.

The past few days have revolved round Lionel, getting everything ready at the house for his homecoming, including moving his bed downstairs, and making sure he gets his medication at the right times. We've all been so busy with him that we haven't been able to think of anything else.

Except that's not true. I can be falling asleep at night, or loading the dishwasher, or sitting on the grass with the sun on my face when my mind drifts to Gabe. Like some bizarre cerebral homing pigeon.

'He's gone up to the Edinburgh Festival,' I add, feeling as if I have to offer an explanation. Even if it's not the full story.

Lionel beams at the thought of all those thespians, artists and musicians. 'Are you going to go up and see his show?'

'No.'

'Oh, right.' He raises his eyebrows.

There's a pause and I can feel looks flying round the garden. 'What?' I demand hotly.

'Nothing, sis,' says Ed evenly and smirks into his mobile. Since his return from America he's been constantly on the phone to Lou. It's only a few weeks now until the baby's due, and Lionel's brush with death has made him realise what's important in life. And it's not football.

'Oh, we don't want to talk about some boring old festival, do we?' pooh-poohs Rosemary. 'Tell us all about that high-society wedding.'

I smile gratefully at her attempt to rescue me, but I've been trying not to think about Lady Charlotte's wedding. 'It's this weekend at Shillingham Abbey.' My mind throws up an image of Daniel, all done up in his top hat and tails. I block it out. I haven't told them the groom is my ex. In fact, apart from Jess, I haven't told a soul. I couldn't bear all the sympathetic glances, and are-you-all-rights because I am all right with it.

Aren't I?

'Oooh, just think of all the celebrities who'll be there . . .' Rosemary's eyes betray an excited gleam. Then she takes a sharp breath. 'Do you think the Royal Family will go?'

'I don't know,' I say. If they do, Brian will think he's died and gone to heaven.

'So, when will you be heading back for it?' Lionel looks over at me expectantly over his glass of Evian.

Oh, shite. How do I tell them I'm unemployed? I try to think of how to explain things then realising I can't, say simply, 'I'm not.'

'You're not?' gasps Rosemary.

I shake my head and glance at Lionel, who's studying me carefully.

'I'm going to be all right,' he says quietly.

'I know you are.' I feel guilty for not telling him the real reason why I'm not assisting Brian at this wedding. But I just can't. They'd never understand. *I* don't even understand.

'I don't need three nurses. I have Rosemary and your brother.'

'And Miranda,' says Ed, who's still on the phone with Lou. 'She's in constant touch with your progress via email. Talking of which, she wants you to send her a detailed plan of everything you ate today.'

'There's plenty of people here to spoil my fun.' Lionel smiles. 'You must go.'

I feel stuck. I'm not worried about leaving Lionel. The doctors are delighted with the progress he's making and I know he doesn't need me to mollycoddle him – Ed and Rosemary are more than enough. I glance at the two of them and feel almost sorry for him. But I can't just call Brian and ask for my old job back. And anyway he's probably got himself another assistant by now.

'Why don't you call Brian?' suggests Rosemary.

I look at her with surprise. I've mentioned Brian over the years but she never appeared to pay much attention. 'Maybe I will,' I murmur.

'You can borrow my mobile,' pipes up Ed, who all of a sudden has finished his call.

I'm suspicious. Since when has he ever offered to lend me his mobile?

Then I catch sight of Lionel who's got that guilty schoolboy look, and get a sneaky feeling that this has been planned. 'Is this a plot to get rid of me?' I take the phone from Ed.

'No, of course not, darling,' says Lionel. 'It's just that Ed mentioned your finances . . .'

I shoot my brother a warning look, but he pretends to be interested in a patch of grass.

'. . . and I know Rosemary was really looking forward to seeing your photographs of all those famous people . . .'

Rosemary flushes guiltily.

With all eyes on me I take Ed's mobile. I feel unexpectedly nervous. Despite what Brian said, I still feel terrible about letting him down at such short notice, and I want to make it up to him. But can I really face being the wedding photographer's assistant at Daniel's wedding? Taking close-ups of a man who broke my heart into a million pieces saying 'I do'?

Yes, you can, Heather, I tell myself firmly.

And all of a sudden I make a decision. So what if I'm dreading seeing Daniel? So what if I'm the one crying in the church this time? I punch in the number. Brian and the business are more important and I'm going to put them first.

'Hello, Together Forever.' It's Brian. He sounds stressed.

I grope around in my head, trying to think of an easy way in to this conversation, then give up and blurt, 'I don't suppose you still need an assistant for tomorrow, do you?'

'*Heather*?'

His surprise is audible.

'Yep, it's me.'

At the other end of the line I listen nervously to him dragging on his cigarette. Then he laughs quietly.

'You're going to need a fancy hat.'

Chapter Forty-four

As it turns out I need a lot more than a hat.

'Lights?'

'Check.'

'Tripods.'

'Check.'

'Two Hasselblads, a Nikon, the reflector, sixty rolls of film and three lenses.'

'Check, check, check, check . . . um . . . check.'

It's the morning of Lady Charlotte's wedding, and we're at Shillingham Abbey in Oxfordshire. The abbey is part of the ancestral home of the Duke and Duchess, and it's nestled in the type of picturesque village you'd expect on a postcard – there's a duck pond, cottages with rambling roses growing round the door, and more Hunter wellies and Barbour jackets than the whole of the Royal Family owns.

'Is that everything?' Brian is asking, looking up from the array of camera equipment laid out on the gravel driveway.

Pausing from unloading cases out of the back of the Together Forever van, I think hard. Then remember. 'Oh, hang on a minute, we can't forget these . . .' I reach into the depths, rummage around and produce a large tub of Vaseline. 'For the lens,' I remind him.

'Oh, of course.' He rolls his eyes skyward as he pops it into his pocket.

'And then there's this.'

'An electric fan?' he scoffs. 'What the blazes do we need that for?'

We exchange a look that says 'Lady Charlotte'.

'Originally she wanted a wind machine,' I explain, rolling up its cord, 'but I told her we could achieve the same effect with a portable fan.'

'This isn't a music video, you know.' He tuts irritably.

'Tell that to her,' I say, and dump it in his arms. Something tells me this is going to be a big day. For all of us.

Since my initial phone call a few days ago, Brian and I have spoken quite a lot and he knows all about Lionel's heart-attack, Gabe's uncle being Victor Maxfield, and my decision not to take the job at the *Sunday Herald.* True to character, he's been a rock, listening supportively, telling me loyally what a great photographer I am, and immediately offering me my old job back. 'Which, of course, goes without saying, but there's no rush, take your time,' he's saying now, as he paces round the exterior of the abbey, taking readings from his light meter.

'Thanks, Brian, I really appreciate it.' Perched on a case, I smile gratefully. With everything that's been happening, I haven't yet made any firm decisions on what I'm going to do about my career. With my dream of working for the *Sunday Herald* over I'm effectively unemployed, and although I love working with Brian, we both know that after six years it's time for me to move on.

But to where I have no idea.

'Oh, it's no problem, no problem.' He takes out a tissue and dabs the perspiration from his face. 'To be quite frank, Heather, after this dratted wedding we're both going to need a rest.' He fiddles with his cravat, trying to loosen his collar, which is so heavily starched that it's like a neck brace. Forced to swap his trusted grey flannel suit for the full top hat and tails, he's been uncomfortable all morning. 'Pity that poor groom, that's all I can say,' he mutters to himself, as he strides over to the van and checks his reflection in the wing mirror.

'Well, that's another thing,' I say hesitantly. There's a pause. Having tried not to think about it, Daniel suddenly rears his ugly head. 'The groom's my ex.'

Brian stares at me, not understanding.

'Remember Daniel?' I say quietly, and feel a familiar knot in my stomach. Oh, God, this is what I've been afraid of.

Brian's jaw would have dropped, had his collar not been nearly strangling him. 'Gordon Bennett, how could I forget? He broke your heart . . .' Wide-eyed, he continues to stare at me, and then, 'You've known all along and you still offered to be my assistant today . . .' His voice breaks off as he gazes at me, his eyes filling up. 'Heather, that's the kindest thing anyone's ever done for me.' He hurries over to give me a hug.

'Stop it, or you'll have me crying,' I protest, my voice muffled by his shoulder. 'And you know I don't cry at weddings.'

He laughs, sniffing away his tears. 'Thank you, Heather,'

'Don't mention it.' I smile, and then, gesturing at the equipment scattered around our feet, say briskly. 'Come on, we've got a wedding to photograph.' And hoisting a tripod under each arm I set off towards the abbey.

We spend the next ten minutes setting up: lights over by the altar, reflector near the pulpit, a tripod at both ends of the aisle. In fact, it's only when Brian pops out to get more extension leads from the van – which means he's gone for a quick smoke – that I take a moment to look at my surroundings.

The abbey is breathtaking. Its sheer size inspires a kind of stunned awe, and I walk round, head tilted back, gazing up at the shafts of sunlight shining through the stained-glass windows, casting a kaleidoscope of colours across the smooth stone floors.

And then there are the flowers: hundreds of thousands in huge elaborate arrangements, cascading from columns, at the end of each pew, strung up high in big garlands. The place is a blaze of pink and white. Though to be honest, I think they've overdone it a bit. Isn't it supposed to be about quality, not quantity? In fact, the more I think about it, the more it looks a bit tacky. I mean, it's so over the top, it's like the Chelsea Flower show in here.

Oh, who am I kidding? It's not over the top, it's absolutely bloody beautiful. I'm just trying to make myself feel better.

I inhale the heavily perfumed air. There's no point in pretending, I have to face up to it, whether I like it or not. This is where Daniel, the man with whom I shared three years of my life, will get married today.

Only not to me.

I feel a deep ache and the stirring of a wishful thought. I banish it quickly. Oh no you don't . . .

Interrupted by the creak of the door I turn round expecting to see Brian with the extension cords. The figure of a man is silhouetted in the doorway but as he starts up the aisle I realise it's not Brian.

It's Daniel.

He's thinner than I remember and a little older round the eyes, but he still makes my stomach flip. And now he's only a few feet from me and we're both staring at each other and my heart's thumping so loudly I'm sure he can hear it. Bumping into your bastard ex-boyfriend who broke your heart is one thing. But the church on his wedding day? Well, you can imagine.

'Hello, Daniel,' I say evenly, summoning up every scrap of composure in my body.

He takes off his top hat and smiles crookedly, 'Fancy seeing you here,' he retorts, but beneath his confident veneer he seems uncharacteristically self-conscious. I smile back and then, not knowing what to say next, fiddle with my hair, waiting for him to speak.

'You look great,' he blurts out.

I feel a ridiculous jolt of pleasure. 'Thanks,' I say nonchalantly.

'And different. Did you do something to your hair?'

'No.' I shrug, but inside I feel like yelling, 'Of course I did something to my hair! I did something to *every single part of my body*. I got up at six a.m. this morning and spent three whole hours getting ready. I even bought a new cream trouser suit for the occasion, borrowed a Philip Treacy hat from Rosemary, and am wearing my gorgeous pink satin stilettos even though my ankle's really painful.'

But of course he doesn't know any of that, and he's not going to.

'So, was this your idea?' Cutting through the pleasantries, I ask him the question that's been bugging for me for weeks. 'Brian and I photographing your wedding.'

'You're the best wedding photographer I know,' he answers jokingly.

'Daniel, I'm the only wedding photographer you know,' I point out drily.

Immediately his face falls and, like a small boy who's been reprimanded, he bows his head and stares contritely at his feet. 'I dunno what I was thinking,' he says quietly. 'I thought it would be great for business. I just mentioned it to Charlotte . . .' His voice trails off as he looks up at me from underneath his brows, his eyes searching for mine, and for a moment I'm sure I see more than just a flicker of regret.

'It's good to see you, Heather.' He sighs heavily. 'I've missed you.'

I stare at him in stunned silence. For months after we first broke up I fantasised about this happening. About him telling me how wonderful I looked, how much he missed me. But now, listening to him actually saying the words, I realise I had confused nostalgia with reality. And the reality is I don't care any more. I don't care if Daniel has missed me, and I don't care that he's marrying someone else.

The only person I care about is Gabe.

Finally I admit it and, as I do, all the thoughts and feelings I've kept hidden burst through my consciousness to the surface. The gratitude I felt when Gabe defended me to Rosemary at the dinner table, the terror when I thought something had happened to him surfing, the wretchedness after we rowed and he moved out. And all the hundreds of fleeting glances, smiles, pauses and moments when I thought something was going to happen, felt something going on between us, but dismissed it. All those tiny fragments are piecing together now and suddenly I feel as if I'm looking at a loved-up jigsaw. Oh, God.

'I'm really sorry about everything that happened. I was a total idiot . . .'

I zone back in to realise Daniel's still talking to me.

'Are you still angry with me?' he asks.

I stare at him calmly. In the beginning anger was the only thing that kept me going but now, looking inside myself, I can't find any left. It's trickled away without me noticing. 'No.' I shake my head. 'I'm not angry.'

'I got your text.'

'Oh, that!' I blush with embarrassment. 'I was drunk.'

'You were?' I'm surprised to see he seems disappointed. 'I can't remember what I put. Was it anything bad?'

He looks at me for a moment, then shakes his head. 'No, nothing embarrassing.'

There's a pause.

'I should go. I've got to finish getting everything ready,' I say.

'Actually, there's been a change . . .'

I look at him sharply.

'What kind of change?'

'Charlotte's had second thoughts about the ceremony.' He's rubbing his jaw agitatedly.

This is the first time I've ever seen Daniel nervous.

'She doesn't want anything conventional,' he's saying, 'so we've decided on handfasting in the woods across the river.'

I look at him blankly.

'It's a pagan ceremony,' he adds in explanation.

'*A pagan ceremony?*' I repeat, staring at him as if he's just grown two heads. '*You?*'

He stiffens.

'So?' he says defensively. 'Why shouldn't I have a pagan ceremony?'

'Daniel, you hate anything alternative. You won't even drink camomile tea,' I say.

'It tastes like crap.'

'That's not the point.'

He stares at me for a moment as if prepared to argue, before letting his shoulders slump wearily in surrender. 'You're right. I hate it.'

And with those words it's as if something lifts and I see him in a new light. This is a man I used to be in awe of. A man who seemed so self-assured, and in control, to the point of arrogance. And yet he seems so pathetic so, dare I say it, *henpecked.*

'Charlotte's got very strong opinions,' he continues.

'I've noticed,' I mutter.

He flashes me a look. 'She's very particular about what she wants.'

'And what Charlotte wants, Charlotte must have,' I answer brightly, trying to keep the sarcasm out of my voice. And failing.

Heaving a huge sigh, he looks at me like a drowning man. 'Something like that.'

I open my mouth to say something, but before anything can come out—

'*Dan-eee-al! Dan-eee-al!*'

Like the siren of a police car, a voice echoes through the abbey. Startled, we turn to see a flurry of white silk taffeta hurtling down the aisle. *Lady Charlotte.*

'Shit,' groans Daniel. 'What's wrong, Bunnykins?' he coos, forcing a smile as she arrives at the altar.

Bunnykins? From a man who didn't believe in PDA and refused to hold my hand? Even when I sprained my ankle.

The muscle in his jaw jumps.

'Elton John's got laryngitis and won't be able to sing at the reception, the delivery of Cristal hasn't arrived, and I don't think I like my new titties any more.' Lady Charlotte appears not to have noticed I'm here. She thrusts out her chest and pouts sulkily. 'They make me look fat.'

'Darling, of course you don't look fat.' He swallows hard. 'Shouldn't you be inside? I thought it was bad luck for me to see the bride before the wedding.'

'Oh, fuck superstition, Danny! This is a crisis!' with a tantrum-style howl she scuttles into the vestry.

A stunned silence settles between Daniel and I like dust after an explosion.

'I should go after her,' he says, after a pause.

I nod, and for a moment we just stand there, the two of us, until I kiss his cheek. 'Goodbye, Daniel,' I whisper.

'Goodbye, Heather.' He smiles, but I can't help feeling I can see real regret in his face, and as I watch his coattails disappearing into the vestry, I feel unexpectedly sorry for him. Yes, he broke my heart. But a lifetime with Lady Charlotte is punishment enough for anyone.

Outside the abbey I find Brian leaning against the Together Forever van, smoking and waiting for me. When he hears my footsteps on the gravel he stubs out his cigarette. 'How was it?' he asks gently.

I flop next to him, tilting my hat to shade my face. 'Good.' I nod, after a moment, overcome with a strong sense of satisfaction. It's like the last few weeks have been a mad roller-coaster ride and now it's all over. Everything's worked out fine. Perfectly fine, I tell myself, trying not to think about Gabe. 'I had closure,' I say decisively.

Brian looks confused.

'It's a girl thing,' I explain.

He peers at me as if I'm from some alien species. 'I spent the first twenty-five years of my life wishing I was straight,' he reminisces, 'and I'm so glad my wish was never granted.' He's adjusting his waistcoat as he speaks. 'Men are much more straightforward.'

'Oh, yeah?' I elbow him in the ribs. 'I take it this means you and Neil are still straightforwardly in love?'

'Of course.' He laughs happily and reaches for his top hat, which he's balanced on the roof of the van, then presses it firmly on to his head. 'Shall we?' he says, with mock formality, holding out his arm.

'But what about all the stuff in the abbey that I need to move? I've left all the lights, reflectors and tripods—'

'The bride's changed her mind,' he says, stopping me in my tracks.

'Yeah, I know, it's going to be a pagan ceremony outside—'

'No, she's changed it about the style of photography.'

My mouth opens, then closes again.

'Apparently she saw some of the stuff I did in the sixties. Now she wants edgy, *paparazzi*-style photographs.' His face is buzzing with delight.

'You mean . . .' We share a euphoric smile. Translated, this means forget putting Vaseline on the lens, using the portable fan and trying to get everyone together for the group photographs. Now all we need is one digital camera to fire off lots of spur-of-the-moment, out-of-focus black and white shots.

'And we still go home early with a big fat cheque.' He whoops, impetuously seizing me round the waist and trying to twirl me round. I say *trying*, because Brian's a bit shorter than me, and I'm quite a big girl. We nearly topple over and have to stagger around for a minute to regain our balance, laughing all the while.

And at my ex's wedding. Who would ever have thought it?

'Here.' I giggle, passing him his old faithful Nikon.

He removes his top hat and slings the camera round his neck, just like old times. 'Ready?'

I finish filling my pockets with film, then adjust the brim of my hat. 'Ready.' I link his arm.

Then we psych ourselves up, as always.

Three – two – one.

'OK. So this is it.' Turning to me, Brian winks: '*Showtime.*'

Chapter Forty-five

'I do apologise, Sir Richard, Lady Kenwood, I'm afraid it's just immediate family in the circle of purification. If you'd like to wait in the marquee . . .'

Behind the abbey, uniformed ushers are trying politely to explain the change of ceremony to five hundred confused guests, many of whom are elderly and a little confused already.

'Circle? What circle?' Sir Richard is booming, gripping his ivory-topped cane and looking backwards and forth between the usher and his wife, who's dressed up like an extra from an Edwardian costume drama, all beaded jet earrings, long silk gloves and bustle.

'Oh, do you mean the dress circle? Are we here for the theatre?' she's enquiring shrilly, in the kind of ridiculously posh accent that, like butlers or cucumber sandwiches with the crusts cut off, you can't believe still exists. 'But I thought it was a wedding . . .'

As Brian and I make our way across the manicured lawns we observe the chaos that's ensuing. Bewildered crowds of people, all dressed in their finest, are being herded into the vast white marquee that was originally erected for the reception, and handed opera glasses so that they can watch the pagan ceremony that is to take place across the river in neighbouring woodland.

I glance at it now as we cross the stepping stones and walk towards a small clearing in which I can see the wedding party and—

'Gordon Bennett,' mutters Brian.

As we enter the clearing a woman in flowing purple robes, carrying a wand, wafts towards us. I'm not joking. It has a silver star on the end.

'I'm the celebrant.'

She appears to be in her seventies, with silvery-white hair down to her waist. If Dumbledore from Harry Potter had a twin sister, this would be her.

'Oh, um, hi. Pleased to meet you,' I say, and shake her hand. A large bell on a long silver chain hangs round her neck. 'It's to ring out the old and ring in the new,' she says solemnly, having noticed me staring at it. Then she fixes me with startlingly blue eyes, and adds, 'In the circle of purification there is no place for superstition or tawdry charms, Heather.'

She knows my name? Any amusement I might have felt at her attire vanishes.

'How—' I begin.

'Now, if you'd all please form a circle,' she interrupts me.

What was that bit about superstition and tawdry charms? Was she referring to the lucky heather? Out of habit I stick my hand into my pocket although I know there's nothing in there, and feel my fingers go through the lining. There's a hole! In the lining of my Marc Jacobs' jacket! I feel a rush of indignation. This jacket cost nearly three hundred pounds! Followed by a thump of alarm as I feel something soft and scratchy. *It's the lucky heather.*

I feel a tingle in my fingertips, like a current of electricity. It's turned up again. I wrap my fingers round it tightly, determined not to lose it again. I've got to get rid of it properly, once and for all.

'That means all of you.'

'But what about the photographs?' I whisper to Brian, who's bemused by it all.

'Photographs break the sanctity of the circle,' the celebrant says. 'Now, if everyone will stand shoulder to shoulder in the circle we can begin.'

I back away. 'Actually, I think I'll just wait over there.'

'Everyone,' she repeats solemnly.

Obediently I stand next to Brian as the celebrant picks up a broom and begins to sweep the clearing in an anti-clockwise direction.

> *'Sweep, sweep, sweep this place*
> *By Power of Air, I cleanse this space.'*

There are a few sniggers from the guests, and expressions of bewilderment, scepticism and anticipation on their faces.

'What's she doing?' asks someone fearfully.

'Casting a purification circle,' answers a middle-aged woman, knowledgeably. It comes as no surprise to see she's wearing Birkenstocks and a pair of elasticated tie-dye trousers.

'Blessings and merry meet. We are here today to join Daniel and Charlotte together . . .'

The next few minutes are taken up by Daniel and Charlotte saying their vows and exchanging rings and, although I never would've believed it, as I watch Daniel kissing his bride I feel . . . nothing. Well, actually, that's not true. I do feel something, but it's for Gabe. I can't stop thinking about him throughout the ceremony.

'Now, if everyone can hold their neighbour's hand tightly, we shall all close our eyes and focus on the circle . . . on its special power . . . it's purity . . .'

Surely she's not serious? I glance around. Everyone looks horribly self-conscious, except for Ms Tie-Dye, who grasps the hands of the startled people on either side of her. But gradually, one by one, people reach tentatively for their neighbour's fingers and close their eyes. Until I'm the last one left and, reluctantly retrieving my fingers from the lucky heather in my pocket, I clasp Brian's hand.

Then something weird happens.

It's like an energy. A force. A power buzzing through me like nothing I have ever felt before. A hot blast of euphoria surging through my body. My breath catches at the back of my throat. Yet at the same time I feel the peace and calm of a lullaby. Birds fall silent and an eerie stillness descends. And for what feels like both a moment and an eternity, nothing and no one makes even the slightest movement or sound. Until the voice of the celebrant strikes up again:

'*The web of life is an endless circle never to die only to change from*
What was begun is now complete
Welcome home these energies borne
The circle is open, never broken
So Mote It Be!'

From out of nowhere a breeze whips up, and as everyone breaks apart I open my eyes to see a dove circling overhead. Gosh, I feel as if I'm coming out of a trance.

I glance at other people, see their self-conscious glances and embarrassed smiles, as if they're not sure what happened, and know instinctively something's changed. Not around me, but inside me. Wiggling my shoulders, I tilt my head to the sky and watching the scudding flecks of white clouds, take a deep breath of fresh air. It's hard to describe it without sounding like the woman in the elasticated tie-dye trousers and Birkenstocks, but I feel different. Lighter. Freer.

Immediately I put my hand back into my pocket. I'm going to get rid of the heather by throwing it into the river . . . Except – I feel a pang of alarm. My pocket's empty. Where's the heather? I scrabble around, feeling into the corners. It's not in the lining any more. Puzzled, I turn out my pockets. It must be somewhere. Out of the corner of my eye I catch sight of the celebrant. She's smiling at me. In my head her voice echoes solemnly: 'In the circle of purification there is no place for superstition or tawdry charms, Heather.'

It can't have just disappeared. *Can it?*

'Lost something?' Brian is dabbing his red eyes with a handkerchief.

'Er, no . . . nothing,' I say. I glance back at the celebrant but she's not looking my way at all. Maybe I imagined it.

'What did you think of the ceremony?'

'I'm not sure.' It was only a few moments ago, but it's already fading fast, like writing in the sand. 'What about you?'

'Load of old hocus-pocus,' he says derisively, blowing his nose. 'But this pagan wedding malarkey is going to be great for pictures,' he adds. 'I'm going to take some incredible shots, especially of that wizard character.' He stuffs his handkerchief up his sleeve and bounds towards the happy couple, snapping away like a *paparazzo*.

'I have to say, I didn't know you were such a good dancer,' I tease later, when we're loading all the equipment into the van.

'I wasn't dancing, I was being kidnapped,' grumbles Brian, his head reappearing from behind the doors. He slams them, then turns the handle. 'Right, that's everything.' He wipes dust off his sleeve. 'Now, can we change the subject?'

'To what?'

'To you.'

'What about me?' I say absently, digging my mobile phone out of my little clutch bag and turning it on to check my messages. I know Lionel's in safe hands but I just want to make sure.

'It's the American, isn't it?'

Startled, I glance up. 'What is?'

'He's the reason you've had that look on your face all day.'

'I don't have a look,' I say hotly, watching the little Vodafone hands appear on the screen. Gosh, it's taking ages. Out of the corner of my eye I can see Brian staring at me. 'Honestly, you get a boyfriend and suddenly you're the expert on relationships,' I mutter. Finally the little Vodafone symbol appears and I dial 121.

'I don't need to be an expert on relationships to know when someone's in love,' he replies.

Is it that obvious?

'You have one new message.'

'Hello, this is a message for Heather Hamilton.'

Prepared to hear Rosemary's polite vowels, I jump as a loud, no-nonsense voice barks down the phone. It sounds like—

'*Victor Maxfield here.*'

My heart thuds. What does he want?

'I've just returned from my fishing trip and found your letter of refusal on my desk. My dear, don't you know the first rule of journalism is to make sure you're aware of the facts? Yes, my nephew Gabriel did put in a good word for you, and, yes, on his recommendation I gave you an interview. But that wasn't why you got the job. You got it because you're a bloody talented photographer.'

My breath catches in the back of my throat. Gabe isn't why I got that job? I'm a Bloody Talented Photographer? My stomach rushes upwards as if I'm on a swing, then plummets down again. And I've been a Bloody Stupid Idiot.

'Gabriel might be my favourite nephew but the Sunday Herald *is an award-winning newspaper and I'm not about to give you a job because the idiot's in love with you.'*

What?

After everything, this curveball hits me in the stomach. Did he just say what I thought he said? But that's ludicrous! Gabe? In love with me?

But . . . Victor Maxfield is still talking and I struggle to listen.

'But, look, I'm a busy man, I've got a paper to run, and I don't take no for an answer. So stop all this nonsense immediately. We're running a piece on the Edinburgh Festival and we need a photographer up there. There's a plane leaving for Edinburgh at five from Heathrow. When you call me back, I want you to be on it.'

And then he hangs up. Just like that.

I stare at my Nokia in disbelief. I've suddenly got a job at the *Sunday Herald* after all, and with it my first assignment – the Edinburgh Festival.

Which is where Gabe is.

I walk round the van, tug open the passenger door and climb in. Brian's sitting in the driver's seat puffing at a cigarette and listening to the radio. 'Everything OK?'

I take a deep breath. 'I need a favour.'

'For you, anything,' he quips.

'Can you give me a lift?'

He smiles. 'Course I will. Where to? Little Venice?'

'No, Heathrow.'

A look passes between us. There's no need for an explanation.

'What time's your flight?'

'In less than an hour.'

'Righty-ho.' Turning the ignition, the van splutters into life. 'Hold on to your hat.' He jams the gearstick noisily into first and as the wheels spin on the gravel, we shoot off down the driveway in a swirling cloud of dust and anticipation.

Chapter Forty-six

We race towards London.

After I've told Brian about my message from Victor Maxfield I discover he's actually a frustrated rally-car driver and rises to the challenge with aplomb, putting the little white minivan through its paces as if he's Michael Schumacher in a Ferrari. With the engine screaming and a cigarette stuck to his bottom lip, he expertly cranks up and down through the gears as we zigzag across lanes of traffic.

We cause quite a stir. People gawp in astonishment as the Together Forever minivan whizzes past in a blur, Brian and I strapped into the front seats in our full wedding regalia. I spend most of the journey glancing frantically from the busy roads to my watch. My heart leaps into my mouth every time we hit a red light, or have to brake at a zebra crossing. What's with all this traffic? And roadworks? And red lights?

But then, after what feels like for ever, I see a sprawl of grey terminal buildings. Heathrow airport.

'Thanks, Brian,' I gasp, unbuckling my seatbelt and throwing open the door. I jump on to the Tarmac and my knees go wobbly.

'Here, you nearly forgot something.'

Brian is holding out one of his cameras. It's digital. 'You'll be needing this. And this.' Scrabbling behind him, he tugs out a black nylon laptop case. 'This way you can email your shots to your picture editor. Just in case you find you want to stay a bit longer in Edinburgh . . .'

My stomach stops jumping around all over the place just long enough for a huge smile to spread over my face. 'Brian, I don't know how to thank you . . .'

He flaps a hand. 'Go on, scram. Otherwise you'll miss your plane. And that Yank of yours.' And giving me a wink, he pulls out of the lay-by and disappears into the traffic.

As I walk into Departures the first thing I notice is the queue, zigzagging all the way back from the ticket desks along black elastic barriers to the revolving doors. Which is where I am.

A queue? I haven't stood in a queue for weeks. I glance at my watch, I sort of hover, not sure what to do, anxiety growing. Fuck. I'm going to miss the flight. Victor Maxfield will think I'm crap, I'll be fired and spend the rest of my life taking pictures of brides with leg-o'-mutton sleeves . . .

I struggle to calm myself. After all, there's no point getting stressed about it, I tell myself. I spot a discarded copy of the *Evening Standard*, snatch it up and start to read it. Slowly we drift forward inch by inch. Column by column. Page by page. Until finally I'm just reading about the hike in interest rates when—

'Next.'

Scrunching up the newspaper I fling myself at the check-in-desk. 'Phew! at last!' I gasp. 'I was worried I was going to miss my flight.'

The stewardess keeps typing into her computer, her fingernails clickety-clicking on her keyboard.

'I'm booked on the five o'clock to Edinburgh,' I gabble.

Nothing.

I stare at the top of her head. Has she heard me? 'I think it goes quite soon,' I add, louder this time.

There's a pause, and then, 'Name?' she monotones.

Finally.

'Heather Hamilton,' I gasp. 'Miss.'

'Uh-huh,' she mutters and continues tapping leisurely at her keyboard. Now, I know they must deal with this kind of thing every day, but can't we at least have some *sense* of urgency?

Apparently not.

She pauses to sigh. 'Oh dear, you might have missed your flight. The gates are nearly closing.'

'But that's what I've been trying—' I explode. Calm down, Heather. Just calm down.

'But if you hurry you might make it.' She passes me a boarding card. 'You're in seventy-five F, a window seat.'

'Oh, no, I can't have a window seat,' I say quickly. 'You see, I'm a nervous flyer and I like to be on the aisle because if there's an emergency and we need to jump out with our life-jackets I can get to the exits quicker . . .'

Fellow travellers throw each other nervous looks and move away from me.

'It's the last seat,' says the stewardess. 'And there are people behind you, so if you don't mind . . .'

'But—'

'It leaves from gate forty-two. You have five minutes.' She throws me a sour look. Fuck.

Running in heels is murder, believe me. My ankles are wobbling all over the place as I rush through Security and dash on to the moving walkway. '*Ow*,' I yell, my injured ankle twists under me. I grab the hand-rail to balance and look down. Shit! My heel has snapped off. Cursing, I slip off the pink shoe and gaze sadly at it, then remember I have a plane to catch.

'Bloody hell!'

I look up to see an air stewardess heading in the opposite direction and staring at me in astonishment.

'Jess!' I gasp, as she glides past. 'What are you doing here?'

'What am *I* doing here? I'm a bloody air stewardess, what do you think I'm doing here? I've just come off a nine-hour flight and I'm going home for some shut-eye.'

We shuffle backwards to stay level with each other.

'More to the point, what are *you* doing here?'

'I'm flying to Edinburgh . . .' I nearly trip over a businessman's briefcase and apologise profusely. '. . . on a shoot for the *Sunday Herald*. It's a long story,' I explain, remembering how I emailed her last week about my row with Gabe and his sudden departure.

'Isn't Gabe at the Edinburgh Festival?' She arches her eyebrows.

'Sorry, Jess, I've got to rush. I'm going to miss my plane.' Cutting her off quickly I hobble off along the concourse. 'I'll call you.'

'You go, girl,' she yells after me. 'Oh and, Heather!'

I glance back over my shoulder, but she's far away now, waving madly. Then she shouts something I don't quite catch. I wave back. I'm not sure exactly what she said, but it sounded an awful lot like 'Go catch some butterflies.'

Staggering on to the aircraft I'm greeted with an atmosphere that at best is tense – and at worst positively hostile. Row upon row of stony faces greet me as I limp down the aisle to my seat. Seventy-five F . . . I'm nearing the back of the plane. Damn, it must be here somewhere. Perhaps I've missed it, perhaps—

And then I see it.

At the very back, shoved up right next to the toilets. Two seats. One is occupied by a man with a beer belly so ginormous it's divided into two – one half being on one side of the arm rest, and the other half bursting underneath, over and around it on the next seat.

My seat.

I squeeze past my neighbour, sit down and fasten my seatbelt. So much for getting upgraded into a nice big squidgy leather seat, sitting next to a handsome stranger and drinking complimentary champagne all the way to Edinburgh. I close my eyes. Still, it's only a short flight. With any luck I can sleep all the way

'Well, well, well, isn't this cosy?'

Oh, no. Please, no.

I've been accosted by a thick Scottish accent. I open my eyes to see my neighbour beaming down at me. 'Hello there. I'm Bruce and you are . . .?

For the next fifteen minutes everything goes relatively smoothly. Well, apart from the constant sound of the loo flushing next to me, and Bruce falling asleep and slobbering over my shoulder.

'Would Madam prefer the chicken sandwich or ham?' A stewardess throws me her well-rehearsed smile.

'Do you have a vegetarian option?' I ask politely.

'No, I'm afraid we've run out. But there's a bit of lettuce and tomato in this one,' she says, inspecting an anaemic-looking baguette through its Cellophane wrapper. 'You can always take out the ham.'

'Er, no, that's OK.' My stomach growls unhappily.

'Coffee or tea?' she trills.

'Coffee, please.'

She passes me a little white plastic cup on a tray and pours the thick black liquid, expertly not spilling a drop.

Out of nowhere the aeroplane gives a little judder.

What the . . .? I shoot a glance at the stewardess. Her face remains impassive as she sways on her navy court shoes and continues to pour. Reassured, I take the cup from her.

See? It's nothing, I tell myself. Just a little a bit of turbulence. Nothing to be worried about. Nothing at—

Aggggh.

Without warning the plane is plummeting and I feel as if we're dropping out of the sky. Terrifying doesn't even come close. I hear children crying, a woman shriek, my heart is pounding and a finger's prodding . . .

A what?

I look up to see Bruce is prodding me with his chubby finger and looking at me with concern through his frameless glasses. 'Och, lassie, it's OK. Just a bit of clear-air turbulence, everything's aal reet,' he's saying, chewing a ham sandwich. 'Well, apart from your troosers,' he adds, gesturing to my lap.

I look down to see a large brown patch spreading across my crotch then transfer my gaze to my empty coffee cup, which I'm still gripping. Just in time to watch the last drop plop on to my lap. Great. Just great. Can things get any worse?

Apparently they can. After we've landed – correction: bumped, juddered and screeched along the runway – I get trapped behind

Bruce and am the last person to disembark. Which means I'm the last person through the arrivals hall, and the last person to join the enormous queue for the taxis.

And now it's raining.

As I watch the drops splatter on to my pink satin shoes, one of which is now minus a heel, I sigh. Where did all the beautiful weather go? It hasn't rained for ages, not since . . . I rack my brains. Since that night I got drenched and met the old gypsy woman who gave me the lucky heather.

A weird feeling stirs. Wait a minute. It's not just the sunshine that's disappeared, what about all the green lights and empty roads? And what happened to never having to wait in a queue? Getting the best seat? The last sandwich? The only cab? What happened to wrinkle-free skin? Good-hair days? How come they've all vanished and been replaced with . . .

With how things used to be, I realise. Because this is what it was like before—

Before what, Heather? pipes up a little voice inside.

And then it hits me.

Before all my wishes came true.

For a moment I stand very still on the pavement, but my head's spinning. Surely . . . it can't . . . *can it*? I rewind back to the wedding, holding hands in the circle, the strange sensation, the lucky heather vanishing . . . As realisation dawns, I feel a tingle of joy spread over me.

'Oh, my gosh, look at this queue for a taxi,' I gasp, with a grin that stretches from ear to ear. *'It's huge.'*

A couple in front of me turn to me suspiciously.

'And it's raining,' I whoop. 'Yippee!'

A few more people are staring at me now as if I'm crazy, but I don't care. I don't care that I'm getting drenched, or that my hair is sticking to my face, and the water is running down my neck.

I feel a sharp pain as someone bangs a trolley into my leg.

'Oh, sorry,' they apologise, expecting an angry response, but instead I throw them a beaming smile.

'It's fine, honestly,' I say. Pulling up my trouser leg, I watch a big purplish splodge appear. I feel a surge of delight. 'I love bruises,' I gush.

They move off hurriedly, just as a taxi pulls up at the kerbside. As it nears me its tyres cut through a large puddle, splattering me with filthy water. I glance down at my jacket. Its pristine creaminess is now all soggy and mottled with dirt. It's ruined. Completely ruined. *Isn't it fantastic?*

And throwing back my head I let out a peal of laughter, letting the rain splash onto my face as I hold out my hands and twirl round and round, getting completely and utterly drenched.

I've never been happier.

Chapter Forty-seven

A couple of hours later I'm sitting cross-legged on my bed in my hotel room, wearing a fluffy white dressing-gown and a towel wrapped round my head like a turban. In one hand I have my trousers, and in the other the hotel's hairdryer. I've just spent twenty minutes bent over the sink with a bar of soap and a nailbrush, getting out the coffee and puddle stains, and now it's just a case of drying them off and I'll be good to go.

I turn up the heat and stick the nozzle up one of the legs so it inflates like a wind sock, then reach for the carrier-bag hanging on the bedpost. I made the taxi stop at M&S on the way over and bought a rather natty pair of tan leather slip-on pumps (I owe Rosemary an apology – I was astonished by how trendy they are these days, *and so reasonable*), a pair of socks, an umbrella and a three-pack of black low-rise g-strings. I tip out everything on to the bedspread and hold up the underwear. To be honest, I should've bought flesh-coloured as I'm wearing cream trousers, but flesh-coloured underwear is so unattractive and, well, you never know . . .

You never know what, Heather? demands a voice sternly.

I focus on my trousers, which are on the verge of scorching and turn off the hairdryer. Honestly, I don't have time for all this nonsense. I can't sit here daydreaming about Gabe and me and us and . . . Oh, shit, I'm doing it again. This is ridiculous. Discarding my trousers, I tug off the towel and begin vigorously rubbing my hair with it. Whatever my feelings, Gabe is just a friend, *was* just a friend, and if I happen to bump into him at the festival then, hopefully, he'll accept my grovelling apology and we can be friends again. But that's all. Just friends. He has a girlfriend already, remember? And after what Daniel did to me, I do not go anywhere near men who are prepared to cheat on their girlfriends. Not even if they do have kind, freckly faces and hang towels neatly in the bathroom, I tell myself firmly.

Feeling all moral and righteous and utterly resolved, I finish rubbing my hair which is now one big frizz. Good. Now that's settled I must concentrate on the real reason I'm here. As photographer for the *Sunday Herald.* I feel a little burst of pride. Even if it will be with kinky hair, I suddenly realise, remembering that I have neither a paddle brush nor a pair of straighteners with me. And switching the hairdryer on again, I tip my head upside-down and start scrunching furiously.

Twenty minutes later I've finished getting ready and, after a quick phone call with the journalist who's writing the article, I hang up and reach for Brian's camera. I loop it round my neck and feel a flutter of nerves. OK, this is it. My first job. Throwing back my shoulders I open the door. *Showtime.*

Any nerves I have disappear the moment I step out into the street. It's still drizzling, but it hasn't dampened anyone's spirits. Everywhere I look street performers are mingling with crowds of tourists and people handing out flyers, and over the next few hours I take picture after picture after picture, until by nine o'clock my new shoes are hurting and I flop on to a bench to decide what to do next.

I've been given fistfuls of flyers so I leaf through them. By now I've resigned myself to the awful fact that I'm going to have to see one of the comedy shows, but the question is, which one?

Gabe's, I think, before I can stop myself.

Heather Hamilton, you're not here to think about Gabe. You're here on a professional assignment. Turning my attention back to the flyers, I try looking for something that sounds vaguely appealing – which is a bit like asking a vegetarian to choose something from the chilled-meats section at Tesco, but I persist.

Finally I get to the last flyer. It's upside-down, and as I turn it over I can't help hoping it might be for . . . But, no, it's for a comedy double-act called Bob and Beryl who, according to the *Scotsman*, are outrageously funny. Hmmm, maybe that will be fun . . .

Oh for godsakes, Who am I kidding? I don't want to see some stupid double-act that's outrageously funny. I want to see Gabe. I have to see Gabe. I'm in love with Gabe. It's no use trying to ignore it, deny it or pretend it's not happening. From the very first moment I set eyes on him on my doorstep, with all those freckles and those big baggy blue eyes, I just knew.

Scrunching up all the flyers I walk over to one of the large cast-iron bins. It's already overflowing with multi-coloured paper and I'm resignedly stuffing mine on top when one catches my attention. A soggy pink and yellow leaflet, with a silhouette of a man's profile that looks just like . . .

ANGEL GABRIEL, SENT FROM HOLLYWOOD TO MAKE YOU LOOK ON THE BRIGHT SIDE OF LIFE. TONIGHT AT THE TAVERN, 9 P.M., TICKETS £7.50. COME AND BE SAVED.

Right on cue I hear the town-hall clock chime and, heart beating fast, hear it strike nine. I waver, ridiculously nervous at the thought of seeing him again – and on stage. I mean, what am I going to say? How he's going to react? He might hate me, he might refuse to speak to me. Perhaps it's better if I don't go . . . *Oh, wow.* With my resolve unravelling at the speed of light I catch sight of something that makes me freeze. A beautiful, shimmering rainbow is arching right over the castle. Now, I'm not religious but it looks like a sign. ''Scuse me.' Twirling round, I stop the first person I see distributing flyers. 'Can you tell me the way to the Tavern? I'm going to see Angel Gabriel . . .'

I run all the way there.

Fortunately the Tavern is located in a back-street five minutes away and when I arrive I discover Gabe's show hasn't started. Due to earlier technical problems everything is running late. I buy a ticket at the door and slip inside.

The Tavern is a tiny bar with a 'Bavarian theme'. I've never been to Bavaria but, judging by the décor, it's obviously a country that favours stuffed boars' heads and stripped pine. I keep my head down and skulk round the side of the dark, smoky bar. Ahead of me is a long, narrow section and at the end a makeshift stage where a comedian is finishing his act.

He's a tall skinny guy, wearing the obligatory T-shirt with a logo – 'Never Mind The Bollocks', which seems to be sadly appropriate. Chain-smoking, he's hanging on to the microphone for dear life and although I don't know much about stand-up comedy, even I can tell he's dying. The room's almost silent, but for the sound of people murmuring to each other, and there's the distinct whiff of boredom.

'. . . and then this pigeon flew off the ledge and landed right on my shoulder . . .' I watch him flounder on until my eyes drift through the fog of smoke towards some familiar-looking pink and yellow posters. Sure enough, there's the same headshot of Gabe in silhouette that was on the leaflet, and the words 'ANGEL GABRIEL' stencilled above.

Seeing them now, I feel a burst of pride. He's done all this. Printed leaflets, made posters, organised a show, come all the way from LA to Edinburgh to perform. I know he told me about it, but now it's real. Impressed, I glance around me. There must be twenty or so people in here, which isn't packed by any means, but it's still a respectable number for such a small space. And they've all paid to watch Gabe, I note, with satisfaction, as the pigeon-obsessed comic disappears off-stage to feeble applause and none of the audience disappears with him.

That means next up must be Gabe.

I scan the room for a place to stand. On the way over I decided I'd wait until after the show to approach him, but I need somewhere with a view to take photographs where he won't see me. He's probably really nervous, I tell myself. And even if he's not, I'm really nervous.

A darkened recess at the other side of the bar looks perfect and I edge towards it past a group of girls smoking cigarettes and talking loudly.

'Oooh, did you see *Puppetry of the Penis*?'

'No it was sold out. That's why we came here.'

'Is this next bloke supposed to be any good?'

'Dunno.'

My ears prick up. They're talking about Gabe. I sidle past slowly so I can listen.

'Who cares? The tickets were free.'

'You mean you didn't pay for them?

'Nah. Some American guy was giving them away earlier.'

She says it so dismissively, so flippantly, but as the words *some American guy* register, there's a sickening lurch in my stomach. She means Gabe. And if he's giving away free tickets his show must be doing badly. My worst fears are confirmed, I hesitate – and then the lights dim. Fear grips and I scurry into the recess. Oh fuck, this is it.

A compère arrives on stage, carrying a pint of Guinness, and takes the microphone. 'Let's face it, life can be pretty dull . . .'

There's a sulky murmur of agreement and some comments about the last comedian that make my toes curl.

'. . . which is why you need the likes of this next comic to rescue you. So, let's hear it for your very own Angel Gabriel . . .'

I should've stopped him. I should've done something – I should've . . .'

As Gabe strides on to the stage I forget to breathe. He looks even more adorable than I remember. I was expecting him to be wearing that awful suit he thinks makes him look cool and edgy, but he's in his jeans and a grey sweatshirt. As usual his hair's all over the place, but he's had a shave and when he pushes his glasses up his nose he looks about twelve. I feel immediately protective.

And utterly besotted.

'Hi there, great to be here, it's my first time in Edinburgh. Anyone here from Edinburgh?'

There's a bored silence.

My worst fears begin to get worse.

'I'm from California, but I've been living in London for the past few weeks. London's great. Big Ben, Leicester Square, though I have to admit I was a bit disappointed by Piccadilly Circus. There wasn't a clown or a performing seal in sight . . .' He smiles – and I must admit, combined with his drawl and languorous delivery, it's vaguely comical. But vaguely comical is not enough to give the kiss of life to this audience, who have been left for dead by Mr Pigeon. I glance around the dark little room. There's barely a pulse.

My heart plummets. I was right. He's going to die on stage. Right here, in front of me. In a Bavarian tavern.

'But seriously, this is my first time in the UK and I've noticed a few things that are different from back home . . .'

As I watch him on stage, lit by that harsh spotlight, I want to rush up there and save him. But I can't. I'm powerless to do anything. I glance round me. No one, but no one, is laughing. Seemingly bewildered by the lack of bitterness and exocet-missile delivery of most stand-up comics, they're looking at each other unsurely. The atmosphere's one of dismissal. They're not prepared to give him a chance. I notice a few people have even started talking among themselves. Shit! Maybe Gabe was right – maybe audiences expect their comedians to be angry and *Angst*-ridden.

'Like, for example . . .'

I look back at Gabe. By now I can tell he's nervous. He's rubbing his nose, the way he always does when he's awkward, and his initial confidence has deserted him. There's an excruciating pause as he swallows hard. Oh, God, I can't watch this.

Ducking, I squeeze past a couple of people propped against the bar, and dash into the ladies' loos. The door swings closed behind me, blocking out his voice until it's just a murmur. Breathing a sigh of relief, I rest my hands on the basin and stare at the plughole. It's quite the metaphor: outside, Gabe's dreams of being a stand-up comic are, quite literally, going down the plughole.

Turning on the taps I splash my face with cold water. I feel so bad for him. All that time and work and effort to be here – and for what? To be ignored? Greeted with yawns? At the memory, I feel a knee-jerk of indignation. Because, despite everything, I believe Gabe is talented. And he's naturally funny. And I hate to think of him, right this very minute, up there on stage, with no one laughing . . .

Right on cue I hear a roar of laughter.

What? It can't be! *Can it?* Tentatively pulling open the door, I peer through the fog of smoke. I can't believe my eyes. I'm not mistaken. People are smiling, and quite a few are actually laughing. Even those girls are nudging each other in the ribs and giggling.

'I was on one of those double-decker buses recently . . .'

Edging out of the ladies' I join the audience, and as he continues talking, I can feel the room warming to him. People stop talking and really listen. Gabe is smiling and moving on with a new confidence.

'. . . and there was this little girl crying. I thought, 'What can I do? I felt terrible . . .' With perfect comic timing he pauses to pull a face that has the audience in stitches.

'Then I remembered I had a piece of candy in my backpack . . .' There's a beat. '. . . and so I took it out and popped it into my mouth. It was amazing. I felt so much better.'

The audience cracks up.

My eyes flit round them, mouths open wide, faces creased, eyes shining. Gabe has their full attention – mine too.

With new-found respect I watch him as he moves from one dry observation to the next without being pretentious or preachy. Hands tucked comfortably into his pockets, head tipped lazily to one side, he delivers his comical observations with a deadpan delivery and an angelic smile that reels you right in. He's so much better than I ever expected. The angry wisecracking comic has gone. Instead he's himself. I feel a tingle of pride. Maybe he took my advice just a little bit.

And then, before I know it, the show begins to moves to its climax like a snowball gathering momentum. The laughs are bigger and bigger, and tears are rolling down faces. I glance at my watch. Only a few minutes to go.

'. . . but I can't leave tonight without talking about a special ginger-haired someone I've got to know pretty intimately over the past few weeks . . .'

What was that? Having listened to an entire show of stand-up comedy – which for me is a tremendous effort even if it *is* Gabe – I've been lulled into a sort of daze, but now I'm jolted wide awake. Oh, my gosh, that's me! He's talking about me! Heart hammering, I wait on tenterhooks.

'. . . a tomcat called Billy Smith . . .'

Disappointment throbs and I feel faintly ridiculous for even thinking he was talking about me. After all, why should he?

Because the idiot's in love with you.

I hear Victor Maxfield's voice again, loud in my head. But I dismiss it. For all I know he's probably confused me with someone else. Men have a habit of passing on information like Chinese whispers.

'I always used to wonder where that saying, "you dirty tomcat", came from but now I know.'

I recover quickly.

'There's me and my roommate every night in our pyjamas, drinking peppermint tea, watching *Sex and the City* on DVD – my roommate has the entire series in a boxed set, sort of like an encyclopedia of men . . .'

Blushing, I glance round the room. There's a lot of smiling and nodding, and I see men nudging their girlfriends, who are giggling with embarrassed recognition.

'I know we stand-ups lead a pretty wild life. Sometimes we cracked and hit the liquorice allsorts!' There's a wave of laughter.

'But Billy Smith?' On stage, Gabe raises his eyebrows. 'There was me thinking he'd be curled up in a basket, purring away, but uh-uh.' Shaking his head, he pulls an expression of astonished awe and respect. 'That cat is an *animal*. You wouldn't believe the traffic that went through that kitty-flap. I swear, he was getting booty calls every night.'

Suddenly I remember our conversation in the kitchen. Gabe is a genius.

'You know what a booty call is, right?'

Gabe smiles conspiratorially into the audience. There's a few sniggers, some puzzled looks, and a lot of people whispering explanations. Until, as people start to get it, there's a swell of rowdy guffaws.

He grins. 'Hmm, thought so.'

People are crying with laughter now and as they wipe away the tears in their eyes Gabe just keeps coming with his all most wide-eyed innocent delivery,

'. . . Strays, tabbies, a couple of Persian blues . . . they were in and out all night long . . .' He pauses and looks out into the audience. At first I presume he's waiting to deliver his punchline but it's almost as though he's searching for something. *Or someone.*

Then he sees me. And as his eyes meet and hold mine, my breath stops at the back of my throat and holds itself tight with anticipation. And in that moment everything around me seems to disappear, the lights, the chatter, the smell of cigarettes and spilled beer, and there's just me and Gabe. Back in my kitchen in London with Billy Smith and his ridiculous booty calls.

His face crumples into astonishment. 'You're laughing,' he mouths silently.

Thinking he's talking to them, the crowd responds with hoots and yells. But it's me he's looking at.

'I know,' I mouth back, a smile on my face as a giggle rises inside me. And then, before I know it, I'm laughing. Would you believe it? For the first time in my life *I'm actually laughing*. At a comedian. In a stand-up comedy club. And as Gabe goes for the punchline I lift my camera, take a photograph and capture the moment for ever.

The next morning, up and down the country, thousands of *Sunday Herald* readers open their newspapers to see the black-and-white image of Gabe on stage at the Tavern staring up at them from the arts pages. Underneath is the heading 'Comedians Taking the Festival by Storm' and an article about the top ten newcomers and their acts, of which Gabe is one. Turns out the journalist was in the audience too, and was so impressed that she rewrote her article to include him, and emailed it just before the paper went to print.

I was pretty busy myself. After Gabe came off-stage there was a lot of apologising and explaining to do on both sides and we stayed up for hours, talking about everything. There were a few revelations. His confession that he'd broken up with Mia being the one that caught my attention particularly. But there were others. How when he'd left the flat early that morning he'd circled the block three times before he could find the strength to drive away. How, after much soul-searching, he'd decided to follow my advice and change his act. It all came pouring out.

And then it was my turn. I told him about Lionel's heart-attack, making up with Rosemary, Victor Maxfield's message. I told him everything. Well, not *everything*. I didn't mention the bit about his uncle calling him an idiot and saying he was in love with me.

But I didn't need to as he told me himself.

Just before we kissed.

'So what do you think?'

Snuggled up in a warm tangle of feather duvet, camberwick bedspread and naked limbs, I look at Gabe across the pillows. It's the morning after the night before and we're in my hotel room indulging in breakfast in bed and the Sunday papers.

I wriggle my toes against his and allow my gaze to drift across his mussed-up hair and eyes all puffy with sleep behind his glasses, and can't help wondering what was I thinking, wanting to read the papers alone without interruptions. I love interruptions. My mind wanders deliciously back to only a few minutes earlier . . .

'Hmmm, let me see . . . "fresh new talent" . . . "sheepish, almost whimsical humour" . . . "one of the funniest comedians to hit Edinburgh".'

I swat him with my half-eaten croissant.

'Ow,' he yelps, rubbing his naked shoulder as if he's hurt. 'That's a mean right hook you've got.'

'I'm not talking about the article,' I protest. 'I'm talking about the photograph.'

'Oh, I see, the photograph,' he repeats, as if he hadn't noticed my credit in the left-hand corner, but his mouth is twitching. He studies it intently, eyes narrowed in concentration. 'Och, he's a bonny wee lad,' he declares, in his best attempt at a Scottish accent. I shoot him a look. 'And the photograph's not too shabby either.' He wraps his arm round me. 'You're very talented, Miss Hamilton.' He kisses me. He tastes of pastry and orange juice, and just as I'm enjoying it I feel something. *Again?*

'You know, I've been wanting to do this from the first moment I saw you,' he's murmuring.

'Hey, you had a girlfriend then,' I reprimand him sternly.

'Well, actually . . .' He rubs his nose self-consciously. 'When I told you we'd broken up I never said when.'

I look at him, puzzled.

'It was actually months ago, before I came to London.'

'So why on earth did you say you had a girlfriend when Jess . . .' It dawns on me. That first night. In my back garden. When she tried to seduce him.

'You were her plan B.' I giggle.

'Plan B?' He looks wounded, then collapses into laughter. 'I must remember that.' He chuckles as he leans over to the bedside table to grab his dog-eared notebook. Untying it he takes the little pencil tucked inside and, as I watch him scribble it down earnestly, love swells inside of me.

'Hey, I've got this great joke for you,' he says.

'Oh, God, please, no more.' Groaning I try to bury my head under the duvet. I love Gabe, but one comedy show is enough.

Laughing, he smothers my hair with kisses. 'Have you heard the one about the comedian who fell in love with a redhead called Heather?'

Peeping out, I snuggle up to him. 'No, what happened?'

'He couldn't get out again.'

I smile ruefully. 'That isn't remotely funny.'

'It's not supposed to be,' he murmurs, pulling me close and kissing me.

And closing my eyes, I kiss him back. Now that has to be the best punchline I've ever heard.

Epilogue

'That'll be three dollars and seventy-five cents.'

I place the magazine on the counter and pull out a five-dollar bill from the pocket of my shorts. The shopkeeper takes it from me and as I wait for my change, I pick it up and scan through the glossy pages. It must be here somewhere . . . I turn over a couple of advertisements. Then I see it. A black- and-white photograph of a woman peeling off her wetsuit, illustrating an article about surfing. My eyes flick to the credit, written underneath in small block capitals:

HEATHER HAMILTON.

I feel a burst of pride. *Scene* is one of America's best-selling magazines and it's my first shoot for them. And, though I say it myself, my photo looks pretty good and that credit isn't tiny. The letters must be at least nearly half a centimetre . . .

'Miss?' The man behind the counter is holding out my change.

'Oh, thanks.' I blush, and stuffing the change into my pocket, I close the magazine and walk outside into the scorching heat.

It's late afternoon but the sunshine is still dazzling. I slip on my sunglasses and look across at the rows of impossibly tall palm trees, with the expanse of blue sky, yellow sand and glittery ocean. *Venice Beach, California.* I breathe in the scent of salt, coffee, and suntan lotion. It's everything I dreamed it would be like and more. Filled with cyclists, girls in bikinis, dudes carrying surfboards, a roller-blading sitar player . . . Grinning to myself as he whizzes past on the busy sidewalk, I turn to my bike and plop the padlock into the little wicker basket. Climbing on to the seat I push off from the kerb. I've just been for a swim in the ocean and, feeling the salt on my skin and my bikini damp beneath my shorts, I pedal lazily, allowing myself to daydream, my mind spooling backwards with every revolution of the wheels.

Back to Edinburgh and that morning six months ago when I woke up in my frilly pink hotel room next to Gabe . . .

As Brian had predicted I stayed until the festival ended. Gabe's show was a sell-out. In fact, he was such a hit that a much larger venue offered him a spot. As his audiences grew, so did the buzz. Before he knew it, all the judges of the comedy awards were coming to see him and he was being nominated for the prestigious Perrier Award.

When he won, I wasn't surprised. Gabe, however, was astonished, as was the whole comedy circuit who'd never even heard of him, but since then he's gone on to even bigger and better things. His win created a huge amount of publicity and he's currently in talks about his own TV series, as well as performing a sell-out show in one of the biggest comedy clubs in LA.

I turn into the network of canals, dismount from my bike and begin to push it along the narrow path running alongside the water. As for me, Victor Maxfield loved my photographs from the festival (even though he was probably a bit biased, considering the subject matter) and it was the first of many assignments. Over the next couple of months I had the most amazing time, photographing all kinds of people, places and events.

Then I quit my job. Again.

Beams of sunlight are bouncing off the water, and I push my sunglasses further up my nose. I let my eyes drift out across the canals as my mind returns to the moment I made the decision to leave the *Sunday Herald*. Only this time it wasn't because of a stupid misunderstanding, it was because of butterflies. All I have to do is look at Gabe and I feel them fluttering inside me. And what better reason could I find for moving to LA than for us to start a new life together?

I pause to watch a family of ducks bobbing up and down on the water. Every so often one tips completely upside-down, its feathery bottom sticking up. It's quite incredible. Just as incredible is the fact that usually in February I'm in cold, drizzly old London, fighting my way through the rush-hour on the Piccadilly Line.

Not that it hasn't been without its scary moments. Letting my flat, applying for a visa, turning freelance – it was as if my life suddenly speeded up. Before I knew it I was packing up my Le Creuset pans, saying my goodbyes and promising to email. And then, of course, there was Lionel.

At the thought of him there's a tug at my heartstrings. As much as I love my new life here with Gabe, I hate being so far away from my father. It's silly, really. I know he's in good hands, and he's only at the other end of the phone, but I do miss him. Sometimes I almost feel like wishing . . .

But obviously I *don't*, I remind myself, feeling a little burst of righteousness. The lucky heather taught me a lesson and I'm a changed person. Take the other day, for example. Gabe and I were on the beach when I saw this girl wiggle past in a bikini: even Cameron Diaz would have died for her bottom, and just as I was about to wish it was mine – I stopped myself. Which wasn't easy, as it really *was* a very nice bottom, and one that was obviously no stranger to lunges. But I'm so glad I did because five minutes later Gabe told me I had the most perfect bottom he'd ever seen. Which proves you really do have to be careful what you wish for.

Although now, with hindsight, I'm not so sure any more if the lucky heather really *was* lucky. Maybe I *did* just let my imagination run away with itself. Maybe it really was all just a string of coincidences . . .

In the weeks following its disappearance a few things happened that made me think it might have been. The scales in Boots suddenly sported an out-of-order sign, and when I asked a sales assistant what was wrong, she told me it had been giving the incorrect weight. *By five pounds.*

And then a dog-walker found my wallet tossed into a ditch on Hampstead Heath and handed it in. As expected, all the cash and cards were missing – except for my organ-donor card, which was how the police traced me. And the lottery ticket, was tucked safely into the inside pocket, where I'd put it. As for the million-dollar question, did I win?

Yes, I did.

Well, *sort* of.

I got four numbers and won a tenner, which OK, didn't buy me an Aston Martin Vanquish, but it did pay for a cab home from the movies. And, as slushy as this might sound, snuggled up on the back seat with Gabe I felt as if I *had* won the lottery.

But to be honest, the more I think about it, the more I don't think I'll ever know the truth about the heather. Part of me wants to believe it was magic, that all my wishes really did come true. But, of course, the rational, reasonable, *sane* side of me knows that's impossible. Things like that happen in fairytales, not in real life. *Don't they?*

Finally reaching a large wooden house painted baby blue, I wheel my bike up the path and lean it against the steps, where a large ginger cat is lazing contentedly on the porch in a patch of fading sunlight. I bend down to stroke him. 'Hey, Billy Smith,' I whisper, tickling him behind the ears. He gives a rasping purr and stretches out like a draught excluder, his small white paws flexing. I smile to myself. I'm not the only one to be enjoying the Californian lifestyle.

I push open the screen door and walk inside. The house is still and quiet. I kick off my sandy flip-flops, pad through the living room and pause to turn on the lamp on the little side table. Next to it is a photograph I took of Gabe. He's standing in front of the Laugh Factory on Sunset Boulevard, and on the sign above him 'Angel Gabriel Live' is spelled out in big black letters, alongside 'SOLD OUT'.

Proudly I rub my thumb across the wooden frame. I'll never be a fan of stand-up comedy, but I'm learning to *appreciate* it. A bit like beer, I muse. Thinking how a chilled one might be rather nice right now. I go on into the kitchen.

'*SURPRISE!*'

I freeze in the doorway.

Ahead, the patio doors have all been flung open and I'm looking out into my little garden. Strung with tiny fairy-lights, multi-coloured balloons and a huge party banner that reads, 'Happy Birthday,' it's crammed with people, whooping and screaming, yelling and shrieking.

Oh, my God.

I steady myself against the fridge.

It's a surprise birthday party.

My first impulse is to run. I hate surprises. I'm not prepared. I've come straight from the beach. I have sand in my hair and a spot on my face that I picked. I look like shit. I need a shower. And at least half an hour to do my hair and makeup.

But, like a rabbit caught in headlights, I'm too stunned to react.

Then I see them. Familiar smiles. 'Lionel . . . Ed . . . Jess!' I gasp, and now a whoosh of sheer joy is rushing up inside me like a firework, and I'm suddenly finding my feet and running out into the garden, flinging my arms round everyone.

'Lionel! I can't believe it . . . And Rosemary! wow! Jess! You sod! Keeping this a secret from me! Oh, and this is your new boyfriend Dominic? Hi, nice to meet you, Dominic! Ed and Lou and – oh, my gosh – is this Ruby? She's so beautiful – Hey, Ruby, I'm your auntie Heather! Brian! It's so great to see you . . . Oh, and Neil, lovely to see you too!'

Breathless with excitement I hug them all, laughing as Brian snaps away, taking dozens of pictures. Lionel looks so healthy, and my little niece is adorable, and Jess seems really happy with her new man and – crikey! I take it all back. I love surprises. Bloody love them.

'Sssh.'

In the middle of all this commotion there's shushing.

What's going on? What have we got to be quiet for? Why are we . . .?

Then I see Gabe. He's carrying a birthday cake. It's all lit up with dozens of candles and as he walks towards me, down the little crazy-paving path, everyone starts singing 'Happy Birthday'.

Oh, my gosh, I'm going to cry. My eyes are pricking with tears and I feel a lump of happiness in my throat. I'm so lucky. Gabe was right. There doesn't always have to be a but.

He puts the cake on the little patio table, turns to me and kisses my lips. 'Happy birthday, gorgeous,' he whispers, giving me a mischievous wink.

I laugh and as everyone gathers round me with their cameras ready, I go to blow out my candles.

When he stops me.

'Hey! Don't forget to make a wish,' he laughs.

Goosebumps prickle. I feel a familiar tingle in my fingers and toes. *No, Heather. Remember, you promised.* I look back at the shimmering candle flames, take a deep breath and close my eyes.

But then again . . .

What's one little wish?